MW01628067

Opening Eden's Gate

Complete Works
Sheri Lindner
Volume I
1990-2012

ISBN: 978-1-60571-179-9
2nd Edition, 2013

SHIRES PRESS
4869 Main Street
P.O. Box 2200
Manchester Center, VT 05255
www.northshire.com/print-on-demand

Building Community, One Book at a Time
This book was printed at the Northshire Bookstore, a family-owned, independent bookstore in Manchester Ctr., Vermont, since 1976. We are committed to excellence in bookselling. The Northshire Bookstore's mission is to serve as a resource for information, ideas, and entertainment while honoring the needs of customers, staff, and community.

Printed in the United States of America

For my husband, Michael, whose love makes possible the presence of poetry in our lives. For Daniel and Joanna, whose journeys are the pulse and meter of that poetry.

TABLE OF CONTENTS

III: **The Blue Thread** 213

I. They Leave the Garden

On Giving Dan a Book on the Occasion of His Becoming a *Bar Mitzvah*

Friday Night, October 1, 1993

As you know, Dan, it has become a custom in our synagogue for parents to present a book to their son or daughter on this occasion. We thought about many different books that had something to do with Judaism and that would interest you.

In the past, you have been interested in ancient Egypt; more currently, you have loved baseball, and have tried very hard to legitimize its inclusion in your *Bar Mitzvah* party through Sandy Koufax and other Jewish players. While we appreciate the importance of each of these areas of interest and exploration for you, we know also that the fervor of these interests may pass as you grow.

We wanted to find a book that you would not outgrow, a book that would capture your soul. And so we give you this book of stories that have not, until now, been written down; but they are stories that have been told dozens of times.

These stories combine the Jewish values of history, continuity, memory, transformation, and belonging, and they are also stories that we know you never tire of. At particular moments in your own growing up, you have asked for these stories. They still retain the power to bring tears to our eyes and to yours as we tell them to you. For these are your stories Daniel, the ones that you created when you were three and a half years old...the ones that you, mommy, daddy, and Joanna used to act out on the floor of your room at 6 A.M.

These stories are about evolving into a human being, and so they are like the stories of the bible and those of fairy tales. In these stories, Jews do not wander for 40 years, finally to find their home; but turtles wander lost in jungles, to be found by pet store owners, adopted by loving parents, and nurtured into human beings. Like all myths, these stories transcend time and place. And though they were the creation of one 3½ year old boy's mind, they are the stories of humanity. And because they are about becoming human, they are also about living as a Jew, for these two are inseparable.

And so Daniel, we present you with this book of children's stories written by a small Jewish boy who used to be an author. There is room here to add more stories as they may evolve in your life. We hope that you will eventually share these stories with your own sons and daughters to help them in their journeys from lost turtles to loving and loved human beings.

Charge to Dan on the Occasion of His Becoming a *Bar Mitzvah*

October 2, 1993

Dear Dan,

I would like to remind you of the story of how you arrived at this day. It did not come about as an inevitable event because you happen to have two Jewish parents. You stand here today as the result of a process that you, yourself, initiated.

To put this story in some context, I remember that before you were born, daddy swore that even if his son begged, he was not going to be *Bar Mitzvahed*. Daddy's feelings about his own *Bar Mitzvah* were so awful that he did not want to inflict these terrible things on you. As with many things in our home, you see who got the last word!

In the early years of your life, we celebrated Christmas more excitedly than *Chanukah*, and hunted for dyed Easter eggs more enthusiastically than making *Pesach seders*, that you, at the age of 4, claimed to carpool mates one day as you were discussing what you all "were," that you were "Cathric." The carpool mother, knowing daddy and me, told you that she was sure you were Jewish. You denied this vehemently. In the end, trying to resolve this confusion, you proposed, "Well, maybe my mother is Jewish, but I'm sure my father is Cathric."

Althougn I know this story embarrasses you, I tell it with a certain chagrin, knowing that the laugh is really on daddy and me.

It would still be several years before we would change our practice of non-religious, homogenized, multi-holiday celebrations. And in the end, the decision to do so was not entirely ours to make.

In the fall when you were not quite 6, we took a family trip for a weekend to the Amish country and stayed with a Mennonite family on their farm. After being an attentive tourist at various Mennonite and Amish museums, and a guest of our hosts, you were pretty clear about what the Amish believed and how they differed from the Mennonites. This education and your uncanny desire to know, to think, and to understand, led you to ask the fateful question: "Well, what do we believe?"

Daniel, you stood on the threshold of your Jewish identity, and by the hand, led daddy and me to the threshold of our own exploration of how we would be Jewish and what that would mean to us.

And so, at *Chanukah* time, you asked for your own Bible and begged to begin Hebrew school. We, as a family, entered a synagogue for the second time in over a dozen and a half years.

As an aside, the first time daddy and I had ever been in a synagogue together was when you were 5 months old and we attended the second *Bar Mitzvah* of my grandfather's best friend, Norman Meyer Kupersmidt, for whom your sister, Joanna Maia, *Na'amah*, was named. At this synagogue visit, you began squawking and cooing loudly enough to be a distraction in the service. As I stood to leave the sanctuary with you, the Rabbi stopped us and said something like, "Ah, the music of God's voice." I guess you had an auspicious and favorable early synagogue experience.

When you did enter Hebrew school, to daddy's enormous dismay, I remember assuring him that it was important to you now, that I didn't care if you were *Bar*

Mitzvahed or not—it didn't mean anything to me—I had no interest in requiring you to go to Hebrew school. You could quit whenever you chose. And I believed I meant it.

I soon came to hope you would continue to love this, because I secretly knew that somehow, within two months of your discovery on a Mennonite farm that you were Jewish, your pleasure and eagerness to understand what that meant (which of course was matched by your enjoyment of snacks at Hebrew school!) had ignited or reawakened for me an equal pleasure. I deluded myself that my enjoyment came only from your enjoyment, and that I was doing this "only because you were into it now."

When I think about the meaning of today I think mostly about the gift that you are to us and the uncountable gifts beyond yourself that you have given us. One of these gifts is the richness of being Jewish again...of embracing something from a lifetime ago that I was sure I no longer needed or wanted. As I stand here with you, today, in 1993, I am aware of being transported beyond our particular time, able to touch not only an ancient past and feel connected to an ancient people, but to touch also a not so distant past and the people who connected me there. I imagine, too, as I stand here with you today, that we are also given the gift of touching, a little, who and what is to come.

We are here today to celebrate and join you, Daniel, as you both step into time, into the dawning of your mature consciousness and thinking and memory and understanding, and step beyond yourself, as you perform and perpetuate this ritual observance. Today, you stand on a bridge between what one poet called the story and the fable---the story of how you will carve out your life in time, how you will make a difference, who you will become, and how your uniqueness will show itself in the world and shine in the faces of those you love and who love you; and the fable of how you will, beneath all of your wonderful uniqueness, experience your humanity, not as different from, but as the same as your fellow human beings, with the same thoughts and feelings and uncertainties...the same need to ask how best to be human.

It had been daddy's and my intention to raise our children without religion. We felt, and felt sincerely, that imposing religion would narrow your field of vision and identity and tolerance for those you might hastily perceive as unlike yourselves. We intended to teach you, instead, about all religions, to allow you to understand the universal human needs that are expressed and met by all religions. We wanted to enlarge your sensibilities and sensitivities to humanity. In short, we had intended to approach this subject intellectually, as adults with our children. But you, Daniel, asked for more than that, not less. You asked for an experience first, and understanding as it would grow out of experience. You asked for a pair of glasses to help you focus this large and complex world. You asked to be raised Jewish, and I have come to see that through this Jewishness you experience enlargement and enhancement of identity, not confinement or diminishment.

So, Daniel, you did not come to this day of becoming *Bar Mitzvah* merely because you are nearing your 13th birthday; you did not arrive here merely because you completed 5 years of compulsory Hebrew school. You did not come to this day unconsciously or because you were required to do so. You arrived here as a result of having made independent and deliberate decisions since you were 6 to learn and live and feel Jewish.

As I remember my brothers' *Bar Mitzvahs*, it was customary for a young man on his *Bar Mitzvah* to thank his parents for fulfilling their responsibility and educating him as a Jew. Today, instead, I would like to thank you, Daniel, for asking to be educated as a Jew, and in making that request of us, allowing us to become Jews, as well. Indeed, you embody the poetic wisdom: "The child is father of the man."

Although I am proud today, this word does not begin to describe my experience of you. I wrote much of what I have said to you today in 1988, 5 years ago. You were 8 years old. You see, it is not only on this one day that I can look at you in your maturity and see you as decent and thoughtful, compassionate and strong. You have been ethical and decent, considerate and compassionate, committed to what is right and unafraid to stand firm in that knowledge long before today. You have stood up to people who were bigger, stronger, and in positions of authority when these people have been less ethical, less decent, less thoughtful, and less kind than you knew they should have been. Your fear of reprisal has not stopped you from mature, but difficult action—action that most adults do not have the courage to take. And you did this as a child. I am moved by the beauty that is you, Daniel, and I am deeply respectful of who you are, who you always have been, and the man that you are growing into. As I acknowledge your maturity I feel today what I have always known since I first held you in my arms, that I am blessed that you are my son.

(1988)
(October 2, 1993)

Joanna's Naming Ceremony the Night Before She Becomes a *Bat Mitzvah* (presentation by Michael and me)

May 31, 1996

Joanna,

Although you were given the gift of your name when you were born, daddy and I never arranged at that time for a public and religious naming ceremony for you. So we thought, the day before you will be considered a Jewish adult, that we'd better name you, officially, first.

Your English middle name, Maia, and your Hebrew name, *Na'amah*, the ones we gave you, were bestowed in memory of Norman Meyer Kupersmidt, my grandfather's best friend and long time family friend. "Mike," as we called him, and Lil had been to all of my family's *simchas,* including my own confirmation, although at the time, I only thought of them as friends of my grandparents. When daddy and I moved to New York, the first telephone call we received in our new apartment was from "Mike" and Lil Kupersmidt, who lived in Freeport and invited us immediately to their home for *Shabbat* dinner. Norman Meyer loved my grandfather, and out of this love, he considered daddy and me his own grandchildren. He and Lil invited us often to their home; they felt themselves to be our only family in New York at the time, and they knew, whether we knew it or not back then, that family connection was important. Out of these dinners and our friendship with them until Mike's death in 1983, came my chopped liver recipe, my noodle kugel recipe, and your name. Although these things appear to be of greatly different levels of importance, Mike and Lil's continuity and memory are preserved in all of them. So, if you ever ask again, "What am I, chopped liver?" we may answer "sort of" and you'll know that we mean this in the most affectionate of ways!

Unlike other people, who have their names given to them, you, in your inimitable way, announced last year that you would like to name yourself. After Apa died, you wanted to take his name in order to hold him within you and feel that loving connection as part of yourself. Each of us was moved to beautiful things in the aftermath of Apa's death. Your way is a tender and sweet act which brings great joy and deep sadness at the same time to me. Traditionally, a Jewish child is given the name of someone who was dearly loved by the family, but who the child has never known. How special, that you not only had that, but also knew the person whose name you now carry as part of your own. I am touched that you knew my father and made it an act of will and choice to maintain your loving connection to him. Now when I hear his name, it not only brings a tear, but a smile, as well. So, in addition to *Na'amah*, you added Apa's Hebrew name. He was Hershel, and the Hebrew feminine of Hershel is *Tzivia*. Apa would have scratched his head and scowled as to why this would need to have been expressed in a Jewish fashion, but he would have been overwhelmed by your act of love.

How fitting that your Hebrew name encompasses deep and long- lasting friendship, the type that is chosen and given so freely and also the wonderful and eternal love of a grandfather for a granddaughter. It is a testament to you and Apa, that you would want to choose his name, and that in his love for you he was worthy of your choice. Together, they express the highest of Jewish values with family being at the center and friendship the widening spread of loving community.

On Giving Joanna a Book on the Occasion of Her Becoming a *Bat Mitzvah*

May 31, 1996

About 2 months ago, Joanna, your *Shabbat siddur* looked a bit like this. We had, for the past year, carelessly marked off the pages of different prayers that you would be learning, by ripping different sized "post-its" and slapping them on the page. We would hastily scribble the names of the prayers, or at least some identifying words. One prayer we named "Snappy" because its tune was so catchy you even danced around your room shimmying as you practised this one. (For all of you who think that studying Hebrew prayers is boring, you should have seen Joanna!)

Besides the post-its marking off the prayers, there were stray, frayed bits of tissues trailing out of some other pages at the back of the *siddur*. These were not marking off things you would **have** to learn; rather, they were placed there privately by you, marking off things that you had discovered for yourself. The tissues marked off poems that you had found that you liked. Some were about death, and I know that you found these consoling and helpful when Apa died. Some were about peace, poems that we read together with our companions in Israel. And some were about journeying through life.

When Rabbi Joy asked you to "clean up" your prayer book before your *Bat Mitzvah*, to make it look a little more respectable, you protested: "But it's well used. I love it this way." I loved it that way, too. There was something so... Joanna about it. It had the look and even the soft feel of your pony, Cuddles, who sleeps under your pillow each night. Your prayer book has been a well-loved and well-used friend. Each night for a year, we have sat together and sung its songs. *Ahava Rabba* has replaced Kumbaya; *Mizmoor shir* has replaced Baby Beluga. Like lullabies, these Hebrew songs are with you as you fall asleep each night. (Even Daddy finds himself humming *nigguns* during the day, and wondering how show tunes and camp songs got replaced by *V'Shamru)*.

So, it would have made perfect sense to give you a *siddur* as our choice for the gift of a book. The problem is, that we had already given it to you.

Our inspiration, for this book, however, came from looking at those trails of tissues hanging out of your *siddur* and from watching what you do each night just after we finish singing and practicing liturgy. You love to read and find poems and quotes that move you. You often read me passages about friendship that you find in your magazines. And you write about your day and your thoughts every night in your journal before you go to bed.

So, this is the book we have chosen for you. It is a book that will, as you write in it, become the book of your thoughts, your favorite poems, ideas that you find, and ideas that you form. How is this a Jewish book? Well, it isn't exactly... yet. Mordechai Kaplan spoke of Judaism as an evolving civilization; this book will become the story of your evolution, from the dawning of your mature consciousness at twelve and a half, and be a record of your explorations, your Truths, your Maybes, your growth, and ultimately, you. It will contain the thoughts that have influenced you and those that, as a result, will flow from you. Like you, it will be a work in progress.

We would also like to give you a copy of this book that we wish also to donate to the synagogue library. We know that in many ways you are not yet ready for this book, but I suspect that as this purple book comes close to being filled, you will then be readier for this one. It is a book on the *World's Religions*, but its subtitle is more apt: *A Guide to our Wisdom Traditions.*

You know that daddy and I have always wanted you and Dan to have an appreciation for all religions because we feel, at least in theory, that religions contain enormous wisdom about our questions in life, our aspirations as human beings, and our experiences of awe in the world. Religion, along with art, and music, and literature represents our efforts to render in some tangible form--whether it be by stories, language, chants, rituals, a marking of the earth's cycles and our own--these questions, these aspirations, and these experiences.

We once thought that you could never appreciate the variety and richness of the many religious systems of thought, if we narrowed your experience by having you grow up identified with only one. But we have changed our minds about that. We now know that your having lived the richness of Judaism will allow you someday to bring to your understanding of other religions a knowing from deep within you that will enrich and vitalize your explorations.

Joanna's Presentation of a Book to the Synagogue Children's Library

I have often been told that you can't judge a book by its cover. But that's not always true. When I was 3, the only books I brought home from the library were small, square, colorful books, all of them by authors whose names began with W (they were on the bottom shelf where I could sit on the floor and pull them out). This was not the most purposeful way of choosing books to bring home, but it sure worked for me.

I must say that I ended up with some really terrific books by this method. One of those wonderful books, chosen by its cover alone, was *A Special Trade*. It was little, square, red, and by Sally Wittman--it was the right size, color, and in the right place. And it was the right book.

This book is a simple book that would appeal to anyone ages 3-103. It is about the love and companionship between a little girl, Nellie, and her elderly neighbor, Bartholomew. Nellie grows up under the loving and protective wing of Bartholomew and as Bartholomew ages, she knows instinctively how to spread her own protective love over him. With names like Nellie and Bartholomew, these are probably not Jewish characters; but the themes of mutual care and love between generations, and the simple wisdom that love and respect freely given allows love and respect to be freely returned are supreme Jewish values, and ones that our community and our family work hard to build.

I still love this book, and I think the children in our Synagogue will too.

Charge to Joanna on the Occasion of Her Becoming a Bat Mitzvah

June 1, 1996

My dear Joanna,

On my closet shelf I have a book overflowing with the "stuff" of your life over the past twelve and a half years. I have catalogued the progress of your life in this book, how many inches tall you are, your first words, your favorite books, and your favorite foods (that one, we know is a very small list!). And I'm not sure how, but there are many pieces of tissues, each with a tiny white tooth in it. I have a special deal with the tooth fairy, so that she returned them all to me after visiting you!

So, I have all these details of your life in that book. But, I must confess to you that there is a page in that book that is blank. It is titled something like: "A word about me from Mommy." It is not lack of time that is responsible for that blank; the problem has been that I have never known at what point to "freeze" you. Which moment in time should I have picked? What time would have represented you best?

Today seems a good moment to choose, to freeze you in time, so that some day you can look back at yourself at 12½, Joanna, on the day that you became *Bat Mitzvah*, and see yourself as you were in the eyes of your mom, and feel, in your memory of this moment, the dawning sense of who you are. I would like to wrap you in my words, as you stand before me, wrapped in your *tallit*. I will begin "my word about you from mom" with your *tallit*.

In one corner are the symbols of *Shabbat*, the time, each week, to pause, and experience a bit of the serenity that your Hebrew name, *Na'amah*, denotes. This is a bit of a problem, because our family does not celebrate *Shabbat* in exactly a serene manner. Our style is more like "Make a joyful noise unto the Lord!" Thank you to Suzanne for helping us over the years make *Shabbat* joyful and noise-ful!. Exuberance, rather than serenity, is more your style, too, Joanna.

It has been a kind of family joke, made by you as often as us, that your Hebrew name, *Na'amah* is not yet fitting for you--that serenity or contentment is something that you will grow into. About a year ago, you decided to choose a new Hebrew name, one that is a better fit for who you are now. You added Apa's Jewish name to your own, a name that means deer or gazelle. This addition to *Na'amah* is perfect for you. *Tzvia* conjures up images of an animal that is swift and graceful, that covers a lot of territory in one leap, that meets life head on.

You are indeed a gazelle that meets life head on, Joanna. Even long before your presence, within, was visible to the outside world, you were engaged in the business of life. We did not know then what you were doing, but you were doing it with gusto.

And you continued meeting life with a gusto, pushing outward all of the walls that would cramp your style. When we strolled, you would flap your arms and legs so vigorously through town, that you would wriggle yourself right out of the stroller. Before you had words, your entire body exuded a boundless delight in the world.

Through these years you have envisioned yourself as many different things when you would be grown-up. A baby holder, a pet store owner, (who would not sell any of the pets), a lawyer (for good causes), a jockey, and a child psychologist, and, only this week, a teacher of kids who have not had the privileges that you have been fortunate to have had.

In these choices, Joanna, are reflected both of your Hebrew names, and both are a vital part of who you are. *Na'amah*, the one that we gave you, in memory of Norman Meyer Kupersmidt, is the part of you who could hold babies and pets and care tenderly for small things, who, if you so chose, could nurture and repair the emotional lives of children; *Tzivia,* the one you chose for yourself, in memory of Apa, is the part of you who could, with words and ideas, spin circles of logic and win justice for others or a telephone for yourself, who could imagine yourself riding like the wind on a racehorse, and who could assert with confidence, "I'm good. You guys could learn a little from me!"

I wish for you, *N'amah-Tzivia*, a lifetime of exuberance and joy, grace and the continued courage to meet life head on, punctuated by and therefore given meaning by contentment and peace.

On this corner is a zoom lens view of our family tree--Ama and Apa, Grammi and Zade, mommy, daddy, Dan, and you. There are branches that come from somewhere we do not know, and there are branches that will sprout and grow in places I will never see. But you will see those places, Joanna. Your leaves will shelter and protect and your branches reach out and embrace. If we could step very far back and see the larger view, we would also see that what makes this tree so vibrant is, in part, the richness of the forest around it that protects and holds it. Our tree, all by itself, would spend a lot of energy on survival. But rooted deeply among others, among all of those who sit before us today, our tree thrives easily.

Today you acknowledge, in becoming a *Bat Mitzvah*, that you do not stand alone, but that you embrace, with affirmation, the responsibilities and commitments, along with the pleasures and fulfillments that are inherent in belonging.

On this corner are your hands. These little hands used to reach for and hold tight to mommy, alone. Your first nursery school teacher, Terry Wolff, may remember prying your tiny fingers from mommy's shoulder so you could stay at day camp. At synagogue retreats you held tight to my side until Sunday afternoon, when you decided you were ready to explore the place with the other kids. I used to wonder if those little hands would ever loosen their grips on my shoulder or leg. Sometimes, it seemed, just before you would catapult yourself into a new experience, you would take 10 steps backward. You would survey the land ahead with a wider view, and then, like a gymnastic vaulter, or a rider preparing to leap crossrails, you would gather momentum and find yourself on the other side, before I even knew you were thinking about it.

And so it happened that one day not long after your fingers had to be pried loose from mommy, in the middle of a lightning storm, you took your sleeping bag and Garfield case from the trunk of the car at exit 10 of the NJ Turnpike and went with Aunt Gail for a visit that you had indignantly demanded an invitation to. You had taken your vault without my looking. In your resolve, you were not even bothered by the fact that the lightning, which so terrified you at home, was fierce enough to have cut off all electricity and phone service at your cousins' for 3 days. You even willingly double-buckled with cousin Brian!

And another day only a few years later, calling from school, you left a message on our answer machine one Monday morning that you had changed your mind about sleepaway camp. Thank goodness, I breathed. I knew you weren't really ready, at age 8 to do this. Never one to allow me to feel complacent for more than a second, you continued, with the confidence of a gazelle leaping through unbounded fields of tall grasses, that you had decided to go for two months, not one! Not little by little, but by leaps and spurts, beyond my grasp and out of my sphere of vision, those tiny hands have learned that letting go, frees them up to embrace a wider world. That is, after all, the only reason for letting go...because the world beckons with "flowers in Eden never known."

Here, these hands, your hands are no longer clenched tight. They are spread and opened. With these hands you are in the world. Your hands, here, are shaped like those of the priests as they deliver the three-fold blessing that you recited in your *Torah* portion today. This shape is meant to resemble the Hebrew letter Shin for the acronym, "Shaddai" meaning "the protecting hand of the Lord." You are one of those priests, and the world will one day be determinedly repaired and gently held by these ready hands of yours.

On this corner is a *Torah,* with the first word of your portion: *Naso*: "to lift up--to take account of." One of your favorite prayers, the first one you learned in studying for your *Bat Mitzvah, Ahava Rabba* is about God demonstrating love for us in giving us *Torah* to study. Although we may not believe that the *Torah* was literally given by God, we value fiercely the capacity to study, learn, and think which is represented by *Torah*. What you, yourself have learned this year will be with you, forever in your soul--the words and melodies of a Jewish prayer service that bind you to a tradition so powerful it allows you to feel the memories of 4000 years as your own. And because they are now yours, you will hold them and breathe your life into them and, when the time comes, I think, hand them tenderly to your children. As a family we have struggled together to understand what your *Torah* portion, a seemingly archaic, useless-to-our-lives portion of the Bible might mean. Besides the content of what we came to understand, what was most important about what we did, was that we thought together, we found meaning where little meaning seemed to be, we learned to allow ourselves to be challenged by material that seemed to be beyond us. This *Torah* represents an openness to being challenged, to "taking account of," to letting the world, its enigmas and mysteries, its terrors, like lightning once was, and its wonders, like hundreds of cicada shells marinating in a pail for stew, make an imprint upon you, fashion you, and open your mind, as your hands in this corner are opened.

And then there are these two verses. The *atara* around your neck contains the traditional prayer, commanding us to wrap ourselves in the laws, the 613 knots contained in the fringes of the four corners. It is a reminder to live by the ethics and morals in which you have chosen to root your life. Between the time you turned 8 and when you were 11, you have developed a strong ethical sense, gaining an understanding that changed you in substantial ways, deepened you forever as a person, and enriched your understanding of real friendship.

This other verse is also a commandment of sorts: "We shall not cease from exploration/And the end of all our exploring/Will be to arrive where we started/And know the place for the first time." These words, which are on your brother's *tallit*, and were Daddy's and my wedding vows to each other, remind us to continue to discover the world and ourselves anew throughout our lives.

I knew that you understood this one January day as you and I stood in the kitchen crooning *Le'hi'la* together. We talked about God's command to Abraham to "go forth." You understood that the *Torah* is comprised of story after story about the Jewish peoples' goings forth, about journeying. **You** explained to me why it is that the *Torah* ends with Moses not being permitted to enter the Promised Land. Life, you said, is not about being perfect, but rather about the seeking; **you** explained to me that being **in** the Promised Land is not important, but looking for it and living a life worthy of it is. And so I knew that you understood T.S. Eliot, and I knew that you understood something essential about the *Torah*, that although it is bound on either end by "land," the Garden of Eden at one end, and the Promised Land at the other, that neither of these is what is important. What is important is having the courage to leave one and engage in the journey toward finding the other. But most of all I knew that you understood something very important about life--like we wrote in our song about our Israel trip--that holiness and happiness do not reside in places or things but in the loving connections we make with others along the way. These, alone, are the real substance of the Promised Land. Today, Joanna, I think that you needn't look very far to find your Promised Land, for it seems to me, that you and I, at this moment, like Moses and Joshua, stand here, with those who make up our Promised Land, before us.

In the center of your *tallit*, is the circle of people blessing one another with the words you read today from the *Torah*, words spoken to Moses who gave them to Aaron and he to his sons... and we to you. You have been enfolded by *tallitot* and been blessed at services since you were small. And now **you** are ready to drape your *talli*t around the shoulders of others.

It seems to me that the *talli*t is a garment in tension with itself. Although it is a bit like a warm, protective shawl, adorned with colors and symbolism, that is not its reason for being. The knots, reminders of what we must do in the world, are the *tallit*'s reason for being. Your t*allit* is a little like mommy and daddy: it shelters and holds you, and it reminds and nudges you all along your way.

I can picture your *tallit* 20 or 30 years from now. Its cloth will be yellowed like the cloth of my grandpa Charlie's *tallit*, here, and its fringes will all be braided (French braided, fishtailed), as you have braided these fringes. It's harder for me to picture who you will be 20 years from now. But, my prayer for you, as you go from Eden to desert to new Edens, is that you see life like a *tallit*--sheltering and comforting, while at the same time beckoning and reminding you of how to live, that the sometimes difficult tugs pulling you into the adult world be always embedded within a sense of safety, fullness, and love.

You will not always find yourself in a synagogue with this special "blanket" of comfort around your shoulders or with its reminders of right behavior hanging at your sides. But my wish for you, *Na'amah Tzivia*, is that even when you are not in a synagogue, perhaps especially when you are not in a synagogue, that you feel wrapped from within in light and warmth, in exhilaration and serenity, in the boundless joys and small contentments of life. I wish for you that you know from within that you can always find your way to the Promised Land of your creation. I wish for you, Joanna Maia, that you carry with you always the knowledge that you are our blessing, that I love you with immeasureable fullness, that we all here celebrate your membership in this community, and that the world awaits your embrace with its arms, for you, open wide.

The following was how our family experienced the Exodus story, as the first 3 children of the next generation, my son and 2 nieces, were preparing to leave home for college.

Exodus in Our Time:
A Story for the Children,
Especially for Those Who Will Begin Their Journeys Soon
for Pesach 5758/1998

You know, don't you, that the Exodus story is about you, you sitting
  around this table.
Tonight, especially, it is your story: Daniel, Rebecca, and Loree,
And soon it will be yours, Joanna, Matthew, Brian, and Julie;
It once was our story, mine and Michael's, Sandy's and Gail's,
  Ronna's, Freddi's and Scott's, Robert's and Cheryl's;
And before us, it was Leona's and Eugene's, and Effie's and
  Harold's;
And it was a true story for those who came before them, too.

But tonight, it is your story
And we will map the ways in which you **are** the Hebrews.

Do you remember how the Hebrews came to be in Egypt?
They came because there was food, life in abundance,
  there for the taking.
It was there that they could thrive, and grow into a people.

You, too, arrived nursing eagerly at the land,
Growing strong on the abundance, there for your taking,
Growing into people.

Eager Josephs you were, who paved the way,
Becoming rulers in your new homelands!
Ready to test and then to welcome your kin,
When they would chance to arrive.

For a long time, 400 years the story says,
The Hebrews and the Egyptians lived together.
We do not hear a word about them for this long time.
We assume, therefore, that all was well:

The Hebrews were not slaves; the Egyptians not oppressors.
Together, they thrived.

So it was in our homes.
For timeless years: uninterrupted living.
Continual genesis.

And then, without knowing exactly when it happened,
The Hebrews feel enslaved.
Yes, a new Pharoah arose who knew not Joseph.
How could it have been otherwise?
For Pharoahs,
Like Josephs,
Change with time.
And the Hebrews are instructed by God that it is time to leave.
They are ready, and they are not ready: Moses equivocates, but knows that he will be ready.

And you? Yes, this happened to you, too.
There was a point in time,
A moment that you probably can not even remember,
When you, too, felt that you were no longer recognizable to us,
That we did not know you anymore.
And though we remember Joseph
(Oh, how we remember Joseph!)
It is not enough,
For you needed to set aside your Josephness
In order to receive the mark that time would put upon you,
In order to respond to the silent call, as irresistible as God,
The magnetic pull that tugs insistently at your body and your soul
And tells you to prepare to depart--the time is near,
And you are ready and not ready, but, like Moses, becoming ready.

What have the Hebrews been doing when we hear of them again?
They have been making bricks.
They have been learning how to build,
To know what is the stuff that protective shelter is made from,
To know how to build a home.

And why, all of a sudden, do they feel themselves slaves,
when they had not begun that way?
Because, all of a sudden, they know how to make bricks,
Well enough;
They do not need to be taught this anymore.
And so the practice, in the narrowed walls of Egypt, stifles.

And you?
Yes you, like the Egyptians, have also been learning about
what Is the stuff that makes a home
And though perhaps you could use a tad more practice with the
toilet seat thing, or the dirty underwear on the floor thing,
Still, you are nearing readiness for your apprenticeship to end.
You are nearing readiness to leave Egypt,
The land that has begun to feel too close, enslaving.
Yes?

What of the plagues? What of them?
The land of Egypt can barely imagine itself without its Hebrews.
The Hebrews' presence has enriched Egypt in untold ways.
The Pharoahs love to tell stories about the old days,
When the Hebrews first arrived,
And the golden years, when the Egyptians and Hebrews lived
a synchronous life.
But these are no longer the same Hebrews.
They do not want to hear these stories--not because they do not
love them--because they do.
They love hearing of former times, when all was well,
When they were afforded places in the palace.
But they know that these stories could lure them from their mission,
Their purpose,
Which is to leave.
And they cannot risk being deterred.

They know that they must
'lose the earth they know,
for greater knowing;...lose the life they have,
for greater life...leave the friends they've loved
for greater loving;
to find a land more kind than home, more large than
earth...[1]

And you? So it is with you.
You will rain petty plagues upon us to help us know that the time
Is right.
And we, like Pharoah, will loosen our hold, as we have been doing
little by little since the beginning.
But we will, no doubt, have you make just a few more bricks,
to make sure you really know how.
You will throw plagues our way to distract us from the real issue
at hand:
That you are leaving.
And we will watch to see how **you** weather your own plagues.
And we will know, when you find your Goshen, your safe harbors
from your own storms,
That it is all right for us, finally, to let go.
And we will.
We will let our people go.
And you will go.

But we will, because we must, follow you to the edge
of the Sea of Reeds.
And there we will remember, because it was only a breath ago
When we stood at the shores
And dared to step our feet into a sea much like this one
And how we thrilled as the way parted for us.
We will remember that we wandered for a time
And then we found our way to our Promised Land
This same place that once you knew as Eden
And only now is known as Egypt
But will forever, for us, be our Place of Promise.
We will remember all this
Because this was our story, too
Oh so long ago
And not so long ago.

We will watch you for a long long time, as you cross
to the other side.
We will be more wise than Pharoah: we will know that where
you go we cannot follow,
And so we will watch
Until even our vision no longer binds you to us.
We will watch

Until all that binds us are the invisible threads of memory's
treasure trove
That will always be filled with the awe, as great as creation itself,
that we both felt
When once we taught, and once you learned
How to make the bricks
That you would someday use to build your life.
We will still watch
Bound by a gigantic and ephemeral hopefulness about the life
that you will build.
We will forever watch
Because of something bigger than memory and bigger than hope
Because of that thing that was the first thing.

And we will whisper a prayer that you will not hear
A prayer for the wandering and the discovering and the creating
that lies ahead for you
As you leave Egypt and begin your desert journey.
Whatever words we use,
We will mean something like this:

We hope that you come to know the desert as the place where
creation begins, a place of utter quiet, ready to echo the
strains of music you will play;
We hope that the oases you find fill you with such wonder and
nourishment that you forget you are in the desert;
We hope that you feel, at each new tent site along the way, surely
this must be the Promised Land;
We hope that you find yourself, one day, in a Promised Land and
not quite be able to remember a time when you were not
always there.*

---

[1] Thomas Wolfe, *You Can't Go Home Again*

*I was tempted to include one last stanza:

> "We hope that you remember Egypt as the place that fed you and held you
> Until you could do this for yourself."

but that would be pulling them back before they had ever left. And I imagine that that is a verse they must write for themselves in a time distant from this one, in a time when **we** may not hear, perhaps when they are holding and feeding those who come from them...or perhaps when they are saying goodbye to them.

Published in *Reconstructionism Today* Spring, 2001, Vol 8, No.3, pp. 11-13

Dear Dan,

Welcome to Israel! You and I have just finished packing and doing our usual dance getting you ready for leaving. I hope it's real cold there so you get plenty of use from your North Face fleece vest! Ha Ha.

On my usual, more serious note, I hope that you have the most evocative, compelling, and personally wonderful experience while you are there. I hope that you feel more of what you began to feel at the Freedom Tibet concert--that your generation is filled with idealistic people of vision who are beginning to take their places in the world and bring their vision to places where it is needed--and that you are a part of that. I hope that the place you are in and the people you are with fill you with inspiration and energy.

For daddy and me, this whole year--your 17th year--has filled us with a knowing that we have been preparing for since you were born, although it was always more abstract than it has become in the moment of this year. We know that you belong more to the world than to us now, and that this could not (and should not) be otherwise. We know that others will come to know you better than we do now and that the best of you is yet to be known. Seventeen is the year for emotional leave-taking, for daddy and I can love you best for who you have been, for the things you once enjoyed with us, for the child you have been. But others in your world will love you for who you are to become. Although we try to see this future you, the you we see before us is somehow always filtered by the you who has always been with us. And we understand (but do not always want to accept) that we will be limited in our capacity to go with you. We will be more wise than Pharoah...but we do not have to like being more wise!

So, Dan, journey fully and explore wonderful places in Israel and in yourself.

We will be in Greece and Turkey from July 3-13 and will write from there also. Hellos to John, Elli, Ben, and Josh.

Shalom, L'hitraot!

Ahava, Mom

February 7, 1997

Dear Charles,

I have held onto this parent evaluation form for a couple of months now, not sure how to answer many of the questions. Some of the questions address themselves to details about the trip, such as Dan's impressions (or ours) of specific leaders. In truth, Michael and I really know little about the details of Dan's *Nesiya* experience. However, we have powerful impressions of the experience itself, and after hosting a small get-together this afternoon with Bradley, we thought we would share these with you.

We chose *Nesiya* because it seemed like the most substantial experience offered by any of the programs available. Other programs offer Israel; *Nesiya* seemed to offer not only Israel, but an opportunity to create community and to find how one is both a 'self' and a member of that community. It was an opportunity to think about important things--not just about one's relationship to Judaism or to Israel, but how to create community, sustain community, and be a contributing member of a community. During our open house today, Bradley felt self-conscious that in speaking about *Nesiya*, there was a "seriousness" that he didn't want people to misunderstand. This seriousness doesn't negate the 'fun' parts of the trip, but I do think that it is an essential quality of your program and one that sets it apart from others. There is an opportunity to grow and to grow up, in the context of a Jewish place and Jewish time together. We think Dan did just that.

On a very personal note, we know that there were issues about Dan having come with many friends, and issues of his relationship with Yael. From our point of view, although these were potential stumbling blocks to him having the richest experience possible with *Nesiya*, they paradoxically became the best building blocks of a rich and deep and enduring experience for him. We are appreciative that you remained open for Dan and you to "renegotiate" your relationship together and for you both to understand the summer experience and resolve what had been left uncomfortable for both of you. Dan is also very grateful to have had the time over December to talk with you. We had the extreme pleasure of hosting Yael, Ayelet, Shani, and Raut and being witness to warm, loving, adoring, and caring feelings that flowed in every direction among the four girls and Dan. In *Nesiya*'s subsidizing their visit here, we understood *Nesiya*'s commitment not only to continued Israeli-American interchange, but to the friendships that were formed last summer, as well.

How has Dan changed? We're not sure, and we're not sure we will ever really know what changes have come with time and which ones *Nesiya* may have been a catalyst for. He was asked to speak before our congregation on the second day of *Rosh Hashanah*, along with 2 other congregants about his relationship to Israel. Our congregation has a tradition of having 2 or 3 members speak on a particular topic each year, and this being Israel's 50th birthday, that was the topic. Dan is the only "child" ever to have been asked to do this. It was a daunting honor. He struggled with what to say. He felt he had many more questions than answers. But he was introspective and willing to engage in the struggle. This, really, is something that we always wish for him: that he be willing to engage himself with honesty and be willing, always, to see and feel an experience as if it is the first time. I think *Nesiya* encouraged the same thing.

When Dan left for Israel we wished for him that he have an evocative, compelling, and wonderful experience in Israel. We wished that he feel himself one of a new generation of idealistic people, people of vision, who would soon take their places in the world and bring their vision to where it is needed. We wished that he find people on his summer trip who filled him with inspiration and energy. We knew that at 17, he would soon belong more to the world than to us, and that others would come to know him better than we did, and that the best of him was yet to be known. And so, the details of his summer trip remain unknown to us, and we can't evaluate them, but we know that *Nesiya/Kehillah* expanded his already blossoming capacity to be a thoughtful, caring person, to be a person who is a loving and loyal friend, who will always create for himself and for those around him a meaningful community, and who will contribute to his community in significant personal ways.

In appreciation,

Sheri and Michael Lindner

P.S. Please accept back Bradley's check for reimbursement of food expenses, and use it toward scholarship funding.

Summer's Art Work: Ode to Emergence

I have been told
That a sculptor can see,
Within a rock,
The shape of the figure,
Whole and alive,
That breathes within,
Awaiting its birth,
If only the rock could be shed
Of its detritus.

Even within the roughest of rocks,
A sculptor feels a living pulse
And knows this being's soul
As if its life had been lived entire
Already.

And the job of the sculptor
Is, with delicate touch
By the gentlest of hands,
To chip and sand
To rub and smooth
Until this figure,
Emerging from its womb,
Shows herself.

We visited such a work of art
This weekend.

We saw,
As if for the first time
(Each time is always as if for the first time
And that is one of life's sacred secrets)
The figure that has emerged
From precious stone,
The figure that has shed

A few more fragments and particles
Just a little stone dust,
The remnants of some placental lifeline
Which only yesterday
Nourished and protected
What today can flourish without it.
And in this shedding
The soul of this figure
Shines articulate on its face
As if the stone
Had been mined from phosphorescent hills,
Possessing unto itself,
Its own light source.

Whose are the hands
That have rubbed and honed
This stone,
Smoothed its edges,
So that it is, at once,
A solid and imposing presence
With the grace and softness of humanity
In every pore?
Whose hands have fashioned
This work of art
Smoothing into its face
Such a luminescence,
And into its being such a soul?

The stone was ready,
Having been washed by
New Hampshire rains
And sanded by soft Armington lake silt,
Warmed to pliability by the northern sun
And firmed again by cool evening breezes.
Such forces of nature, year after year,
In such a select place,
Readied the stone

Which always held the gift within,
So that all that was left to do
Was for you to say yes
To all those artists' hands
Reaching to lock their arms with yours
As you make your way, together,
On berooted paths.

And in these sanctified summers
These times of mythic remembrances,
In the double embrace
Of nature and of friendship's love
You are born.

to Joanna with love

Reflections on the Gambol

It is a daunting task we do. By June 25th we will transform the entire gymnasium, so that not one inch of gym, other than the floor, will be visible. The entire ceiling will be draped with hundreds of panels of fabric, pinned together and hung over wires that will be strung from window gratings 30 feet high; the walls will be covered with 4 foot by 8 foot flats of wood, painted, wrapped, and decorated around a chosen theme. Air conditioning vent work will be temporarily wired to the ceiling, for this one night only. The entire facade of the school will be changed, and the entry and lobby and hallway to the gym will all be transformed.

This is the Gambol tradition in Port Washington, and it has been so for around 30 years. The themes are never duplicated. This year's theme is "Puttin' On The Ritz." The gym will become a ballroom from an art deco hotel; the facade of the school will become the entry to this art deco hotel, looking something like the Chrysler building; the lobby will become a lobby of a hotel, with palm trees reaching to the ceiling, a piano, a mahogany check-in desk, stained glass chandelier, painted poster art worthy of a gallery lining the hallway, each with a brass museum light above it, indirect sconce lighting along the walls. The themes and the decorations are inventive and endlessly creative. It is incredible what can be done with twelve foot long carpet tubes. The talent of some parents is inspirational.

But that is just the end result. The process is as much the phenomenon as the result. Beginning on the Saturday after the Gambol of the year before, the junior parents "tear down" the Gambol of the night before and store all of the decorations, flats, equipment, down to thousands of screws and pins. Then within months, they are senior parents and they begin meeting in October to determine a theme for their children's Gambol night. The theme is determined and the shape of it emerges--what the gym might look like, what the lobby will be, and how the facade will tie all of it together. And how all of that transformation will come about. This year, carpet tubes with Christmas lights inside, figure prominently, with silver reflective paper wrapping the flats, whose graduated angled and pointed tops will complete the art deco look. There will be details that haven't even been thought of yet, even as late as mid-May. And a cadre of parents has worked each night at an old elementary school building, to make these details.

There are others, working on fundraising, food, invitations, waitering and waitressing, hostessing for the evening, party favors, raffle prizes (anything from a trip for 2 to the Bahamas, or a computer, to massages, free coffees and pizzas).

And what is this year of work all about? The quick answer is that it is our gift to our graduating seniors--an evening from 10 PM to 5 AM of fun, dancing, food, and safety, where no one is driving and, for those 7 hours, no one is drinking. But that is only the quick answer.

If you were a fly on the wall some Tuesday, or Wednesday, or Thursday evening at the Salem School, you would see a small group of 6 or so women, and an equal number of men (rarely is the same family represented twice in these volunteers), painting flats, sawing wood, hauling, cutting, wiring, re-painting, and finishing carpet tubes, making hundreds of palm leaves, cutting out huge green shapes around a pattern, straightening lead coil, recycled from some former Gambol, taping it inside a double leaf and gluing the twins together, cutting out wavy brown patterns that will be wrapped around other carpet tubes, to look, magically, like the bark of a palm tree.

And you would hear each night many threads of

conversations. Some of us know each other well, and some of us are casual acquaintances from some play dates our children had in kindergarten, our paths not having crossed again until now. And some of us, even in this small town with a graduating class of 320 kids, have never met before. Early in our work, we talked of the colleges our children had applied to, and then where they were accepted, and then where they were going. Some nights' conversation focuses on whether they have dates yet to this event, or whether they will be extending the Gambol into the weekend at a beach. As our time together has increased, we have ventured into more uncertain territory, like how we've handled drinking and parties. It is good, finally, to share thoughts about this with those who are not necessarily our closest friends, and to feel a camaraderie in knowing that we all have had to chart our course through these waters, regardless of what path we have chosen to get us, and our children to this place.

One night the realization hit us that the work we do together is a lot like nursery school--we cut and paste and paint. We laughed at ourselves that as our children move ahead, we take such pleasure in doing these young activities again for them, decorating a party for them, as we may have once done in a time long ago.

More recently, a group of 4 of us working on those palm leaves inevitably found ourselves in the territory of menopause: of irregular heart beats, of irregular body temperatures, of irregular moods, and irregular periods. It is no wonder we wandered into this topic, for our children are graduating high school, and whether this is our first child to reach this milestone or our last, we all hover somewhere around the age at which this inevitable thing happens to our bodies. But while we commiserate with one another's symptoms, we are subliminally aware, that there is something else happening here, and this is where the quick answer--about what this gift to our children is about--is insufficient.

That is, in the quiet, manual work we are doing together, we are slowly reconciling ourselves to the near future when our children will be leaving, when our nests will be a little emptier. We are awed and humbled at how quickly the time went—the time of our childbearing years, which, as our menopause-conversation signals, are coming to a close, and the time of our children's childhoods. Some of us admit to the fantasy of having another baby; some of us admit to an unequivocal relief that there will be no more babies. Much as we loved babyhood, or childhood, or teenagerhood, we are aware, each of us with a complex mix of emotions, that there will never be a going backwards, that we will not have babies and young children again, and, especially, that we will never have these particular children in this particular way again. Our Gambol work allows us to linger over this wondrous moment in our children's and our lives--for a whole year. While they drive to concerts or to jobs, while we hardly ever see them anymore even though they still live at home, we hold them to us in our cutting of leaves, folding of fabric, painting or wiring of tubes, in this final month of their childhood lives.

And there is one thing more. We are aware, as we off-handedly share with one another where WE went to college, that this, after all, has small meaning in the scope of what our lives have become. We, a generation of women who thought that career would define our lives, have learned something precious over these nearly 2 decades of raising our children. What we do in our day jobs may be very interesting, it may fulfill a part of us, we may enjoy it, but it is not what we find ourselves talking about together. It is not, in the end, what has defined our lives, after all. Our jobs, whatever they be, are linear, taking us in one direction or another. But this other thing we do, motherhood, is cyclical, taking us backward into our own histories and forward into futures filled with yet-to-be-discovered important relationships. This motherhood job links us together, whoever we are and wherever we've come from.

Perhaps there was a time when some of us would have rolled our eyes and felt a certain disdain for women sitting around each evening, making leaves and talking about their kids. We might have mistaken what we saw for narrowness or a sense that there should be something more in these people's lives. But each night, as we work together, as we talk about who has her dress and who will be sharing which limo, we are, in some deep place, aware, that we are talking about the most important thing there is to talk about. We are talking about that moment when our children will belong more to the world than to us; we are talking about the fact that others will come to know them better than we do; we are talking about the fact that where they go, we cannot follow. We are talking about the utter fullness that has been ours in having had and raised these children, and we are talking about the overflowing fullness we feel in letting them go.

Published *in Port Washington News* June 24, 1999, Vol. 66, No. 46

Gambol Night

Chomping on gum, like carefree cows
who might as well own the world on which they graze;
Wobbling and strutting, like newborn gazelles propelled
and restrained by only their newness in the world;
Raising fists and arms, like revolutionaries pledging solidarity
in their promise to go forth and make a better world
They arrive.

Arm in arm they support each other,
Or they walk courageously alone
As they confidently or tentatively steer themselves toward the
place where they will enter.

Before the welcoming, watchful, wistful eyes of their town
They emerge.

The youngest of the town are the fashion critics,
Commenting on each gown, on hair, on tux,
Fashioning fantasies of what they, themselves, will wear, and
who will walk beside them when time will tell them it is
their turn.

We are next, we who look with awe and bafflement and
fullness
Upon that which is exquisitely familiar and yet barely
recognizable,
Upon those whom we and time together have created.
And we are inarticulate in the face of what is before us,
For the sum total of what was given by us and what was
given by time
Does not equal what is before us.
They are unfathomably more.
Possibility electrifies them:
It sprouts from their heads in beards or braids,
And overflows their gowns which can barely contain

Their bountiful youth.
There is something unutterably hopeful
In the faces and the bodies that walk before our eyes
And captivate our hearts.

The elders watch, too,
Enjoying the pomp, the entrance, the evening.
And memory is stirred,
And knowing is stirred,
As if it were actually memory, already,
Of a time that is not yet,
A knowing that is not filled with bafflement
But with trust and certainty
Because it has been known more than once.
The elders know why it is that the town gathers and watches,
And as the new ones' emergence is announced, we—all of
us—in a moment know it, also:

We know that these people, chewing or stumbling, or
celebrating their way to the entrance,
These people ripe with the possibility of everything
Will continue what has been begun.
These are the people who, very soon, will cease chewing,
and will no longer stumble,
But will, we all hope, celebrate, forever, what has been
handed them,
Joining it to what they will discover,
And to what they will create,
Until the time, a long time hence,
When they will look lovingly at the new chewers.
And when they do this, they will know, because **they** will be
elders then,
That the chewing and the stumbling are those sweet
moments
Before the new ones take up the business of the world.

(June, 1998)
Published in *Port Washington News*, June 24, 1999, p. 26

To Dan: on Leaving for College

A parable: When I was a little girl I used to spend long days in the late summer and early fall collecting acorns and hickory nuts. I'd keep them separate and fill lunch bags full of each. My brother and I would have contests about who had collected the most nuts. I loved the smell of the hickory nuts and was thrilled when I'd find a huge one. When winter came, we would each count out 10 of each kind of nut and place a neat and careful pile, each day, at the foot of each tree in our back yard. We were taking care of the squirrels, to make sure that they had enough food for the winter.

No one told me then something that I would come to know 40 years later. By collecting up all that was needed, and doling it out, no matter how generously, the squirrels would learn one of two things: either they would leave our yard, seeing that there were almost no nuts to be had (all of them being in Sandy's and my lunch bags), not knowing that they would magically reappear when **we** thought **they** would most need them; or they would stay and not ever be able to leave our yard, becoming dependent on our system of neat nut piles, and losing their ability to store up their own nuts in their own way.

So I know now that squirrels will come and go freely when nut trees grow freely, and when they can find them, eat them, store them as **they** need to, according to their instincts.

This has been the thing that daddy and I have struggled over more than anything else in helping you grow up--how much do we put under the tree for you and how much do we let nuts of opportunity lie in front of you, knowing that some will blow away before you have found them, some will be buried under leaves, some rotted under snow, and

August, 2000

Dear Jo,

I hope you get this before you leave Israel. I am going to send it special mail, so that you will. I feel badly that I even tried to explain Charles' motivations today when you called. I know that you were telling me something really important about what you had observed and how appalled you were that an adult in his position could act like he did to a 15 year old kid. I very much appreciate your view of the incident and I trust that your perception was quite accurate (it usually is). I'm sorry I didn't respond with a more supportive understanding to you—I knew as soon as we hung up that you had needed that from me and that I disappointed you. I disappointed myself in trying, somehow, to take Charles' point of view. Since we hung up I have been composing a letter in my head that maybe I'll write and maybe I'll send (long after you're home) that tells him how he missed about 180 opportunities (or however many kids are under his supervision this summer) to turn kids on to something really special. How he tainted Israel, study, service by assuming the worst about kids, rather than assuming the best. How kids probably acted out a little because they were treated disrespectfully. Daddy and I talked to each other about how Charles could use a psychological consultant for him and his counselors to help him and them understand what is normal, healthy, desireable, in teenagers, and to understand that his restrictions and rules undermine your experience there, rather than enhance it. We intend, at the very least, to demand that he not use our names as recommendations. We will wait until we have had time to digest all of this with you before we do anything, but we are behind you and feel very badly that what should be a wonderful, full, enriching summer has been smudged with this other terrible stuff. I only hope that you pull out of the summer, as you did last year, something good to take with you. Last year was also difficult, yet your memory of it emerged triumphant. I hope it is possible to have something like that this summer, too. You are experiencing far too much of the schmuck theory in your summers!

I can't wait for you to call again. I hope all of the kids in the group are a strong support to one another. Don't even pay attention to what Charles will try to tell you on the last night—that you all don't matter. In the long run, Charles has proven himself to be a person who doesn't matter, who is not true to what he says, and who seems to misunderstand his own mission. I picture that when he wants to engage you all in some discussion at the end about how the people in the group don't matter, etc. , and when he baits all of you to get angry at him, that if no one even responds at all—if you all just sit there and refuse to let him go down that path—he will get very frustrated and upset (but he will have failed to get you guys upset), and that maybe that will be your triumph over him.

Well, babe, I just needed to tell you that I love you and support you and am sorry to have disappointed you today on the phone. I focused on the wrong thing.

Hold onto you and don't let anyone, most especially a misguided adult, unplant your feet. Stand firm in what you know is important. I have faith in you.

Love, Mom

Eden Lost

There was a moment in time
Before time even began
When all was Eden,
Was just as it should be.
But then arrived a serpent
(Had been there all along)
The instrument of betrayal, some say.
No, more mundane than that.
Merely time
Undulating its way toward us
Silently ticking
The inevitability
Of moving,
Of leaving Eden
Which was, all of a sudden,
Eden no longer.
But the serpent was always there
And had, at some point,
To have been seen,
And once seen
Engaged;
And once engaged,
Understood
As the destroyer of worlds,
The opener of gates.
No, not in the manner of Oppenheimer,
Do not misunderstand.
More mundane,
And more inevitable,
Like a womb,
In time,
Must expel its residents.
Like that,
As ordinary,

And inevitable,
And important
As that.
There was yet another moment in time
Long after time began
When time was frozen
And Eden was again,
When the waters of Armington
Fed your soul
Like a garden of unforbidden fruits.
No serpent there,
Yet lurked the blessing
(Always present)
Of warm, summer days
That would unfreeze time
Which would take you by the hand,
You latter-day Adam,
And once again,
Lead you out of Eden.

So, you will go forth
Out of this Eden, too.
But carry its godly imprint
Like DNA threads
To replicate the spirit of this Eden
Where'ere you go,
Serpents and thirteen year old boys
Notwithstanding.

for Dan with love

Seventeen

It is the year when we awaken for the first time
and know ourselves as ourselves—the self we will remember
from here on out;

it is the year when we long to walk away
from the Eden
that can no longer contain our dreams;

it is the year when we turn from our mothers
who have loved us for who we have been,
who are strangers now,
unable to imagine what we may become;

it is the time when our ripeness overflows
the tiny tank tops and too short shorts
we wear;

it is the time when sex is always a moment away
whether it is or not.

It is the time when we seek our soul's mate
the one who will take our hand
as we walk together
from seventeen
to forever.

(January 19, 2001)

Who Knows Where the Time Goes

The large vinyl record
Spins slowly and unevenly
Beneath the relentless scratch of the needle.

From nearby speakers
Comes a crackling static
Attesting to the age of the record,
The warped swirl of the spin
Defining its overuse
In a time gone by.

There was a time that I listened to this record
Over and over,
And then a lapse of twenty years
When time was telescoped
Like a Dopler wave
Compressed as it approaches you,
The noise of time
And the close clustering of the busy-ness of life
Obscuring reflection.

But of late
I think of the record often
And look forward to pulling it out
With a needy anticipation,
Like a lover on her way to a secret rendezvous.

Words come:
"Hello, hooray
Let the show begin
I'm ready."

But these are not the words I am waiting for,
Though they are right, too.
The ones I need come five songs later:

"Across the morning sky
All the birds are leaving.
Oh, how do they know
It's time for them to go?"

Just last night
As she sat on the counter top
While I made a cup of tea
My daughter said,
"What are you going to do, now that all your..."
She paused, feeling a little silly about what she was about to
say,
But drawn to say it nonetheless,
"...now that all your little birds will have left the nest?"

She began to laugh and then
As the perfect symmetry of crystalline snow flakes
Warms indistinguishably to muddy rain,
Her laughter slid down the length of her face,
Mascara tracks marring the smooth surface,
Their etchings bearing witness to the woman replacing the
young girl.

She was sad for me
But was transported into her own disbelieving realization
That soon she would never live here again.

I turn on the old record player
And ritualistically set the needle.
The diamond head etches its way across
A thousand tiny mars
Inscribed by time and a young girl's love of a song
"Who knows where the time goes?
Who knows where the time goes?"

(February, 2001)

An Introduction to a Passover Poem: on Jo's Leaving

The story we have just read is about many things. At its most obvious, it is about a people freeing themselves from slavery.

But it is also about a people growing up, becoming strong emotionally together in preparation for the moment of departure.

It is about Moses, who grows up, and comes to define himself as who he is.

It is about Moses, unable to lead, unable to leave, until he finds his voice.

It is about Pharoah whose heart softens in response to the loss of his child.

It is about the birth of a new definition of a people, the beginning of a new life.

There are many of you here tonight who stand on the edge of a new beginning. Our Passover gathering will celebrate your new beginnings.

I would like to share a poem, that is not a Passover poem, *per se*, but it is a poem about all of the things that Passover is about.

It is entitled: "I Always Thought That I Would Not Miss These Things, But Now I Think That I Was Wrong About That."

It is dedicated to Joanna, who stands on the brink of her exodus.

(April, 2001)

I Always Thought That I Would Not Miss These Things; But Now I Think That I Was Wrong About That

Canto I

It is 3:30
The bookbag finds its way,
Like a moth to the porch light,
To the center of the first step.

The jacket slides off of the wrist—
Not the fingers, no,
That might have triggered a primordial response
To clutch the coat, using that great evolutionary
achievement,
The opposable thumb;
And that, in turn, might have triggered a higher, cortical
response
To place the jacket, with intentionality,
Where jackets belong—
No, it does not happen this way,
But bypasses fingers, altogether,
Bypasses the possibility of cortex thought,
Slides right from the wrist,
And drops dead, there where it lands,
Somewhere about a step below the bookbag.

And I? I approach
With laundry basket overflowing
With things dirty and things that found their way into the
basket because tossing them there was easier than
folding,
All obscuring my vision.
I approach naively thinking that the way is clear,
That safety reigns within my home's borders,
Not suspecting that I am seconds away

From an imminent tumble and a possible break of some large
and important bone in my body.
But hey, it would only be a one step fall.

Everyday at 3:30 P.M.
For years
There was no doubt
That I would not miss the littered step
When you left for college.

But now, I am not so sure.
If the bookbag is not there,
If the old yellow or red jacket
Stays put on the hook,
Then it means that you are not here
To tell me about your day:
About the frustratingly outrageous things that Mr. Jones said,
The fight that you and Hill had,
The way you outsmarted the security guards
Who thought you were a senior for 4 years and let you off
campus
(Who thought you were Danielle Lindner, with a white van)
The fact that the class average on a physics test was 54,
making your 55 a perfectly stupendous grade,
How you have avoided "tank time" for 4 years,
How you are sure the guy who sits behind you in physics likes
you.

No, if the bookbag does not threaten my life,
It means that I am eating chocolate alone at 3:30 in the
afternoon.
And do not know who has broken up with whom
Who has a crush on whom
Who might ask whom to the prom.

Canto II

Years ago
We packed up your girlhood books
And put them in the attic
To be saved and enjoyed by your daughter(s) someday.

We put them in their series, In boxes:
A hundred and three Sweet Valley Twins and High books
All in order;
Twenty some Thoroughbred books
All in order;
A dozen or so Saddle Club books
All in order;
However many Peanut Butter and Jelly books were written
All in order;
A slew of Babysitter Club books (80?),
All in order.

We labeled each box and interflapped the lids.
Catalogued and clear; nice and neat.
Dormant for the next 20 years.

But no,
You request
That I wake up these dormant boxes,
Rummage through these books,
And pick "some good ones"
For you to read again.
And again and again.

I thought
That when you left for college
I could finally put books from your youth
Back in their boxes,
All in order,

And close those lids
Once and for all.
And that this would feel real satisfying,
Nice and neat.

But I think I was wrong about that.
I will miss your forays into your youth,
Your memory of horses and California girls with blue-green
eyes,
Of the lucky little girls of divorced parents,
Who got to live in two houses,
Of the times when we laid together in your bed
And I read to you
Long after you could read for yourself,
So that you could twist and sniff your pony's tail and suck your
thumb,
And drift into a dreamy state of relaxed consciousness.
I will miss how unabashed you were
At 16, still requesting 4 or 5 Sweet Valley books
And reading them all in one night.
I am sure that no one has read One More River more times
than you.
You sure got your money's worth out of a book,
And you are as fiercely loyal to your beloved books
As you are to Mary and Cuddles and Moosie
And all the newcomers daddy has added
Even though they have not had time to absorb the lore and
smells of your girlhood days.

No, it will not be satisfying to pack those books away
Knowing that it will be a very long time
Until they are read again,
And that when they are
You will be in my place.
It is a long time for books to stay asleep.

Canto III

Could you get me a glass of water?
It is the classic refrain,
The classic stall tactic,
The classic dawdle technique
Of a 3 year old.

It is, in our house, an art form,
Honed and chiseled to perfection for 15 years.
Just when I think we are ready for the final tuck,
The kiss, the hug, the song,
Ready for me to go to sleep myself
After an hour of bedtime rituals,
Comes the request: "Can I have a glass of water?"

I was definitely sure I would not miss this,
This ritual of fetching how many glasses of water
Since you were 3?

But, yes, I will miss this too.
Because if there is no one to fetch a glass of water for,
It means that you are not here to tuck into bed:
To knead into bread;
To sing "Hillmen" to;
To sing the soothing lullaby, "Eve of Destruction" to;
To give an alcohol rub to;
To give a foot massage to;
To sing a hundred Hebrew prayers with;
To sing *Yerushalayim shel zahav* with;
To sing *Lu y'hi* with;
To try and sing *Asher Yatzar* and *Elohai elohai* in two parts
    together;
To debrief about your day with;
To pretend to hit you over the head so you could fall asleep;
To go and make a cup of hot chocolate on Sunday night to
    conquer "Sunday night insomnia";

Somehow going to sleep, just like that, is far too easy.
And the days of singing "Hillmen" with daddy,
Are too long gone.

Canto IV

It has been my secret challenge
To use up the last dregs of hair conditioner,
Shampoo, body wash, toothpaste,
Those dregs that you did not have the patience to squeeze
out,
Or the frugality to mix with water
So that every last drop could be used,
And not a pinch wasted.

There were times that I had 4 different kinds of conditioners
And 3 old, defunct razors (with a summer's supply of blades)
All things you had to have, but then found a better brand
When you were 9/10 of the way through with one.

As loyal as you are to your books,
You are that fickle with hair products or cosmetics.

So, it was my job to use those last drops, that somehow,
Like miraculous Chanukah oil,
Lasted weeks and even months,
Instead of the 2 days' worth that it seemed was in there.

I was pretty sure that when you left for college
I could have one bottle of shampoo,
One bottle of conditioner,
One tube of body wash
And that the bathtub would not look like a Genovese display
case.
How simplified a bath would be.
And I could finally choose my own favorite brands,
Instead of using up your dregs.

But, I'm not so sure.
If there are not 16 hair and bath products on my tub's edges
It means that you are not showering in there nightly.
Oh, yes, my bathmat will be dry
But I will not be able to sneak into my room
And listen though closed door
To your uninhibited, unwarbly, clear, sweet voice
Crooning your favorite songs, unaware that you have a
    secret audience.
It is a large bathroom for only 3 or 4 bottles of bath things,
    really,
And its vaulted ceiling was made for echoing song.
And I will miss your song.

Canto V

Will you blow my hair out?
The set-up alone
Takes half an evening:
Six bottles of Redkin things named
Str-8, Frizz Complex, Smooth, Stay, Groom
Things for before the blowing
Things for after the blowing
And an hour of separating, clipping, yanking, pulling.
These hands that were not trained in beauty school
Attempting to coordinate themselves with blower, globe-
    sized circle brush, and small segment of hair
Surely a formula for carpal tunnel syndrome.
And the result, after an hour, is never quite as good as when
    Yessi does it.
But when Yessi does it
You do not sit for an hour and sing with her 27 verses of the
    song we wrote to *Bagadi Katan* to remember our Israel
    trip.

It is a wonder to me
That you do not see your hair
Those free, and unfettered, abundant and full curls
As the perfect expression of the all that is untameable about
you.
While you are busy piercing various appendages
And tatooing others
Finding strange foreign languages with perfect human
messages
To ink into your body,
While you eagerly await a jump from a plane
And a free-fall to earth,
While you seek freedoms and expressions that all say
something like "Don't tie me down cause I'd never
stay"
You will also sit for hours and try to shackle your hair into
behaving in ways that you, surely, would never stand
for!
Ah, but this is you, in all your contradictoriness.

And while soon my hands will relax at night,
Surely I will lose some dexterity if I am not called upon to
coordinate 3 things in my 2 hands,
And I may soon forget those 27 verses if I do not practice
them with you,
And I will miss the pleasure that we both took in sitting for an
hour
And sharing random thoughts and songs,
Just us two girls, doing your hair,
In the bathroom together.

Canto VI

Ah, the room.
Has the Una-bomber been here?
We've been vandalized.
Someone has turned your room upside down

Looking for some top secret, classified spy information.
Couldn't have been robbery as a motive...
Because he left the 20 crumpled dollar bills and loose change
right out there on the dresser top...and floor.

This one, I definitely will not miss.
I have craved a gorgeous, spotless room
Where the deep blue carpet shows off its plushness
And the Golden Oldie distressed pine furniture
Is content to have been distressed a long time ago
And not today.
Where the Imelda Marcos shoe collection remains lined up
Two of a kind
On the closet floor.
Ah, how I looked forward to those days
When I could get my hands on your room.

But, alas, how empty it will be
(Do I dare admit this to you before you leave?)
If the clothes stay put in drawers and on hangars,
The shoes in pairs in place
If the empty rewetting drop tubes have all found their way
into the trash
And the eyeliner and lipliner pencil shavings have joined
them there,
Then it means that you are gone.
It means that Amy and Dara and Hillary and Jessie have not
been here recently
Trading wardrobes in order to combine just the right tops and
bottoms and boots
To maximize the slutty look.
I will miss tripping over Dara's size 8, 9 inch high platform
boots, that all of you figured out a way to fit into;
I will miss knowing when Amy's mom has been to the Gap, so
that we all can share in her newest acquisition;
I will miss having you and Hillary switch your tankini tops and
bottoms, so that you end up in red and blue again, just

like those days, so long ago, when you were twin
Buckley girls;
I will miss Jenna's bathing suit for a year;
Marlyn's pants that you figured you'd just keep;
Julia Trinko's red hooded shirt, that she never knew you even
had;
And our shared pants from Express that began crisply folded
on a hangar in my closet,
And ended up with all the others, on your floor.
I will miss the moment when your hanging chair was clean
enough for your friends to sit and swing on, as you
gossiped an evening away.

If it is too clean, then none of you is here, getting ready for
some evening out
Trying on every pair of jeans in your combined closets
Because the nuance of difference between one and another
pair Is large enough to make empires topple.

Yes, in the end, I will miss this too,
Though I might not be quite as sad while I am missing this!

Canto VII

The large plastic file box
With multi-colored, hanging, file dividers
With brochures and booklets peeking out above each
temporary wall
Sits patiently but beckoningly on the guest bed.

And on the booklets
Are the names:
Connecticut
Haverford
Middlebury
Pitzer
Pomona

Washington
Wesleyan

The names of places
Any one of whom might claim you for its own
By the time the leaves have all fallen
Within the next 40 days.

The purple lid has been
Home to half-completed papers,
Gridded check lists of dates
Looming like hooded henchmen
With axes poised.

I wonder if the purple lid
Has felt rejected,
(Though I know it was not personal)
On all those evenings when you,
Practicing an ancient adolescent
Style of meditation
Intoned your mantra;
Not yours alone,
But a mantra shared by thousands of other seventeen year
olds
Each fall,
Across this great land of ours:
"Not tonight."

And, I,
Like a dutiful Buddhist postulate,
Endured the frustration
Of that which I could not control.
The frustration
Of wanting to be done with applications, already;
Of wanting the spare bed clean;
Of wanting to be the benevolent donor
To some needy family

Of 2 Fiske catalogues,
And a host of other tomes;
Of wanting to put a pink check mark
And the word: "Sent"
In every column.

But I learned
The acceptance of a lama
Because I learned
That "not tonight" meant
You were still percolating
Your thoughts;
That if I rushed you,
It would be like pouring weak coffee from a barely-warmed
urn.
And best of all,
If I let it go
The richness of what would eventually pour forth from you
Would be like witnessing a holy act of creation
Worth the wait and more.

I learned that my daughter is a poet
With the treasure trove of myth and metaphor
To anchor her unique expressions upon a canvas that is larger
than her.

I learned that coded on a 3.5 floppy disk
That she had forgotten about
Was a cache of golden words
Made all the more precious
For having been written by her 14 year old self.

I learned that every essay she would need
Had already been born
And that she and I together had only to wait
For her to remember that she had already given birth
And that her words were grown enough

To set them free.

Like everything else
If your college applications are finished
Your disk full
The essays all written...
If the purple box lid is empty
And the file box is now mine
Then it means that you are on your way.
And the next application
In your life will be filled out
Not in this room
On the green and purple bedspread
And not with my editorial eye,
But by yourself.

Canto VIII

So, Jo,
Your essays will be done,
Your room will be neat,
I will be using my own, chosen shampoos, conditioners, and
razor brands,
I will become a beauty school drop out,
Your Sweet Valley books will be put away,
You will have a roommate who will probably not give you a
foot massage and not tuck you in,
Your jacket and bookbag will not threaten my life on the front
hall steps.

And, as this moment of orderliness draws closer,
I know that I will miss
The careless scatter of the things of your life
All over the spaces of my life.
And, oh how I will miss the scatterer!

But, truly, I will learn to live with everything in its place

Though when that happens I will love it less than I would have imagined.
The real solace and pleasure will not come from the orderliness,
But from knowing that
When everything here is in its place
It will mean that you, too, are in your place
And that is what we,
And you,
Have lived for
All along.

What We Will See at the Gambol...

Tomorrow night, hundreds of beautiful, elegant young women and handsome, dazzling young men will arrive by coach to a waiting throng of spectators, and walk up a pathway that will lead them forever away from us. The crowd will murmur and applaud as each, in his and her radiance, walks before their eager eyes. And what is it that we will see, as we watch them enter their high school for the last time?

We will see, pulsing right beneath the surface of their womanly or manly faces, the roundness and softness of a 2-year old's face.

We will see the little hands of unselfconscious 4 year olds who could while away an afternoon detaching the empty hulls of cicadas from every tree and fence on the block, filling whole buckets for "cicada-shell stew."

We will see the toothless grin of their 6-year old selves.

We will see 13 previous Gambols when six flushed, young girls would walk home across the Willowdale Bridge at 11:45 PM, not tired at all, excitedly designing the Gambol dresses they would wear more than a decade from then, and assigning which boys would go with which girls.

We will see compact 8-year old bodies that rode horses and danced in pink tutus.

We will see the miraculous transformation that happened to 11 and 12 year olds, when their tadpole bodies changed so that they could become the princes and princesses who walk before us now.

We will see the moment when they became taller than we are, and wonder at what moment it was, precisely, when they left us behind.

We will see our familiar children, and somehow, barely recognize them.

We will see, in alternating focus and haze, a past and a future parade before us.

We will see, in each one, children whom we once knew, and adults we have yet to meet.

We will see the moment when this dream of ours began, some 18 years ago and think, hauntingly, of a song that marked our own 18th year, and find ourselves singing unconsciously for the next few weeks: "Who knows where the time goes? Who knows where the time goes?"

We will see bounty and ripeness, possibility and hopefulness.

Yes, we will see all this, as we watch them walk into Times Square, their Gambol world, a world that we created for them, for this one night, alone.

And the next day? We will see them walk into that other world, the world that they will create for themselves.

But for this one night, we will linger with the sweetness of their youth, and hold them, if only with our eyes, this one last time.

(2001)
Published in *Port Washington News*, June 21, 2001, p. 26

August 24, 2001

Dear Jobie-Wan...

Welcome to ConnColl! I imagine that right now (12:30 AM Thursday night) you are crying with Jessie, and that you spent a few hours before this crying with Dara and Hil and Zan. I hope you got to see everyone tonight and say goodbye.

I know you have felt sad over these past few weeks about all that you are leaving. And you've felt anxious about the vast unknown that lies before you (but that you are smack, dab, in the middle of right now as you read this). But, while it is sad that this is the end of something that has been long and luxurious and wonderful and maddening at times, it is, once again, time to leave. You have been in this place before—on the threshold of leaving, you have written about this moment, but I know it does not make it any easier to do it once again. In a way you are not much different from how you were when you were 2. At the moment of leaving, you are terribly ambivalent about leaving and almost want to turn the clock back. But once you've made the break, you are more than fine, and you look forward instead of back.

You might misunderstand what I'm about to say, but I hope that you've left your home friends far behind. They are not forgotten and they never will be, and you will all rejoin in a few months, but for now, it is OK to let go of them so that you can "become" the you that will be living this new life. And that is both the gift and the burden—that you (and they) will continue to evolve into new selves in a life that you guys don't share any longer, and when you do rejoin, you will all be different a little. That is a little sad, but if you are not all a little different, that will be even sadder.

So, I'm thinking about you as you are letting go of the "this" that you have known for so long in order to prepare for the "that" that is not yet known. But in a way, you are not really letting go, but rather drinking in one long, deep, final drink of the best that these 17 years have given you, so that it is all within you and you will digest it and take it with you wherever you go. And yes, when you bring it back, it will have changed and will be different; just like food and drink, you cannot take sustenance and nurturance and grow from them unless you change them as you take them in.

So, Jo, go from strength to strength, within you, ever Eden, and before you always, the place of Promise.

We love you and already miss you.........

Love, Mom and Dad

I'm a *Dawson's Creek* Junkie

I am a *Dawson's Creek* junkie. And *Felicity*. You might assume, from that initial confession, that I am somewhere between the ages of 15 and 25. No. I have another confession. I am 50. And I love these shows.

I am a little embarrassed, I must admit, when a friend or my mother-in-law calls on Wednesday night between 8 and 10, and I have to say, "I'll call you back. I'm in the middle of *Dawson's*." But only a little.

I love Joey, and Jen, Dawson and Pacey and Jack. I am growing to love Joey's new roommate, Audrey. I love Felicity and Noel; I don't love Ben, but I do want good things for him—just not Felicity. Sean and Megan have grown on me. I adore Javier.

Here is why I love these late-adolescent, young adult characters so much. My own two late-adolescent, young adult characters have recently left home. When my daughter was home last year, she and her cadre of friends would have "Dawson's parties" where they would congregate at someone's home and watch together. I, of course, was banned from such gatherings. So, I only watched Dawson's one or two times before this year. Now I am hooked. I want them all to flower into confident, comfortable people who carry each other in their hearts and move forward out of 18 into a world that they create for themselves. I want them all to fall in love and feel so content and radiant, so full and alive, transformed from their still plump-cheeked, juicy, sweet, sapling selves into the bloom of graceful, fully flowering maturity.

If you are a *Dawson's* or *Felicity* watcher, you may have noticed that although they are all in college now, there is little time devoted to what they are learning. No, this is not a flaw in the script writing. It is, I think, a given, that they are learning. Felicity has found an important artistic talent and identity, switching from pre-med to art, at the grave risk (and reality) of being cut off financially and emotionally from her parents for this independent and necessary choice. Ben has moved, finally, and passionately, from being directionless to pursuing a pre-med program, in his senior year, no less. Dawson, having always been of single vision about his future, dropped out of his film program early on. And Joey may be a writer, if she is willing to forego some A's along the way and struggle through to find her voice. And Pacey has developed his culinary talents, and even, recently, chose to turn down that offer of a lifetime on a sailing boat, knowing inside that the possibilities were deeper and richer, if not broader, right there at home. Oh yes, they are learning, whether they are in college or working. They are either allowing or resisting the forces around them to chisel and shape them, as they, simultaneously, figure out how to place their imprint upon and change the shape of their world.

But no, the main story lines of both shows are not about college classes. They are about love: falling in, falling out, searching for, yearning for, feeling cheated by, feeling chosen by. It is painful to watch, sometimes, and at these times I pick up the phone and call Joanna, who is watching with her new friends 200 miles away. Exasperated, I proclaim, for the 4th year in a row: "Why doesn't Felicity know that she's in love with Noel?!" "Why can't she see that he is right for her, that Ben doesn't really love her, that Noel does?!" It is our joke. Joanna has always had a thing for Ben and his green eyes. I contend that his eyes are blue and Noel's are green. I'm a sucker for Noel's sweetness and boyish cuteness; Joanna likes Ben's aloofness and tendency to be a 'bad boy.' We both know whom each of us is rooting for. But really, we're rooting for Felicity. No, actually, I think we're rooting for Joanna, for while she does not yet have a Noel or a Ben in her life, it is what she will be looking for. It is, partly, what this stage of her life will be about, every bit as much as thinking and learning. She is ready to be sculpted by love.

So, I want to know what will become of Joey and Dawson, Pacey and Jen, how it will end with Felicity, how it will begin for Joanna.

B'reishit

Rose-petal velvet
wraps itself around engorged, pebbled hardness,
creating a vacuum seal
so fierce
its whole body might be supported by this, alone.

And then:
tug,
tug,
tug—
will not accept no for an answer—
this tiny softness
causes hot prickles
to crowd themselves into the place
I already thought was too full,
just before that sweet let down,
which, like the burning bush, unconsumed,
leaves me full, though I am emptied.

Not five thousand, seven hundred, sixty-four years ago,
not fourteen billion years ago,
but now,
this:
this waggling bud, transplanted right from Eden,
this charged pulse, reaching out like that finger toward Adam,
this biggest little bang of all.

Not yet sixty seconds old,
this organ of silk
with the tensile strength of steel,
that does not yet know
how to shape itself
into declarations of war,
knows how to do this:

to suck for dear life,
bringing forth into the world
far, far more than milk.

(February 27, 2004)

On the Wisdom of Not Considering Every Possible Contingency

The first warm day
spears of lime green
push
from a place of mystery
parting soil
that only yesterday
was packed tight with snow.
As quickly as a newborn's
intake of air
fragile flowers bloom
in pre-ordained sequence:
snowdrop, crocus, daffodil, tulip.
They did not wait
for perfect solar alignment
or the surety of winter's end.
Days later,
snow, again,
filigreed and light
as spun sugar
draped upon
quivering pink blossoms
of the rhododendron
that had rushed
headlong into spring
heedless of the possibility
that winter's last hurrah
was yet to come.
And even had she known
there would have been
no other choice,
no better choice.

(March 29, 2004)
(March 14, 2009)

On Observing a Dog in a Meadow

Gravity loses its grip:
Back legs tuck up under her
Like landing gear
Retracting into the belly of a plane.

Front legs reach out far
Into space she does not yet possess
Becoming wings
Creating her own updraft.

She flies across the meadow
Like my favorite dream:
Suspended above the grass
In aerodynamic ecstasy.

She shows you how it is done:
To reach into the
Yet-to-be known
Refusing to let earth
Or any thing less worthy
Hold you back;
To leap without
Perfect knowing
Trusting your legs to
Touch down
In a place
That just might be
A Promised Land.

(April 17, 2005)

Published in *Jewish Currents*, May-June, 2007
Published online in *Soul-Lit*, November, 2012

December, 2005

Dear Jo,

I've been following yours and daddy's conversations and just wanted to insert my thoughts. One of the things I LOVED about my teacher in high school is that she never belittled our idealism, but loved us for it. It was frustrating that most other adults did that polite smile thing and dismissed us as immature for thinking we could change the world.

I think that that is the supreme pity of adulthood. It has saddened me that your generation seems to have generally missed or skipped the idealistic phase of life--many of them jumping into monied positions, accepting jobs that do not better the world but only their own circumstance, and accepting the shackles of reality way too soon. I LOVE your idealism (and I know daddy feels the same). It is not immature or silly or unrealistic. It is from such dreams that the holiest aspirations of humanity spring. Without our youth being idealistic and showing us reflections of our hypocrisy and the ways we've sold out, we would be even less civilized than we are. Youthful idealism isn't a phase to grow out of. It is the time of life we see clearest how things should be, when we want better for humanity, when we are charged with such passionate energy that we just might be able to move a mountain--even the tiniest bit, and maybe thereby shake the world into sense. There are many things about adulthood to aspire to....but the capitulation to reality is not one of them. For me (and I think dad too) the profession we chose allows us to hold that idealism--yes, people CAN change, and love CAN be had and felt, and we surround ourselves with children who hold all that possibility for the future. So, surround yourself with people who will nurture your idealism, who will add fuel to your passion for equality and rightness within the world (not by making you justify it, but by saying yes yes yes that is how it should be). Your idealism is one of the most exciting, alive, fertile (no laughs here please) electric things about you. Reality will intrude itself, and you will come to accept some of that too--but unlike Rudy, I say, don't let the flame of your passion and vision go out too quickly. See if maybe it can remain a steady light, to illuminate your way as you go and heal the world.

Love,

Mommy

Sonnet for Joanna on the Eve of Her Departure for a New World, a New Life

Like the moon that circles tightly 'round the earth
Tucked safely within gravity's embrace
You, a knowing orbit long have traced
For light years, since the moment of your birth.

A different orbit now you shall describe
Like comets do, both near and far from source
That draws them back and sets them on their course
Launched on new paths that they'll inscribe.

So as you look to heaven's huge expanse
And chart your stellar course anew this eve
Putting trust (and hope) in sun-riped, honeyed chance
Unsure to the core of what you may receive

Let gravity briefly pull you again in tow
Then I with you shall weep, rejoice, let go.

(February 7, 2006)

The Transmission of Tradition: an Australian *Amidah*

L'dor v'dor...and they shall go forth from their native land, from the house of their father and mother, and go to a land that they will show us, and if they take with them the courage of their fathers and the wisdom of their mothers, we need not fear.

In her blog—www.orble.com/no-place-like-oz/--of September 26, 2006, she writes that ten years ago, on the occasion of her becoming a *Bat Mitzvah* she was told she was now a Jewish woman. But, she goes on to say, she really, officially, became a Jewish woman last night in a home she is creating for herself eleven thousand miles away from her native land.

There, she went on an urban hunting expedition, criss-crossing an entire city in search of the cut of meat that we call brisket; there, she unearthed every appliance in her shared apartment kitchen, mixing together sour cream, vanilla, fruit for noodle *kugel*, using broken-up lasagna noodles because I had forgotten to tell her to buy egg noodles; there, like a potter molding her clay, she massaged into existence *matzoh* balls, and made chickenless chicken soup, fit for her Hindu vegetarian friends; there, because she had no electric processor or even food mill grinder, she improvised, with mortar and pestle, like some medieval apothecary, the making of her great-grandmother's healing potion: the liver of a chicken, mixed with other secret ingredients; there, she shared the family challah recipe with one of her more curious friends who had volunteered to help her with the cooking, who would bake his first loaves of bread and say the word *challah* for the first time. There, she 'convened' a 'congregation' of twenty-five fellow graduate students, representing at least 5 major religions, from all over the world, twenty three of whom had never tasted a morsel of Jewish food before, to share this holiday meal with her as she celebrated *Rosh Hashanah*.

She called us at eleven o'clock that night—her time—which was still the morning of *erev Rosh Hashanah* our time—to report the meal's huge success, that even the chopped liver, which she thought was an acquired taste, went—right off the bat, that Ross's circular, braided, shiny-egg-brushed *challahs* were almost too beautiful to eat.

She said that she now understands that ten years ago, as she chanted *trop*, and interpreted *Torah* through the eyes of her dozen years, and led the congregation in the melodies and words of a Jewish prayer service, she was really absorbing a community's confidence in her, that someday she would stand where she stood last night, in a home of her own making, and celebrate a new year, placing, as our ancestors did with the fringes of their *tallit*, her own signature on the ritual. She said that last night, she felt herself to be, legitimately, a Jewish woman.

She did not go to synagogue last night. But she performed an *Amidah* standing in her kitchen, invoking her ancestors in the form of recipes, handed from generation to generation, those holy texts, as sacred as the other one—parchment stretched lovingly like strudel dough, between two wooden rolling pins.

(October 1, 2006)

Lech L'Cha
Go Forth

It is a long way from Eden to Canaan
from that dimly perceived place
that was
before memory
to the one yet unformed before your eyes.

As you sojourn from one to the other:

Be Eve:
hunger for knowledge
and walk through the gate
that will close forever behind you
so that you might know blossoms and fruits
unknown in Eden;

Be Abraham:
struggle with impossible choices;
look around you
and look again;
try mightily to understand
what you are to make
of a ram in a thicket;

Be Jacob:
dream ladders to heaven
and invite encounters with angels;
welcome life's imprint upon you
so that you are Jacob and no longer Jacob;

Be Nahshon:
walk into the water
knowing that the sea does not part
until one person steps into it;
not from the shores, from the edges of experience

do such wonders happen;
the sea does not transform
nor will you
until you enter;

Be Miriam:
when you are covered in mud
having made a crossing against all odds
mark that moment;
gather about you all who are your people
and sing and dance for all you're worth.

Be Moses:
when you find yourself atop a mountain
having come so far
and gaze upon what you cannot have
revel in your soul's understanding
that it is a long way from Eden to Canaan
and the distance left to travel
was always asymptotic
ever closer but never meant to intersect.

Do not yearn to arrive in the land.
Do not regret leaving the garden.
Journey forth,
within you...always Eden,
and before you ever...the place of Promise.

(October 23. 2006)

Leaving

For My Daughter, On Her Need To Remain In Australia

I understand that
you are pulled
like a compass needle to its magnetic pole
to this path
that has carved its trace
in spite of nature's urgency
to seed it over,
this path that is obstinate in the face of
the wind's imperative
and the bird's scat.

I understand
that you can not turn away
from this road that grass and time
will not swallow up,
this road that if rejected now
would frequent your dreams
from which you would always
awaken just before knowing
where it leads.

(June 5, 2007)
Published online at
http://womenspiritualpoetry.blogspot.com/2013/05/leaving-by-sheri-lindner.html

Yellow Lilies

They are not like us
no,
they turn their
butterscotch sexuality
inside out
arching their waxy pointed petals
with saucy grace,
poking their honeyed, threaded stamens
as far into the world as they can reach,
their only purpose:
to be seen,
these buds that open in reckless succession
these marvels of fecundity.

No, they are not like us,
but our teenage daughters—
they understand the lilies.

(December, 2007)
Published in *Jewish Women's Literary Annual,* Volume 9, May, 2013, p. 26.

Transitions

Consider the tree,
my dear impatient one.

Fall and spring cannot happen together

there is always a space between—

even the briefest of winters.

After her blazing flamboyance
the tree lets go her leaves,
releases them for no good reason
except that it is time,
then gathers them close around her root source
and patiently, patiently
pulls in their nourishment
for new buds
that are only a short season away.

(August 30, 2007)

On the Bridge

Clipped to the steel cable that ran like an artery
up the open-treaded steep stairs and all along
the narrow grated walkway,
we threaded up the arched suspension
        of Sydney Harbor Bridge
arriving at the pinnacle
in time to hold the sun
for a suspended moment

before it continued on its way
settling beyond the far horizon,
casting the city in amber glow that faded to sepia,
as the harbor's turquoise darkened.

Swaddled together in dusk
with you secured familiarly between us
it was easy to fend off knowing
what else that sun was setting upon,
easy to fend off knowing
that when we climbed back down
you would unlatch yourself
from our shared cord.

Breathing in that July winter sunset
I understood why you fell in love
with that land called Oz
that has pulled you
from the place you have always—until now—called home.

Even so, please hold on to the ruby slippers.

(November 29, 2007)

Dear Jobes,

As 2007 draws to a close, I am thinking about what you have just completed. It seems very fitting that you chose to write about the fluidity of identity, as I can't think of a person who exemplifies this better than you. Yes, indeed, identity is a construct that must always be in flux, growing, changing, evolving, and your thesis, it seems to me, expressed this with passion from a place of very personal knowledge and experience. As you have continuously experienced yourself anew, recreated (or attempted to) some form of home or Promised Land for yourself in each new place you move your bed and with each new group of people you meet and embrace as friends, you seem to have come to understand that countries, too, stagnate (or worse, sow the seeds of the destruction of their founding dreams and ideals) if they do not also allow themselves to change and grow. Somehow your conclusion of your thesis was almost inevitable and a fairly perfect reflection of you, the author.

So, as you ring in 2008, still in a foreign land, I hope you continue your grand exploration of your life, remaining open to the possibility someday of arriving where you started, and knowing the place for the first time.

I love you and miss you. Happy New Year, Mommy

On Being Mom and Dad

The answering machine bubbles
with her excited news:
the visa granted.

We tell ourselves that the journey cannot begin until
the knife edge severs the binding cord.
We tell ourselves that there is no story
until Eden's gate is opened
and closed behind them.
But still...

We are, just then,
like the tide at the instant of turning,
unsure
whether it is going out or coming in,
retreating or swelling
and for just that moment
surrendering
to be tugged in both directions at once.

(September, 2008)

Christmas Eve:
the air is charged
with quiet
expectancy
snow cascades right on cue
past rainbow lights that wrap houses
against the solstice dark.
I must be outside!
there where transforming is happening minute by minute
Grabbing my husband
and the Irish fisherman sweater
my mother has made for me
(the only thing now that fits),
I step into this miracle-night
where all things are possible.
In spite of the heavy weight that goes before me
that precedes my every step
as we slip along
slickened
neighborhood streets
tasting and blinking snowflakes
I have never felt more perfectly balanced.
Soon after 11:04 the next morning
I phone my mother to wish her happy birthday,
and call her grandma for the first time.
The unconscious is something:
has slipped right in,
commandeered the ship,
chosen this day, three weeks early,
for the birth of my first child
a magnificent gift to my mother
to seal—once and for all—her esteem.
It works,
for a time.

And then, it does not matter.

(November 1, 2008)

Return

Like Odysseus, you may someday return
To the Ithaca from where you set your course
In a time before you knew that you would go
When home contained the wonders of the world.

From Ithaca you set your compass course
And raised your sail to catch the fairest winds
Though home contained some wonders of the world
You heard the call of all that lay beyond.

You raised your sail to catch the fairest winds
And took your tread from its familiar hearth
And listened to the beckoning urgent call
To shape your life according to its truth.

You took your tread from its familiar hearth
And learned to set your footprint by your soul
To shape your life according to its truth
The gods could not have granted more than that.

You learned to set your footprint by your soul
And steer where you, alone, know you must go
The gods could not have granted more than this
To anchor in a harbor you'd call home.

You steer where you, alone, know you must go
As fair winds grace you, keeping your course true
Until you find your harbor, though it be
In seas that hug the far curve of the earth.

As fair winds grace you, guide you on a course
That you and we could never have foretold
Your heart keeps time with the far curve of the earth
Far from where we in Ithaca remain.

No, you and we could never have foretold
The glorious curve, the route your ship would trace
Yet, we who stay in Ithaca still yearn
That like Odysseus, you may someday return.

(March 29, 2009
August 4, 2009
August 17, 2009)

Awarded First Place in the Nassau County Poet Laureate Society Poetry Contest, April, 2013

To be published in the *Nassau County Poet Laureate Society Review*, Winter, 2014.

Published in *Jewish Women's Literary Annual*, Volume 9 2013, p. 24.

Quickening

Weeds are pulled
grass mowed
lawn edged
your room tidied and scrubbed
right down to the window sills
and as I write this
very moment
a cake rises in the oven
climbs up the sides of the pan
almost overflowing.
Except for the cake
you will probably not
notice the other preparations
just as you did not
register them the first time
but still they had to be made
then, as now.
Nesting, it is called
and I hardly know
what to do with myself
these next twenty-one hours
as you traverse the endless sky
above the Pacific and then
the continent that once
you called home.
This that I do in readiness
is like putting on a *tallit*
to prepare for prayer
or perhaps
it is prayer itself.

(July 22, 2009)

Customs

These next two weeks
I will be very careful
how I use the word
Home
knowing that
home
refers to a different place
now.
But I can't do anything
about the custom's officer
who, when she sees
your weary shining eyes
and places her metal stamp
on one of your passport's pages
will surely say
Welcome home.

(July 23, 2009)

First Date

You don't remember our first date
but I do, you
in that kelly cabled sweater
that made your hazel eyes
as green as new clover.
We stroll through town, find ourselves
at the corner European patisserie
nearly empty at this hour.
Across from each other
at a small round table,
there is nothing
pressing we have
to do this fine afternoon but
sip hot chocolate
and blot each other's
whipped cream moustaches.
After, we stroll some more
until you tell me urgently
that you have to go.
There is no choice, nowhere to turn
but to duck around the next corner
and just go.
The cop does not have a sense of humor
and I'm guessing no small son
who has just shed his diapers
and drunk too much
on his first date with his mom.
Today you asked
her the question,
gave her the ring,
and I, who was her place holder,
remember that first date
that took up quiet residence
in your cells
and in mine. (October 14, 2010)

iGod

Neither of us believes
in God
yet each time she flies
she sends a text:
boarding now
off I go
mwah
and then:
landed
Honiara, Jakarta,
back home in Canberra
and, best:
at gate JFK!
We two skeptics
know that it is these
little prayers—
tapped by thumbs
that once, when sucked,
were all
that was needed for
homeland security—
offered up to ether
and beamed down to me
that keep her safe.

(December 5, 2010)

November 25, 2010

My dearest Jo,

I was glad yesterday when you wished me a happy birthday too. Because this day was very much a birth for me, also. Twenty seven years ago at this moment I had not yet met the tiny being that was to change my life. While I hadn't met you yet, I can't say that I didn't know anything about you. I knew your elbows and knees, your determined heels, your hands, like Marcel Marceau, testing the boundaries of your containment, learning where those boundaries had some give and where not, and I imagine in some way those brain synapses were already firing to plot your exit from that containment.

I think you were far more active in that than I. My body just went along with what was planned for it. (Ah, so early did we establish that!) In under 3 hours from the first inkling that this would be your day, you were here! So like you! And little did I know what new world lay ahead for me from that day forward.

Oh, yes, I was already a mother, and being Daniel's mom already changed my life forever and filled me to the very top. I could not have imagined what else was possible beyond that top. Being a part of your growing up, and now, your inviting me to be part of your adult life, takes me to places that actually did not exist until you did. Your life in Australia, while very real and amazing, is a perfect metaphor for those places. A place so far away--places within so deep and rich. As I watch your own life blossom into color, and as you share with me the deep roots that have taken hold within you, of a self so solid, so open (kicking and screaming, but, yes, so open) mine does the same.

I hope that Dave has begun to know this phenomenon--that his life, in response to who you are--is about to (or has already begun to) undergo a burgeoning, like embryonic cells, so that he might hardly recognize the him that existed before you and him. I know that yours, in response to him, has and will do that, because you will not permit anything less of yourself.

So, blossom away, my little one, my grown woman, who gives new life to everyone who is part of hers. Celebrate this 27th anniversary of that first day. And I will celebrate, too.

Wishing I could take you in my arms, like that first day. It makes me happy that you will be in Dave's arms today!

Love love love, wowwy

February 8, 2011

Dear dear Jo,

What a gift we awoke to this morning, receiving your email reflections on the 5th anniversary of when you "took your tread from its familiar hearth." I have so many responses...

The first was that I felt terrible frustration and regret at not having taken your call last night when you called, forgetting that it was a day to be marked. But then, I wondered if you would have sat and pondered and reflected if we had spoken on the phone. Remember when you said, a few nights after 9/11, walking across Conn's campus on the phone to me that you doubted that your generation would produce any orators like the one you had just heard? And my thought was that that might be because your generation doesn't enjoy engaging in quiet, reflective time, but rather often chooses to talk immediately and keep those feelings and responses more external to the self. So, with all that in mind, maybe it was OK that we didn't talk and you wrote what you wrote. I hope it was as gratifying for you to write as it was for us to read.

My next thought is that you are so much like a mythic or Biblical, or fairy tale person...having undertaken this epic journey in search of something not quite named and then finding far more than you even knew you were looking for. You seem to have known, consciously or not, that, like those characters (Ariel, Odysseus, Hansel and Gretl, Dorothy, the Jews), your growing needed to occur in a place away from home. And what you found, you already knew, though it was like arriving where you started, and knowing the place for the first time. And I think that what you have discovered is not about adventure or novelty, but more about the most essential things: finding your own feet, your voice, your essence, your place within a larger world, and loving someone and being loved. Indeed, the gods could not have granted you more than that.

Although we could not have predicted all this, I had some sense or fantasy or hope in some vague, unarticulated way, that these were the possibilities that were before you as you left that February day in 2006. Although I've said this in many ways to you over the years, I will say again, that I really had little desire to hold you back from this. I knew that what was possible was far greater than anything more we could give you here, at that time of your life. I did not know how we would manage our contact and maintain our connection but I guess I didn't have worries about it and felt secure enough that we were not losing you. I've missed you immensely and it's sometimes a sad missing but mostly it's a full missing that doesn't feel depleting to me. I still feel most of the time that I have you. I've noticed recently that you don't talk to me as much about Dave and you, and I assume that that means you and he can do that more together now and you need me less as a sounding board for things in your relationship together. That's a good thing for the two of you.

I love what you've created and I love that it's clear to you that it's all within you and is portable.

I will attach again, the poem called *Return*, as it says all of this better than I feel I'm saying it now. I love you and thank you for the gift of you that you give so freely to us,
mommy

Toast on the Occasion of Erica's and Dan's Wedding

October 1, 2011

We first want to thank all of you for coming here and joining us on this wonderful occasion. Everyone has traveled to be here, but some have traveled great distances to be here, (Joanna and Dave, you seem always to win that contest!,) and we appreciate all of you being here, regardless of the distance you covered.

All of us, whether family or friends, have shared loving connection with the Snow or Lindner families, and with Erica's and Dan's lives, some from the very beginning, and others after they stepped out of their childhoods and into their adult selves. Each of you adds to today's joy, as our happiness would be incomplete without this sharing.

And of course the poignancy of today's occasion is deepened by our love and memory of those from all our families who are no longer here and who would have so loved to be here, and who are dearly missed. I know that if my parents were here tonight, they would be turning inside out with joy, and Erica, they would have loved you in an instant. This celebration is but one small link in the eternal chain of creation, that started long before us and will continue way beyond us, and we honor and appreciate those who led us here, just as we happily anticipate all those who will follow us.

It is no secret that Dan has delighted us since his arrival. His dazzling passion for life, his beautiful soul, his sweet, loving charm, his intense enjoyment of people and the bringing together of people (that's code for party planning) have been part of him since the beginning. Where Dan is, people want to be. More recently, he gave us the immense pleasure of having Erica in our lives. From our very first meeting, we knew many of the reasons Dan chose Erica. She is a beautiful young woman who exudes quiet maturity and wisdom. We have learned to appreciate that inside that quiet is a steady, clear voice and her values are guide posts for them as a couple. Beyond that quiet is a sharp wit, a stunning awareness of people and their contradictions, and a clarity of who Dan is. In her, Dan has found someone worth listening to, and whose advice he respects and follows (did we get that right, Erica?) This is a good thing! Erica has become a treasured addition to our family, and we take much pleasure in knowing that Dan has been embraced and folded into the weave of the Snow family with love and great affection.

As the planning of this wedding celebration unfolded, we witnessed how Erica and Dan managed it all, involving both families at crucial moments, and working together as a couple; we came to feel a deep respect for this process as their process, and recognize this as a defining year for them as a couple. They have expressed from the beginning, their awareness that their wedding represents each of them as individuals, both of them as a couple, and still, something larger than simply themselves. They have grown, in honorable ways, and have given us the great gift of being witness, once again, to the mystery of how two people, each seemingly sufficient unto him and herself, come together and are made even more whole because of it.

We thank you, and offer you our dearest blessings:

May the Universe be kind to you and shine its loving face upon you.
May you always feel easy love and kindness between you.
May your love for each other guide you and amplify your own individual selves.
May laughter fill your home.
May the unexpected find a comfortable place in your lives.
May your happiness in each other be your protection.

May your dreams be within reach because you are together.

We love you and congratulate you, and together we raise our glasses to toast the life upon which you embark.

II. Inside the Words: *D'vrei Torah*

Isaac on the Mountain: a Legendary Tale of Development

Much of classic children's literature addresses itself to the issues of maturation and development (Bettleheim 1976). Certainly, one sees this core theme in children's stories varying from Grimm's Fairy Tales to the Curious George (Reys 1941) stories, from the Wizard of Oz (MGM 1939) to the Bible. In all of these tales, the maturational process is the underlying or unconscious meaning of the story. This process leads to the emergence of an independent and separate self, which comes only after an arduous effort. Frequently, this emergence is tied to the character's ability to disobey and remove himself from the grips of parental authority. Blind obedience is rarely associated with growth and development.

This prevalent literary theme in classic children's literature is consistent with clinical child observations as well as theoretical teachings (Mahler, *et al.* 1975; Blanck & Blanck 1974) that separation and movement away from the safety and security of the maternal/symbiotic orbit are essential for development to proceed. Psychoanalytic understandings have clarified that what is appropriate and adaptive at one age must be left behind at later ages.

Given this thematic agreement between classic

children's literature and psychoanalytic theory, we are confronted with the Biblical story of the near-sacrifice of Isaac, the traditional interpretation of which is concerned with Abraham's **obedience** to God (Maimonides 1135-1204; Spiegel 1967; Ginzberg 1968; Leibowitz 1972). Although this interpretation serves a religious function of glorifying unswerving faithfulness (Kierkegaard 1843), as a psychological statement it is antithetical to the principles of development which psychoanalysis has recognized as crucial.

It is impossible to imagine that the story of Isaac, so central to Western civilization for thousands of years, could have endured based only on its manifest content, which has been the apparent basis for its traditional interpretation. We would like to explore a developmental, psychoanalytic interpretation of the underlying, unconscious, thematic material.

What, then, is the story of the binding of Isaac about? Is this a story about obedience to authority, obedience to a God who orders infanticide, as the manifest story and traditional religious interpretations suggest? How could it be that blind faith, faith that would drive a father to slay his son, could become a cornerstone story of Judeo-Christian inheritance? Are we, truly, to aspire to Abraham's model of blind faith? Alternatively, is this a historical story pertaining to the end of child sacrifice, as God stays Abraham's hand and prevents him from sacrificing Isaac? If this were its most profound message, its impact would not be as universally compelling, it would not speak to generation after generation, and it would not have endured.

We approach this story with an assumption that it has endured for so long because, like all art, it must speak to what it means to be human; it must represent our struggle to understand our own humanity, and the inner conflicts which must be negotiated on our way toward our own humanness (Smith 1971). We assume, therefore, that this is not merely a Judeo-Christian story, or necessarily a historical story, but rather a mythic story whose embedded message is one that is nurturant to children and can be absorbed in a productive way. It is, therefore, emblematic of humanity in its largest and most universal sense.

To try to get under the surface of this story, we undertake a careful textual analysis, following a process similar to that of dream analysis where the different characters are recognized as representing different aspects of a central, dreaming self.

You may have wondered why or perhaps taken offense that we have placed this story in the genre of children's literature. The reason for this lies not only in its thematic similarities, but also in its structure, which is similar to that of fairy tales. Let us first examine this structure.

Fairy tales, like this Biblical tale, are often rather stark in details, conveying motivation and relationships through a series of actions, which may have magical, extreme, or unrealistic qualities. Frequently, the action takes place long ago and far away, enabling the listener to project his own inner conflicts into the story by providing a safe distance between the manifest story and the inner workings of the reader or listener.

As with our Biblical story, in fairy tales, the action begins *in medias res,* in the middle of things, when the protagonist, almost always a child, is faced with a dire situation. We are compelled to deal with the action of the moment without getting involved in preceding context. We may assume that what happens before our story is of little interest; it is the moment of change which is to occupy our attention. It is only with conflict and its resolution that a fairy tale concerns itself.

Since our story begins at the moment of conflict, we can assume that all went well enough up until our story begins, and that the protagonists are "ready" for what comes. They have been prepared developmentally for the "hard times" which have erupted; they have a store of emotional resources which are untested but which must now be activated.

Fairy tales, traditionally, have bad parent figures (step parents, witches, goblins, giants, etc.), conveying the sense of the protagonist as victim to a hostile environment, from which he must escape. In mobilizing his resources for this escape, the protagonist repudiates his own passivity along with the formerly experienced parental protections. It is the bad parent figures that allow the audience to feel that the protagonist is justified in his upcoming rebellion or deception. (It is easier for a child to become independent and repudiate his parents if they are experienced as bad. We may even go so far as to assert that all parents must be experienced this way for a child's growth to occur).

In fairy tales, the way in which a parent is viewed as bad has several layers of meaning. On the surface level the "bad" parent usually tries to kill the child/protagonist. On an underlying level this same action by this same parent may be viewed through a different lens. The parent is experienced as "bad" precisely because of her demand for change. Paradoxically, it is this parent who recognizes the child's readiness for change and growth. Thus, the parent who responds to her child's increased capacities, a parent who refuses to allow a continuation of the *status quo* of regressive passivity will be experienced as frustrating and "bad." What later turns out to have been timely and appropriate impetus for growth, was, at the time, experienced by the child as life threatening and terrifying. In essence, the "bad" parent does "kill" the child, in requiring that the child leave behind the dependencies of childhood. We will see that these same mechanisms appear in the story of Isaac.

It is not a coincidence that in many fairy tales it is the loss of food, the drying up of the cow, the depletion of money for food, or some near "oral" catastrophe that initiates this conflict and begins the action of a fairy tale.

Fairy tales also use the mechanism of "splitting' (Kernberg 1974), where characters are all good or all bad, enabling the child to project unidimensional and unmodulated bad feelings about himself and others onto the bad characters while preserving the integrity of his good feelings and his good internal images of the parents and the good self.

The end of a fairy tale usually involves the transformation of the protagonist and often the gaining of a kingdom. This may be understood as the kingdom of the "self," of moral, sexual, interpersonal maturity through which wholeness is achieved. It is important to note here that self-actualization, alone, is not usually the ultimate end of a fairy tale. The kingdom is not attained without a marriage or a reunion of family. The protagonist does not ride off into the sunset alone. This indicates that a fairy tale deals with the maturational transformation of a human being which enables that person to unite with another human being. Participation in the community of humanity is thus the fulfillment attained in a fairy tale and is available to the audience as a message of what Erickson referred to as "generativity" (1950).

These are some essential elements of fairy tales. Now let us turn to the story of Isaac.

Like a fairy tale, our story begins *in medias res*. We know only that Isaac was born, that there was a circumcision, a party, and that he was weaned: "And the child grew, and was weaned. And Abraham made a great feast on the day that Isaac was weaned. And Sarah saw the son of Hagar the Egyptian..." (*The Holy Scriptures,* 1964, "Genesis," Chap 21, 23). At this point the story shifts abruptly to Hagar and Ishmael being cast out. Why?

If we approach all elements of this story as having meaning beyond the apparent story, then this shift from Isaac to Ishmael may be seen not as a diversionary story about Abraham's other son, but as a continuation of the same, larger story, with Ishmael representing a different aspect of Isaac (or more aptly, both children representing phases of a more universal "child"). The sequence of the story suggests that Ishmael may be seen as the representative of Isaac just after he was weaned, as this is when we first meet Ishmael. We are reminded that, as with all children, Isaac's inner experience is that weaning is tantamount to being cast out. Similar to a fairy tale, it appears that weaning provides the propulsion for the action of our story.

Interestingly, the name Isaac, meaning "laughter," (Webster 1966) supports the interpretation that the time prior to the action of the story was conflict-free. The name Ishmael, meaning "God hears," (Webster 1966), suggests that it is this moment to which we are to harken; it is this moment which introduces the conflict or developmental task which must be met.

It is Sarah, not Abraham, who demands the casting out of Ishmael. This is consistent with life where it is the mother who closes off access to her body which has been the child's Eden. When we read chapter 20, traditionally, we squirm that Sarah's jealousy is so powerful and murderous, and that against this Abraham is so weak. But when we look deeper we see that Sarah is doing only what mothers must do -- support forward movement of her child to foster maturation. The child needs to grow; in being set on the course that will foster growth, the child feels cast out.

Abraham is grieved. God reassures him that Sarah's plan of action is the right one. In this interchange God may be seen as the force which guarantees development, an understanding of God not terribly unlike the "predicate theology" of the Reconstructionist movement in Judaism (Kaplan 1962; Schulweis 1975).

Abraham, however, seems not to understand the necessity of Ishmael's departure, of loss as a precedent of growth, or the larger plan of which God has spoken, (which maturation demands). He attempts to sabotage the child's progressive movement by providing Hagar and Ishmael with water and bread upon their leaving. Of course, like all regressive gratifications, it only temporarily fills a void and cannot sustain movement and growth. It all runs out in the desert. Ishmael and Hagar are eventually on their own, as maturation (God) demands. It is ironic that Abraham's inability to understand God (maturation) has driven him unknowingly to delay the child's progressive movement; development cannot proceed simultaneously with regression. Abraham tries to hold them back or delay their end, yet it is this end which is crucial for development, as the end of infantile gratifications is a necessary precondition for the emergence of a more mature self. Abraham does not yet appear to understand this maturational process. He still aims to provide for his child in a way that the child no longer needs. In accord with the mechanism of simplification, the character Abraham, here, embodies the seductive, false "Paradise" of dependency. It is a further irony that in the manifest story Abraham's action appears to be "good" and Sarah's appears "bad." In examining the latent content of the story, however, we may see that the reverse is true.

With this understanding, we see this story as not just about the sacrificial binding of Isaac, but as a much larger story of the universal human struggle to free oneself from regressive binds, parental protections, and the infantile needs which cause us to cling to them. While maturation holds many possibilities of new, exciting, wonderful things--"a great nation," (*The Holy Scriptures,*1964, "Genesis," Chap 21,23) it also feels frightening.

So, up to this point we have: a child for whom the earliest years of development presumably proceeded without remarkable incident (Isaac); we have the same child who has just undergone the developmental and conflictual event of weaning, and has suffered the loss (Ishmael); we have a person who represents the ambivalence of letting go and moving on (Abraham); we have a parent who sees the way towards growth but whose vision feels bad to the developing child clinging to infantile dependencies (Sarah); we have the parent whose image is utilized to form a transitional object who will eventually become fully internalized and thus provide an ever-present source of self-nurturing and self-protection (Hagar); and we have the force of development (God). Unlike traditional renderings of this story, ours understands it not as a tale of Abraham's or Isaac's or Ishmael's life as the manifest content implies, but rather the much grander story of the development of a human being, of all human beings.

In the next scene Ishmael is dying in the wilderness of Beersheba. Hagar is with him but abandons him under a tree, to die alone. In this action that appears on the surface to be unbelievably cruel and criminal, Hagar, as an internalized good parental image joins God's plan (maturation). The child must exist autonomously, regardless of how difficult it is for the parent to witness, regardless of how difficult it is for the child. She sets him down cut off from her view and protection. Ishmael is alone, with God; the child is alone to exist relying upon his own internal resources and the power within him of developmental urgings. "And God was with the lad and he grew" (*The Holy Scriptures*, 1964, "Genesis," Chap 21, 23).

The traditional reading of this scene sees Hagar's

weeping as grief over the imminent death of her child. When Ishmael is seen from our perspective, as one representative of a larger Isaac (or all humanity), we understand that Hagar, as the nurturing mother of infancy, is struggling to allow her child to exist and mature without her, in spite of her pain over her loss.

In a telling scriptural anomoly, God hears "the voice of the lad" when it has been Hagar who has been crying. This apparent discrepancy suggests that what we, the reader, are privy to in the surface story is not what God is witnessing. It further suggests that Hagar, the protector and nurturer, is now internalized, and that it is the child's development to which God is attuned. Maturation (God, in this story) concerns itself with the forward growth of the child, not the holding-on of comfortable but infantile protections. In development the child can only proceed forward if a necessary sense of security has been built from earlier good developmental experiences and has become a reliable internal resource. Only then is the push forward timely. If it comes too early it is traumatic and mitigates against healthy independence; if it comes too late dependencies have already been established, ego development retarded, and regressive gratifications will have begun to restrict growth. Just as loss is the prerequisite for maturation, so, too, is this internal acquisition of support and nurturance.

As in many fairy tales, this story has the image of the mother split into the good, giving mother (Hagar), and the bad, casting out mother (Sarah). While the "good" mother provides the child with the necessary internal securities for maturation and future integrated identity, it is, paradoxically, the mother who is experienced as bad who provides the child with the propulsion for continued development (Sarah). They are, of course, both one and the same, but the mother who weans is experienced very differently from the mother who nurses. (Sullivan 1953). Both mothers are appropriate to Isaac/Ishmael's developmental needs at different times, and all mothers have been perceived as both Hagar and Sarah, if you will, at different times.

It is at this point in the story that we return to Isaac, a different Isaac from the earlier, newborn Isaac, and from the Ishmael/Isaac who was cast out. What is noticeably different about this segment of the story is that it includes only men. Sarah is conspicuously absent. Many commentators upon the story have felt unsatisfied with this omission and have devised rationalizations which allow her to be arbitrarily injected into this segment, either crying and mourning her son, or taking initiative to change the course of perceived history (Wilner

1989). However, from our developmental/ psychoanalytic perspective it is appropriate that Sarah is physically absent. Some may argue that it is a sexist parable when the mother takes only an early nurturant role and the father takes the later developmental roles. We do not agree. In the development of the child the mother exists first as the sole embodiment of the universe, then slowly, as the child perceives more and more of the world, other aspects of reality, both of the self and others, come to play a greater and greater importance in his development. The interpretation which claims sexism minimizes the role of the early mother as the representation of all of the world, and as the foundation upon which all the rest is built. The men in this part of the story are symbolic of the identification which Isaac must make in his development toward a fully integrated, autonomous, identity. In the earlier chapter, inhabited by women, Isaac's task is to move beyond the nurturance, to incorporate it as part of his own internal resources. To linger further in this earliest stage would be to perpetuate not this positive connection, but rather a crippling dependence, passivity, and neediness in relation to the world. The child must make this move beyond the maternal core-forming experiences for development to proceed.

In this Bible tale, as in fairy tales we have entered at the cusp of the expulsion experience. This suggests that autonomous identity, and with it personal, conscious memory begin in the conflict of giving up and letting go. Perhaps the expulsion from Eden is the Biblical prototype of this emotional milestone.

It is apt that we now find Isaac with Abraham and with two young men, ascending a mountain in the land of Moriah. Theodor Reik (1961) contends that this is a representation of an adolescent/puberty initiation ritual and that Isaac's near-death is the symbolic death of the child Isaac and the rebirth of the adult Isaac. We do not disagree with this, but feel that this interpretation clings too closely to the manifest content, and in doing so does not touch the deeper unconscious themes held within this ancient tale.

We do not think this segment of the story is essentially about a father about to kill his son. Nor is it about a passive, weak Isaac who would allow this to happen (Ginzerg 1968, 280). This story, we think, is about a child whose foundation experiences are strong enough that he may progress in his own development. It represents nothing less than the emerging identity and humanity of a person. In this way it is archetypal of the birth of humanity.

We note that in chapter 22 Abraham responds with the words, "Here am I" three times--to God, to Isaac, and to an angel. These words do not really indicate **where** Abraham physically is. His whereabouts are known. Rather, they indicate the very fact of his being. The shift in focus to Abraham paralleling the Isaac/Ishmael shift, which indicated developmental changes, reflects the story's progression to adult phase development. Abraham no longer undermines development, but now, working as God's agent, fosters it.

Putting aside for the moment the laws of *kashrut,* God here appears a bit like the big bad wolf in *The Three Pigs*. As the wolf eats each successive pig, the audience knows, that it is only a symbolic devouring; the next pig comes on the scene and speaks the same words as his brother before him. In that manifest story, the wolf, like God in the *Akedah,* tests the pigs' ability to survive and in doing so brings about their demise. At a deeper, unconscious level we understand that the pigs at each successive developmental stage must be gone for development to proceed. Incidentally, the more widely known Disney version of this story, in which each pig takes shelter with an older brother, and all remain alive at the end of the story, robs children of the opportunity to work through their own conflictual letting go and moving on. It gives them the message that they can continue to be infantile and mature at the same time. Would that development were so easy!

So, if God is the big bad wolf, he is so to the extent that he demands progression that upsets comfortable equilibrium, but which is necessary for fulfilling our humanity. The essence of this story is not that Abraham brings his son to a murderous, testing God; it is that Abraham harkens to God, the force of human developmental progress. That the child Isaac must be sacrificed is the necessary prelude to the emergence of an autonomous adult.

Where is Isaac at the end of this scene? "So Abraham returned unto his young men, and they rose up and went together to Beersheba; and Abraham dwelt at Beersheba" (*The Holy Scriptures*, 1964, "Genesis," Chap. 22, 25). It is important to remember that Abraham is not Abraham, just as Isaac is not Isaac. At this point, Abraham represents the sum total of all accumulated development which has so far been enacted by each and every character in the tale. Maturity has been achieved through the developmental process reflected in the evolving amalgam character of Sarah/Hagar/Isaac/Ishmael/ Abraham. In the manifest story, each has enacted God's plan (maturational movement), and portrayed a crucial aspect of development.

The story reaches its ultimate fulfillment in one of two places. It is either on the mount in Abraham's total acceptance of his bond with God (his total acceptance of life's terrifying necessities) or it is in Abraham's return to Beersheba, as a transformed man, at one with God (reconciled to development's necessities) and to the recompense of mature human connection.

Following the first possibility, maturity finds its ultimate achievement in a fully autonomous individual. As Abraham faces his greatest challenge in the manifest story, we understand that to become a truly integrated individual, one must renounce childlike securities (the sacrifice of the child Isaac) and be capable of existing autonomously (Abraham on the mountain after the sacrifice of the ram).

Following the second possibility, maturity finds its ultimate achievement in that autonomous individual's connection to a common humanity. The events above are a necessary precedent, but not sufficient in and of themselves. It is only in the return to Beersheba, where Abraham joins with others, that the preceding events are fulfilled. This interpretation is supported by verses 20-24, in which ongoing generations, the ultimate symbol of generativity, unfold.

If this story is not really about a mean, testing God who threatens death and demands blind obedience, why is it cast in such horrifying, and primal terms? It is because these are the metaphors of our inner world, just as characters are cooked, eaten, blinded, etc. in fairy tales. This is also the language of dreams; it is what a child feels.

The story is cast in terms that address our most fundamental fear--annihilation--because that is always what we experience in some form (fear of death, fear of loss of love, fear of bodily harm, fear of humiliation or embarrassment or failure, fear of disappointing oneself) when we move from security to newness. Although, in the words of Judith Viorst (1986), it is a "necessary loss," it is, nonetheless, a loss, and is often felt by all of us, and most certainly by children, to be **the** loss.

From our point of view, this story has never felt satisfying when read as a "real" story, the way a fairy tale, if read as a moralistic message about how children **should** behave, falls short of richer and deeper meanings. These stories, the binding of Isaac included, are not about how we **should** be but about how we are. The emotional truths that emerge are inescapable.

These truths harken back to the first Biblical story containing human beings. We must all leave Eden. And we all do so because the world "out there" beckons with treasures beyond those experienced in Eden, and because it is our nature to do so. While the parental nest is warm and protective, it does, eventually, become too small. It is relegated to a special place in memory and revived in our children becoming caregivers to their own. However, this process of having our own integrity, and becoming thoughtful, knowing human beings, of leaving one nest and building another is undertaken with inevitable ambivalence and fear.

This story of Isaac is a prototype for all of us, of our own stories. It is about expulsion from, and sacrifice of Paradise. It is about leaving security and entering a world where conflict and imperfection abound, but where choice and humanness are possible.

One foot in Eden still, I stand
And look across the other land.
The world's great day is growing late,
Yet strange these fields that we have planted
So long with crops of love and hate.
Time's handiworks by time are haunted,
And nothing now can separate
The corn and tares compactly grown.
The armorial weed in stillness bound
About the stalk; these are our own.
Evil and good stand thick around
In the fields of charity and sin
Where we shall lead our harvest in.

Yet still from Eden springs the root
As clean as on the starting day
Time takes the foliage and the fruit
And burns the archetypal leaf
To shapes of terror and of grief
Scattered along the winter way.
But famished field and blackened tree
Bear flowers in Eden never known.
Blossoms of grief and charity
Bloom in these darkened fields alone.
What had Eden ever to say
Of hope and faith and pity and love
Until was buried all its day
And memory found its treasure trove?
Strange blessings never in Paradise
Fall from these beclouded skies.
--Edwin Muir (1956)

References

Bettelheim, Bruno. *The Uses of Enchantment.* New York: Alfred A. Knopf, 1976.

Blanck, Gertrude & Blanck, Rubin. *Ego Psychology: Theory and Practice.* N.Y.: Columbia University Press, 1974.

Erickson, Erik. *Childhood and Society,*N.Y.: W.W. Norton and Co., Inc., 1950.

Ginzberg, Louis. *The Legend of the Jews.* H. Szold (Trans.). Philadelphia: The Jewish Publication Society of America, 1968.

Grimm, Brothers. *The Complete Grimm's Fairy Tales.* N.Y.: Pantheon Books, 1944.

The Holy Scriptures (According to the Masoretic Text). Philadelphia: The Jewish Publication Society of America, 1964.

Kaplan, Mordecai. *The Meaning of God in Modern Jewish Religion.* Wyncote, Pa.: The Reconstructionist Press, 1962.

Kernberg, Otto. *Borderline Conditions and Pathological Narcissism.* N.Y.: Jason Aaronson, 1974.

Kierkegaard, Soren. "Eulogy on Abraham," in *Fear & Trembling,* Trans. H.Hong & E.Hong. Princeton, N.J.: Princeton University Press, 1843.

Leibowitz, Nehama. *Studies in Bereshit (Genesis) in the Context of Ancient and Modern Jewish Bible Commentary.* Third revised edition, Trans. A. Newman. Jerusalem: World Zionist Organization, Department for *Torah* Education and Culture, 1972.

Mahler, Margaret, Pine, Fred, & Bergman, Anni. *The Psychological Birth of the Human Infant.* N.Y. Basic Books, 1975.

Maimonides, Moses. *Guide to the Perplexed in Studies in Bereshit,* N. Leibowitz. Jerusalem: World Zionist Organization Department for *Torah* Education and Culture, 1972, p. 188-189.

Muir, Edwin. *Collected Poems.* New York: Oxford University Press, 1965.

Reik, Theodor. *The Temptation.* New York: George Brazier, Inc., 1961.

Reys, H.A. *Curious George.* Boston: Houghton Mifflin, 1941.

Schulweis, Harold. "From God to Godliness: A Proposal for A Predicate Theology." *Reconstructionist,* 41.1 (Feb., 1975).

Smith, Norris. Personal communication, 1971.

Spiegel, Shalom. *The Last Trial: On the Legends and Lore of the Command to Abraham to Offer Isaac as a Sacrifice: The Akedah.* Trans. J. Goldin. N.Y.: Schocken Books, 1967.

Sullivan, Harry Stack. *The Interpersonal Theory of Psychiatry*. Eds. H.S. Perry & M.L. Gawel. N.Y.: W.W. Norton and Co., Ino., 1953.

Viorst, Judith. *Necessary Losses.* New York: Simon and Schuster, 1986.

Webster's New World Dictionary of the American Language. N.Y.: The World Publishing Co., 1966.

Wilner, Eleanor. "Sarah's Choice." *The Reoonstructionist* LV.1 (Sept.-Oct., 1989), 16-17.

(September, 1991)

Presented to the Reconstructionist Synagogue of the North Shore, *Rosh Hashanah*, Day 2, 1991/5752.

Presented to The Long Island Institute of Psychoanalysis, March 20, 1992, East Meadow N.Y.

Presented at the American Psychological Association meetings, August, 1992, Washington, D.C.

Published in *Reconstructionist: Journal of Creative Jewish Thought,* Vol LVIII/No. 1 Autumn, 1992/5753, pp. 5-8.

Presented to the Unitarian Universalist Society, Spring, 1994, Manhasset, N.Y.,

Lindner Family *D'var Torah* *Naso* June 1, 1996
Presented to the Reconstructionist Synagogue
of the North Shore
in honor of the *Bat Mitzvah* of Joanna Lindner

Joanna:

Picture this:

The four of us, sitting at a table in the dining car of an Amtrak Metroliner. Across from us sit 4 men drinking and laughing. At our table, we sit reading and discussing *Torah*. If a picture is worth a thousand words, we have a full manuscript here!

This is how we began to tackle *Naso*. For each of us, our first reaction to this *Torah* portion was disappointment.

I said, "Can't we do the portion that's near my birthday instead?" That would have been the story of Joseph and his brothers, you know, one of the good stories.

Dan: I said, "Just summarize it for me. Don't read all the boring, repetitious parts. Just tell me the basic idea."

Dad: I said, "Doing a *D'var Torah* isn't as meaningful as doing a good project. We should go back to doing the projects."

Mom: I said, "Maybe we shouldn't have been so excited about June 1st. I was thinking about nice weather, but I hadn't bargained for the Book of Numbers."

None of us had yet gotten all the way through *Naso*. We did not know that it contained the words of the "priestly blessing":

Jo:	*Yi-va-re-chi-ha adonay v'yish ma re-ha*
Dan:	May God bless you and protect you;
Jo:	*Ya-air adonay panav ayleha v'yi hoo ne ka*
Mom:	May God's face shine upon you and be gracious to you;
Jo:	*Yi-saw adonay panav ayleha v'ya same l'ha shalom*
Dad:	May God's countenance be lifted towards you and bestow upon you peace.

We did know, however, that Joanna had wanted on her *tallit*, a group of people, draping one another with their *tallitot*, as they offered this blessing to each other, as we do in our service. She did not know that this was in her *Torah* portion; she only knew how much she looked forward to having her own *tallit* in order to participate in this ritual, not just as a recipient of blessings, but as a grantor of blessings, as well.

Joanna: We knew we had the option of speaking only

about this small section of the portion, but it bothered us that 9/10 of the stuff here seemed to be useless. We really wanted to figure out what this could mean.

Let's look closely at *Naso*. This portion is divided into 7 sections, each appearing to be about something different. We didn't understand why these 7 sections were grouped as one portion, and how they might be related.

Dan :

Section 1: The Tabernacle and Census: In the first part, God tells Moses to count all of the members of the Gershonite and Merarite clans of the Levite family, and outlines the specific duties of each clan regarding the Tabernacle.

This section is only about a few clans of the Levite family. Each family's responsibility sets it apart from all the others, and each is needed to ensure that the community runs smoothly. This first section seems to set the groundwork that the whole portion may be about how individual families come together and work as a larger society.

Joanna:

Section 2: Putting out lepers from camp: In the next section, the community is supposed to put out any person who has leprosy, or who has come in contact with a corpse, so he or she does not defile the camp.

In those days, people thought that this disease might be contagious, so it makes sense that they would want to put out the afflicted. But this hurts those who need to be cared for most.

Rashi said that these people had their leprous condition because they had engaged in "evil gossip." Having famous *Torah* scholars tell us that it is OK to blame the victim, seems dangerous. What kind of community, with these rules, is being established here? Why is caring for one's dead considered a defilement? Why is caring for those in need not a good Jewish value?

Dan:

Section 3: Righting Wrongs: The third section outlines how one should make amends when he has wronged a fellow human being. He should confess his guilt, and pay back the amount plus one-fifth to the victim or his family.

This section outlines a simple and logical value system by which a society can function. It also makes the assumption that people **will** "sin" or do wrong to their fellow human beings, and that such wrongs can be easily repaired.

No grave punishment is necessary and the community does not fall apart when people do things they shouldn't. They have a way to deal with it.

Joanna:

Section 4: Jealous Husbands or The Problems With a Patriarchal Religion: Well, I get all of the "fun" sections! This section outlines what will happen if a man suspects his wife of being "with" another man. Whether she has or hasn't, she must undergo a ritual where she drinks a potion, made of bitter water and earth from the Tabernacle. The priest casts a spell on her, and if she is guilty her belly will swell and her thigh will sag. If she is innocent, she will be able to "retain seed."

If the wife is innocent, why doesn't the husband get punished for wrongly suspecting her and putting her through humiliation? Why does the wife have to prove her innocence but the husband doesn't have to trust and believe in her or apologize once there is "proof" of **his** error?

Maybe, like earlier sections this is also about how to maintain a society. The jealous husband must not vent his rage upon his wife. He must control his anger and allow the community to deal with the matter. This is like our own laws that prohibit an individual from taking justice into his or her own hands.

When we first read *Naso*, this section seemed really outdated and oppressive. However, all you have to do is read the newpaper to see stories, everyday, of domestic violence to see how **our** society deals with these issues. It certainly caused me to wonder which society is more "primitive."

Dan:

Section 5: The Vows of the *Nazirite*: The next section is about a person who wishes to take the vow of the *Nazirite*-- to dedicate him or herself to God. He or she must refrain from eating anything made from grapes, must not cut his or her hair, and must avoid contact with the dead. Part of the vow also includes making a "sin" offering or ritual sacrifice. A *Nazir* could terminate this vow at any time.

Commentators have dealt with the question of why a *Nazirite* must make a "sin" offering. What could be the sin in dedicating oneself to God? Wouldn't that person be even holier than most?

Maimonides says that the decision to separate oneself from the community is itself a sin-- the *Torah* commands us to enjoy life, and that in taking such a vow the *Nazirite* is guilty of abstaining from the joys of life. Nachmanades argues that the sin is when the *Nazirite* forsakes the vow and returns to the joys of life. Astruc says that the *Nazirite* takes such vows in the first place as a way of imposing control over bad habits.

Although the *Nazirite* vow sets people apart from the business of living, in some ways, the *Nazir* is not forbidden from all pleasures or involvements with the community. For example, there is no rule against sexual relations. This at first seemed odd, if the intent of this holy separation is to abstain from human pleasures in order to serve God. Clearly, the message seems to be that to serve God, one must remain involved in community with others.

We were confused also, that alcohol was prohibited, but sex was not. This seemed inconsistent with our own modern morality (which may have been influenced by a later, Christian morality,) which somehow links them together. I thought that it might be that alcohol takes you more into your own experience and further away from others, whereas sex involves at least one other person!

This reminds me of a great joke... uh... later.

O.K., back to *Naso*... So, there are even prescriptions about how to separate oneself from the community. Even in separation, one remains involved with community both directly and indirectly, through an acceptance of these rules. As in the other sections, there is a statement here about the tension or balance between the individual and the larger group.

Joanna:

Section 6: The Priestly Blessing/ The *Birkat HaKohanim*: And now we come to the Priestly blessing. Much discussion exists among scholars about the fact that **God** does not bless the people directly, but rather does so through designated priests. Bradley Artson, in a contemporary commentary, says that the *Kohanim* are no holier than any other member of the community, but that God has an "otherness" that is higher than all people. Abravanel says that God's blessings are different than those bestowed by people, in that people's blessings are not "real gifts." (in Leibowitz, p. 63).

I disagree with Artson and Abravanel.

As Reconstructionists, we understand that we are all both priests and servers. **We** are given the responsibility as priests, to bestow blessings on one another, but we must also live our lives so that they are worthy of being blessed. We do not believe that God lies in "otherness," but within the individual, within the community, and within the kinds of lives we choose to live. The aspirations which these human choices reflect, indeed, are godly gifts.

<u>**Dan:**</u>

<u>**Section 7: The Bringing of Gifts:**</u> The final section of *Naso* describes what each tribe gives as gifts for the dedication of the sanctuary. Over the course of 12 days, each chief, one per day, gives a list of identical gifts.

At first it was boring to read, twelve lengthy, identical lists. The repetition is **so** redundant, **and** repetitive, **and** it says the same thing over and over!

I think that in keeping with the theme we have been looking at, of the individual and the community, there is something special about each tribe giving identical gifts. The repetition acknowledges that each tribe is separate and individual. The sameness of the gifts suggests that each is now a part of one cohesive whole. In having become a People, no tribe would be more important than another. For the sake of community, each foregoes some form of individual choice over its gifts.

<u>**Joanna:**</u> This kind of community, at the end of *Naso*, is different from the one at the beginning. In the first section,

each clan was told what to do, but in the last section, the clans' leaders are not bound to any given formula. The middle sections describe the movement from one kind of order to another, from the necessity of being told what to do, to being able to choose freely. Choosing as the tribes did, suggests a more mature, more developed kind of community.

Like Milton's angels, the tribes might have said, "Freely we serve, because we freely love."

Michael: It does appear as if *Naso* reflects a movement in the nature of community from the beginning to the end. As Dan and Jo have pointed out, each section seems to describe things having to do with the ways in which an individual can be part of a community, and ways in which community ought to function to serve a common good.

Recognizing this led us to wonder if this portion might also be about how one comes to be an individual in the first place, and how individuals live in community with others.

Sheri: Through our study we became aware of another level of interpretation that is not immediately obvious from the overt content of what we were reading. Each time we have embarked on *Torah* study, we have been surprised to find embedded within the story deeper suggestions of how a human being becomes a human being. We believe that it is this link to deep qualities of humanness that has kept the *Torah* alive.

Embedded within the words and seeming fragmentation of *Naso* lies, for us, an underlying order that conveys the story of an individual growing up.

Michael: The first section of *Naso*, appears to correspond to the earliest stages of human development. The portion starts out with mandates that the clans accept fully. There are no clauses included about what will happen if a clan fails in its duty. In this light, the Tabernacle might represent infancy. It must be cared for in specific ways, which are absolute. There is no tension between need and its gratification.

Sheri: In the second section the leper may represent someone who **feels** cast out of camp. At a certain stage in life, when parents attempt to curb the child's impulses, and demand increasingly more civilized behavior, a child will feel cast out of the parental protection that was effortlessly his or hers until this point.

As Joanna pointed out, commentators have focused on what the leper must have done to bring this upon himself, which seems always to have something to do with uncurbed impulses. The tension between the child's desires and the parents' demand for modulation and inhibition cause the child to feel like a "leper," unwanted, cast out.

Michael: The third section is suggestive of the years of middle childhood, perhaps 6-11. This is a time when children move slowly out of the family orbit into the world. There is, as Dan mentioned, the assumption that one **will** make mistakes in the process of growing up, and they are easily dealt with: make reparation, and give even more to show true regret. Like the "Latency" period of development, this section deals with socializing.

Sheri: The next section, as Joanna said, is difficult. Maybe this is not exactly about husbands and wives. Marital issues are not really the focus here. It does seem to be about sexuality and its control. In this section, emotions run high, and consequences feel dire: different from earlier sections, no redress for mistakes is possible. Relationships are intense and may be weakened and rejected by petty emotions.

The issues of intense and fluctuating emotions, of relationships that can so easily be doubted, and of society's desire to impose restrictions and consequences of sexuality are all suggestive of the developmental stage of adolescence.

Michael: The next section of *Naso* might correspond to the late adolescent/early adult stage of development, which entails the absolute rejection of things worldly.

As the *Nazirite* grows his hair long, abstains from alcohol, and seeks to dedicate his life to things spiritual, we may recognize our high school and college aged children, who sometimes become vegetarians, explore meditation and Eastern philosophies, reject materialism, and attempt to lead a self-imposed life of asceticism. The sense of invulnerability and immortality of youth, is suggested by the prohibition against being involved with death.

It is interesting to note that the *Nazirite* does not have to abstain from **all** things physical, can terminate this vow, and can cut his or her hair, drink wine, and re-enter, fully, the world of pleasure at will.

Children, like the *Nazirite,* who advance to this level of

maturity, come to impose their own restrictions on their own impulses, rather than requiring society or external authority to do so. They come to experience themselves as quite different from all others around them, by imposing sometimes idiosyncratic rules upon themselves. However, in this continued process of differentiation, they ready themselves for the future developmental achievements of adulthood.

Sheri: The next to the last passage is the priestly blessing, which represents the young adult's re-entry into community--into the world of work, productivity, relationships, and procreativity.

Many commentators have noted that the blessings increase in length from 3 to 5 to 7 words, interpreting this as movement from the material to the spiritual.

For us it makes more sense to understand the gradually increasing length of this blessing as corresponding to the increasing awareness of the self and the world outside of the self.

In the previous, "*Nazirite*" stage of development, there is an implicit criticism and partial rejection of the world and its values, and an attempt to repair the world by self-abnegation and attention to the spiritual. In this "blessing" stage of development, there is the willingness to participate in the world, to **receive** from the world what might be good. This maturational stage, is marked by a beginning sense of balance between what we receive from the world and what we can give.

Michael: The final segment of this *Torah* portion concerns itself with the giving of gifts. This appears to us, in the developmental *schema*, to represent further maturation into adulthood. As Dan said, there is a choice here-- to accentuate one's uniqueness and in doing so, stand out from the group, or to recognize one's link to a common humanity and sameness, and support the community.

Up until this point, the portion has concerned itself with particular clans, with Levites only, with particular situations-- the jealous husband, the leper, the *Nazirite*. The final two sections concern themselves with the entire community of Israel, and with the way in which all of the tribes support that community.

Sheri: These sections, which earlier seemed to be barely connected, now appear to follow a pattern: from total identification with one's family; to feeling cast out of the parental Eden, as infantile demands become less tolerated, and gratifications less available; to entering a world where one **will** err by continuing to take gratifications inappropriately, but where repair of this greed is easily accomplished; to a time of intensity of emotions and relationships, in which there is great tension between the desire for self-indulgence and the restrictions of society; to a rejection of the world and its prohibitions, and with this rejection, the imposition of self-regulation; to a rejoining of the world with acceptance and participation.

There was a time that I would have thought that it took courage to live alone, that being an individual apart from community took more strength of character. Figuring out how to be an individual, and yet make choices that take account of things larger than the self, seems now to be a choice that demands a great deal of courage and thought.

Joanna: Our family has learned about how to be a part of something larger than ourselves from being a part of this synagogue. Here, we participate in a community that asks us to study and think, that teaches us how to give to and care for one another, and that aspires to nurture all that is good in each of us.

The Little Mermaid and *T'fillah:* A Presentation to the Reconstructionist Synagogue of the North Shore February 11, 2000

See Appendix for Supplement

Before proceeding in this article, it would be helpful if you have familiarity with the Disney movie ***The Little Mermaid.***

I've gotten some really odd looks about this topic whenever I've presented it—looks that have made me feel somewhat apologetic about this whole idea. It doesn't help that when I first wrote this, several years ago, my earliest critic, my daughter had the response: "Mom you have WAY too much time on your hands." More recently some of my friends who are usually more supportive and pretty expressive, have, upon hearing the topic, said, "Oh." If I read that "Oh" correctly, it has meant something like: "You're going to compare services to *The Little Mermaid*?" as if comparing something so significant to something so childish, is ridiculous, and maybe even a little heretical.

So, I decided I had better begin with some concluding remarks. I think the comparison of *Shabbat* and *The Little Mermaid* is not so different from Mordechai Kaplan's (the founder of the Reconstructionist movement within Judaism) own seminal experience of finding holiness in two worlds. As I understand his story, when he was approaching the shores of America, as a new immigrant, on Friday night, July 4, there was holiness and necessity in his *Shabbat* observance, below decks, with his family, but there was also holiness in the explosive expressions of freedom that lit up New York Harbor . Whenever I've heard that story, I've always felt it from a child point of view, that it was a shame he had to miss "the fun" up above on the boat. But I understand now that the fireworks were not just fun. They were "the other civilization's" expression of the same impulses that were being expressed, in different language and different form, down below, as *Shabbat* was awakened and welcomed.

So, that is how I will introduce this presentation. *The Little Mermaid*, far from being just "fun" or a childish fairy tale or cartoon, expresses the **identical** impulses to those we express each *Shabbat*. These impulses, to help orient us as we begin, are: our sense of awe and wonder about our world, about ourselves in the world, about our ability to perceive and comprehend ourselves and our world, about our capacity to be in the world, our capacity and obligation to create beauty and fineness in the world, our capacity to love another and to find reflected in that love, the face of God. This is what *The Little Mermaid* is about, no less than a *Shabbat* service. Beyond the thematic similarities between *Shabbat* and *The Little Mermaid*, there is also an astounding parallel in their sequential elaboration of these themes.

The two civilizations, and perhaps, all civilizations, converge in their need to express these things. For some, *Shabbat* liturgy may be the more accessible form of this expression. For you, I hope that this presentation will introduce you to *The Little Mermaid*'s holy potentials; for others, *The Little Mermaid* may be the more accessible language. For you, I hope that you come to think of Ariel's book, and her need to "know what the people know" when we take out the *Torah*, or that you envision King Triton's rainbow when you say, "*Oseh Shalom*."

A brief synopsis of *The Little Mermaid* follows. Ariel, a mermaid, daughter of King Triton, ruler of the sea, discovers many artifacts of the human world and is fascinated by them. Upon seeing a human, Prince Eric, above, she yearns to go up into the human world and become a human, herself. Her father forbids this. She seeks the magic assistance of the evil sea witch, Ursula, who agrees to make her a human in exchange for her voice. In order to remain a human forever, she must obtain the kiss of true love within 3 days. Otherwise, she will be returned to mermaid form, and become one of Ursula's slaves, forever.

[p. 584 and 585 in Appendix] Our *Shabbat* service begins with us extolling the wonders of our awakening in the morning with *Birhat Ha-shahar,* the morning blessings. In these morning prayers we express gratitude for, among other things, waking up, standing up, walking firmly, and having strength. [point to 1st 7th, 8th, and 10th blessings]. Our evening welcoming of *Shabbat*, similarly asks us to "Arouse yourself, arouse yourself,/your light has come, arise and shine,/ awake, awake, pour forth your song,/on you now shines the Glorious One. [5th verse of *Lehah Dodi*, p. 44 of *Kol Haneshamah*].

Ariel, also, begins her story this way. It is not long before we become aware that we are dealing with an awakening in *The Little Mermaid*. The awakening occurs both in the sea, with Ariel's awareness of the world above, and in the world above, with Prince Eric's search for love. If we take liberties with the spelling of what might be the root of Ariel's name, and use the Hebrew letters of *ayin* and *resh,* which spell *Ar*, Ariel's name, itself, might mean to awaken or arouse oneself (p. 236 of Ben Yehuda's Pocket English-Hebrew dictionary). [1] The Hebrew verse of *Lehah Dodi* uses this root, (*Uri*), calling for us to awake. Thus, we must be fully awake to welcome both *Shabbat* and *The Little Mermaid*, and to release the latent potentials in both.

The movie opens with praises for nature's wonders, in a scene where human beings are plying their way through the seas in a boat. Similar to *Birhat Hashahar*, the opening song is a song of praise for the sea, the wind, the salt air, and the mysteries of the fathoms below. There is a dramatic tension, however, over who is master of nature: humans or the gods. Although our liturgy eliminates this tension, it is, for many of us, part of our experience, especially in those moments when rational thought and ritual practice intersect. **[video clip #1]**

In the video clip, some of the humans believe that we must respect and pay homage to King Triton, ruler of the merpeople, while others believe that such a notion is mere "nautical nonsense." It is fitting that the sailor who is comfortable on the sea and in harmony with the sea, and reaping the rewards—fish—of the sea, is the one who understands what must be respected. The other gentleman, clearly no sailor, is made sick by the sea and is out of harmony with it. He is even reprimanded by a captured fish, who, in the process of gaining his freedom and leaping back into the sea, slaps this man in the face, perhaps, attempting to awaken him to that which must be attended.

[p. 586 and 587 of Appendix] Returning to our service, our *Shabbat* liturgy continues with expressions about the wonders of our bodies and souls which allow us to appreciate creation in *asher yatzar* and *elohai neshama*. We move, after this, to praises that focus on the wonders of nature that those bodies and souls allow us to appreciate (such as in *mizmoor l'David*, p. 185 *Kol Haneshamah*)

After Ariel's first glimpse of Prince Eric, she moves, as our service did, to a prayerful song about the wonders of what bodies allow us to do and feel. She wants feet to walk, and the capacity to breathe out of the water. She wants to lie warm on the sand. She wants to revel in nature's joys, and experience them through the new senses that she yearns to have opened to her as a human being. These words are Ariel's *mizmoor l'David*, and *asher yatzar* prayers. Notice, in particular, what Ariel does as she says the words, "I want to know what the people know." **[video clip #2]**

Ariel embodies the sense of wonder and awe about her world and especially about a world just beyond hers. She is a collector of treasures from the human world, and, in scenes recollective of Adam, she is hungry for her friend Scuttle to give her the names of her treasured objects and tell her of their uses. As they are named and given function, she begins to yearn, irresistibly, to go above and become part of the world that created these things. The idea that humans are to be co-creators is highlighted by two of her most special objects from the human world: the fork, which is a miniature version of her father's trident, the instrument of creation; and the pipe, which Scuttle tells her is an instrument for making music, as is her own voice. In these two objects, Ariel will embrace both mastery over her own fate, as well as her obligation to create a world of beauty (through music, symbolized by the pipe and actualized in her own voice, and through the fork, which, when used as a comb, as Scuttle insists is its function, brings about human beauty). **[video clip #3]**

The *Shabbat* service then moves to prayers in which we rejoice in our ability to study and learn, and in the gift of *Torah,* expressed in the prayer *Ahava Rabba*. Ariel, in the song that she had been singing (Part of Your World) asserts: "I want to know what the people know; Asking my questions and get some answers." As she sings this, she takes out a book, her *Torah* equivalent. Her consciousness follows the same course as ours does in our service: from awakening, to gratitude for our bodies to perceive nature around us, and gratitude for the nature around us, to passion for knowing more than what our senses permit us. And, like us, she wants to understand more than just things; she wants truly to be, as her name suggests, if we spell it this time *aleph, vav, resh*, and assume that "*Or*" is its root, [2] "illuminated" by the understanding of how to be a human being. This Hebrew spelling of Ariel's name harkens back to the verse noted above in *Lehah Dodi*, where the "light" of *Shabbat* has come. In that same verse we are also commanded to "pour forth [our] song," an activity that Ariel engages in passionately.

[p. 588 and 589 of Appendix] Essential to this first portion of our service and to the movie, is the function of words. We are taught: "In the beginning was the word." It is words that give creation form and meaning. We are reminded on Friday evening, in *Asher Bidvaro,* that it is God, speaking the word "evening" that actually brings about the evening. On *Shabbat* morning, it is *Baruch She-amar* that acknowledges that the word of God was necessary for all things to come into being. As Arthur Green elaborates, "our word, like God's, gives expression to a depth beyond language."[3] It is through language that we are able to come close to identifying feeling and expressing it. However, as Green suggests, there is much that is inexpressible in language, which is, at best, only approximate. We express our awareness of this shortcoming in *Ilu finu,* where we understand that even if our "mouths [were] oceans of song, our tongues alive with exultation like the waters' waves, our lips filled full of praises like the heaven's dome..."[4] yet we could never express sufficiently our wonder at our world and its creative potentials. And yet, we are commanded, in the *V'ahavta,* nonetheless, to speak our praises, to express words of love, whether they are adequate or not, when we lie down and when we rise up, and to teach these words to our children.

The Little Mermaid understands the enormous importance of words, as well. We are introduced to King Triton's daughters, whom we must know by their names. In their names they are created (in quite literal imagery in the movie, as each emerges from a shell as she is introduced). It matters little whether we think of Ariel's name as meaning awakenings, light of God, or city of God (as in Ir –iel), for they are all essentially the same. To be illuminated is to be awakened to the dwelling place of God. What is important here, is that Ariel is not in her shell, to her father's and tutor's great dismay; this alerts us not only to the conflict that is ahead, but more importantly to the fact that this conflict is inherent in her role as a messenger of God's light, of awakenings. Her name is not spoken in full at this point, only "*Ar...*"perhaps not unlike how the name "Adonai" is not revealed in that form upon God's first introductions in the *Torah*. And Ariel does not emerge from a shell, as do her sisters, for she is not fully created yet. It is "iel" portion of her name, that is not spoken yet. Whether she is the illuminator, the awakener, or the dwelling place, she is not yet "of God." This might parallel the fact that God's potentials, early on, are not fully comprehended by humanity. **[video clip #4]**

Ariel is elsewhere, as she needs to be. She is elsewhere learning the names of things and praising their existence with her words and song. She knows that "a world that makes such wonderful things can['t] be bad." Even as she asks periodically: "what's the word...?" no one tells her; she finds each word within her. With fork in hand and words from her mouth, she begins the Godly work of creating and defining her universe, and in this process, creating and defining herself.

At this point in *The Little Mermaid,* something dramatic occurs. Ariel's father reprimands her for going above and being fascinated with the human world. He dictates: "As long as you live under my ocean you will obey my rules. Not another word!" **[video clip #5]** Having established how important is the word, we know that Ariel's choice is set by his *dictum:* she can either leave his ocean, or not speak what she must speak. As it happens, to do one, she must do the other, as well. She is driven from the sea by necessity: her father will not permit her expression, and Ursula, the sea witch, whom we are about to meet, will exact from her her voice as the "toll" to "cross the bridge" into the human world. Interestingly, Ariel's friend, Flounder, loses his capacity to communicate clearly at this moment, also. As he tries to explain to King Triton why they were late to the concert, he stutters and is unable to express clearly and effectively what he wishes to. Meanwhile, on land, Prince Eric, whose life Ariel has just saved during a hurricane, searches passionately for "the voice" that he had heard singing to him when he was unconscious (and without speech). **[video clip #6]** Although Ariel has been prohibited from speaking in her sea world, there is one place where her voice is sought, and that is on land, by the prince. Like the Israelites, whose path of liberation was through the sea and onto land, Ariel's destiny is set.

[p. 590 and 591 of Appendix] It is fitting at this point that we insert the *Hatzi Kaddish*. The *Hatzi Kaddish* signals an end to one phase of the service, as it is a prayer that one recites at the conclusion of study. It appears in the service to divide parts of the service, and let us know that we are moving from one phase to another.

Ariel, herself, alerts us to a change that is about to occur: **[video clip #7]** She does not know where, she does not know how, but she knows something's starting right now. A *Hatzi Kaddish* is about to occur in *The Little Mermaid*. The plot of *Little Mermaid* picks up speed at this point, as Ariel makes her dramatic and life-altering decision. Let us summarize what is about to happen. Ariel, the mermaid, longs to become a human being and live on land. She is willing to sell her soul, in this case, her beautiful voice, in order to have her dream. Enter Ursula, a mauve-colored, enormously globular octopus, who is a fallen sea queen, now, apparently, evil incarnate, who barters in such important currency. The catch (no piscatological imagery intended!): Ariel must get the prince, above, to kiss her within 3 days, or she will be returned to the sea to live out her life in the lowly form of one of Ursula's slaves (an important parallel with the image of slavery and liberation we are about to sing of in our service). With her voice, this task would have been a piece of cod, uh, cake for Ariel; without it, well, there is the dramatic conflict. **[video clip #8a]**

This moment, the *Hatzi Kaddish*, is actually, what began this whole idea of comparing the service to *The Little Mermaid*. For several years now during services, my husband and I have noticed that the melody of the next-to-the-last line of the *Hatzi Kaddish* is identical to the melody that Ursula, the sea witch, sings to Ariel, in *The Little Mermaid*, as she takes her voice from her.

> "*Le'ela min kol birhata veshirata.*"

[video clip #8b]

> "*Palooga* sarooga come winds of the Caspian Sea
> Now *rainsus glaucitis et max laryngitis, la voce* to me"

Interestingly, the content of the line from the *Hatzi Kaddish*, and the content of Ursula's incantations, as ridiculous as it might sound, are not so different. The *Kaddish* line expresses that holiness is higher than all blessings, praises, or songs that we could utter. This line, essentially, says that our voices and songs are inadequate to express the holiness of God. Ursula is about to express this same idea, by commanding Ariel to sing as she takes her voice from her. Ariel is instructed to find holiness (love) which lies beyond her voice (as we are commanded to find and feel holiness that lies more deeply than the words our voices can utter).

Just as the *Hatzi Kaddish* signals movement, our parallel *Kaddish*, Ursula's Latin-esque chant, functions in this same way for Ariel in the story. The moment she sells her voice, she begins her "trial" life on earth. She is now proto-human, and is given three days as a human being (minus voice), to get the prince to love her. Ursula's intonations, indeed, signal a shift in Ariel's potentials--from mermaid to human. In metaphoric terms, of course, Ariel, as a mermaid, represents childhood, like a tadpole, when bodies are not yet fully defined and "voices" must be found. Physical transformation, expressive capacity, and the capacity to love are what we are dealing with here--in short, the maturation into a human being. So, our service and our movie are in wondrously precise synchrony as we are alerted to the transformational movement from one phase to another. Perhaps Ursula's switch to Latin, and the service's switch, in the *Kaddish*, from Hebrew to Aramaic, further underscore that we are on different territory now (quite literally, in both the movie and our people's historic journey across the sea).

[p. 592 and 593 of Appendix] As a mirror to Ariel's emergence, our service neatly moves to the *Mi Chomocha*, the song that offers praises for our having emerged safely from the waters of the Sea of Reeds and been able to set **foot** on dry land. The parallels here almost need no words! As Ariel sings for Ursula, and relinquishes her voice, we are reminded of Miriam and the women singing on the far side of the Sea of Reeds. While Miriam's song celebrates the safe arrival on dry land, Ariel's celebrates the moment of decisiveness. According to one *midrash*, deliverance and redemption, transformation, occur only in the moment when they are expressed in song.[5] However, using Ariel as a model, and recalling *Nahshon ben Aminidav* who, according to another *midrash*, made the decision to step forward into the sea, perhaps redemption or transformation do not occur **after** we have crossed the sea, but rather in the moment in which the decision is made **to** cross. Ariel's wordless theme that pours forth from her soul as she gives up her voice, is her *Mi Chomocha*, her affirmation of going forward, of no turning back. For the Hebrews, the ultimate finding of the Promised Land is both assured and redundant, as the commitment to go forward is the transformative moment: "the awakening." The Land is merely the concrete representation of this decisive moment, the place where holy "awakening," holy "illumination," and holy "dwelling place," *Ar, Or,* and *Ir,* converge and are fulfilled. Similarly, Ariel's finding of love is assured, by her having committed herself fully to going forth. It does not matter that she does not obtain the kiss within 3 days. (Parenthetically, Ariel feels the certainty of her place in the world, and is able to sing **before** the reward is obtained, her song celebrating her commitment. She does not need to know when or how; she knows only that she will go forward, conquering whatever obstacles are before her. The Israelites, at this point, do not sing until after their commitment has been rewarded by a safe crossing.)

Ariel can look back at the recent moment in her own personal history and offer thanks for her emergence from water, which threatened to suffocate her psychological development and then threatened to suffocate her literally, once Ursula took her voice and gave her human shape. As Ariel emerges from under the sea and gasps her first breath of air as a human, we are reminded of the word *neshama*, meaning breath or soul. Although she has no voice, she has a human soul which is inspirited, graphically, as she arches from the water into the air and greets her new human world with her first intake of breath. **[video clip #9]** As she emerges from the water, her sea friends know that she is different, but they are not sure quite how. **[video clip #10a]** She begins to be less recognizable to them, as her path diverges from the one she has been on until now. She is no longer fully recognized by her past world, nor is her identity yet known in the human world into which she seeks membership, but her internal knowledge of herself is firm. For now she is thankful for her ability to step, with **feet,** on dry land--the place where she will wander for a time (not quite 40 years, but an ordeal of time, nonetheless), moving steadily closer to her promised land, symbolized by the fulfillment that will be hers through love. As he continues to seek her voice, Prince Eric plays Ariel's motif, almost a kind of *niggun,* on his pipe. This *niggun* functions for him, as ours does for us: he becomes ready for Ariel's arrival, ready to integrate something new into his life, ready to find what he seeks, ready to know it when he finds it. **[video clip #10b]**

[p. 594 and 595 of Appendix] The *Amidah,* which is sometimes recited silently, without spoken words, is essentially a prayer in which we express our desire to be open in a total way--open to knowing who we are and where we have come from, especially in our connection to our ancestors. During the *Amidah,* we wish to remain open to everything that is available to us here, now, from each other and from within ourselves.

This silent reflection is part of Ariel's journey, at this moment, also. In her transitional moment, just before she signs her "contract" with Ursula, she realizes that her move will mean that she will never see her father and sisters again. She looks backward, briefly, here, remembering from whence she came, and **we** know that what she is leaving is within her, and will carry her forward. As with the *Amidah*, Ariel enters her three day trial with no voice, but with a soul exquisitely open to what is around her, for this is a world that she feels religiously compelled to know. During this time she must meditate and reflect on what is around her, on where she fits in this scheme of things, on how she will bring herself into this world and create holiness in her life in this world. Sebastian, her tutor, reminds us of our role in the world: "You want something done, you gotta do it yourself." While some of her ancestors are within her, others are still, in reality, with her during this ordeal, as Sebastian, her crab-tutor, Scuttle, her seagull friend, and Flounder, her fish-friend remain with her. Representing harmony between land, air, and water, their presence effects changes in her world, as they attempt to set the stage for Prince Eric to kiss her. The past, present, and nature harmonize (quite literally) to bring about love, as Sebastian calls for "percussion, strings, wind, **words.**" **[video clip #11]** The presence of her "ancestors," her important connections to her pre-human life, support her and allow for her continued metamorphosis during her silent moments. In Prince Eric's desire to know Ariel's name, and his first utterance of her name, we see reflected the beginnings of love. It is such love that our liturgy intends to evoke in us, when we read the letters of the tetragrammaton, and utter the name of Adonai.

We should not overlook the fact that the *Amidah* is a standing prayer. For Ariel, standing, on her own feet, is a holy act. In this act, she pays homage to her human world and her human self, and its potential for Godliness, even if her voice is silent. Our recitation of the *Amidah* is the same.

[p. 596 and 597 of Appendix] The service draws to a conclusion with the *Aleynu* in which we acknowledge our obligation and role as co-creators. Interestingly, the traditional (as opposed to the Reconstructionist) version of the *Aleynu* resonates more fully with Ariel's experience. The traditional *Aleynu* expressses our gratitude for having been created differently from others, "situated...in a different spot, [with] our daily lot another kind from theirs..."[6] Although the common interpretation of this centers on the Jews as "chosen" above others, we could better understand this, here, to refer to our differentness as human beings from other forms of nature. For we have, indeed, been "made different... situated...in a different spot" with a daily life and destiny that are also different from that of other creatures.[7] It is of interest to note that one alternative *aleynu* praises the creator for "giving life to all...peoples, the **breath** of life to all who **walk** about"[8] [emphasis added]. These two emphasized attributes, are, of course, central to Ariel's physical transformation. The gift of feet, the capacity to walk and breathe as a human, are, indeed, to be praised, but most especially as they represent her more significant psychological transformations and our own potential for consciousness.

It is appropriate at this point that Ariel becomes aware

of her differentness from other creation. She completes her differentiation as she says goodbye to her sea friends. Although this is a poignant moment, we know that they remain as internalized "ancestors" who will forever sustain her. We, as well as her father, recognize that the differentness **she** has chosen could not be unchosen. She could no more remain a mermaid than a baby remain floating in its mother's womb, for each of these states is a "threshold" experience, a state where one becomes ready for expulsion, ready to fill one's lungs with the breath of life, ready to begin. We understand such threshold moments, for both Eden and Egypt were such places—places in which the goal was readiness to leave, readiness to become. Perhaps our gratitude in the *aleynu* is really for the human capacity, different from other "nations" (read as: other forms of creation) to **become** different as we grow, and to recognize ourselves as different from our former selves. In this, we are unlike all other creatures whose consciousness does not permit this self-awareness. This may be, after all, what chosenness means: that we are chosen as human beings, above other creatures, to exercise responsibility through consciousness and conscience. In this, both we and Ariel, and even King Triton are awed and humbled.

[p. 598 and 599 of Appendix] Mourners' *Kaddish,* at the end of the service, again is a prayer in which awe and holiness, reverence and peace, life and harmony are extolled. It is recited as a conclusion. It is recited for one whose study has come to an end, through death, and who, therefore, cannot conclude her study for herself. It is a solemn moment, and although its words are not about loss, we, the reciters, are filled with what we have had and what we have lost.

Ariel's father recites a version of *Kaddish*, and his version, like Judaism's, is all about reverence and love. He acknowledges to Sebastian what has become inescapable to him: that Ariel really does love the prince, and that there is only one thing to do about it. In a supreme act of paternal understanding, of Godly affirmation, he turns her back into a human (she had been reverted to a mermaid by Ursula, for not obtaining the kiss within 3 days). **[video clip #12a]** His mer-daughter is lost forever to him, now. His words, however, are not about her loss; his words are for the ending of her study as a child, under his parental tutelage. He has, after all, done his job well; she has emerged, she is formed, she is full, and she has the capacity to love and be loved. It is not random that Ariel has no mother from the time in which we enter her story. From this, we knew from the beginning that her story would be one of moving from the womb-like fluid protection of her watery world (which is, prototypically, the mother-world), to the larger world beyond her protected home (the father-world). In parallel, Prince Eric has no parents, only loving mentors, suggesting his readiness, also, to find loving connections beyond his family. One significant phase of Ariel's study is ended, and her father, King Triton, understands this. His words, like the *Kaddish*, evoke sadness, but they are also, like the *Kaddish*, celebratory of the world of which his daughter has now become a part, and the human being which she has become. Whatever shape she takes, he cannot fail to recognize within her adult self, his former child. And he cannot fail to let her go because, after all, she has found the thing he would have had her find. His final act, before diving back into the sea, is to paint a rainbow, a kind of protective covenant, from the sea to the heavens, embracing Ariel and Eric and all that is in their world. This act is King Triton's wordless, but loving rendition of: *"Oseh shalom bimromav hu ya'aseh shalom aleynu ve'al kol yoshvey tevel ve'imru amen."* ("May the one who creates harmony above, make peace for us and for all who dwell on earth.") **[video clip #12b]**

[p. 600 and 601 of Appendix] The service ends with songs of celebration about what is enduring (*Adon Olam*). While the words of *Adon Olam* are about the enduring and harmonious aspect of God, the *kavanah* or intention of this prayer centers us on those aspects "of reality which elicit from us the best that is in us and enable us to bear the worst that can befall us."[9] This is a fitting ending, not only for a service, but for *The Little Mermaid*, as well. For Ariel has discovered and created a reality that has elicited from her, already, her humanness, and that will sustain her in her new world. She has also created something larger than herself, as the merfolk come to the surface to meet the human world, formerly, their enemy. In a moment illustrative of our Reconstructionist understanding of our human partnership with the divine, the divinity of the merfolk, King Triton, and the divinity of the humans, Prince Eric, bow to one another in respect and peace. Their mutual fear is at rest, and the realms of earth, air, and water are at harmony.

What are we to make of these interesting parallels? Why would a prayer service resemble a fairy tale? Does this diminish our praying?

There are some who may take offense at this comparison, and feel that this trivializes the inspirational work of the prayer service that would urge us toward the divine. Far from diminishing liturgy, it is elevated and expanded. Its meaning is surely deepened when it can be understood in its "mysterious fathoms," when we understand that the language that carries its meaning is like a road, but that we are not to focus on the road. The road is only our human attempt to make a path that will follow the river, the mythic waters that all peoples yearn to follow. The river follows a timeless path cut by necessity, a path that knows the way without us.[10] We may think of liturgy as one road, perhaps just to the east of our river, and *The Little Mermaid* as another road, just to the west. It becomes, then, no surprise that their course is the same, for they are both following the ageless way of the river.

And, what more important theme is there than the

theme dealt with in *The Little Mermaid* and in liturgy? How could we not be awed by the recognition that these themes/stories have been part of our collective memory trove for hundreds or thousands of years. Clearly there is deep meaning and profound import which would lead us to carry such stories for generations, and lead us to ensure that we "teach them to our children" so that they will walk with **their** children along the roads that run closest to the river, also, and if fortunate, have the river always within sight, and its inspiriting nourishment always available. I would contend that the river comes into our place of focus and we become most available to its guiding path, when we recognize or create those holy moments in time—those moments that we sometimes find under the protective, sheltering wings of *shekinah*, and those that we sometimes find at the tentacle tips of a mauve octopus that would urge us—indeed, propel us--forth away from the protective, comforting shelter to encounter the world and ourselves.

To be compared to a child's tale is to be held to the highest standards, for it is there that all journeys begin. What else do children, or we for that matter, need to understand from any story or service or inspirational experience, than to have it touch the truths of our lives: the pain and necessity of leaving safety, of leaving behind our "shadowy selves,"[11] of wandering and discovering, of reveling in the bounty of what is possible, of creating new and sacred ties, and of being able to live with others in the sanctity of what we have created?

Notes

1. Ben Yehuda's Pocket Hebrew-English Dictionary. New York: Washington Square Press, 1961. p. 236.

2. *Ibid*, p. 6.

3. Arthur Green commenting upon *Asher Bidvaro* in Kol Haneshamah Prayer Book. Wyncote, Pa.: The Reconstructionist Press, 1994, p. 59.

4. Kol Haneshamah Prayer Book, translation of *Ilu finu...* Wyncote, Pa.: The Reconstructionist Press, 1994, p. 236.

5. Arthur Green, Translator and Interpreter, *The Language of Truth: The Torah Commentary of the Sefat Emet, Rabbi Yehuda Leib Alter of Ger*. Philadelphia: The Jewish Publication Society, 1998, p. 100.

6. Kol Haneshamah Prayer Book, translation of *Aleynu* (traditional). Wyncote, Pa.: The Reconstructionist Press, 1994, p. 445.

7. *ibid*.

8. *ibid*., p. 444.

9. Mordechai M. Kaplan, *Journal*, 1933. Cited as *kavanah* for *Adon Olam* in Kol Haneshamah Prayer Book. Wyncote, Pa.: The Reconstructionist Press, 1994, p. 458.

10. Edwin Muir. *The Collected Poems*. New York: Oxford University Press, 1956.

11. John Milton. *Paradise Lost* (XII, l.303) in *The Complete Poetry and Selected Prose of John Milton*. New York: Random House, 1950, p. 384. The original quotation is: "From shadowie Types to Truth."

On the Custom of *Niddah**: a Talmudic Response

After studying this custom in a *Rosh Hodesh* women's group

Codified commentary on n*iddah*, recognized as authoritative by the Jewish community at large, is nearly 1000 years old. The students of *Rav* Jodi offer contemporary commentary on original text as well as the words of subsequent commentaries often referred to as authoritative.

Student Judith claims that the laws pertaining to *niddah* can find no meaningful application to men or women of the time period of the twenty-first century. According to Judith, it is a generally accepted custom, outside of Orthodox Jewish circles but pertaining to nearly all Western cultures, that men and women occupy equal status and that the free exchange of consensual sexual contact between a man and a woman in an evolving relationship is customary. Because the nomenclatures of 'clean' 'unclean' 'purity' and 'impurity,' as well as those having to do with 'defilement' are not characteristics that find applicability in relation to sexual contact, the parallel classification of '*niddah*' is also a description to be relegated to antiquity. It follows from Judith's statements that the consequent necessity for the use of the ritual cleansing, as first outlined in Leviticus 15, and endorsed and elaborated by every commentator since, is nullified. [Miodownik, Commentary on Lev. 15]

Student Michele observed that the laws of *niddah*, as elaborated by Rashi and Maimonides serve to contradict other, more fundamental customary practices which prohibit the embarrassment of one person by another. *Rav* Jodi responded that the particular practice of the total separation of the genders at all times, as adhered to by the Orthodox, was for the specific purpose of not embarrassing a woman. If a man had to ask a woman if she were menstruating before touching her, this would violate the custom of avoiding *hay-vee bim-vu-cha*. Student Michele, observed that, in fact, the opposite occurs, and the law of total gender separation as practiced by the Orthodox, especially Orthodox men, engenders *m'vu-cha*, by implying that women are perpetually 'unclean' and, therefore, 'untouchable.' Such a practice imposes continual embarrassment and humiliation upon women, and therefore violates the custom of *kvod habriot* which should take precedence over any laws of *niddah*. It is Michele's claim, then, that the laws of *niddah* not only are antiquated, but, more importantly, and of necessity in their practice, violate other laws that have greater priority. [Weiden, Commentary on Lev. 15]

Student Sheri offered that the laws of *niddah*, as all *halacha* in the twenty first century, remain within the province of Orthodoxy, which remains frozen in Rabbinic and Medieval time periods of one to two thousand years ago. She proposed that the students of *Rav* Jodi undertake a limited updated responsa to previously codified commentary, of which this current document is the first. She further proposed, in an effort to begin that process, that the laws of *niddah* might be transvalued in the manner of Reconstructionist practice, rather than discarded as non-pertinent to twenty-first century Jewish practices. Following this Reconstructionist exploration, which itself has roots deep within the ancient tradition of study and 'chewing' upon, and digesting and re-integrating the meanings that are often obscured within original text and subsequent commentary, it was suggested that such an undertaking has the potential to re-enliven and breathe life back into text which an Orthodox tradition has ossified and caused to remain static. To this end, Sheri suggested that the practice of *niddah* might not be objectionable, if the language of *niddah* were to be altered to reflect other practices that form the foundation of Jewish law and custom. If *niddah* were understood as a ritual separation of the sacred and the secular (words such as 'profane' having no pertinence when applied either to sexual abstinence or sexual indulgence), then this practice would closely mirror, in a monthly cycle, the weekly cycle of *Shabbat* and *Havdalah,* a separation of sacred time from mundane time, the value of which is more easily recognized and acknowledged. According to this revaluation, sexual contact, far from engendering uncleanliness such as that referred to in Lev. 15:16-18, would be relegated to 'sacred' time. Paradoxically, and importantly, the 'separated out' time in which couples would agree to refrain from sexual relations, would also be considered 'sacred' time, as it would provide time for reflection. In this way, an ongoing and evolving clarification of separate self and conjoined selves—of each person in relation to him or herself and both people in relation with one another—would be effected. This understanding of the practice of *niddah* further allows for the sacred and the mundane to be intertwined, with value residing in both, rather than enforcing an arbitrary splitting of that which naturally co-exists.[Lindner, Commentary on Lev. 15]

**Niddah* refers to that time of the month when a woman is menstruating and until she has been to the *mikvah* 7 days following the conclusion of her period. During this time, according to Jewish law, sexual contact between husband and wife is prohibited.

The Plagues: a Developmental-Psychological Interpretation

When my son was about four, I read him the story of *The Frog Prince*. As I approached the end of the story, I quickly did some on-the-spot editing, reacting in horror at the apparent message of this tale. A little girl promises anything to a frog who will fetch her golden ball from the well. Once he makes good on his end of the bargain, she attempts to renege. Her father, however, admonishes her that she must grant the frog what he wishes, which is to eat at her table and sleep on her pillow. In an act of defiance, the girl disgustedly takes the frog and throws him against the wall, whereupon he becomes a handsome prince whom she marries.

I did not want my son to think that breaking promises was acceptable, or that throwing things against the wall was all right. I did not want him to think he should defy his parents the way the girl in the story defies hers. So I made this into a moral tale about being reliable, about obedience. I could not understand why the girl got rewarded for such seemingly bad behavior.

Over time, I came to understand that I had made a grave error in editing *The Frog Prince*. I had edited out exactly what was crucial, and had made it a static, rather Puritanical story, robbed of poetry and metaphor. It is precisely in the act of defiance, in the little girl's assertion that she will not be held accountable for a promise made through the naivite of her childishness, in her disgust at oral/dependent greediness implied by the frog at her plate, in her awareness that she is not ready for the sexual encounter suggested by the frog on her pillow, and in her rejection and redefining of the rules imposed upon her for her growing up, that she, in fact, grows up. The frog's transformation into a human being is a metaphor for her own parallel transformation, and her ability, through that transformation to be, now, accountable to fellow human beings, represented by her capacity to love the prince, and accept him as her life mate. ***Now*** she is ready to honor her promises, and participate in a relationship based on mutuality--not before. How little I understood when I first read this, of the richness of experience it offers children. It is not about a message or a moral--it is simply, or not so simply about what is--about life.

Of late I have gone back to the Exodus story to try to find out if I have similarly missed some crucial element. What is this "I'm-stronger-than-you" game that God plays with Pharoah?

Is this story of Moses and Pharoah and God about power and obedience and submissiveness, as many commentators suggest, and as I thought *The Frog Prince* was about parental authority? Is it about morality that is effected through fear? Or could all of this be a metaphor for something quite different?

I approach Exodus as if it were not so different, after all, from *The Frog Prince*, or other tales that deal with emergence. And if the Exodus is about being thrust out of one world and into another, then the events immediately preceding the Exodus--the plagues--must lay that groundwork, must prepare for the transformation that will enable the Israelites to emerge.

The portion *Vaera* [Exodus 6:2-9:35] begins not with the Israelites desiring their freedom, but with God deciding that they are ready. God cites past history, reminding Moses that God had appeared before Abraham, Isaac, and Jacob, but not in the same guise, as *Adonai*. God further reminds Moses that he had promised to give Abraham the land, which he now intends to do.

From this brief introduction we understand a few things. First, that Abraham, Isaac, and Jacob were forerunners, inchoate forms of what is now to come to fruition. God did not appear to them the way he will appear to Moses. Therefore, whatever force this God is, was also not fully formed, but nascent, awaiting its time. This is further suggested by the fact that God did not bring Abraham and his immediate descendants into the land; in some important way they were not yet ready to receive the land, nor God ready to give it. Thus, the stage is set for a story about growing, in which all characters, including God, represent parts of this motif.

The frame is also set for conflict around the issue of growth, for neither the Israelites nor Pharoah wants it to happen. Like parent and child, there is comfort, for both, in the securities of sameness, of protection, no matter how stunting that protection may be. God, however, represents the force that impels maturation. It is time--and God knows it--for slavish dependencies to end, for the Israelites to leave their temporary home, to find the land, the place in which they belong, the place where selfhood is at home, free to flourish into thriving community.

God instructs Moses to speak to the "children" of Israel; they do not heed him. God then instructs him to speak to Pharoah; perhaps the parent will be an ally in effecting the necessities of maturation. Movement is frozen for a moment, as the Israelite "children" seem content to live in their father's home, in Pharoah's land. As the maturational, psychological timetable unfolds, Moses will come to represent the path that each human being must traverse, with God representing development's necessities, nudging him forward, and Pharoah representing parental protections, anchoring him. At this point, however, Moses remains a sapling, suggested by his impeded speech. He is unable to speak clearly, to communicate effectively. He is not yet a full human being, until he claims his voice, and it becomes an instrument of effective expression. So, Moses is not ready, the Israelites are not ready, Pharoah is not ready, but God is ready. The process of maturation must be set in motion.

Following the introductory verses, the text reviews the generations of which Moses and Aaron are a part, to assure us, seemingly, that the Moses and Aaron to whom God has spoken are the same Moses and Aaron who are the descendents of Levi. Surely we do not doubt the identities of Moses and Aaron. Why the digression here? Following the current line of interpretation, this family tree helps us see, in telescopic form that people grow from being "begottens" to "begetting," from being sons to being fathers, from being daughters and sisters, to bearing children. This, again, underscores our interpretation of *Vaera* as being about the movement from potentiality to actuality, from childhood to adulthood, from the slavery of dependency to the freedom of independence.

What follows are the plagues. Although there are many ways in which to view the plagues, for our focus on development and growth, we examine each plague in light of three interwoven dimensions. The first is the most apparent one--the content of the plagues themselves. The second dimension concerns who enacts the plague, and the third concerns who is affected by each plague. There is progression along each of these dimensions, and each contributes to the motif of growth and development.

PLAGUES 1 and 2: Blood, frogs [*Exodus 7:8-8:11*]

Content. Thematically, the first two plagues form a cluster, along with the "pre-plague" demonstration of turning the rod into a serpent. Looking at this pre-plague, we witness a transformation of something inanimate into something writhing with life. This alerts us to a theme replayed throughout the plagues: the lifeless, or rudimentary life becoming transformed into fully emergent life. The not-too-subtle phallic-sexual overtones further contribute to this interpretation. We are dealing with the potential for life, with the not-yet consummated. In the first plague, too, the image of the Nile's water becoming blood represents a transformation in the direction of life, and the suggestion of womb fluids is evoked. Thus, we have both male and female procreative images as our first encounters between Pharoah and Moses and Aaron.

The second plague, that of frogs, continues the transformational imagery, as frogs are animals that change their physical form in the maturational process. That we are dealing with procreative processes is further underscored by the emphasis that the frogs will "enter your palace, your bedchamber and your bed." *[Exodus 7:28]* This recalls the image from *The Frog Prince*, in which the frog extracts a promise from the girl that he will be able to sleep on her pillow. Regarding content, therefore, the first two plagues, and the pre-plague may be viewed not as destructive acts, but as displays about the possibilities of creation, of making life, and of growing into fully mature life.

Agent of Action. For all three of these displays, although Moses speaks to Pharoah, Aaron is the one who actually enacts each display. However, because God, who may be seen as the propelling force of growth, speaks to Moses, and not Aaron, we know that Moses is the story's main character, not Aaron. Why is Moses not the performer of these plagues from the beginning? It would seem that Moses is not yet ready. Aaron, as the first born, is ready, but we are not so interested in him, perhaps because there is no conflict surrounding Aaron and growth. He is already competent in front of the Pharoah/father. Having arrived is much less interesting than the journey that still lies ahead for Moses.

Thus, the second dimension, that of who performs the act, also represents potential for growing. As the tadpole must grow legs and lose his tail and acquire the capacity to breathe in both water and air, so Moses must learn that he not only must speak, but act, and acquire the ability to replace Pharoah/father as an adult.

Effect. Pharoah is not terribly bothered by the first three displays. His magicians can do as much. This may suggest that in the earliest stages of growing, parent and child have congruent experiences. In psychological terms, this experience may be what Winnicott calls Primary Maternal Preoccupation[1]--the emotional state where normal adult needs are suspended, temporarily, as a mother-to-be and new mother experiences her own needs as being totally congruent with her baby's. In our story, at this point, Pharoah, like a patient parent, ignores his children/Hebrews: "Pharoah turned and went into his palace, paying no regard even to this." *[Exodus 7:23]* The Hebrews' actions are premature "stabs" at differentiation, not really meant to cause the parent to relax his protective vigil over them. They are not really ready to "grow up," as seen by the fact that Moses does not perform the actions himself. and Pharoah "knows" this. However, even the child's earliest forays away from security are important preparations. The Nile remains red, suggesting that developmental movement, even at this stage, cannot be undone.

PLAGUES 3-6: **Lice, insects, pestilence, boils** *[Exodus 8:12-9:17]* *Content.* Unlike the first few plagues, which represent images of life, the next four plagues represent parasitic elements--things that "feed" off, or derive their sustenance from, other living things. These may be apt metaphors for the next developmental stage, where there begins to be divergence between the needs of parent and child. We may recall here images from *The Frog Prince*, cited earlier, of the little princess grabbing her ball back from the frog and running off without fulfilling her end of the bargain, or of the frog sitting slimily on her plate and smarmily on her pillow. These plagues seem to be about the stage of development when the growing child greedily takes from the environment and feeds off of it.

Agent of Action. Moving to the second dimension, we see a shift, although not a perfect one, in the agent of action. Aaron performs the first plague of this set, bringing on the lice, but his role is coming to a close. For the plagues of insects and pestilence, God acts in communion with Moses, performing the action, while Moses continues to do the speaking. Gradually, Moses undergoes a transformation from speaker to agent of action. By the 6th plague Moses is the agent (although Aaron is still ready in the wings). God instructs both Moses and Aaron to take a handful of soot and throw it toward the sky. The dust that settles over the land will cause boils. While we may assume that both brothers take the soot, only Moses throws it up. Although the courtiers have begun to take notice, it is not until Moses finally **performs** this action, his first, that Pharoah's people are afflicted. When the child finally takes action, the parent must take notice.

Effect. As these four plagues unfold, Pharoah's magicians no longer can match the feats, signaling a change from the first cluster of plagues. Parent and child are no longer in synchrony. At first, for the plague of lice, even though Pharoah's magicians are outperformed, Pharoah is not particularly bothered, and does not ask Moses to stop. Here, again, we have an incomplete transition from one stage to the next on the part of the parent, who seems unable to recognize that a significant shift has occurred in the child, an increase in capacity that is moving him beyond the parental orbit.

By the second plague in this cluster, this shift becomes clearer. This change is underscored in God's literal separation of the Israelites from the Egyptians. Child and parent are now on divergent paths; however, they share the experience of ambivalence. While the child protagonists/Israelites are pulling away, they, nonetheless remain attached to the parent in their continued need for protection and sustenance. The antagonist/parent Pharoah hangs onto the child, trying to abort separation and growth, but he, also, ambivalently, and with no real conviction, begins to consider the necessity of permitting separation. After the plague of insects, Pharoah agrees to let the Israelites go and sacrifice to their God, if Moses will remove the insects. Of course, Pharoah does not uphold his end of the bargain, but we do not expect him to, as we are only midway along our journey's path.

This may be a way of understanding the motif that is repeated throughout the *Torah* portion, that God hardens Pharoah's heart. If we continue to understand God as the guiding principle of maturation, then God ensures that Pharoah will not let go too soon--he cannot let go until his child, Moses, and by extension, Israel, is ready.

PLAGUE 7: **Hail** *[Exodus 9:18-35]*

Content. The final plague in the *Vaera* portion represents a partial culmination along all three dimensions of exploration. Hail is a different kind of plague from the parasitic ones before it. Hail is a kind of environmental inevitability that comes about as a result of natural forces in conflict. It is less "personal" than those preceding it. Because it is formed as a result of a clash of elements, hail represents an apt continuation of the metaphor we are following. Until now, we were dealing with two forces--Moses and Pharoah--neither of whom was ready for a life independent of the other (the fact that Moses was literally raised as Pharoah's son further underscores this interpretation). Both were preparing themselves for this inevitability: Pharoah, by not acting prematurely, but waiting for Moses/Israelites to "grow up" and demand their independence, with voice and action unified; and Moses, by his gradual accession to the forces of maturation (God), his gradual assumption of adult responsibilities (his replacement of Aaron), and his eventual ability to leave his father's (Pharoah's) home.

Agent. For the first time, at the seventh plague, Moses, alone, both speaks and acts; Aaron no longer is the understudy. This may be key to understanding why the weekly *Torah* portions were divided as they are. It certainly would have made sense to group all of the plagues together in one portion. However, perhaps *Vaera* concludes with the seventh plague because it is a turning point: Moses is ready.

Effect. Although Moses is ready, dad is not. Parent and child are on separate, but compatible tracks--the Israelites in Goshen with life forces intact, and Pharoah in his region, with his cattle and slaves and Egyptian men and women protected indoors from the hail. This could be a turning point for Pharoah, if he could do what a parent needs to do to foster the development of his child. In truth, he is not allowed to yet. God continues to "harden his heart," to ensure that Pharoah will not yet gratify Moses' demand for independence. Is this because Moses is not really ready? Or is it because Moses, too, like Aaron before him, is only a representative? Perhaps this is the reason that the story must shift again, from Moses to the Israelites, who themselves must become ready before Pharoah will be permitted by God, by the inevitability of human development, to let go.

The plagues that are presented in the next portion of *Bo* continue the metaphor of development. Locusts are insects that experience a stage of prolonged, subterranean incubation prior to their emergence as mature adults. Both larva and pupa stages signal moments of imminent transformations--from the wingless to the winged, from immobility to the effectiveness of the fully formed adult insect. In addition, locusts often migrate great distances in their search for what they need to sustain life. The parallel of this image to the Israelites on the verge of their own stepping forth, is striking. Furthermore, the locusts consume all vegetation "so that nothing green was left," *[Exodus 10:15]* suggesting the necessary disappearance of what is young and green and budding in order for full maturation to replace it.

The next to the last plague represents the mythic descent into darkness that classically precedes the emergence into light which heralds rebirth. The Israelites are ready for their "coming of age" as they remain in light during this plague *[Exodus 10:23]*. Pharoah, the parent, must wrestle with himself ("people could not see one another"), preparing to accept the maturity that will soon stand before him.

By the end of the plagues, in *Bo,* Moses will again speak to the Israelites, as he did at the beginning of *Vaera*. This time they will heed him. Their readiness to listen is a reflection of the fact that Moses is different now. He has claimed his voice through his actions and is worthy of being heeded. We will also come full circle with the image of blood (on doorposts) that began the plagues, with its life affirming presence and meaning made manifest.

God's decree to destroy the first born recalls Pharoah's own similar decree earlier. But, in keeping with our understanding of this story, the son that Pharoah loses in the final plague is not his young Egyptian son--that son is only a metaphor. The son that Pharoah loses is Moses. And he does not lose him to death, but to life. Moses has carved out his own identity, different from his Egyptian father's, but similar, after all, to his Hebrew father's. These two fathers, Pharoah and Amram, are split screen images for Moses' final differentiation, where some parental values are rejected and some embraced. This is the hallmark of real maturation: that identification does not happen *in toto*, but rather selective identifications are "digested" and synthesized into a new and distinct personality.

Like the pre-plague which foreshadowed the final plague, one son, one serpent, must be gone for the other to emerge. If both sons are metaphors for development, it is not sad that Pharoah's young son "dies" while Moses lives. Like the frog in *The Frog Prince*, the earlier "incarnations" must disappear for the next developmental stage to unfold. One cannot move on to maturity while remaining infantile. Letting go and giving up are prerequisites for movement.

In the end, it is not death that forces Pharoah's hand, but life. Although Pharoah experiences Moses' life, his independence, his emergent adulthood as the ultimate loss of his "son," he finally lets go. And Moses, like each of us, finally leaves his father's home: "to find a land more kind than home, more large than earth..."[2]

During our next Passover *seder*, when we spill a drop of wine for each plague in sadness at the suffering of innocent Egyptians, we might view this ritual through a different lens. It may be, after all, that we are not diminished by the deaths of the Egyptians, for the Egyptians might be understood not literally as a separate nation, some of whom perished at the bottom of a sea, but rather a metaphor for a state, within--our earlier tadpole selves, which we had to relinquish in order to grow beyond. While the relinquishing may have been accompanied by ambivalence, the loss which is crystallized in our memories and our myths, is balanced by the recompense of fuller life. Perhaps the drops of wine may be seen as remembrances of steps along our way, remembrance that each plague only **seemed** to be about destruction--that the process of growing up, with its harsh demands, its wrenching separations, its moments of frightening insecurity are often experienced by us all as being dictated by a cruel and arbitrary authority; at another level growing up is always about the possibility of continued life and movement. In our ritual remembrance of our people's mythic history, we understand that slavery and freedom and the journey from one to the other, are the external metaphors for the internal odyssey that we each must make to become a human being.

Notes:

1. D.W. Winnicott, "Primary Maternal Preoccupation," (1956) in *Through Paediatrics to Psycho-Analysis* (New York: Basic Books, Inc., Publishers, 1975).

2. Thomas Wolfe, *You Can't Go Home Again,* (New York: Harper and Row Publishers, 1968), 57

I am grateful to my congregation, the Reconstructionist Synagogue of the North Shore, who received this paper so warmly and enthusiastically on January 20, 1996.

Published in *Kerem:* A Journal of Creative Explorations in Judaism, No. 5, 5757/1997, pp. 7-16.

Parashat ***Vaera***
Exodus 6:2-9:35

PLAGUE	AGENT	EFFECT
A. rod turns to serpent	Aaron does	Pharoah's magicians do also
1. Blood	Moses speaks Aaron does	Pharoah's magicians do also Pharoah does not ask Moses to stop
2. Frogs	Moses speaks Aaron does	Pharoah's magicians do also Pharoah begs for respite; deceives
3. Lice	Moses speaks Aaron does	Pharoah's magicians cannot do Phaorah does not ask Moses to stop Courtiers begin to be afraid
4. Insects	Moses speaks God does	Pharoah begs for respite; deceives God separates Israelites from Egyptians
5. Pestilence	Moses speaks God does	God separates Israelites' cattle from Egyptians' Pharoah does not ask Moses to stop
6. Boils	Moses does Aaron back-up	Egyptians are afflicted Pharoah does not ask Moses to stop
7. Hail	Moses speaks Moses does	Israelites and Egyptians separate Pharoah could save Egyptians; begs respite; deceives

Next week's parasha ***Bo***:

8. Locusts	Moses & Aaron speak Moses does	Pharoah begs for respite; deceives
9. Darkness	Moses speaks Moses does	Israelites have light
10. Death to first born	God does	Moses speaks to Israelites again Blood is symbol again

On the Heels of His Brother: the Inevitability of Jacob Receiving the Birthright

Toldoth

Like all *Parashot*, the portion called *Toldoth* does not easily yield its meanings. What is Esau's offense that he should be robbed of his birthright? Why is apparent deception on the part of mother and son rewarded?

In *Toldoth* we are dealing with a familiar theme: one person/generation must pass to make room for the emergence of another. Indeed, this mantra: "l'dor v'dor" figures prominently in the collective experience of our people, in its liturgy, history, and memory. So our portion opens with the identification of our characters, stressing their ages, setting the stage that our story will focus on the passing of these characters as they are inevitably "replaced" by those who follow.

This same theme is replayed on a smaller stage, like a play within a play, by Jacob and Esau. One brother arrives on the heels of the other, an expression whose vernacular suggests replacement of one by another. As their births are announced, Isaac's age is given, and he is now 20 years older than when he married, surely underscoring the rapid progression of age and its consequences.

As in many stories (particularly fairy tales, of which this and all Biblical stories are variants)[1] the unavailability of food spurs the main action of the story (in the *Akedah*, "Isaac was weaned.") Here, Esau is hungry. In psychological, symbolic terms, hunger in stories often signals the need to act, to grow up, to provide for one's self. Both brothers, however, are capable of doing this: Esau can hunt his own food, and Jacob can cook. Where is Esau's offense that he should lose his birthright? It is only in this: that Esau came first. He is the earlier incarnation of 'son,' perhaps representing a more primitive (though not less moral) form of humanity. Esau hunts yet is still hungry. There is the suggestion in the description of Jacob as being "mild," that his ability to domesticate, to cook the hunted food, is a higher developmental level than merely acquiring food.

Such a suggestion is seen in the less lofty but perhaps more accessible story of *The Three Pigs*, where the eldest pig has access to apples at the fair, but must use forethought in order to have his food and not become lunch for the wolf. In *The Three Pigs*, the earlier incarnations of brothers must be gone, before the mature version of pig can emerge. In a moralistic revision of the original, the youngest pigs are described as lazy, and only wanting to play, which is, of course, their downfall. In the original, however, no such moral commentary is necessary, for we, like our children, understand that such behavior is totally appropriate for the young child but that it must give way, in time, to more mature, thoughtful behavior, in which gratifications are delayed.

So it is with Esau and Jacob. They are two embodiments of one idea--the idea of an integrated, mature human being. We know this because they are twins--in some important way they embody a unified idea (just as the pig brothers in *The Three Pigs* represent different embodiments of a unified idea, as each echoes the others' words: "not by the hair of your chinny chin chin.") In *Toldoth* we see this unity again, as Isaac prepares to bless his son. Jacob, at this point becomes the carrier of both his brother's and his own identities: "The voice is the voice of Jacob, yet the hands are the hands of Esau." In this blending of mental and physical capacities, Jacob represents an evolutionary advancement over Esau. Jacob's supplanting of Esau is an inevitability--it does not come about because of wrongdoing or error on Esau's part, or deception on Jacob's part. It is, simply, what must be.

Interestingly, the biblical paragraph that follows Isaac's blessing, underscores this interpretation, for the brothers' identities become merged by the end of the *parasha*. Esau is now able to prepare a dish; he, too, can cook. At the end of the *parasha*, the fusion of identities is complete: each has the capacities of both. Isaac instructs Jacob not to take a Canaanite woman as his wife, as this would displease Isaac. Esau, follows suit, wishing also not to displease his father. Like Jacob, he, also, will not take a Canaanite woman for a wife.

It is a kind of evolutionary necessity that Jacob replaces Esau, and all of the characters in *Toldoth* participate in effecting this necessity. No one, really, is deceived. Rebekah does her part to ensure that evolution proceeds; Isaac seems to know, also, that Jacob is to receive the blessing of continuity, for he does nothing about the fact that he knows it is Jacob's voice before him. Even Jacob and Esau seem to 'know' this. Jacob, is, after all, the one who can provide during hunger, and it is this capacity, as a psychological symbol, that marks emerging maturity. By the end, Esau has merged his identity with that of Jacob, in his capacity to cook and in his choice of whom to marry. We do not hear of Esau again, for some time, because he has been 'absorbed,' so to speak, within Jacob.

Biblical commentary often takes the form of moral imperative. There is an assumption that the Bible is to teach us right from wrong, to teach us what we should or should not do. When we approach the Bible in this way, it often makes little sense, as we are left with deceivers (Jacob) or braggarts (Joseph) who 'win' out in the end. *Midrash* that emphasizes one character's assumed or interpolated blemish is frequently not satisfying, as it imposes negative qualities on the 'vanquished' characters to explain why they had to be 'vanquished,' even when these qualities are not present, in either suggested or explicit forms.

Biblical stories do not need to have moral referents in order to lead to important insights about humanity or to resonate with truth. I do not think that the point of this Biblical tale of two brothers is that we should be like Jacob—clever and deceiving. I do not think that the point is that we should avoid being like Jacob—cunning and thieving. I think it is, rather, that we **are** like Jacob; this is not to say, we are like the "good" Jacob or the "bad" Jacob, and we should learn a lesson from one or the other. We are like Jacob, because we were once born, and being born, we replaced those who came before us, not in the manner of a sibling rivalry, but on a larger canvas. Our being born, like Jacob's is, of necessity, a usurpation. Indeed, it is the parental job to ensure that children are ready to be usurpers, to step into the parental place, to take over the business of the world. When he becomes ready, Jacob steps into his place; he does no less and no more than this. His brother is only the incarnation of one who came before him, no more and no less. The story, when viewed in this way, is not driven by morality's imperatives, but, simply, by life's imperatives.

B'Hukkotai: D'var Torah

At first glance, the *parasha B'Hukkotai* appears to evoke images of a vengeful God who demands obedience...or else. The *parasha* begins with four brief paragraphs outlining the benefits to the people if they "follow [the] laws and faithfully observe [the] commandments." These paragraphs are followed by twice as many that detail, with significant elaboration, what will befall the people if they do not "obey [God]," and "observe all these commandments." On a manifest level, God holds many threatening cards, each to be played at the first sign of a lapse in our obedience. God is in charge; God is punitive; we are subservient.

But that is only on first glance. A closer reading of the text yields different understandings. Above all else, *B'Hukkotai* is about a covenant—an agreement. By nature, a covenant can only be established between two equal parties. Each agrees to give to the other something desired in exchange for something desired. The equality is established at this level: each is in need and each possesses something desired. If equality is the basis of covenant, then God and the people can be imagined to be standing face to face, equal partners in this agreement.

It is clear what the people have to gain by this covenant. The first four paragraphs address this. But, what possible gain could there be to God, that this covenant should be so important? Only this: that if the people agree to this covenant, then "I will be your God." Thus, what hangs in the balance here for God is God's very existence, definition, and being, perhaps the very things that hang in the balance for the people. Beyond the symbiotic necessity, we might even argue that the people and God have interchangeable identities.

If we approach this exploration from another angle, we might argue that, in fact, God is independent of us, and in need of nothing from us.

Let us proceed with both of these premises before us--that God does not stand to benefit in any significant way from this covenant, and that there is a type of commutability between God and the people. It would follow, then that the covenant is actually between the people and themselves. God instructs the people to follow the laws, not because it is good for God, not because God needs this, not because God is boss, but because it is only through submission and obedience to a set of shared principles that a civilization can emerge and be sustained. It is essential to follow the laws and commandments not so we can be rewarded by God, but so we can flourish as a society. Indeed, the content of the first four paragraphs focuses totally upon images of fertility and strength, of reaching a critical mass that allows us to be "a People," and of having the strength to sustain this "Peoplehood." Conversely, if we fail to obey these laws, it will not be God's vengeance that we will have to face; we will have sown the seeds of our own destruction. This interpretation is supported by much of the text elaborating what will befall us for disobedience. Many of these images are either of internal distress (such as eating but feeling unsatisfied [Leviticus 26: 26] or "fleeing...though none pursues" [Leviticus 26: 36]) or of being dissociated from the anchors of family and familiar custom (such as "you shall be delivered into enemy hands" [Leviticus 26: 25] or "I shall loose wild beasts against you, and they shall bereave you of your children..." [Leviticus 26: 22] or "And you I will scatter among the nations." [Leviticus 26: 33].

Disobedience to our own governing laws causes both internal turmoil and distress ("The sound of a driven leaf shall put them to flight" [Leviticus 26: 36] and external distress through the severing of our own connectedness to conventions and ties that bind, but in that binding, nurture. Of course the laws are restrictive and limiting, but without them there can be no shape, no definition, no peoplehood. Covenantal engagement must be the starting place for the emergence and sustenance of a people.

So, God stands to gain nothing from our obedience. We, on the other hand, stand to gain everything. God loses nothing from our disobedience. We, on the other hand move toward self-destruction and total loss when we break with this covenant, that is our own covenant.

Perhaps, there is something more. If we hold to this covenant, we flourish in such bountiful ways, our basic needs are so fulfilled that there is space for the contemplation of a God. It is in this, that God's statement: "I will be your God and you shall be My people" has great resonance. A covenant with ourselves makes room for God. And when we break our covenant, which we are wont to do, it will never be annulled: "I will not reject them or spurn them so as to destroy them, annulling My covenant with them...I will remember in their favor the covenant with the ancients..." Even in a time of lapse, we will be compelled back toward repair, as **we** remember our need for covenant, our need for life to be good enough, our need to be part of a people, our need to have connective threads held, so that we can find again, the awe that our ancestors once called "God."

B'ha-a-lot'cha

D'var Torah
Presented by invitation to the
4th adult B'nai Mitzvah class
Reconstructionist Synagogue of the North Shore, June 2, 2007

I would like to thank the members of the *b'nai mitzvah* class for extending to me the honor of an encounter with today's *parasha*.

I will focus my words today on three related themes that are present for me in my reading of *B'ha-a-lot'cha*.

The first theme derives from the name of the *parasha* itself: *B'ha-a-lot'cha*: *when you rise; to raise up*. I will take some liberties and extend this definition to include *when you awaken*.

This broadening of definition is not too far a reach, when we consider that the reading begins by describing a sensory event that is tied to awakening. It is fitting that today's portion opens with instructions on how to "raise up" or "mount the lamps"—how to make and position light. This introductory paragraph sets the stage that we will be dealing with the shedding of light—not only that our eyes may see, but that our vision—aimed behind us to our history, before us to our destiny, and deeply inward to the core of what it will mean to us to be human and how we will fulfill our humanity, may also come sharply into focus. With light mounted, we are awakened.

Chapter 10 details another sensory reference to being awakened, as Moses is instructed on how to make the trumpets that will be used to call the community together. Here, again, we move quickly from the **sound** that will call us to rise, to the more complex reasons for rising: to assemble, to move forward, to insure safety, to invoke memory, to offer gratitude.

Being awakened now, we can read the rest of the *parasha* with eyes and ears focused and with our emotional receptors that process and digest this information, ready to make sense of what will be seen and heard. Let us catalogue some of the particulars found in this passage and the way in which each is linked to the theme of rising up or being awake.

There is the designation of the Levites who, in performing service to the Tent of Meeting, represent those who will unify the group, who will maintain the place where the "spirit" of the group, the force that will move this group forward in their growing up, resides. In Biblical parlance, this force is called God, though I think that the word "God" has come to be a somewhat sloppy shorthand, allowing us to be careless in its use, but that is the subject for a different *d'var Torah*. The Levites' service is intended to maintain the Tent of Meeting, that place where we take the base metal of concrete, sensory information, (literally, the gold of the lamps and the silver of the trumpets) and transform it, alchemistically, into the precious currency of consciousness...and where we, in turn, undergo the transformative, awakening process of becoming fully, rather than barely, human.

There is the listing of all of the troops of Israel by division and commander, suggesting the importance of "joining ranks," of belonging, of rising up and taking one's place in the march so that we can get from here to there in as orderly and civil and supported a way as possible.

There is Moses' quandary about how to lead such difficult people, suggesting the necessity of stepping forward, again of rising up, of taking responsibility beyond one's self, for steering humanity in the direction of "promise."

There is instruction about when and how to perform the Passover ritual, suggesting that memory and the honoring of origins is worthy, is necessary for remaining awake to who we are, to where we have come from, in order that we may chart our journey's trajectory from there to here...and on to there.

There are instructions about when to journey on and when to remain encamped, helping us understand that the Promised Land, to which we were and ever are heading, always was and always is, a place within, and not a destination, a place to be created in the small accretions of ordinary experience as we move forward in our lives and in the quiet moments of rest, which, in their own way, also move us forward. Wakefulness propels us into life whether we find ourselves encamped on a new patch of soil tomorrow, or whether we are able to see this same patch newly tomorrow.

The second theme that emerges from all of the various sections of *B'ha-a-lot'cha*, is that all of them deal with ways in which identity is built: by knowing our past; by moving forward into a future; by journeying between the two; by resting which gives time for reflection; by inviting others who are "not me" into one's journey (as Moses does when he invites Hobab a Midianite to come along with them); by feeling moments of one's limitations (as Moses does when he feels incapable of leading); by learning from others (as Moses does when he is helped by the 70 elders); by feeling apart from the group (as Miriam does when she is temporarily set apart from the community for speaking ill of Moses); by being alone at times (as Miriam is); by being readmitted into the group (also as Miriam is). In our tradition, as is made clear in this portion, identity is always defined in the context of more-than-self. Listen to these words: "The Lord spoke to Moses saying...Let the Israelites lay their hands upon the Levites, and let Aaron designate the Levites before the Lord...You shall place the Levites in attendance upon Aaron and his sons..." The first chapter of *B'ha-a-lot'cha* is dense with such references in which we find: God (which we will continue to define as the thrust that keeps us moving forward, as that creative force which allows, demands, necessitates, makes possible the type of regeneration within us so that we are ever growing); we find Moses, an individual; we find Aaron and his sons, a single family unit; we find the Levites, a larger, clan unit; and we find the Israelites, a community of creative, vibrant, individuals, families, and clans who are journeying, discovering, and "becoming" together. While it may seem to us to be a quintessential Reconstructionist *parasha*, it is actually perfectly emblematic of what it means to be Jewish—to be a part, concentrically, of many rings within this buzzing, lively hive.

The final impression that I would like to share emerges in this *parasha's* depiction of God as incredibly flexible and moderate. Different from descriptions of God as exacting and demanding, rigid, or punishing, this *parasha* images God as being wonderfully reasonable. Placed as it is, between *Naso* and *Sh'lach L'cha*, *B'ha-a-lot'cha* expresses something important about our "readiness" for this kind of God. The Israelites have just undergone an accounting of themselves, and have received the *Kohanic* blessing in *Naso;* and some of them, in *Sh'lach L'cha* are about to go out, to scout the land of Canaan, to lay eyes on this Promised Land for the first time since Joseph's family sojourned from there some 402 years before. Perhaps in their growing up, as the Israelites near the mythic place toward which they have been heading, they are ready for a God who understands, along with them, the vicissistudes of life. Let us keep in mind our former "definition" of God as a generative force. God makes clear, the text makes clear that there is no single way in which connection to this generativity must occur—only that it **must** occur.

This is a God who commands Moses to perform the Passover ritual in the first month, on the fourteenth day of the month, at twilight, in the wilderness of Sinai; but, if he misses this time, OK, so he can do it in the second month. We can have our *seder* on Sunday night instead of Monday night if this will allow all of us to make the offering.

This God asks the Levites to serve only between the ages of 25 and 50—service is not to be experienced as bondage, only as necessity in that time of our lives when we are most able.

When we are on our journey, it is not important to "get there" with single-mindedness and blinders to all else. This God sends a cloud our way during which we are not to move forward, but to remain "encamped" allowing, perhaps, this time to be *Shabbat*-like, like the "pauses between the notes" to quote Greenberg. And if no cloud is sent our way, I suspect we are to manufacture one, ourselves, in order to remember that like life, the moments--and not the completion of the moments-- is all.

This God lets us know that there is no necessity to be xenophobic, to remain insular, only keeping to ourselves in order to be a People; we are to invite others in, not of Our People, who may know the way even better than we (as Moses said to Hobab: "Please do not leave us, inasmuch as you know where we should camp in the wilderness and can be our guide.").

This God tells us we need not shoulder responsibility all by ourselves, as Moses is instructed by God to choose 70 elders to help him lead this sometimes oppositional group.

This God tells us to be moderate in meting out consequences, and to allow each other to repair what becomes cracked in relationships. When Miriam is removed from the community and stricken with scales for speaking ill of Moses, Moses entreats God on her behalf to heal her, and the community does not leave her, but waits until her 7 days of isolation are done, readmits her, and then sets out again.

This is a God I understand.

While we often think of the prescriptions, laws, rituals, and sacrifices that are enumerated in the *Torah* as rigid, demanding perfect adherence, this *parasha* seems to suggest, at its heart, that rigidity is to be eschewed, that one need only to "sign on," to be a part, to agree to take this journey, and, perhaps, most important, to remain awake on the road from here to here.

What a perfect *parasha* (perhaps they all are) for you:

the troop of Belfer commanded by Karen, daughter of Elaine Neidorf Unger and Barney Unger;

the division of Kaynard, commanded by Ann, daughter of Ethel and Meyer Ostrow;

and Meryl, daughter of Hannah Ostrow Kaynard and Sheldon/Sam Kaynard;

the troop of Kliman, commanded by Bernice, daughter of Rebecca Shulimson Widgoff and Leo Widgoff;

the troop of Lehn, commanded by Joan, daughter of Henrietta Kanner Adler and Barney Adler;

the troop of Pitkow, commanded by June, daughter of Ruth Reinhold Rosenberg and Robert Rosenberg;

the tribal troop of Pulver, commanded by Lauren, daughter of Jeanne Hirsch Pulver and W. Howard Pulver;

the troop of Schaffer, commanded by Barbara, daughter of Rhala Opper Yates and Eugene H. Yates;

the troop of Walowitz, commanded by Jeanette, daughter of Rachel Sutten Zonana and Victor H. Zonana;

the troop of Weinberg, commanded by Naomi, daughter of Florence Ashinsky Miller and Irving Miller...

for in signing on to become a *bat mitzvah* today, you have fulfilled the prescriptions outlined in *B'ha-a-lot'cha*: you have lighted the lamps; you have sounded the trumpet; you do not need to be Levites to have performed service to our Tabernacle in making it a place of assemblage today, a place where we find and create our best selves; you have performed this ritual—if not at 12 or 13, then at 50 or 70; you have done better than Moses, for you have enlisted the help of elders **and** youngers, of your teachers and families, and fellow congregants knowing that wisdom comes from many sources. You have allowed us to be an essential part of this with you, creating a binding covenant for us all. You have said "yes" to this passage that has raised you up before us, this journey that will point you toward promise each day 'when you rise up.'

Isaiah: an Interpretation

For *Yom Kippur Haftarah* reading September 18, 2010

If we fast today
with no thought
of how we will meet tomorrow
and every day that follows tomorrow
then this ritual fast is as hollow
as the dry shrunken gourd
from last year's *sukkah*
barren, unmoored
from the lifeblood of meaning
or, worse
if our empty stomachs
fill us with the righteous illusion
that today's hunger, alone,
makes us good Jews, good people.
We may fast for many reasons
but, on this day, only one matters:
that this fast, like the blasts of the *shofar*,
unmoor us
from the familiar place,
the stasis of our packaged selves
making it impossible for us not to see
what is needed
making it imperative for us
to share in some manner, in some measure
the abundance that graces our lives.
If we fast today
with no thought
of how we will meet tomorrow
and every day that follows tomorrow,
then today is as any other day,
and we might as well return home
and feast on a noonday meal.

(September 14, 2010)
Presented to the Reconstructionist Synagogue of the North Shore
Congregation on *Yom Kippur*, September 18, 2010/ 10 *Tishrei* 5771

A Play in One Act for *Yom Kippur*

The Actors: One goat, who has all the speaking parts (known sometimes as the *Azazel* Goat);

The Congregation, who does not yet have a speaking role

The Setting: Here

The Time: Now

Goat: You may be wondering why the cast of characters is so small. I'm sure you've noticed that there is no High Priest, no bull, no blood, and maybe, most controversial of all, no God. And you're probably feeling more than skeptical about listening to an old goat, the likes of me, narrate your *Yom Kippur* drama. The truth is: I shouldn't be in this play at all.

But you have insisted on my presence here, chosen me. And none of us can argue with the fact that for thousands of years, you have trusted me with what is most private in your lives, most disturbing to your sense of your own humanity, with things unspoken even to your most intimate of partners. I have borne the weight of your hearts on my horns as I've wandered in the wilderness. I know you. I know what you would not wish anyone to know. Who else could possibly narrate this story?

You read this ritual-- the one where you slaughter a bull and another goat, where your High Priest splatters the blood in prescribed directions, counting in specified ways, where he wears prescribed clothing, enters the Holy of Holies, and where you send me off into the wilderness with your sins on my head--with some mixture of fascination and abhorrence, honoring it as your history, rejecting it as your destiny. You can't embrace it, and you can't let it go. I will be respectful of that tension. Perhaps the destruction of the Temple was a catalytic gift, propelling you up a developmental ladder where you moved from killing and blood splattering to reading and telling about these things, from real to imagined.

So, the obvious question is: after nineteen hundred forty one years, is there a next rung on this ladder? And if there is, what is it? And are we ready for it?

Let's go back to our cast: me and you. A small cast, but still many parts to be played. Because I'm in charge of this play, I can tell you that I will not be playing the usual role assigned me. And you will take on a bit more than what you might have done in previous *Yom Kippur* dramas.

I'm actually going to assign you all of the roles in this drama, even mine.

First, you will be the High Priest. I know you have showered and chosen special clothes for today. And like the High Priest, you feel both awe and fear on this day when all is sealed, as you have your own encounter with God. I'm guessing that you even have symbolic ropes tied around your core that allow you to pull away when you get too close to important Truths. And along with the rope, I'm also guessing that you know well how to drop incense on a burning coal to create smoke that blinds you from seeing Truth, from seeing the face of God. You are so like the High Priest; you can play this role without rehearsal.

Our play could certainly not proceed without the Holy of Holies. It is where the climax of our drama is enacted—the place where you come closest to God. This Holy of Holies: it is within you. You have called it many things: your heart, your consciousness, your soul. The name you use is not important—

the inner knowledge of The Place is supremely so. So, you are the High Priest, and you are the Holy of Holies.

Next, we must figure out how God is to be part of our play today. From several thousand years of *Yom Kippur* attendance, I know this is less straightforward than your liturgy suggests. But, one way or another, God must be with us today. I imagine you have been spellbound by the abiding Symmetries of the Universe, have seen Beauty that has brought you to your knees, experienced Consciousness too deep for words, known the Unutterable, been born of the Mystery of Becoming, felt Love that took your breath away, stretched forth your most Awakened Selves toward Holiness. This is what we might mean by God, the Idea of a thousand thousand facets, ungraspably complex, eluding language. But because our lives are bound up with all this as much as they are bound up with air, we breathe, like air, one Unified Word, to hold for us all that is beyond holding but must be held, nonetheless. It is in this holding that God might be found. God, therefore, must be played by you if God is to have any real presence in our play.

And me. You know, surely, that even when you transferred those sins to my head and sent me off, I still lived. That *midrash* that you find both comforting and repellent—the one where I am pushed off a cliff to obliterate me and the all of you that I carry—that never happened. I was always set free; it's there in Leviticus, the unwritten understanding being that your sins were alive, because I was alive, and because you would never know how near to your camp I might find my way back, you would need to do the continual work of keeping sin away. So, in the end, you are the goat, too, and this play has only one actor: you.

All the roles have been assigned.

Now, what is our drama to be today? Scripture tells us that the High Priest must prepare to enter the Holy of Holies by sacrificing a bull and another of my brethren, and ultimately, banishing me to the wilderness with the weight of your disowned failures on my horns. *Midrash* describes several ropes—one around the High Priest and one around me—to pull us both **away** from the Ultimate, the center of life's pulse. Today's play must unfold differently. I will help you find the end of the tether that has always bound you, and I will hand that end to you, so that you may lead yourself **into** all that is Holy. You have never needed a High Priest to go inside the Holy of Holies; in fact, only you, alone, can enter that sacred realm within yourself.

This is where I leave you, poised upon a ladder rung, to answer for yourself: Can you open to the Incomprehensible All in your life? Can you take hold of this tether and lead yourself into your Holy of Holies? There is, after all, only one *Yom Kippur* sin: to live your life behind that smoky veil, behind the incense-dropped-on-hot-coal-curtain that shields you from all that is bound up in that word God. The only sin: not to live fully in the Presence or Awareness of the sacred, without which, nothing is Illuminated.

I take my exit here.

This is the Holiest Moment; Your Ark, the Holiest Place; Your Encounter, the Holiest Encounter. When you enter your Holy of Holies, what do you find inside? When you emerge, who stands there? Let the play begin...

(August, 2011)

Presented to the Reconstructionist Synagogue of the North Shore Congregation on *Yom Kippur*, October 8, 2011/ 10 *Tishrei*, 5772

III. The Blue Thread

Thoughts on a *Tallit*

The first time I ever put on a *tallit* was six years ago on *Rosh Hashanah*. I had volunteered two months earlier to prepare a *Torah* reading on the second day of *Rosh Hashanah*. I was not yet a member of the synagogue even though my family and I had been participating in synagogue life for over a year. There was a kind of grace period or trial period during which people were welcomed to be part of the community prior to making a commitment to the community. As neither my husband nor I had been inside a synagogue for 16 years, it seemed an unlikely place for us to find ourselves, let alone find ourselves with pleasure.

So, the fact that we had been around the place for at least a year and attending family functions at the synagogue fairly regularly, a mistake was made and an *aliya* extended to me with the assumption that I was a member. After some controversy about his, the decision was made to allow me as a non-synagogue member to be called to the *Torah*. Someone shared with me his rationale that maybe the experience would make my decision clearer, easier, less filled with hesitation and doubt.

That someone was very wise.

I'm not sure how it happened that I had inherited my grandfather's *tallit*. I have two brothers and three male first cousins who shared my grandfather, and an older sister, any of whom might have been considered first. Although my brothers wives are not Jewish, and although my husband is Jewish, we had hardly made any kind of commitment to being Jewish together or raising our family with a Jewish education or Jewish practices. In retrospect it seems unlikely (that word, again) that the bag with *tfillin* and *tallit* should have come to me. But for many years now, since my grandmother died, I have had this religious bag tucked away on a shelf in a dresser, not sure what I ever would do with it except keep it.

I am also not sure what "possessed" me to don this *tallit* the day I would read from the *Torah* for the first time in my life. It seemed "acceptable," as our congregation is led by both a female and a male rabbi, and some women did wear them. I watched the men who ascended the *bimah* for *aliyot* touch the *tsitsi* of their *tallit* to the *Torah*. It seemed that I should do the same. Yet, I must admit, it also felt strange, a little pretentious. For I was not a woman who really knew what this meant, what this was all about, how I felt about it. I was not yet even sure whether my first High Holiday service in 16 years would be my last or merely the first of my adulthood.

Nonetheless, I did wear my grandfather's yellowed and worn *tallit* that day, and each High Holiday service since. I must confess still that I continue not to know what it means, but I am growing into my feelings about it. When I wear it, I remember my grandfather in the primitive way that memory has of weaving its way into the present. I smell Gorham's silver polish and feel the pleasure of being allowed to polish my grandmother's silver for the holidays (I do not remember the actual holiday dinners, except *Pesah*, but I do know I polished the silver for many other dinners now lost to my memory). I remember the delight in seeing the tarnish come off of the spoons and knives (the forks were always harder), and rubbing them until they were bright and gleaming. I remember helping to roll the bagelah dough into snakes, curling them around, dipping them into the mixture of pulverized almonds and sugar. I do not know which other grandchildren helped make bagelah, but I think I may be the only one who still makes them. I remember the taste of tea with sugar that I sat and drank with my grandparents when they got home from services Friday night. I do not remember if I went to Friday night services with them or just slept over their house very often on Friday nights. I do not drink tea with sugar now, but when I prepare a cup for my son, and sneak a taste, a flood of sweetness and memory is mine. I remember watching my grandmother, with both fear and fascination, give my grandfather his insulin shot in the morning. My Saturday mornings with my grandparents ended as I walked down to synagogue to sing in the children's choir for services. That is how I learned the rhythms of the service.

As I put on his *tallit* year after year, I do not have a sense exactly that I bring him alive, but it does feel as if I find an historic part of myself. As I am enwrapped in his *tallit*, I feel as if I infuse a kind of vitality into this cloth that makes it live and feel right on my shoulders. And the reverse feels true, as well. In wearing this thing that was not worn for 28 years, I feel an intimate connection to my grandfather and his religious life, and through this connection, my own religious sensibilities are more available. I think this *tallit* has become a metaphor for bringing alive something that was dormant for a long time and keeping it alive. It does not really bring my grandfather into the present, but it does transport feelings, smells, and rituals associated with him into the present.

And from here? As my son prepares for his *Bar Mitzvah,* it feels appropriate that I pass the *tallit* to him, as he may become someday the torch bearer of Judaism to his own. But I know he wants his own *tallit*. Perhaps he will wear it for his service, until he is given his own. And perhaps my daughter, too, will do the same. I guess it is fitting that they have their own, for that is really what I am passing to them—the desire to possess this religion and make it their own. I do not feel the desire to have my own *tallit*,* and I am acutely aware that the one I wear is not my own, but rather mine to hold and keep and wear until someone else takes it over. I am *tallit*-sitting for awhile. If wearing a *tallit* means anything to me, it is in this that it has meaning: that I will pass onto my children the smells and tastes and melodies and pleasures that will make up their Jewish memory trove, and that these will be at once as real and tangible as the *tsitsi* on my grandfather's *tallit*, and as intangible yet indelible as the yellow of its cloth.

(May, 1993)

* Fourteen years later, I did want my own *tallit*, which my parents made for me. See the piece that follows.

Tallit

And the daughter who was herself beyond two score and ten
saw that the woman's fingers had begun to twist like
branches of an ageless tree
and she asked this of the woman
and the woman said
yes
and the woman took up
the tool of her ancestors
and set to work,
made
thousands
of perfect stitches
each nestled snugly to the next
like lovers spooning in exquisite fit.
On the virgin white cloth
that the woman cursed for its slipperiness
the stitches multiplied
in mitotic unfolding
as if the silken threads
were spun from the very tips
of her fingers.
The story rose off the cloth,
a sculpted *bas relief*
that could be read by touch as much as by sight
spun for the younger one
as unique as a fingertip's whorl
and mythic as the song sung on reedy shores
when being came into being:
begotten and begetter
beloved and lover
seeker on her way from Eden to Canaan
carried on the tides of history, the shoulders of her people
her own feet wet from the crossings made.

And the older woman gave the garment
to the younger
a swaddling cloth of pictographs
that wrapped the girl season upon season
in the gift of her own life.

(November 3, 2007)
Published online at
http://womenspiritualpoetry.blogspot.com/2013/05/tallit-by-sheri-lindner.html

I Find Myself Thinking about Jewishness in the Strangest of Places...

On Father's Day of 1995 my husband, Michael and I took our 14 year old son, Dan, and a friend to a Grateful Dead concert at Giants Stadium. Before going I was actually somewhat excited--I had never been to one, and I liked the folksy music that Dan listens to of the 'Dead.'

It did not take long for me to realize that Michael's and my presence there was anachronistic, and Dan's was precocious. In short, this was not yet a place for a young adolescent, and most definitely not an event that one goes to accompanied by one's parents. But that is for another editorial.

What I spent my time doing there, however, was watching and thinking. What I watched was people engaged in tribal and ritualistic activity that was both familiar and estranging. It struck me that here were 35,000 people who were rejecting "mainstream" or adult values (whatever that is, which is also for another essay), and were creating their own sub- or counter-culture, which I suppose is mainstream for adolescents. But this counterculture (or whatever) group recreated, in different form, the very values that had been ostensibly cast aside.

To begin with, there was the chain of neon necklaces, about 30 of them linked together that were passed around the stadium. Since these were not on sale anywhere that I could see, someone or several someones had clearly brought them with them. I have since been told that they represent a song: "The Unbroken Chain." The goal, it seemed, was to see how far around the place this chain could be passed, and maybe, how many people could touch it as it went around. At one point, the whole thing was tossed up to the tier above, to which many thousands cheered when it was caught. In a bizarre moment of transvaluation, I thought of the *Torah* being carried around the congregation and touched by many hands...the sense of community ownership...the thing brought by someone, but given over to the community...the thing becoming a link, literally, here, that binds this 35,000 together, and the more people who touch it and "claim" it, and then share it, the better. Of course, I couldn't quite image a "*Torah* toss" up to the top tier, but this inconsistency did not ruin the analogy for me! The same thing occurred with balloons. I watched someone behind me blow up a huge balloon and set it "free," sharing it with this large community. I watched his sense of pride and good feeling at having "contributed" and given to this community.

Then there was the ritualistic rolling of joints and the passing of them around with a sense of largesse and general good will. You'll know that I was not exactly transported by the music when I tell you that I was thinking that this is like tearing off a piece of challah and passing the rest around. Yes, transvaluation is a good way to pass the time. The "Dead Head" behind us, who was 'religiously' following the group around the country on its spring tour, even benevolently offered us a drink of water from his water bottle, as if strangers drinking from the same bottle were not at all strange. I guess the point was, that as part of a community, we did not feel like strangers to him, really. And anyway, we offer wine or grape juice around from our *Kiddish* cup to any who join us for *Shabbat*, and this does not feel strange to us.

Just after a lengthy intermission, all of the lights went low in the stadium, to signal that the band was returning. Many thousands lit their lighters to create a rather pretty sight of candle-glow spread throughout the arena. Everyone knew his/her cue, what to do, when to do it. A *Havdalah*-like ritual.

The guy behind us asked Dan and his friend if he could

borrow one of their ticket stubs to get his girlfriend in. My instinct was to caution Dan not to give his ticket away, as we needed them each time we re-entered the seating area from the concession area. I felt suspicious and afraid that he wouldn't get the ticket back. I thought of the ritual chairperson of our synagogue and our yearly discussion of and rejection of requiring High Holiday tickets! I felt very old and foolish, when Dan's friend gave his stub away, the guy brought his girlfriend in, gave the ticket back, and offered Dan's friend a few bucks for a souvenir. Of course, Dan's friend turned the money down, as this would have ruined the spirit of his having given. I used to understand about this stuff, and used to participate in it, but I had forgotten for the moment, that inclusion into the community was what this was about. Everyone who wanted to should be able to partake in this experience.

While there was so much that was familiar, I was estranged from this community. I saw danger lurking everywhere; I wondered if the huge chocolate chip cookie we had bought in the parking lot had been made with "something" in it. I looked at the long brown tunnel that we would have to cross with 35,000 others, at the end of the concert and thought about crowd crushes. I remembered reading about 7 people getting killed at a concert. I witnessed the free and easy access to drugs and the allure and seeming normalcy of their use. Although I was never in the center of this culture, I had been near the center for a while. There was a time when I would have felt at home in this group. I wondered when I had become more at home with "*ha pores sukkat shalom*" than with "peace, man." When did it happen that thoughts of *Torah* ritual come spontaneously to mind while at a rock concert?

Our exit through the tunnel that night was easy--we left early and missed the crowd. Nothing bad happened; the experience was benign, interesting, and a look at a community with many of the same elements as our own synagogue one. I even asked Michael if he thought that these were future Reconstructionists. (He answered: "future Republicans!"--always the cynic).

I was naive enough not to have expected such an alien experience. I guess I exited that world without even realizing I had done so, just in time for my children to enter it. I wonder what influence our family and our synagogue, the prototypes of community for my children, will have on their creations of and participation in their own new communities. It is somewhat reassuring to remember that after all, what will be rejected by my children will be the very thing they will reestablish, on their own terms...that after all, we all yearn for the same things from one another.

Appeared in the *Shaliyah*, Spring, 1995

Editorial for *Shaliyah*

For those of you who heard Michael Lindner speak on the second day of *Rosh Hashanah*, these musings here might be considered a kind of Chapter Two on his journey as a Jew.

As I am typing this newsletter it makes me smile to know that downstairs in the basement and outside in the yard, Michael is fashioning two tablets that look like those Moses carried down from Sinai. With a great deal of love and care, he is bullnosing two pieces of oak, and joining them with a Star of David "butterfly" connection. He occasionally calls me down to ask my aesthetic opinion about the shape of the tablets, the grain of the wood, the fit of the butterfly stars. One need not believe in God to feel that he is engaged in Godly work right now.

It is not just that doing craftsman type things is a creative act, and therefore is imitative of "the" creation; Michael has a mission that today has to do with *Hiddur Mitzvah*. Last August neither of us knew what those words meant. Now, his first day out of bed from a severe cold, he is laboring to create something beautiful to commemorate a *mitzvah* having to do with *Torah*, that he doesn't even believe in. While he always has loved creating things (furniture, hope chests, decks, stained glass, brief cases out of leather, belts, chair seats, macrame) the creation of things Jewish might not always have seemed worth the effort or the time. Within the past week he has spent whole days with his tongue sticking slightly out from between pursed lips as he concentrates over stained glass *mezzuzahs* and oak tables of the covenant.

These efforts are not the contradictions they seem. Michael has always been zealous in his thirst to learn and know, though things Jewish have for a long time been behind a wall whose address was something like "hypocrisy" or "rigidity" but not "knowledge." Dr. Eric Ray, a master scribe who visited the synagogue and spoke to a small group of very fortunate 7th graders and their families on April 17th easily spoke through those chinks in Michael's Judaic armor. Dr. Ray is a man who loves God and his life and life's work radiate that love. This is a man who thinks about the meaning of life and who he is. There was a time that his strict ritual observance would have diluted Michael's respect for his far-reaching knowledge and learnedness. Instead, Michael has written down every explanation of every process that comprises writing a *Torah* so that the whole congregation can share what we had the privilege of sharing, and he is making an oak replica of the laws on which to display the implements that are used to write a *Torah*.

It is not just Dr. Ray who inspired this activity, because those *mezzuzahs* were made with the *Bar/Bat Mitzvah* class a week before Dr. Ray's visit, and Michael made 4 *tzedakah* boxes months before. As I began writing this, I thought it was going to be a "tribute" to Michael, whose Jewish artistic endeavors warm me, though somehow do not surprise me. But I think really this is a tribute to all of you--our community. It is in the context of our community and for our community that my husband downstairs is engaged in preserving for all of us a piece of our tradition. One need not believe in God to engage in Godly work. Belonging to our community is sufficient.

Appeared in the *Shaliyah*

Religion and Our Family ~ June 1, 1996, read by Dan at Joanna's *Bat Mitzvah* service

There is an ongoing debate in our home--or rather, usually, in our car. This debate surfaces on *Rosh Hashanah* and *Yom Kippur,* and on those infrequent occasions when my parents have been called upon to read and interpret *Torah*. The debate goes something like this:

My father will assert, in terms stronger than he is usually prepared to back up, that religion is pathology, that it is the "opiate of the masses," that it is the conceit of small minds and that it is meant to appeal to small minds. Or maybe he would say that it is meant to keep men's minds small, and therefore in control. He would say that it is needed only because people are barely civilized without it. If he had it at his fingertips, he might quote Schopenhauer, that "religion is the masterpiece of the art of animal training, for it trains people as to how they should think." He would cite history and argue that belief in God allows for passivity, complacency, or worse, persecution in the name of God. He would quote such quotable quotes as "more people have been murdered in the name of religion than saved in it." He would talk about the repetition and laboriousness of the text as substantiation that people don't listen, don't think, or they need to hear something dozens of times before a kernel of it seeps in. It is clear to my father most of the time, that religion is an expression of the worst of mankind. Somewhere, his "famous" '*schmuck*' theory would come in: "everyone's a *schmuck*."

However, the irony, I'm sure, escapes none of us, that my father has passionately devoted his life to helping people feel deeply, live honestly, create dignity and integrity in their lives, and be able to find, give, and receive love. But you know my father, and you are all much more polite than my father is, in not pointing out to him, every opportunity that you have, how hopelessly and adorably inconsistent he is, and how, like his father, he really has a deep, and yes, religious, belief in the highest capacities of people. But we'll just keep that our little secret.

My mother, if she could, would quote Hume that "religion arose...from a concern with regard to the events of life." She would say that religion expresses our highest potential, and that the idea of god (not God, mind you), urges us toward ethical and decent behavior. She would assert that religion is an idea that springs from humanity's capacity to think about itself in relation to the world. She would talk about humanity's unique and amazing ability to create myth and legend as a way of crystallizing our experience into symbolic expression; she would continue, as if she were invited to join Moyers and Campbell, that the mythologies of religion are like poetry--metaphorical and imagistic, pitching us beyond the world of words into "what can be known, but not told." At some point she would concur with my father that religion and mythology are often reduced to theology, that what is symbolic and ritualisitc is meant to remain fluid and lyrical, but often becomes ossified and rigid, that most people become concrete about religion, and think that the myth is something to be accepted rather than understood, that many people use religion as a weapon rather than a beacon. But, she would say, that is not a statement about religion; that is about some people. Oops! She would have backed herself right into the 'schmuck' theory... but only for a moment. It is clear to my mother that there is in humanity something noble and glorious, that religion encourages us to be not barely human, but exquisitely human.

And my sister and I? We used to tell them to stop arguing. It would seem to us that my father must be right, after all, about religion, if, over a set of ideas, my parents could be sitting there arguing. But then they would laugh at us and say that they loved these discussions, that this was wonderful and they were enjoying themselves. Maybe my mother was right--maybe religion appealed to the best in people.

Nowadays we still tell them to stop arguing, but mostly because we want to get back to listening to some good music on the radio. We recently found out that one of the first discussions my parents ever had when they met at the ages that my sister and I are now, was about God. It's hard to believe they are still talking about the same old stuff!

What **is** true is that my mother almost always wins these debates. I suppose we wouldn't be standing here today if my dad won. My sister and I used to wonder--did that mean one point for religion or one point for mom? Now we understand better how to keep score. Mom and dad seem forever to be tied. We win.

Observing the Ritual Elimination of *Chametz*: a Revaluation

Recently, I have been re-examining my thoughts about the elimination of *chametz* for Passover. For most of my life, *chametz* remained exactly where it was, and we just ate more *matzah*

during *Pesach*. Then when my kids were small, we removed the cookies and crackers from their shelf, wiped down the shelf well, even used the little feather, but merely relocated the *chametz* for the week. We haven't even done that in a long time. But I am thinking of actually discarding "most" of my un-used *chametz* when *Pesach* rolls around this year. Has being president of the congregation brought "religion" into my life, you ask? Not exactly. It happened like this.

One day this mild winter, Joanna wanted to bake a cake. Having providentially prepared for any apocalyptic event I had several boxes of cake mix in the cupboard. When she opened one, there were tiny worm-like critters in the mix. This has happened to us more than once (one time even in a box--a new box--of *matzah* meal). Now it's true, I do not look at expiration dates very often (and even if I did, I might feel bad to throw away an unopened, perfectly good-seeming box of cake mix). I guess there haven't been quite as many of those hurricane-snow-can't-get-to-the-store-for-a-month-days as I had been prepared for.

I don't know if this next thing happens to you or not, but do you ever get small winged, moth-like things flying around your kitchen? I have come to think that they are the cousins of those worm-like things (maybe even the "developmentally advanced" incarnations of those critters). When they begin to swarm, I look around to see what has "gone bad" in the cupboard. Usually, I find an unopened bag of whole wheat, sesame seed, health-food-store pretzels, or a package of flatbreads, again unopened. You see, Michael, who has not eaten a carbohydrate in 2 years (well, if you don't count the Dunkin' Donut(sss) on vacation, or...) still has sugar plums and pretzels dancing in his head. When he goes shopping, he usually comes home with oodles of boxes and bags of snack foods that **he** can't eat, but that he thinks **we** would like. It makes him feel so good to do this for us, and especially because all of these boxes and bags have the word HEALTHY on them. Understand, these are things that he wouldn't really enjoy even if he were eating carbs, but he likes to think that we are the kind of people who could really sink our teeth into these "no-fat, no salt" snacks. So my cupboard is full of such snacks that he just had to get for us, even though none of us eats these. And me, I don't throw these away immediately...I feel compelled to keep them until the bags begin to undulate with those little wormy things, or until my kitchen looks like a new-age plague of swarming, teeny moths has descended.

Not to blame all of this on Michael's *mishagoss*, I must confess that there are also boxes of certain cereals that I purchased, oh, around 1986 or so when Dan decided he loved Frosted Mini-Wheats. I wouldn't want you to think my child is indulged in his every whim or anything, but I did go out and buy "multiple" boxes of these things, to have on hand, for my then 6-year old. Now, there are a few that have never been opened, so I figure, they must still be fresh, right? Such a shame just to throw them away. Maybe when he's 18 he will like them again? Maybe a friend of his or Joanna's will sleep over and say, "Do you have any Frosted Mini-Wheats? I LOVE them!"

In my continuing journey toward self-actualization, I have come to realize that I don't even want to **see** what's in **those** boxes, and that I would be doing no favor to starving children anywhere to continue to keep them around, even **if** my grandchildren one day might like Frosted Mini-Wheats!

I think the redactors of *Torah* probably, at some time in their travels, opened up a big ceramic jug when spring came and were not happy about what had been hatching in there all winter. Maybe they just picked out those "extras" and kept quiet to their kids (the thought **did** cross my mind, knowing that Joanna was **really** in the mood for cake...but I just couldn't). Maybe those jugs looked really disgusting and they just knew that they should chuck its contents, clean out the jug, and start all over next harvest with some fresh stuff.

So, with this new understanding this year, I will be observing the tradition of discarding *chametz*. Those of you who have ever had cake at my house might decide that we'll meet at the Landmark Diner from now on. Those of you who might get assigned to my house for future Progressive Dinners might call up the dinner-planners, and ask, discretely, to be reassigned, no offense. But you should feel assured, that all the carbs in my house, after April 10th this year will be fresh!

Happy *Pesach* (do I dare sign my name?)

Appeared in the *Shaliyah*

Afikomen

Seated at the piano
I rummage through books,
long neglected,
of old favorites.
From between the pages of Chopin's nocturnes
slips a satin-wrapped piece of *matzah*.
I do not know from which year this *matzah* hails:
which year it was that children grown or grown-ups
lost the penchant for the search;
which *seder* it was that we completed incomplete,
this broken half left,
like a lost, forgotten tribe,
unransomed,
as we left the table with chocolate in our mouths
instead of the taste of this one particular *matzah*.
Stale as it is,
I cannot throw it away
before placing a small corner of it
on my tongue
and letting it
slowly dissolve.

(December 1, 2006)

Published in *Jewish Currents*, March-April, 2008, p. 10

תשליך

The Reconstructionist Synagogue of The North Shore

TASHLICH
5758 – 1997

Tashlich, a relative newcomer in our catalogue of traditions (appearing first around the fourteenth century), is a somewhat controversial practice because of the concreteness of our act during *Tashlich*.

The Rabbis understood that emptying our pockets or aprons of symbolic sins should not be a substitute for doing the real work of changing ourselves, and they feared that many would feel "done" with their sins after performing this act. The pocket-emptying action that we perform during *Tashlich* is a little too close to transferring our sins onto a scapegoat (or a scape-stream) and feeling cleansed in the process.

So, why do we continue to meet for *Tashlich*? Perhaps because it is good to be outdoors together, in between two long days of being seated indoors. Perhaps, also, it is because we affirm, together, that change does not happen as a solitary activity. How, after all does one transform oneself, and why, especially, does one do this, if not to bring this changed self to the world of fellow beings, and experience this change in the context of the world? As our acknowledgment of our need to look into ourselves and confront our shortcomings is done communally, so is our symbolic act of casting aside that which we wish were not part of ourselves. In meeting together, we affirm that really, it is only in relationship and in repairing relationships that transformation is meaningful.

Although the word *Tashlich* means to "cast out," the place in which we do this act seems to be at least as important as the act, itself, of casting away that which we wish were no longer part of ourselves.

Different groups of Jews do this casting out differently--not all do it by emptying their pockets. Some send little boats down a stream. But water--that is the universal place where Jews meet to perform *Tashlich*. Traditionally, water has been understood to be cleansing. Liturgically, we are to "cast our sins into the bottom of the sea," according to a passage from Micah. Perhaps we can understand water also as a perfect symbol of transformation. A stream is always new--accepting from its source new and fresh input; allowing what was, to exit--letting in the new, ridding itself of the old, while nearly always retaining its shape and path, though even these, too, may be changed.

So perhaps we gather by the stream as a way of saying that we wish to be like this river: purity and cleansing may not be the goal, really, but transformation and a sincere interest in renewal and openness may be. In emptying our pockets, let us not imagine that our sins have magically disappeared into the bottom of this stream, but rather that we pledge not to keep ourselves hidden from ourselves, not to tuck away or sequester parts of ourselves from this transformation process, to turn ourselves inside out so that next year we will not empty the same pockets of the same debris. Next year the stream that we stand before will surely be different; may it be so for us, as well.

בָּרוּךְ הַמָּקוֹר מִנַּיִן אָנוּ שׁוֹאֲבִים כֹּחַ וְאֹמֶץ לֵב לְשַׁנּוֹת

Blessed is the source, from where we draw strength and courage to change

בְּרוּכוֹת הַתְחָלוֹת וּבְרוּכוֹת הַמְשָׁכוֹת

Blessed are beginnings, and blessed are continuings.

לְשָׁנָה טוֹבָה

Used by the Reconstructionist Synagogue of the North Shore for *Tashlich* observance from 1997-2008.

Introduction to Loree's Thoughts on Passover
April, 1999

I am submitting this piece on my niece's behalf. The child of a Jewish father and Christian mother, Loree was raised observing several Christian holidays a year, Christmas and Easter, and one major Jewish holiday a year: Passover. This year, it looked as though our family would not convene for Passover. My father's brother had just been moved to a nursing home for his degenerative condition of Progressive Supranuclear Palsy; Loree's mother had just had major breast cancer surgery on the first night of Passover and would still be in the hospital; and my other brother's children, who attend a Quaker school, were not off from school on Wednesday, Thursday, or Friday. Given the fact that we usually travel to Delaware--from New York, Washington, and Pennsylvania, it looked undo-able this year.

And then Loree began e-mailing us all. She really wanted to have the seder, and she wanted to host it. She was aware that this might be the last time the 25 of us who live in the NY-DC corridor would be together for some time, as the first 4 children of her generation (herself, among these 4), will leave for college in the fall, and as Uncle Lenny's health was so fragile. She wanted us all to be together for this seder. And she wanted to learn how to make a seder. So, while she delegated out many dishes to be brought, she asked some of us to come early enough to teach her how to make the traditional ones. And she wanted to uphold Aunt Nan's tradition of having the head table continue to be all male. Even as the one who brought us together, made bowls of fruit salad and flan, mixed fresh horseradish root into horseradish sauce, she did not need to have more of a voice, not even as a first-born (which our aunt, once, made concession for at the head table). Being together and sitting at the "kids' table" was more than sufficient expression and fulfillment for her. She did all of this at the age of 17, while her mother was one day post-op, and in spite of the fact that she was not raised Jewish.

There are studies that link Jewish continuity to three experiences: Passover seders, Jewish summer camps, and trips to Israel. Loree did go to Jewish summer camp with several cousins, all of whom are also the children of one Jewish and one Christian parent. But this piece, written by Loree several months before this Passover, attests to the power of a Passover seder in the formulation of Jewish identity. And beyond a Jewish identity, it attests to the power of religious ritual...religious ritual that links us to the rich landscape of larger time, in deepening and expanding a sense of oneself. Our family had gone on a cruise to celebrate my parents' 50 wedding anniversary several years ago. While this was a great deal of fun, and the cousins were all together, this experience was not what Loree remembers as pivotal when she thinks of who she is. She revealed herself to us this year as a woman of valor, a person who helped us grownups remember that even if we all travel different, busy paths in our lives, it is important for us to come together. She revealed herself as a person of substance, whose depths have been forged by the intangible thing that happens in ritual time, once a year, like steam rising off of a bowl of matzah ball soup.

Reflections on the Children on *Shabbat*

They are coloring, or painting, or dressing Barbie dolls, or clicking away at hand-held Nintendo games. They come in and out of the sanctuary. They look as if they are not paying attention. But do not be fooled.

The *Shabbat* service that is taking place around them is not merely background noise that they are filtering out. It is, rather, background in the way that air is background. And they absorb its sounds, its rhythms, its pacing, its movement in a way similar to breathing. They take it in without thought, without consciousness, but with all of its life-giving or life-affirming or life-enhancing qualities, just like air.

And though they have not been paying attention, have not appeared to listen, have been absorbed in their play things or in each other, they are, in a flash of a moment, on the *bima*, ready to open the ark. No one told them it was time; no one called them up. They were, though, propelled by an inner call, an inner ear that brought them, at just the right moment, into consciousness, that it was time to open the ark. And they are there, ready. They have run to the ark as if they own the thing. It **is** theirs. They have raced forward in betighted or bestockinged, or bare feet. They are so comfortable with this awesome and honorable job. They wiggle their hips or twist their bodies back and forth; they hug each other or hold hands; they whisper in one another's ear. They are engaged in the irreverent lusciousness of childhood—an irreverence and a lusciousness that are transformed, as they stand before the ark, into a moment so replete with holiness that we, who watch them, overflow with the presence of God.

And while they wiggle or whisper they know just when that ark must be opened. They do not need to **listen**, really; they **hear** with finely tuned ears and finely tuned souls the rhythm of the prayers and melodies, and they just know—better than many of us who sit decorously in the congregation—just what moment it is when they need to open the ark. And they do it, just right.

They parade around the room behind the *Torah*, and the symbolism overpowers us. Without them, behind the *Torah*, the *Torah* would cease to be. They are the very soul of the *Torah*—which is why we are compelled to reach out and touch them as we affirm our ownership of the *Torah*. In a way, it is really more natural for us to touch them, pat their heads, give a hug. We know this more instinctively than we know how to touch *Torah*. But really, in the end, they are the same.

They raise their high child voices so loudly in song, that we hear "*Etz Hayim*" come from those four voices more than from the 10 or 20 of us adults in the congregation. And again, it feels perfect that it should be that way, for they are our Tree of Life, and the green, young, strong branches that will take over the embrace of whatever is essential about *Torah*. And then, they recite "*Bo-rey, p'ri ha-a-gofen*" one sneaking the teensiest sip from the *kiddish* cup, and together they sing the "*Ha-motzei*," wiggling all the while.

There are many reasons to come to *Shabbat* morning services at the Reconstructionist Synagogue of the North Shore. But I, for one, felt restored, renewed, sweetened, and uplifted by the presence of our regular *Shabbat* attendees: Rebecca, Shoshana, Sari, and Aaron. Our future feels secure, and our present full of joy.

(January 29, 2000)
Shabbat Yitro

Appeared in the *Shaliyah*

Published in *Matzoh Ball Soup*, Spring, 2002 pp 76-77

Sukkah Thieves

Gourds and flaming Indian corn swinging from tenuous
beams
autumn vines woven to lintels
quilted cloth vegetables strung from corner to corner
new year's cards girdling this temporary home
like a ribbon enfolding a gift
and I, a chieftain,
surveying my harvest home one last time
before the tribal gathering.

My eye catches the ruin—
our *sukkah* has been vandalized!

I can see just how it was:
the Saturday night news traveling with the speed of impulses
across arboreal synapses from branch end to branch end:
Party: 2 A.M., the Sukkah!

Like restless teens they must have come
daring each other to perch in precarious balance
as they nibbled the swinging corn cobs
gnawed through tough orange pumpkin skins
gorging themselves
becoming drunk on multi-colored Indian kernels
that must have been harvest liqueur
after their usual fare of acorn maple hickory
and then one petty vandal coming to his senses
seeing the cobs shorn of their copper and golden nuggets
exclaiming in horror:
Oh my god, guys, look what we've done!
the pack leaving in a guilty rush.

I imagine just how much fun that frenzied fete must have
been
and how much better it is for cobs to stand empty

and predators full
than the other way around
those bitten pumpkins and perfect
denuded corn cobs
testament to our shared pleasure in nature's bounty
the squirrels and I.

I will not press charges.

(December, 2007)

Lessons Learned from Ten Women
Aged 29-88
Who Share Themselves Monthly
in Celebration of a Moon That Was Not Lost After All

After the blood
And the milk
What then?

For forty years
(A biblical duration)
Our bodies poured forth
The fluids and substance of life.
And after the forty years
It stops.

What is left?

Are we diminished by the loss of what was given to us when
we were twelve,
When we were ill-equipped to know the enormity of the gift?
The loss of the biology that had come to define us:
The wombs and breasts that filled and emptied
Over and over
In yearly, or monthly, or hourly cycles,
Engorging to contain and nourish creation, itself,
Contracting again to cradle only itself?
Do we lose our sacred connection
To these bodies that ebbed and flowed
With the godly awesomeness of possibility?

Or are we strengthened for having come to know the
Monthly waxing and waning of the spaces within us
As the tidal power
That allowed our bodies to be as the seas
From which all creation would spring?
And, are we, now, like dendrites primed for reuptake

Ready to reabsorb,
Into ourselves
And be affirmed
By all
That once we gave away?

We Are Very Much Alive

I haven't been to services in awhile. But last night, we did the "synagogue thing," ushering in *Shabbat* with a catered meal and Eric's study group, and staying on for services. When I've been away for awhile, I often forget what being present is like. Here is a collage of my experience this past Friday night:

Eric's study group is a blend of people who have young elementary school aged children, and those who might have young adult grandchildren. There are 3-year members and 33-year members. This group, last year, was attended by 6 people on an average *Shabbat*. Last evening there were 22 of us. Eric knows all of our names, and each of us extends the reach of whom we know, and, of course, what we know.

I don't imagine that our service is like any other synagogue's. It is an hour and a quarter before we get to the *Borechu*. We have begun with a discussion of how the Hebrew people in Egypt could "know" God. Rabbi Lee responds to one comment with: "I really like that thought...I don't love it, but I like it a lot." There is openness and acceptance here, but there is also a challenge to clarify our thinking. We have, after all, just been taught about the power and importance of words in the act of creation, and so we are nudged along by Lee, who urges us to create with our words a thought we may never have had before. What is also remarkable about this discussion is that Sam Blumenthal responds to Daniel Altschuler,* and Dan Fink is responding to Harriet Feiner. I try to imagine where else such a discussion could occur. *L'dor v'dor* unfolds before our eyes.

I have come into the sanctuary late and am sitting in the back row. Michael is falling asleep next to me. I encourage him to go take a nap. He leaves the sanctuary and falls asleep, curled up into half his size on the small bench outside of the office. When I check on him I wish I had a camera. Far from being a "no-no," it feels so right that our synagogue can simultaneously spark a spirited discussion about the nature of God, and cradle an exhausted, slumbering ex-president at the end of a long work-week.

Next to me now, is Mickey Warshawski.** He leans over and whispers a comment to me every minute or so. This could be annoying, while I am trying to hear un-microphoned comments made at the front of the room. But, it just isn't. As Lee keeps trying to focus the discussion: "So, how did the Israelites know God?" there are root systems sending their runners all over the room. What Mickey is doing is happening with dozens of congregants seated next to each other all over the sanctuary. We are all, simultaneously listening to one speaker offer an answer, while at the same time leaning to our neighbor, excitedly thinking out loud. And then, Mickey leans over and says something like, "We are having the same discussion 3300 years later that the Israelites were having." He almost has tears in his eyes. I respond, "Yes, this is how we know God; we are talking about how our people have known God." As far as we two are concerned, we have stumbled upon the culmination of the discussion. We both understand that God is in that moment, at 9:10 PM on January 11th, 2002, right there in our discussion, as we continue to define our relationship with God. Holiness is found in this moment. Harriet Feiner clarifies that this holy moment is doubly validated, as it immediately passes into history, becoming the most recent link in the continuum of our people.

The service, itself, is brief. It is hardly needed after our discussion. We have already traversed the terrain of creation, revelation, redemption, the stepping stones of our service as Eric has taught us. We have talked about God and we have talked with one another. The threads of history and the possibilities of future are palpable in this community.

But, there is more. Sam has written new music for the *V'shamru*. It is being debutted this evening, with Sharon*** singing it. Sam introduces it for us, sharing that his grandfather lived for *Shabbat*. He alerts us to listen for a repetition of the words "*et ha-Shabbat.*" Mickey clenches his hands, and holds his breath, knowing when the high notes are coming, silently cheering Sharon. The music feels like a love-song. *Shabbat* is caressed. There is passion in a moment, but mostly there is exquisite tenderness. Sharon's voice encircles the words, embraces *Shabbat*. There is something liquid—and luscious—, and we feel, with Sam's grandfather, that truly, nothing can compare with *Shabbat*. Sam is proud. We are radiant with him. What a gift we are given.

We eat cake and drink coffee together.

In the quietness of a *Shabbat* evening, we are so very much alive.

*Sam, in his 80s, a founder and patriarch of the congregation; Dan, a young teenager in the congregation;
**Mickey, a survivor of *Auschwitz;*
***Sharon, Mickey's wife.

Appeared in the *Shaliyah*

The Shofar Blower*

Illuminated
iconographic
he stands,
the light upon his dewy face
coming from an unseen source.
Left arm outstretched to its farthest reaches
right arm bent,
his body a sailboat keeling to catch the best wind,
lists toward port.
Eyes closed
lips pursed
he forces a huge amount of breath through
the narrow place.
The wail:
an exhalation of pure defiance
an affirmation like a baby's first cry.
No one's attention drifts at this moment.
In the midst of these Days of Awe
there is much that is ordinary,
but this is not;
for once there were those
who would have stolen away this breath
this breath inside this man
this man who is us.

Rapt,
we listen
we bear witness
to this one who holds the ram's horn
this latter-day Isaac who was not sacrificed
as he breathes forth
the soul of his people.

(December, 2007)
Used for several years on the website of the
Recontructionist Synagogue of the North Shore

* for Mickey Warshawski

The People of the Hands

The People of The Book? Perhaps. But I think we should be called The People of the Hands. Nearly everything really important about us has occurred through hands.

Take, for instance, Abraham. He was the first one of us. But in order to have become the first one of us, the story goes, he had, first, to take up, in his hands, his father's statues, and with his hands throw them down. Perhaps, in order to become the first one of us, he had to destroy all that was from before. That is often the way it goes with fathers and sons. And later, as he knelt upon the mountain with his own son, Isaac, his knife-wielding hand raised above his son, perhaps he was still thinking that he had to destroy, in order to be the first one of us. But, (thank God), he figured out in time what his hands needed to throw away, and what they needed to hold onto. I think it was in that moment, in the frozen arm above the son, in the confused moment that resolved itself into clarity, that Abraham became the first one of us—not in the statue-smashing moment. The smashing was important; but the figuring out what to hold onto was more important. That is what made him worthy of being the first one of us, our father.

Then there was Jacob, who reached forth his hands toward his father's unseeing eyes. Did he become the third of our famous ancestral triumvirate because he used his hands to deceive? No *midrash* around has yet made this make sense. Maybe we invoke the pretender with the hairy hands because he is a graphic reminder to us of our capacity to go backwards, away from our own domestication toward our more primitive, less civilized selves. Maybe the birthright is given because Jacob knows well this capacity for primitivity and the need to keep it tamed. Perhaps, too, he is honored as one of our firsts, because those hands, covered by the hair of animal skins, acknowledging our primal selves, are the same hands that wrestle with angels. Not as the great deceiver, but as the one who, in his own hands, takes us from the dirt of the earth to the canopy of the heaven—for this he is worthy to be called ancestor.

And Moses. Not among the first of us, but the one who made us an "us." Even Moses had hands that could both raise a rod and strike a rock, or raise a rod and split a sea—hands that could get what they wanted by force, and hands that could effect a miracle.

Yes, we are definitely People of the Hands. And if we close our eyes when we invoke our ancestors, we know with primordial familiarity what it feels like to use our hands to smash, deceive, enact primal urges, strike. But if we have paid attention, we might know also, as did Abraham, how to stay our hands; we might, like Jacob, have the courage to wrestle with heavens' possibilities; or like Moses, to use our hands to change the very shape of our earth, to reverse the direction of forces that appear impossible. Do we, the People of The Book, The People of the Hands, yet know what to let go of, and what to hold tight to?

(October 16, 2002
October 10, 2006)

An *Amidah* Moment

The *Amidah*, so I've been taught, is that time in the prayer service when we move from public to private prayer, when we pray from a place within, in silence. We begin this prayer by remembering our ancestors, in an effort to send our root-runners deeply into the rich loam of our past, to weave these newest of shoots into the ageless, clustered, rope-braids that hold us so firmly upright, in anticipation of opening ourselves to the wonder and awe of all that lies before us and to the possibility of all that lies within us.

But as I stood for the *Amidah* this *Rosh Hashanah*, I did not meditate upon the words contained on the 20 or so pages that comprise this core prayer in our service. For standing in the row in front of me, *kippah* askew so that it nearly covered his eyes, stood a young boy of barely 9 years old. I watched as he took within his hands great bunches of the multitudinous, slippery *tzitziot* of his father's *tallit* and ran them through his fingers over and over again. And then, in a way that was almost too intimate for public display, he raised a handful of these *tzitziot* to his face, and brushed them slowly, softly, sensuously across his cheek again and again. He did this for the many minutes' duration of the *Amidah*.

I did not turn my *siddur's* pages. I did not need to. I stood, witness to a living *Amidah*, as I watched this young pray-er be simultaneously transported beyond himself and perfectly present in the rapture of this moment. His silent, wordless, enactment could not have come any closer to the liturgist's intention.

I do not imagine, 30 years from now, that this boy will remember this *Rosh Hashanah* moment, when the *Amidah* was alive within the webs and tips of his small fingers, this moment when he planted his child-seed-pod self in the soil of his father's land. But it will not matter. For the memory of this moment will have been transformed into something else. I think, however, that there will be evidence that this moment existed. I imagine, 30 years from now, that this moment will be present, as a young one, standing at this one's side, reaches, almost unconsciously, as the gentle brush of fringes grazes his hands, and this new one, I imagine, will take up those *tzitziot*, those ancient signature-seals, and raise them to his cheek, and know the soft kiss of a thousand thousand fathers and mothers.

(September 27, 2003)
1 *Tishrei*, 5764

Appeared in the Reconstructionist Synagogue of the North Shore *Rosh Hashanah* supplement of readings 5765/2004, Reading 7

Published in *Kerem: Creative Explorations in Judaism*, No. 9. 5764/2004, pp. 1-2

Published in *Poetica: Reflections of Jewish Thought*, March, 2009, p. 22

Solomon, The Wise

(I Kings, Chapter 2)

He did not see,
But we saw
The unravelling
That comes
When sons follow paths
Set before them by others.

And so he did as he was told,
He spoke the words
That sent Benaiah
To strike Adonijah down
And to strike Joab down
And to strike Shimei down.
He did these things.

No, he did not know
What sequent line would
Issue from the loins of his words.

He did not see,
But we saw
The heaps of hollow skulls
And charred, gray bones
Twisted together
Like so many rotting sticks
Amassed carelessly for
The pyre
That would be the torch light
Forever
Of human history.

He did not see all this
That we have seen.

How could he have known?

Because he was Solomon
And he should have known.

(December 8, 14, 2003
Midrash Workshop with Alicia Ostriker)

The Unseen Son

A father's glazed unseeing eyes
Blinded by the knife edge glare
Or perhaps no sun is there
And blindness comes from fog of faith.

Blinded by the knife edge glare
Held poised above the young son's head
Himself webbed in the fog of faith
Trusting his father to light the way.

Held poised above the young son's head
The paralyzed hand that can not act
A freeze-frame light to find the way
The choice between stark faith and life.

The paralyzed hand that can not act
Resolves to clear, unclouded eyes
That see the choice, so clear, of life,
The ram that was there all along.

The clear, unclouded, seeing eyes
Now work with aged but nimble fingers
That grab the ram ensnared in brush
Then loose the binds that hold the child.

The aged, gnarled, but nimble fingers
No longer stopped by indecision
Loose the child from the altar
Of his father's dreams for him.

No longer stopped by indecision
This son, a father now himself
Dreams of blessing his first born
But the younger comes instead.

This son, a father now himself
His hands upon the son that's there
Blesses the hairy one who kneels
Before his father's glazed, unseeing eyes.

(April 1, 2004)
Published in *Jewish Currents*, September-October, 2005, p. 48

Acrostic

Alone, Abraham asks:
"...but....but..."
Can't comprehend careless
dreams, damning death demands,
enslaving edicts, enunciating
fettered faith. Father's faith-filled faggots
grace-given. Ghastly God.
Heart-hacked, he holds
Isaac
jeopardized. Jackass jostles,
kicks knowingly,
lumbers, loaded,
mountain-meanders
nearing nexus.
Offspring,
progeny pensive,
quiet, quivering.
Renegade ram revealed. Released
son
tethered, tied
untied.
Vacuous vows.
Weary, world-wounded, winnowed,
xenogenic.
Yahweh yields.
Zachar. Zeal
ablated. Aching, alone, Abraham asks: "...

(March 9, 2005)

A Mixing of Metaphors:
Haiku* for *Rosh Hashanah

Knife blade hanging high
Boy's face twisted in terror—
What a dreadful God!

Blind, beclouded eyes
See the nothingness of faith—
Ah! There's a ram there.

Bewildered and stooped
He stumbles down the mountain—
Best leave the boy there.

We hear it again
This ghastly, shameful story—
Can't we be done with't?

We'll read it each year
To know how easy it is
To kill in God's name.

(September 10, 2005)

Abraham:

this man of faith
who seduces his son
as he walks him to the mountain's top
and lays him across the altar
of his father's delusions,
the blade of faith held close against his neck,

our patriarch,
our paragon.

We were always meant to keep our eye on Abraham.

It is easy enough to do;
he walks among us, undisguised,
in the garb of God men all over earth:
head wrapped in layers of cloth
or a black streimel
or a dusty cowboy hat,
neck stiffened by the starched certainty
of a pure white collar.

Beware Abraham
who brandishes God's Truth
and in whose presence
our sons are not safe.

(September 21, 2005)

What I Do During *Rosh Hashanah*

From the front of the sanctuary, the choir place, I spend a lot of the service looking at you. And, because of this, my eyes sometimes land in your most private moments. I want to apologize, that I have seen what you would not have had me see: the furtive wipe of tears as they spill the levees you hoped would hold them. As **you** dab the corners of your eyes with a finger tip; **you**, with a tissue; **you**, with the back of your hand, I know you do not wish to be seen in this moment. I know I should look away.

But when I see your jaw begin to tighten and your eyes swell like lakes, there is something unseen that draws me to you, and I choke on emotion that began as yours, but somehow becomes mine. I imagine that your tears come as awareness washes over you of the grace in your life in loving the person next to you, or those who have settled far away; or that a yawning ache opens within you as you know in this moment all that you could lose, or all that you have lost. Your tears flow, unbidden, like the weeping rock beneath the Temple Mount, the rock that is said to be the center of the world.

They come with *Avinu Malkeinu* or with *B'rosh Hashanah y'ka tei vun*. The ancient melody haunts as it penetrates and possesses, and we stand in *shul*, strangely strengthened even as we are saddened, knowing both the full measure and the fragility that is our lives.

I know you are glad to be looking at someone's back, hoping that your eyes will dry before you are noticed. But what I want to tell you is this: you are having the only experience worth coming to synagogue for. As a spectral angel, the *Rosh Hashanah* moment has entered your soul and escorted you into the Holy of Holies. And there, **you** stand in your aloneness, sending memory out to the edges of eternity, where, for the intake of a breath's time, you have again what you have lost; **you** reach beside you, lacing your fingers into those of the person who always stands beside you; **you** brush the smooth, young face of your grandson, unable to let go his cheek for the whole of the *Amidah*, until you can wrap him in the prayerful protection of your *tallit*. And I, I watch you touch God.

(October, 2005)

Appeared in the Reconstructionist Synagogue of the North Shore *Rosh Hashanah* Supplement of Readings Day 1, 5768/2007, Reading #7

National Council of Jewish Women Writers' Conference

It was the first real snow of the year. Beautiful at 7 AM; gray-brown slush-mess by 9 AM. It was the kind of day on which we are glad not to have appointments and schedules, so that we could part the curtains, glance out the window, and make the quick, guiltless decision to go back to bed, or, at least, remain in our pajamas all day.

But on this Sunday, which held visible promise of so little, there were about 100 women, whose median age was probably 70, who did not stay in the warmth and comfort of their homes. They converged on Hebrew Union College from Pennsylvania and Rhode Island, from Massachusetts and Vancouver. They came in search of one thing: words.

While the conference that took place on December 4, 2005 at HUC, sponsored by the National Council of Jewish Women, was in celebration of Jewish women writers, the preponderance of attendees at the conference identified themselves proudly as "readers." To be sure, there were nearly two dozen writers featured at the conference (Pogrebin, Ostriker, Jaffe, Klagsbrun, Leegant, McDonough, Moore, Rapoport, Resiman, Richler, Sandor, Schwartz, 2 Wolitzers, Eidus, Felman, Fuchs, Glickfeld, Hacker, Hautzig, Horn), as well as an uncounted number of not-yet-so-well-known writers, as well as many would-be writers, but this status and these distinctions blurred, as it became clear that every participant was there because she was in love with words and the ways in which words can be sculpted by writers who become the dream merchants of our humanity.

The individual stories of many of the featured guests, were captivating: how, for instance, Esther Hautzig was exiled to Siberia from Vilna, how she was denied a teacher's license after graduating from Hunter College because her English (one of her 6 languages) was accented, how she once wrote to Adlai Stevenson upon learning of his visit to her village in Russia, sharing her remembrances, how he wrote her a personal letter back, his own perception of the place affirming hers, how he encouraged her to write a book about her experience, how she did, and became an author.

But, writers' individual stories, fascinating as they were, were not the point of this conference. The ostensible theme of the day was how being a woman and being Jewish informed or defined the work of the featured writers. The keynote speaker, Letty Cottin Pogrebin, focused her address on the process of writing, itself, targeting three "rules" of writing. The first, with apologies to Grace Paley who advised to "write what you know," was to " write what you don't know." The most interesting writing, Pogrebin proferred, comes from asking the "next question after the one you know." Her second point was that a writer must represent no one but herself, must not yield to the "yoke of any doctrine." Her third precept for writers was that the most specific is the most universal and that "sense is catalytic to memory and meaning." While she did not directly address the impact of gender, culture, and religion in her own writing, she set the stage for the featured writers to take her three precepts to focus their own discourse about the ways in which their writing has been influenced or defined by gender and culture.

Five panel discussions, each featuring four authors, were presented following Pogrebin's keynote address. Nearly a dozen "conversations with authors," each hosted by two authors, were available in the afternoon. Presentations and conversations throughout the day articulated two apparently contradictory "truths": being female and being Jewish were inescapably coded genetic and psychic imprints, whether an individual writer had begun with this conscious acknowledgment or not; and, these two facts did not mean that the literature created could be narrowly categorized as either feminist or Jewish. Nessa Rapoport, for example, spoke about her passion for "the word" as having its origin in her Jewish roots. Francine Klagsbrun, similarly, described that her passion is for "text"—not prayers or God, necessarily, but for the tradition of combing text for meaning. Her work, being informed by deep tradition and Biblical text, is not *about* being Jewish, but rather is "infused" with the Jewish influences which have become part of the definition of who she is. Marjorie Sandor credited her belonging to the Jewish people as the source of her appetite for "discovering." She described that her writing is fueled by remaining "an amateur, a neophyte—always open to the awareness of discovery."

From the panel discussions and conversations I attended, as well as the opening and closing speakers' remarks, more discussion focused on the influence of religion than the direct influence of gender. I found this particularly curious, in light of the fact that several of the writers had spent the better part of their adult lives as advocates and activists for the legal, social, and cultural reforms that would allow their daughters to consider the word "feminist" to be part of historical lexicon, as they comfortably became rabbis and physicians, lawyers and bankers. It was also impossible not to notice that here was gathered a group of women, nearly all of whom had long since left behind their monthly acquaintance with that other stream of creative potential. Though this was not addressed among this middle-aged to senior group of women, I wondered what role the experience of forty years of biologically generative potential exerted on all of our yearning for continuous creative endeavors. While the direct influence of gender was not clearly articulated, its imprint seemed to me to be inescapable.

What became clear was that the twin identity-lenses of female and Jewish allowed writers to focus their experience; rather than confinement or diminishment, their creations, thus focused, are enhanced and enlarged. By leading us carefully into a precise time and place, into an individual person's life, these authors catapult us beyond the specific, and we touch a place that is, ironically, too deep for words, as the particular becomes the signature of mystery.

Though I write this for a secular Jewish publication, I cannot avoid relating that attending this conference was something of a "religious" experience, refracted through Judaism, though extending far beyond Judaism, as well. The women who came to this conference seemed to me to be pilgrims, paying homage to creation. Pogrebin, referencing Cynthia Ozick, joked that each time one writes, she is violating the second commandmant—usurping God's role in creating a world. That appears to be the point, exactly, and in Ozick's comment there are liturgical resonances. Creation becomes manifest when words are spoken: "God said…and there was light"; "Blessed are you…by whose word the evening falls." Our words, no less than "God's," have the capacity to transport us to "depths beyond language" (Arthur Green), to silent places where potential is poised on the brink of eruption, where creation begins. In Ozick's comment, we understand that creation was not once and nevermore, but an organic, self-renewing process, the template for which can be understood in our tradition's (and, universally, in all traditions') foundational stories and mythologies. It is this template that finds its way into our psyches as an undeniable urgency in each of us, whether we are writers or not, to touch the wellspring of this creative fountain. Madeleine L'Engle expressed it thus:

> It's all been said better before. Of course.
> If I thought I had to say it better than anybody else,
> I'd never start.
> Better or worse is immaterial.
> The thing is that it has to be said—by me…
> We each have to say it…in our own way…

Good or bad, great or little:
That isn't what human creation is about.
It is that we have to try:
To put it down in pigment, or words, or musical
    notations,
Or we die.

And so these pilgrims came, hungry for the transportative and transformative experience—where letters are combined into words, and words into stories, stories that, even if saturated with female or Jewish sensibilities, are emblematic of our profoundest human story. These pilgrims whether readers or writers, are forever hungry...for the words that will open the way in. So they willfully pluck the apple and open the gate and are on their way, as they join the holy act of creation, finding the words that will loosen us from our comfortable moorings and pitch us into the place of the wordless known, a place where, for a brief time, our pulse beats in time to the music of the spheres.

(December 4, 2005)

Published in *Jewish Currents*, July-August, 2006, pp. 36-37

The Last Commandment

I am scouring the Bible for it—
the last commandment,
the 11th one.
I know it must be here
because it's the one that has guided
humanity
for its whole history,
the most popular one, really,
if popularity is defined by degree of obeisance.
The 11th commandment:
the one that says
we must kill each other in God's name.

(August 25, 2006)

Shiva

I know nothing about this man.
I should look away
but I cannot take my eyes from him.

Gathered in his daughter's house
in the brief time it takes to recite the *ma'ariv* service
here are the handful of things I come to know about him

He does not hear well
I know this by his unmodulated voice
rising like punctuation
now and again above the group

He is so old
I know this also by his voice, tremulous and coarse
accented from an old country
broken

He is just a little disoriented, I see,
as his daughter trades *siddurim* with him
giving him hers turned to the right page

I know that there are no words hidden
within his 97 years' worth of cerebral folds
to describe the newly empty place,
that cannot even be located

But there is this
this he can say
sad and sonorous
elemental and enduring:

Yisgadal v'yiskadash sh'mey raba…

(April 17, 2008)
Inspired by Joan Cardell's father

Preparing for *Rosh Hashanah*

The smell of Gorham's silver polish
releases memory
tucked ages ago into
crenulated brainfolds,
pathways to the soul
that pink butter
dabbed on a soft gray cloth
massaged into forks, knives, and spoons
my hands lathered with graying paste
as I rubbed away history,
the tarnish laid down
by time and touch
until they were as pristine
as creation's beginning.
It's funny that we did that,
Gram and I,
funny, because we Jews
like to remember,
hold on to time's imprints,
caresses from generations of fingers,
and we were wiping all that away,
all that I didn't yet know
I was not supposed to forget.
Memory holds that six year old
there, standing
on a chair at the sink,
head to head with Gram,
rubbing those stains away
to start the new year seeing
myself and my grandmother reflected
in the cradles of her silver soup spoons.

(October 7, 2008
September 22, 2009)
Appeared in the Reconstructionist Synagogue of the North Shore
Rosh Hashanah 5771/2010 Supplement, *Erev Rosh Hashanah* Reading 1
Published in *Jewish Women's Literary Annual* Vol 9, 2013, p. 59.

God's Screed

How did I fail so utterly?
Do not try to mollify
I have failed, most certainly.

Like your mother or your father
I was only supposed to walk in front of you
For a brief time
Until you would go: "*Lech l'cha,*" remember?
You were to drink me in
Grow strong and sure
In love
Grab my hand when you fell
And learn to right yourself
But you suck at my teat still
You cower at my feet still
You compete for my affections
Over and over and over
Deadly parodies of a childhood that does not yield.

You build altars and worship
A God as primitive as you.
Why would you imagine that I wanted
Flat, blind, static faith?
You have the capacity to imagine me
As the best of you
And if my most palpable presence
Exists in your imagining
Why image me as petty, vengeful?

Obedience was never the point
Be done with Abraham.
He failed my test.

(June 9, 2009)

Hold the Date: Extraordinary Speaker

June 20th Friday night services

Lawrence Bush, former editor of *Reconstructionism Today* and current editor of *Jewish Currents* will be discussing his recently released book: *Waiting for God: the Spiritual Explorations of a Reluctant Atheist* in which he explores the turn toward spirituality and religion on the part of baby-boomers. He examines the influences that "have left so many of [us] enamored of spiritual practice when so much of the rest of [our] experience should point...in the other direction." "He identifies the anxiety often generated by the multiplicity of cultural options and the loss of certainty created by modernity" as one source of the resurgence not only of fundamentalism and orthodoxy (in Judaism as well as other world religions), but also of the resurgence of interest in religion and spiritual practice. Lawrence Bush also takes on Reconstructionism and poses challenges to us "for narrowing ourselves into one more religious denomination." The evening promises to stir us out of our comfort zone nudging us to dislodge ourselves from the compromises we may have made to sustain our uneasy relationship with religion.

If you would like to read the book before this evening, you may purchase it at www.benyehudapress.org for $16.95

Introduction to Lawrence Bush's Address to the Reconstructionist Synagogue of the North Shore

June 20, 2008

It is my pleasure to introduce tonight's speaker, Lawrence Bush. No stranger to Reconstructionism, Lawrence was, for 13 years, the founding editor of our movement's magazine, *Reconstructionism Today*. Presently, he edits the 61 year old *Jewish Currents*, the publication of the Workman's Circle, and he edited the millennial edition of Leo Rotstein's *TheJoy of Yiddish*. Lawrence is a poet, essayist, visual artist, and former rabbinic speech writer.

While I cannot tell you that I know Lawrence well, I will tell you a little of what I know about him beyond his credentials. I know that the first page I turn to when I receive a new edition of *Jewish Currents* is Lawrence's column called *Religion and Skepticism*, whose logo: "I Deny Adonai I Dunno" conveys perfectly what Lawrence does best—combine fabulous irreverence and absolute respect as he explores the narrowing enslavements and the expanding enhancements that coexist at the heart of religion.

While Lawrence may reject much of the doctrine, practice, or ritual that defines Judaism, the religion, he has not rejected what I, and I imagine many here tonight, would consider to be the most essential foundation of Judaism, and that is "the conversation." This he embraces fully, willing to be honest, risking censure, but never allowing us—or himself—to settle into lazy complacency, as his book *Waiting for God: The Spiritual Explorations of a Reluctant Atheist* attests. He will, I suspect (and hope) challenge us this evening to dislodge ourselves from the compromises even we Reconstructionists have made to sustain our uneasy relationship with religion. He may have rejected belief in God, but, the very existence of his book is testament to the fact that he refuses to do so flippantly, casually, rigidly, or because it is trendy; he does so in the manner of Jacob, renamed Israel, and in this he is worthy of being counted among the "God-wrestlers"; in this he honors what is most important about being Jewish. Lawrence Bush…

Intermarriage

How could the intermarriage of a Jew and a Catholic
be considered a bad thing

The congregation extends condolences to the Giovanniello family on the death of Joe's father, Joseph Giovannniello

when from such a union springs this
announcement:

The wake is Wednesday 7-9 pm and Thursday 2-4 pm and 7-9 pm at Flinch & Bruns Funeral Home

delivered with no sense of self consciousness or irony

The funeral will be at St. Raymond's Church...

about the juxtaposed incongruity,

Shiva will be observed SUNDAY, September 12th... MINYAN at 4:30 pm. at the Kesselman-Giovanniello home...

this announcement that, despite its sad content,
holds the surest promise of eventual world peace.

(September 10, 2010)

CONTEMPLATIVE WORDS FOR ROSH HODESH

As we gather together on a schedule set by the moon, may we take as our example the moon's journey each month, learning from this orb that is always in metamorphosis, the universe's archetype of transformation. May we observe the moon closely, the steadiness of her climb from new to full, seeing that she does not clamber to reach her pinnacle, but daily, and only bit by bit, brings another portion of herself to light. May we observe and understand, also, that the moon does not covet its own full measure, but relinquishes it, even if, in doing this, it appears to be lost. By the moon, we come to know of waxings and wanings, rising tides and receding tides, blood-rich wombs and unready wombs, and always, always about the surety of change, the requisite food for our souls.

We honor the dynamic condition of the universe that we see reflected each month in the moon's face, and that we embrace within ourselves as the capacity to change and grow.

אֲנוּ מְכַבְּדִים אֶת הַמַּצָּב הַדִּינָמִי שֶׁל הַיְקוּם שֶׁאָנוּ רוֹאִים אֶת
הִשְׁתַּקְּפוּתוֹ בְּכָל חוֹדֶשׁ בִּפְנֵי הַיָּרֵחַ וְשֶׁאֲנַחְנוּ מְאַמְּצִים לְתוֹכֵנוּ
אֶת הַכּוֹחַ לְשַׁנּוֹת וְלִצְמוֹחַ

Transliteration: Anu m'chab-dim et ha-matzav ha-dee-na-mee shel ha-y'kum sheh-anu ro-eem et heesh-tak-foo-to b'chal hodesh bif-nai ha-ya-ray-ach v'she-nach-nu m'am-tzim l'to-chai-nu et ha-ko-ach lish-not v'litz-mo-ach

—Sheri Lindner October 18, 2009

Used in 2009 by the *Rosh Hodesh* group of The Reconstructionist Synagogue of the North Shore
Published online in *The Ritual Well,*

***Kaddish*, traditional**

Reader: Let God's name be made great and holy in the world that was created as God willed. May God complete the holy realm in your own lifetime, in your days, and in the days of all the house of Israel, quickly and soon. And say: Amen.

Congregation: May God's great name be blessed, forever and as long as worlds endure.

Reader: May it be blessed and praised and glorified, and held in honor, viewed in awe, embellished and revered; and may the blessed name of holiness be hailed, though it be higher than all the blessings, songs, praises, and consolations that we utter in this world. And say: Amen.

May Heaven grant a universal peace, and life for us, and for all Israel. And say: Amen.

May the one who creates harmony above, make peace for us and for all Israel, and for all who dwell on earth. And say: Amen.

***Kaddish*, re-valued**

We stand before the Idea God
by which we mean
all that holds us spellbound within
the abiding Symmetries of the Universe
Beauty that brings us to our knees
Consciousness too deep for words
the unutterable Known
the mystery of Becoming
Loving that takes our breath away
the stretching forth
of our most Awakened Selves
toward Holiness
This is what we mean by God
the Idea of a thousand thousand
facets ungraspably complex
eluding language
but because our living is bound up
with all this
as much as it is bound up with air
we breathe like air
One Unified Word
to hold for us
All that is beyond holding
but must be held nonetheless
Gratitude compels us
to vow before this Incomprehensible
All
and to Each Other
to safeguard
Minds that can imagine
such an Idea
Hearts that can open to
such an Idea
our own precious Humanity
that will forever refuse
to be vanquished by
such an Idea.
God
Amen.

(November 22, 2009)
Published online in *The Ritual Well,* July 19, 2010
(http://womenspiritualpoetry.blogspot.com/2013/02/kaddish-re-valued-by-sheri-lindner.html

Synagogue Retreat, May 23, 2010

If I were asked to describe how the retreat was, I would say that this is what happened over the weekend that 57 of us spent at Camp JRF:

-some of us felt a deep sense of regret for never having gone to summer camp;

-some of us felt a wonderful nostalgia and immense gratitude for having gone to summer camp;

-some of us felt grateful to have given the gift of summer camp to our children;

-some of us just breathed the air at Camp JRF and unpacked the selves that had awaited all winter for the time when they would return to that place;

-some of us (and others of us watched this happen) just lived as they were meant to live, knowing beyond all words that here is where the self they long to be will blossom into its full flowering;

-some of us witnessed the affirmation of unfolding individual and communal identity, where body shapes and sizes, intellectual capacities, quiet and not quiet personalities, and all measure of other differences were embraced and, like our studied *Torah* portion this week, *Naso*, lifted up and honored;

-some of us (well, actually one of us), pushing the age of 6, became an instant leader, assuming, Moses-like, a staff and leading his people. Always out in front, hopping from rock to rock, this one became our tireless leader, reminding any stragglers not to be "slow pokes." If we ever again needed to leave a place in haste, this would be the one to follow!

-some of us, pushing 80 or better, hiked right behind this little leader, defying anyone's inclination to think of them as slow pokes;

-some of us sat together quietly beading or braiding string or gimp, making bracelets, lanyards, earrings, with the 9 year olds being teachers to the 70 year olds;

-some of us studied *Torah*, coming to understand the essential qualities of those who become community leaders, those who tune their hearts to the readiness of their community, who lead and inspire simultaneously;

-some of us got pretty competitive in 3 legged races, wheelbarrow races, sing-offs, hoola hoop contests. Yeah, some of us probably had some difficulty moving certain body parts the next day;

-all of us were reassured about the future of humanity, seeing before our eyes the awesome awakening, the stepping of feet into places where no certainty is, the sublime transformation, that is far more miraculous than any splitting of a sea.

That's how the retreat was.

Appeared in the *Shaliyah* June, 2010

From 2 to 18

Fifteen years ago, as they paraded through the hallways of RSNS, the attributes we might have identified would have been these: they were adorable beyond measure; their parents were committed to their Jewish connection; their parents had both a pioneer spirit and a deep trust in this new nursery school program, and were willing for their children to be its first enrollees.

Watching them parade onto the *bima* last night evoked almost inexpressible feelings for all of us. In what congregation do so many high school students remain so involved after they have become *b'nai mitzvah*? And it is not just "involvement": these are kids, no, these are young adults who are clearly deeply committed to caring about and repairing the world; they harness their intellect, which is substantial, and their talent, which is gorgeous, to express important ideas and ideals, and, perhaps most touching, they care sincerely for and about one another. They have had fun together, real fun. They appear not to have been numbed to the powerful, human stirrings within them, by overfocus on superficialities, or by falling under the spell of popularity. These are the nearly grown children who will allow us to sleep soundly at night, knowing, as we hand over the world to the next generation, that they are capable and worthy to safeguard the precious gift.

And so, the generation that entered *Gan Shalom* when its doors first opened, now graduate high school. So fast this happened, from 2 to 18. And not all by itself did it happen. Daily, yearly, they watched their parents, their teachers, the visionary founders of *Gan Shalom*, their Rabbis, each other—shepherds all—models of questioning, wrestling, welcoming, embracing as they grew from seedlings to blossoms. May they go from strength to awesome strength. They are a blessing to each other, to us, and to the world they have already stepped into.

(June, 2010)

Why Abraham? Why Not Jacob?
A Reconsideration of the Covenant of Circumcision
(A Draft)

In previous publications (*Reconstructionist* Vol LVIII, No. 1, Autumn, 1992 and *Kerem* No. 5, 1997) I have put forth that Biblical stories and fairy tales share the same structural and thematic progression. Structurally, both employ particular and sequential literary conventions. [1] Thematically, both Biblical stories and fairy tales move a protagonist from a state of helpless dependency to a developmental place of wholeness where the protagonist is ready to assume both the rewards and the responsibilities of this attained maturity. This movement never occurs in the context of obedience. It is only in the act of defiance, in the exertion of one's individual will, that development is propelled. This can be seen no more clearly than in the Biblical Garden of Eden story, where no movement, indeed, no story, would ensue, without Eve's curiosity, her desire to know, that leads to inevitable disobedience, that opens the gate to multi-faceted life.[2]

Lest the reader take offense, or feel that this author makes an unholy comparison between Biblical stories and

---

[1] The common structural elements include: settings that are removed in time and place ("long ago and far away"), stark details, the conveyance of motivation and relationship through a series of actions which may include magical, extreme, or unrealistic qualities, beginning the story in *medias res* (in the middle of things), where the protagonist is propelled by some crisis, (often the loss of food), the use of an evil character from which the protagonist must escape, the use of the psychological mechanism of "splitting" which allows a young reader to hold tight to good, uncontaminated by bad, the use of "fused" characters, where many characters represent various facets of one central character, and a resolution where wealth, wholeness, fertility, and love are abundant.

[2] For a fuller development and comparison of Biblical stories and fairy tales, see "The Binding of Isaac: A Psychoanalytic Developmental Exploration" by Sheri Lindner and Michael A. Lindner, *Reconstructionist*, Vol. LVIII, No. 1, Autumn, 1992, p.5)

fairy tales, it is important to establish that both Biblical and fairy tales resonate in the deepest places not only for our children, but for us. These stories endure because they contain what is "true" as opposed to what is "real." Biblical stories need not be historically accurate or "real" any more than fairy tales, for them to find a way inside us, ring psychological bells within us, and hold emotional valence for us. Real is for a moment; true is what finds reverberations with our inner knowledge of ourselves and our humanity.

It is important to understand, also, that neither "real" nor "true" have anything to do with morality. Fairy tales and Bible tales are stories about maturation and development. As such, they are not about morality; they are about necessity, about what *is*. Many Biblical stories are interpreted as teaching us what we "should" do, how we "should" behave or think or believe. These interpretations are both limiting and, in more important ways, miss the mark, in the way that striking a bell while holding onto it eliminates the resonance of the sound.

Clearly there is deep meaning and profound import that leads each generation to carry these iconic stories, which are almost always about journeys (*lech l'cha*), and the outer travellings, like a moon, always reflect the inner transformations that are at each story's heart.

The thematic movement from not-ready to ready, from incomplete to complete, outlined above may be seen not only within individual Biblical tales (such as the *Akedah* story recounted in Genesis 21-22) but between and across stories, as well. Indeed, the overarching frame of the Five Books of Moses, moves us from pre-existence to readiness to enter the Promised Land. It should be possible, therefore, to read the stories of the lives of our three patriarchs, and discern a developmental movement and character transformation from Abraham to Isaac to Jacob.

In order to create the framework and psychological landscape for this Biblical analysis, I will begin with an explication of a well-known fairy tale. In the original story of the Three Little Pigs we have an old sow with 3 children pigs. The story begins that she has no money to keep them, (can not provide food, one of the common structural conventions that sets the story in motion) and so sends them off to seek their fortune (not "fortunes," note, but "fortune," in the singular). This grammatical singularity, and the fact that the pigs are brothers establishes not only their relatedness to one another, but the underlying fact that there is something of a shared identity. Their unity of identity is further underscored by the fact that each is spoken to in identical words by the wolf, and each speaks identical words to the wolf. The wolf says: "Little pig, little pig, let me come in" to which each pig replies: "No, no, not by the hair of my chinny chin chin." The first pig builds his house of straw. It is the easiest to make and the least durable. Some moralists like to warn children that this pig was lazy and just wanted to play and so got eaten by the wolf. A different and more psychologically resonant interpretation is that this type of house is fitting for the youngest aged pig to build. It has nothing to do with laziness and everything to do with what is perfectly age appropriate. The impermanence of his house reflects the transitory nature of childhood; we would no more want this pig's house to endure than we would want the earliest stages of childhood to go on forever. Yes, he is eaten by the wolf, but this act, operating at metaphoric levels, expresses that youth, by necessity, must be gone, must give way to emerging maturity. Thus, while the youngest pig is "gone" (childhood yields), the next pig brother now comes on the scene to encounter the wolf (life's vicissitudes). The identical words are used to describe his acquisition of building materials and his encounter with the wolf. He builds a slightly sturdier house of sticks, again, age appropriate to his maturational place. That we are dealing with the same pig as before, at a different developmental level, is revealed in the identity of his words to the wolf. He is the same pig, but his ability to manage life's vicissitudes has developed beyond what it previously was. Finally, the third pig builds a brick house. We, and our children listening to this tale, are not really saddened by the disappearance of the two previous incarnations of pig, unconsciously understanding that they must be gone for maturity to emerge.[3] One cannot be mature while holding onto infantile or childish impulses. The story concludes with the eldest, now mature pig continuing to foil the wolf by using higher level thinking processes, often referred to as "executive functions," that include the capacity to plan, to direct one's thinking, to delay gratification, to tolerate frustration, to maintain alertness, to persevere. These were not available in the same magnitude, to the earlier pig incarnations, and these capacities more than recompense us for the loss of the earlier two brothers. We see this in our children's (and our own) delight in this pig's cleverness and ability to meet life's vicissitudes with planning, pluck, and confidence.

With this (apologetically unkosher) framework, let us turn to our patriarchs: Abraham, Isaac, and Jacob.

Abraham, as our first patriarch, represents the earliest incarnation of our "founding father." Except for his challenging of God in Genesis 18: 22-32, (chastising God for being willing to destroy all of Sodom, even if innocents were

---

[3] Importantly, the Disney version of *The Three Pigs* misses this crucial feature of the story, having each pig brother, as his house is destroyed by the wolf, go and join the next brother, with all three being alive and together in the brick house foiling the wolf at the end. This version makes the assumption that children are not capable of letting go of their infantile selves, are not capable of internalizing and "metabolizing" their own early selves, and are not capable of tolerating momentary sadness of loss, and transforming it to developmentally sturdier forms of self competence and independence. It robs children of the psychic, poetic, and essential maturational "work" that can occur when being read a fairy tale.

present there), his alliance with God is characterized by submission. If being like God is to be a creator, Abraham surrenders, symbolically, his procreative powers to God by agreeing to the covenant of circumcision. Not only does he "hand over" a part of his organ of procreation, but he enacts his willingness to hand over also, the product of his procreation, his son, Isaac. Abraham's relationship with God is hierarchical in nature.

According to the schema of development being explored, Isaac should move us forward, so that the relationship with God continues to develop. Little exists in Genesis about Isaac's relationship to God except that God commands him to remain in Gerar, assuring him that He will be with him and fulfill the oath that was made to Abraham that "your heirs [will be] as numerous as the stars of heaven...inasmuch as Abraham obeyed Me and kept My charge." Isaac remains in Gerar only temporarily, moving outside of Gerar and then to Beer-sheba when water rights are contested. Thus, it seems that Isaac submits to God's will when he can, and takes care of business when he has to, regardless of God's command to remain in the land. Developmentally speaking, we have moved from full submission to the prerogative that obedience may be partial, supplemented by Isaac's own personal judgment.

Like parts of Abraham's story (like the Three Pigs story), Isaac's story continues its movement through the tale of his children. As with the three pig brothers, who, as we saw above, were three incarnations of one developing pig, Isaac's two sons also share an identity. Though they are described as opposites in many ways, Esau and Jacob are twins. Esau emerges from the womb first, Jacob second, "on the heels of his brother." ("holding onto the heel of Esau"). The stage is set for us to understand that Esau (earlier incarnation) will need to yield to Jacob (later incarnation). We must not lose sight of the fact that, like the pigs, they are meant to be the same, reflecting merely different stages of development. In nearly all ways, Esau (hunter, hairy) is described as more primitive than Jacob (domesticated, a chef, civilized). In keeping with this understanding, Jacob does not "steal" the birthright; rather, the birthright must, of necessity, go to the more developmentally advanced place, the more mature representation of the central Esau/Jacob character. This is underscored in two ways. The first is that Esau fairly willingly trades it for food (food, especially the lack of it, again being the "crisis" that propels the action of the story). Esau yields to Jacob effortlessly. Furthermore, Isaac's words: "the voice is the voice of Jacob, yet the hands are the hands of Esau" underscores that Esau and Jacob comprise a unity of identity, with Jacob blending both the physical capabilities of his brother, and his own mental and verbal capabilities. As such, Jacob represents a kind of evolutionary advancement over Esau. The birthright is not denied to Esau because of some wrongdoing or moral laxity on Esau's part (as commentators often assert) or because of deception on Jacob's; rather, it is inevitable that it be given to the character who represents integration of what went before with developmental advancement of what is to come for the next generation. Here, as in the Greek tradition, Isaac's blindness perhaps is only an outer blindness that belies his inner vision. Isaac appears to understand, intrinsically, that "voice" (words, thought made articulate) replaces "hands" as civilization continues to take shape. In this, he actually mimics God's own creative process, where words were the vehicle that effected the action of the creation of the world. At the end of this part of the story, the merging of Esau and Jacob continues, as Esau learns to cook (like Jacob) and decides not to take a Canaanite wife (as Isaac has instructed Jacob not to do). In bestowing the birthright onto Jacob, Isaac assures that primitivity will not be our inheritance.

Continuing this analytic trajectory, we would expect Jacob to represent the most fully developed representation of patriarch. We can point to two events that support our thesis. First, Jacob takes over the procreative process with a vengeance, fathering 12 sons who will become a "People" / a great Nation. (Though Abraham also eventually fathered 6 additional sons with Keturah, these sons did not partake in the inheritance). Second, he has a dream in which he wrestles with an angel or a man or God, after which he becomes "marked." Having initially rejected the God of his father as he was receiving the birthright ("...because the Lord *your* [italics added] God granted me good fortune") he requires of himself that he undergo his own personal encounter with this God. He is not submissive, nor does he merely accept, as his father's inheritor, God and God's demands or commands. Unlike Abraham, for whom submission and obedience were enough, Jacob demands that he engage in a process of "knowing" God (hand to hand, as it were, which is, perhaps, as close to face to face as is possible). For him, submission is not sufficient. Also unlike Abraham, who brings his son to God, God initiates the visit with Jacob, engaging him not with a command but with an encounter. A dynamic, rather than hierarchical relationship ensues, as Jacob lays down the conditions upon which he will accept the Lord God as his own ("If God remains with me, if He protects me on this journey that I am making, and gives me bread to eat ...the Lord shall be my God"). Jacob comes to know God nearly as an equal, and takes back fertility prerogatives, seen not only in his own prolifically numbered progeny but in his ability to increase the fertility of his flocks. Jacob has insisted on a personal, corporeal encounter with God before being willing to consider a relationship. Like Abraham, Jacob is "marked" after this encounter and undergoes a change of name from Jacob to Israel. In some ways, not only has Jacob/Israel reclaimed unconditional (pro)creative powers, but has, effectually, replaced God; in the Joseph story that follows

Jacob's, "the Lord God is neither active nor articulate." (*God: A Biography*, Jack Miles, New York: Vintage Books, 1995, p. 78).

Given this developmental progression in Biblical patriarchs, the question arises as to why we continue to adhere to the covenantal prescription made of the most primitive patriarchal incarnation by the most primitive divinity characterization? Our patriarchs and God evolved in their relationship to one another. Why, therefore, do we continue to adopt the most primitive "marking" custom, rather than the more mature "marking" of Jacob? Abraham's marking was done in submission; Jacob's in relation. Which of these should constitute or define *our* sacred, covenantal relationship with God?

I would propose that we, as Jews, have overlooked this progressive movement in the Bible, and that circumcision is a regressive custom that fixes us in the moment of Abraham, as if we are saying that we revere the primitivity beyond which our ancestors developed, and beyond which we seem loathe to develop. I would propose that a more meaningful "ritual" is one that honors not Abraham's submission, but Jacob's God-wrestling—a willingness, with full mature intentionality, to have an encounter with, to engage in the process of coming to know, God. It is not the knowing that is to be revered here, anymore than the submission, but rather the willingness to engage in the process.

I can imagine a new Jewish ritual, of a small tattoo[4] marking upon one's hip or upper leg, that acknowledges one's willingness to engage—throughout one's lifetime—in this God-wrestling process. (This might be a *yud*, the Hebrew first letter for *Yisrael*, the word for *God-wrestler*, and also the first letter of the unutterable sacred name of God). This would not be a ritual, like circumcision, that one's parents perform upon their children. It could only be done in adulthood, with one's full intention as a sign of commitment to the process of wrestling with the ultimate Idea. I imagine that the ritual would involve the person, himself or herself, gathering 10 other adults who have also committed themselves to this wrestling process, in witness of this commitment. This community of witness bearers would underscore the understanding that God-wrestling cannot occur outside of the context of "people-wrestling"—that one cannot engage in relation to God outside of the context of relation to fellow human beings. And, as important, the convenantal marking of our relationship with God would honor not the more static, hierarchical Abrahamic-God connection, but rather, the dynamic, interactive Jacob-God wrestling.

(October, 2010)

Presented to the *Rosh Hodesh* group of the Reconstructionist Synagogue of the North Shore Spring, 2011

---

[4] Despite the prohibition in Leviticus 19:28: "You shall not make gashes in your flesh for the dead, or incise any marks on yourselves: I am the Lord," a small tattoo would be no more in violation of this verse than the "gash" of circumcision.

Terezin: 2012

Like walking in a parade
both sides of the street
vying for attention
waving, cheering
(though it was empty, silent, you see)
and me, looking
right, left
for a signpost to point the way
on the right: *Krematorium*
the left: pizzeria,
arrows pointing in the same direction.
Desecration of this place
hallowed by desecration,
or consecration, like trembling
new grass shoots
that inevitably
blanket even the
newly covered grave?

(July 1, 2012)
To be published in Poetica, Spring, 2013

Saved

This is how it happens:
the man, a stranger,
has just completed surgery
on the other man's wife,
notices the numbers
branded into the pale
underside of the husband's arm,
does not pretend he
has not seen what he has seen,
says how very sorry he is for what
his countrymen did
decades before he ever existed,
and the husband,
who, from the age of 16,
and despite all he would
hope of himself,
has had one particular
hate branded into him
as inextricably as those numbers,
feels the Universe shift
with a force not unlike that
of the first day, and
darkness is separated from
light.

(October 5, 2011)
For my friend, Mickey

To be published in *Kerem*, April, 2013

IV: For Those Who Lead the Way

For Karen Denton: on Her Retirement

written February 25, 1998

"Bliss it was in that dawn to be alive,
But to be young was very heaven."[1]

That dawn was 1968-69, and the world was embroiled in conflict--a half a globe away and in our own places of higher education. While our slightly older peers were reading newspapers and becoming aware of the world of politics, we, the lucky ones in Karen Denton's Clarion English class, were **also** preparing to enter the currents of adult awareness and adult consciousness and adult humanity. But our world, in 1969, was not filled with noise or protest or napalm...our path into the adult stream was quieter. We opened books and sat with Karen, and began our struggle to understand humanity's deepest impulses, humanity's highest needs for creation and connection, humanity's capacity "to see a world in a grain of sand."[2] For some of us, our sit-ins barely one year later, would be more tangible acts, but, I think, they could never begin to touch the significance, to have the import or impact or imprint of those transformative years when Karen Denton was our teacher.

We stood on a threshold, we 17 year olds, and she stood with us. She would usher us to "lands more kind than home, more large than earth."[3] How did she do this?

She filled our heads with words, with the beauty of language. I would put my honor on it that many of us can still, on a long car ride, in a traffic jam, or on a sleepless night, quote the first 18 lines of *Essay on Man*, or the first 18 lines of the Prologue to the *Canterbury Tales* **in** middle English, or words from *Meditation 17*, or lines from *To A Skylark*, or passages from *Paradise Lost,* or any number of Blake's or Wordsworth's verses. There is great power in the memorization of such language. We, the lucky ones, had neural pathways forged in our brains and our synapses filled with poetry. And while we are likely this hour to forget where we put our keys or our glasses, we will have with us always the lyric wonder and promise of renewal of: "Whan that Aprill with his shoures soote"[4] etched deeply within us, claiming a place of permanence in our memory's treasure trove.

But beyond the grandeur of words, we were ripe, and she knew it, for the meanings of those words. We began 11th grade with the adolescent arrogance that let us know, with asurity, that there **was** nothing, larger than ourselves, worth being a part of. We were

"Calm, indifferent, cross-legged
or on elbows half-lying in the grass--
how should the great dead
tell [us]of dying?
[We] will have time for poems at last,
when [we] have found [we] are no more
the beautiful and young
all poems are for."[5]

But she, who was so young, herself, 25, maybe 26, knew of our imminent emergence. She knew, and we would come to know, that the "great dead" indeed, understood us well and had much to tell us--not of our dying, but of our living. We were, all of a sudden, not indifferent; we were filled with

"Chaos of Thought and Passion all confused; [6]

We were

In doubt to deem [ourselves] God[s] or Beast[s]"[6]

She introduced us to the great ones, who introduced us to ourselves, and in this knowing we fell in love with the world of thoughts and ideas, to which we would, soon, in our turn, become contributors. And we wanted, desperately, to find our places in that world. We looked above and contemplated God as Wordsworth's

> "sense sublime of something far more deeply
> interfused,...
> A motion and a spirit, that impels
> All thinking things, all objects of all thought,
> And rolls through all things."[7]

We looked within and reveled in our own minds' capacity to

> "become...a thousand times more beautiful than the
> earth
> On which [we dwelt]...In beauty exalted, as it is itself
> Of quality and fabric more divine."[8]

We looked toward each other, we who had spent every day of our timeless childhoods together, now no longer "islands, entire [unto ourselves],"[9] and as we parted that summer of 1969, to take our places in the world, we trusted that we would "find strength in what remain[ed] behind."[10]

Other teachers helped us chart our course through the topographies of history, of chemical and quadratic equations, of cells and laws of motion, of foreign idioms and conjugations. These are no small tasks, and their successful accomplishment is not trivial. But Karen was a cartographer of a different sort: she gave us sextants and maps (of words and images and metaphors, of poetry and art and human urgings) so that we could chart the quiet, essential streams that flowed deeply within us, streams, that in the end, would be the only true paths by which we find our way. Most of us, before then, had not even known of the existence of these subterranean sources of nourishment that bubbled deeply within us, whose rich silt would come to fertilize our souls.

But there was more than words and more than words' meanings that happened to us that year. There was Karen, herself. For some of us, 17 was the year that we would turn from our mothers, and turn toward Karen as the model for our yet-to-be-coalesced selves. For our mothers could love most what we **had** been, what we **once** enjoyed, the child they had always known; but Karen loved us for who we were to become. She had a vision for each of us, and her vision was always of a better self than we felt we were at the time, and we each wanted to be the person of substance and integrity she thought we already were. And if she could look at us and see our better selves, then we could look at humanity "from [its]golden side"[11] and envision ways to repair our fallen world. Unlike other adults in our lives at the time, who had made their peace with reality, she did not scoff or smile at our narrow idealisms, for she understood that from such dreams spring the holiest hopes for humankind. She nurtured each moment of perfection and hopefulness that we could imagine.

From wthin our knotted tangle of silk threads, she, better than anyone, it seemed, could find the end strand, and hold it gently away, so that we could dance and spin out of our cocoons. And as we sought to feel at home with these newly emergent selves, we often became like Karen, adopting her soul for awhile, as we were growing into our own. Some of us wore Avon Charisma perfume, as she did; some of us played piano for hours, learning Rachmaninoff's *Rhapsody on a Theme from Paganini*; some of us learned to play this without ever having played the piano before 1969; we listened to classical and romantic music, allowing ourselves to be disturbed and moved by it; we drove with her in that great blue Corvair, singing "Let The Sun Shine" and "Grazin' In The Grass" through five states, as we made our sacred pilgrimage to Stratford, Connecticut to see as many Shakespeare plays as could be seen in 24 hours; we became pantheists; we became Presbyterians; some of us abandoned our synagogues and went to church with her, to find the same sources of inspiration that touched her; we drank black coffee late into the night, breaking curfews to linger over one more cup at Lundy's; and we read **everything** she mentioned: *Manfred, Alastor, Prometheus--Bound and Unbound; Paradise--Lost and Regained*; *The Prelude*; *Look Homeward Angel,* and, prophetically, *You Can't Go Home Again.* And we arrived at Pierre S. duPont High School twice a week at 7 AM bursting to talk of what we had read.

Although in time, we would find our own brands of perfume, or come to enjoy cream and sugar in our coffee, yet there remains a legacy of deeper significance than these soul-shaping, but transitory identifications. We became teachers of English, ourselves, loving forever, literature and learning, and loving young minds on the verge of consciousness--ourselves unable to imagine a more fulfilling, exciting thing to do than to paint a dawn, and then gently to nudge the minds of 17 year olds into wakefulness. "What we have loved, /Others will love, and we will teach them how."[12] Long before ecology awareness, we understood how and felt compelled to recycle and renew the precious gifts she had bequeathed us.

There is a *midrash*, a parable, about the Israelites as they stood at the Sea of Reeds, the Red Sea, on their departure from Egypt. The story is told that the sea did not part until one person stepped a foot into it. Not from the shores, from the edges of experience do such wonders happen. Had Karen walked us to the shores and shown us what lay on the other side, this alone, would have been enough; had she taken us there and told us in great detail all about what lay on the other side, this, too, would have been a sufficient gift. But this was not her way. Rather, she filled our minds with gorgeous rhythms and melodies, and awe for what is possible in language; she filled our hearts with the poetic and powerful yearning to understand our own human nature, a yearning that has touched, immemorially, every human being; she filled our souls with her glorious vision of who we were. She put her arm around the shoulder of every single one of us, and then she with us, and we with her, stepped our feet into the sea. And the way parted for us. Legend calls it a miracle that the **sea** so changed in shape. Oh, but it was **we** who were sublimely and irrevocably transformed.

"There are in our existence spots of time,
That with distinct pre-eminence retain
A renovating virtue, whence...
Our minds
Are nourished and invisibly repaired."[13]

Such a spot of time was our time with Karen Denton, and such nourishment and repair still ours these 30 years later.

---Sheri (Lipstein) Lindner, Class of 1969
Pierre S. duPont High School
Wilmington, Delaware

1 William Wordsworth, *The Prelude*
2 William Blake, *Auguries of Innocence*
3 Thomas Wolfe, *You Can't Go Home Again*
4 Geoffrey Chaucer, *The Canterbury Tales*
5 Robert Wallace,"In A Spring Still Not Written Of"
6 Alexander Pope, *Essay On Man*
7 William Wordsworth, *The Prelude*
8 William Wordsworth, *The Prelude*
9 John Donne, "Meditation 17"
10 William Wordsworth, "Ode To Intimations of Immortality"
11 William Wordsworth, *The Prelude*
12 William Wordsworth, *The Prelude*
13 William Wordsworth, *The Prelude*

Dear Joy and Lee,

First, I want to thank you both for the gorgeous *mezzuzah*. Not only is it just beautiful to look at, but it feels very fitting in a symbolic way--it seems so delicate and fragile, and yet it contains words that are at the foundation of our religion, which has endured through so much that should have destroyed it. It also makes me feel that something very fragile yet very substantial has been entrusted to me. Other *mezzuzot* that I have on doors around my home do not make me feel this way--they are merely beautiful or interesting. So, thank you for that.

Beyond this gift, I feel that you both have given another gift to me. You have given me a place in which to continue to grow up. There was a time--it feels long ago--that I thought belonging to a synagogue must be the biggest waste of money. I couldn't imagine why anyone would want/need this. I was interested in my smaller world, comprised of Michael and me, and eventually Dan and Jo. This seemed enough for me. Now I think a lot, as we talk of "new members" who don't "get it," about how smug I felt at mooching off of our synagogue for several years before paying money to join. I did not feel the sense of responsibility, I did not feel I was doing something wrong, I was profiting and enjoying the belonging without feeling that I should be giving. It was still about my smaller world/family, and what we could gain from you. Eventually, without anyone ever censuring me for it, I learned by example what needed to be done, what were the right things to be done, and came to feel that this was now part of my ethic as a synagogue member. I am a little embarrassed about where I had come from, but also feel forgiving of those who may be there yet.

And, even more recently, when called upon to give to the college, I felt like I was not ready, yet, to move beyond the smaller-but-somewhat-bigger-world that I had by now embraced. I felt that the synagogue was my world and I was responsible for it and its building (besides feeling the necessity of saving for my children's college years). I felt somewhat put-out by being asked to support the "larger" institution of the Rabbinical College. It was not just that I was afraid, financially, to let go of what my family might need, but also that I could not see my way clear to being a part of something beyond what I am a part of now.

Jodie Siff's talk on Saturday inched me into the larger world. It caused me to wonder what I and my children take for granted from our extremely narrow vision of our part of the world. And it caused me to look at the joy I take (and sometimes take for granted) in scenes like the following:

--conversation with Joanna and Danny Seigerman in which Danny offers to fix her up with a friend of his from school, and she says fine...he doesn't have to be American but prefers that he be Jewish! (where does this come from--you know we don't talk about this);

--Dan walking by the living room while I teach Lee Chait the *V'ahavta*, and saying, "Oh, are you learning the *V'Ahavta*? That's my favorite prayer because it's the first one I learned--and then singing it for her--only to be joined by his friend (his first Jewish friend). They continue singing it as they walk out the door to go play basketball.

So perhaps this is still about my own small world of Lindner people, but I feel as if I am becoming aware that as these Lindner people move out into the larger world, I would like them to be able to find there the same welcoming and accepting "forces" that have shaped their identities so far, and I know that beyond our family, a significant shaper of their identities has been our synagogue. I am always aware of how lucky we are to have you both and this place. But I think in my naivite I have assumed that my children will find this wherever they go. This may not be so, unless my generation helps to make it so.

A few years ago...as a matter of fact, the *Pesach* after Dan's *Bar Mitzvah,* I had a dream. It was that I was on the Exodus march out of Egypt. Lee, you were in the dream, too. We were thousands of people walking along the side of a hill, snaking our way across land, with a vista that was endless. I was ecstatic at how exciting this was. Lee, in the dream, you were looking down, depressed, kind of grumpy, and complaining. You were annoyed with me that I was chattering; you did not see much to celebrate about this long, arduous, and difficult walk ahead of us.

At that time, I laughed when I woke up. I understood the dream as one about my own going forth, about my having come of age in my family-of-origin's eyes. You see, my siblings had asked me, just after Dan's service, "When did you grow up?" In their eyes, I am frozen at 12 years old. In that family, we are all stuck in assigned places. And by the way, my mother's name is Lee, so your presence in the dream was as a stand-in for a different relationship in my life. To the consternation of my original family, I made Exodus and founded my own new land, and it took 20 years (not quite the 40 of the Hebrew wandering) for them to see that I had gone.

Today, I see more about this dream. Two years ago I chuckled that I was dreaming in Jewish Bible stories! It was only funny to me. Now, I think it is significant that I dreamt in Jewish symbols. I think that it is in the framework of Judaism that I have continued along the path of growth. Many, many years of psychoanalysis launched me on a more private, if you will, exodus path--one that was about me as an individual, as a person who loves Michael, and as the mother of my two children. This helped me create my small world. But my synagogue connection has launched me beyond that small world and given me a consciousness of responsibilities outside of that world. Only a few years ago, I would have thought that going over someone's house for *shiva*, if I hadn't known the person well, was fraudulent and hypocritical, or that it wouldn't matter to the person, since I was not a close friend. I see that differently now. I was most touched when Michael's dad died by those who came and sent cards who were not close. They mattered a great deal. And I feel that I must do this for others, not because I **have** to, but because it matters.

So, you see one reason why I gravitate toward themes of maturation and growth. Not only do I love watching Dan and Jo growing up, but I feel very much that I am doing it, too. And I am still thinking (kvetching?) about what becoming a *Bat Mitzvah* means to me. I think I had been focusing on the wrong things all this time. When people would say to me that I must be so proud of my accomplishment, I couldn't really say yes or even feel "pride." I was looking at the "skills" involved in the process, most of which I had already had. Because I had them, I wondered why I was doing this. I did not feel like I needed to "show off" my skills, but sometimes it felt as if that was what I was doing. This feeling bothered me, because I do not feel that I "worked" at acquiring these skills. I have enormous respect for those women in the class who really did work, and recently learned Hebrew. For them this was an accomplishment that made me proud and moved me. For me, I am still not sure what it was, but I know that it was something.

I am thinking that it means something about what I have been saying here. That in some important way I am still growing up. It is a bit of a strange phenomenon that in a month Joanna will consider herself a Jewish adult, and I am also just beginning to consider myself a Jewish adult.

So this was a very long thank you note, that I had

intended to handwrite and it was supposed to be shorter. I thank you for not needing me to know before hand why I was becoming a *Bat Mitzvah*; for knowing, in some way I was not yet aware of, that I had been becoming a *Bat Mitzvah* for a long time now. I think my mistake on the post-*Haftara* blessings is a metaphor for all of this. I was aware, as Toby and I were singing the wrong tune, that it was wrong, and also I was very aware that you did not sing behind us to correct us. I was not aware of feeling embarrassed to be wrong. Rather, I felt grateful that you let us find our way back through the words and the song that was in our veins.

(April 22, 1996)

Dear Joy,

This is a long overdue note to you with thanks (and thoughts) about June 1st, Joanna's *Bat Mitzvah*. I figure that for the most part you are keenly aware of the influence you have over/on our kids (not just mine, but lots of others, as well). But I also know that it is easy for you to feel undervalued and to lose touch at those times with how much you are appreciated.

So, at the simplest level, this is a thank you note for Joanna's *Bat Mitzvah*. It is hard to enumerate the precise "things" for which I am thanking you, but I want to share with you some sequelae of Jo's *Bat Mitzvah* that both linger on our surfaces and burrow themselves more deeply within.

Joanna asked us at her camp's visiting day to send up your talk to her. In her own words, "I love Rabbi Joy's talk to me and I want to be able to read it whenever..." On one of those car rides to the mall, the day after she got home from camp, she told me that she "used" your talk a lot this summer. It helped her get to the top of Mt. Washington. Throughout the hike, she kept saying to herself that she was a kid who would "get there," and she very much wanted to get there. All year she had been saying that she would opt out of that hike--that it was too hard, it intimidated her, she didn't want to do it, who cares. As late as visiting day, she said, "I don't know if I'll do it. Maybe we'll all do an easier hike." So, you did not know it, but you were on Mt. Washington also this summer, and your words allowed her to find herself, stretch herself (and more easily to embrace my values!), so I thank you for both of us.

Now, climbing Mt. Washington might not seem like a terribly important follow-up to a *Bat Mitzvah*, but your talk to her also reverberated more deeply than this. Jo's bunk had a counselor who was not middle-class, not privileged, not

Jewish, not white, and who none of the kids could relate to. The counselor was strict and serious, gave the girls a hard time, seemed not to enjoy them or be able to relax and have fun with them. The girls hated her. Joanna felt uncomfortable disliking Dee and did not want Dee to feel that it was because she was black. Jo wrote to our friends in Cleveland and to us and asked for advice on how she should handle this and what she should do. On that same mall car ride after camp, Jo said that she felt like the whole situation with Dee was like "getting lost," and that it was important that she find her way in and through it all. Your metaphor and your story and your history with Jo touches her, guides her, she remembers it (could probably quote most of it)...and loves it.

So the next part of this now famous to-the-mall car ride was Dan talking about **his** hike up Washington, in which he and his best camp friend brought up the rear of the group because they were discussing religion and concepts of God/godliness. Dan finally convinced his conservadox friend to at least be interested in the Reconstructionist understanding of godliness, while his friend convinced him of the value of more traditional observance. So now, I have two kids in the car wishing we were Kosher and more observant (though getting anyone home for *Shabbat* dinner is harder and harder these days, and I'd wager valuable possessions on the fact that 3 *Rosh Hashanah* services will still be too much for them). And then they both say, as if each has come up with this thought independently, that they think they will be Rabbis when they grow up.

Now, I will not wager anything on what they will actually choose to do as adults, but I do want you to know what an enjoyable moment it was for each of them and for me, just to know the loving connection they both feel not only to Judaism, but to the models that you and Lee have provided for them.

Just wanted to share that with you. Thanks.

Michael and I would love to give you something as a thank you, but it hasn't occurred to us yet what it would be. If you have a Rabbinic or personal wish list, we'd welcome your help here--no need to feel awkward about letting us know. If not, just know that we haven't forgotten; we're waiting to be inspired.

(September, 1996/5757)

Dear Joy,

This is a very belated thank you gift from us for the occasion of Joanna's *Bat Mitzvah*. It is a token of our thanks for your allowing us and encouraging us to explore the Jewish streams that bubble around us and that course within us; to express ourselves creatively about them; to forge meaningful, deeply pleasureable, and abiding connections to them; and to re-create ourselves and our family in the context of them.

With great affection,
Joanna, Dan, Sheri, and Michael

(November 2, 1997)

In Memoriam: Richard Koebele

(Principal of Shelter Rock Elementary School) March 11, 1999

The details of a person's life are easy to collate, and it is usually those details that figure prominantly in a eulogy. But the facts of a man's life do not equal the sum of the man. Beneath the eulogy "catalogue" of Richard Koebele's life accomplishments, there is a legacy that is both quiet and colossal, unassuming and monumental.

It is not necessary to go further than the 40 classrooms of over 750 children at the Shelter Rock Elementary School to understand the ripples created by one stone being thrown into water. These ripples are a testament to the impact of Richard's public life on those he came in contact with day after day, year after year. For one student, Mr. Koebele is remembered as the first person to whom he ever spoke English; one remembers a reassuring squeeze of the hand just before the student was to make a classroom presentation; many remember being called into Mr. Koebele's office to receive a sticker for a job well-done—whether that job was a project or respectful behavior in the hall. These are individual identity-forming, life-shaping memories, and they abound among Shelter Rock's students.

But there are collective memories, shared by an entire building of people, and beyond that, by an entire generation in Manhasset. These memories are about the smile that greeted nearly 800 students each morning as they entered the place where they would spend 7 years of their lives—their bodies and their minds changing so dramatically that they would be barely recognizable, upon graduation, as the same people who had so tentatively entered Shelter Rock so many years before. Richard's smile and greeting gave them the courage to enter and the confidence to continue. These memories are about his noisy camera that he thought he could keep quiet by putting it in his jacket pocket as it wound its way back to the beginning. These pictures marked ordinary and extraordinary moments in the daily life of Shelter Rock school, and they would become the catalogue of a generation of children's lives. Mr. Koebele was the keeper of their delicate, young histories. These memories are about his fantastic ties—a silly quirk, it would seem, to those outside of Shelter Rock. But these ties were part of the literal and communal fabric that bound together hundreds of people—children and adults, alike. These ties, if one could read between the patterns, told of a man who stayed in touch with what would delight children, of a man who knew that humor must be present at the heart of this serious business of educating children, of a man who wanted our first reaction upon entering school to be a smile.

Such small acts, these things that Richard Koebele did. And yet, in these days when our culture so often criticizes what is **not** done in schools, and the ways in which education fails our children, there are no acts that could, by any measure, be larger.

Dear Mrs. Aufses,

I have just heard that you will be leaving Schreiber next year, and I wanted to take this time to write you and wish you well. And, selfishly, I must say that your good fortune in your new job is very much our loss. I had hoped that my daughter, Joanna, would have had the opportunity of having you as a teacher. You have made a difference in Dan's life.

It is true that a picture can so efficiently and elegantly stand in the place of many words. And so I have this image in my mind--a frozen frame in time--of Dan reclining in his bed reading *Song of Solomon*...after he no longer has to. Not such a big deal, you may think. But Dan is a person for whom reading has always been a labor, and rarely a pleasure. It has not been something that he would ever choose to do as a relaxation. While he loves ideas, and the discussion of them, he has, throughout the years, retreated from reading that was not required. I think that reading is still a labor for Dan; you did not change that. But it is a labor that feels very worth the effort now, and that **is** your doing. And the labor opens doors to ideas that feel worth the effort, and that, too, is your doing.

Our kids encounter many teachers as they move along their path to becoming educated, and perhaps, someday, wise people. Many of these teachers are fine, helping our children chart their course through the topographies of history, of chemical and quadratic equations, of cells and laws of motion, of foreign idioms and conjugations. These are no small tasks, and their successful accomplishment is not trivial. But there are other teachers--cartographers of a different sort--who give our children sextants and maps--of words and images and metaphors, of poetry and art and human urgings--so that they can chart the quiet, essential streams that flow deeply within them, streams that in the end will become the only true paths by which they find their way. Such teachers love the kids, certainly, as much as they love what they teach. While I do not know you directly except for the briefest of conversations, I recognize, in my child's affection for you and for your subject, a teacher who adores young minds on the verge of consciousness, who loves to nudge the minds of 17 years olds into wakefulness, who loves kids and loves what she does. As I have watched Dan this year, his enjoyment of literature has only partly been about enjoying a story or a character or an author; what has seemed important is that through this process, he has gained insights and understandings that help him know himself and begin to find his place in the world. And it has been joyful.

And so, I thank you for the gift you have bequeathed our son. Our best wishes to you as you continue along your way...

Warmly,
Sheri Lindner
(June 17, 1999)

For Joy, Upon Her Leaving

There is a story that we all know well--a story that nurtured us in our growing up and that we treasured with our children for their growing up. The story is about a young girl who gets lost and who wants to find her way back home. She does not know the way. But she journeys forth in search of one who will show her the way. And when she reaches this wise person, he tells her this: that he cannot tell her the way. She is disappointed...and she is angry. But then, with his next words, he gives her a gift, the gift of the wise man. He tells her that she has always had the power to find her own way back home. And she knows, in that moment, that it was not the wizard whom she sought on her long journey to Oz; it was always her self. She did not need the place, Oz; she needed the time, when her feet would be planted firmly enough in the kingdom of herself, that she could look down at them and know how it was that she would go home.

Dorothy was certainly a step ahead of the Lindners. We did not know, for a long time, that we sought home. Red poppy fields lured us; green castles excited us. But one day we stumbled inside the castle of the wizard, and there we, like Dorothy, were challenged to blend cognition, with compassion, with courage, and in this process we would discover the ruby slippers that had always been on our feet. This was the gift given to us: we found ourselves at home in the Judaism we had left long ago.

For many of us in this congregation, Joy has been our wizard. She knows, before we do, when we are ready to look down and take note of our feet, of where they are pointed. She knows, before we do, when we are ready to have the ruby slippers take us to places to which we thought we dare not return. She understands things about us that we only gradually come to understand, as her words to us, delivered in a sanctified ritual moment, reverberate sometimes years later. She taps us, uncannily, the moment **before** we know we are ready, and our trepidation and intimidation are transformed by her faith and certainty in us. She believes we can write *d'vrei Torah,* when we barely know what *Torah* is--and we write *d'vrei Torah;* she believes we can deliver high holiday talks and impart something of importance to the entire congregation when we are sure we have nothing of importance to say--and we find within ourselves the passion and the purpose to address one another; she believes we can learn Hebrew when we can not even remember where we put our housekeys--and we learn Hebrew; she believes we can sing and be cantor to *ha-minyan*, when our voice warbles uncontrollably in nervousness except in the shower--and we become cantors who lead others in song; she believes we can be president of a 325-member congregation, when we find the charge of 4 people in our own families daunting--and we become presidents; she believes we can live as Jews, when we are content with our own homogeneous assimilation --and we find ourselves living as Jews, with lives richer than we thought possible.

Your energy, your creativity, your vision, your capacity to seize a moment are qualities that are practically legendary about you, Joy. They are qualities that we adore, qualities that have infused excitement into and enlivened our community. They are some of the things that drew some of us to this place. We know that you have wondered, in moments of self-doubt, whether these things are seductive Emerald City lures that dazzle and delight us and leave us dependent on you and your vision of Judaism for sustenance. We wish you to know this, Joy: these **are** among your extraordinary and inspiring talents; these **are** qualities that have challenged us to follow your model and invigorate our ritual observances and saturate them with thoughtfulness and feeling and meaning; these **are** qualities that have awakened us to Judaism's unimagined possibilities and invited us to create our families and our lives in the context of this Judaism; but be assured, Joy: your **true** gift to us these 13 years has been in showing us that **we** always had, each of us, the ruby slippers upon our feet, and that really, we were home already.

May the Place of Promise remain ever within your vision and your grasp...

With great affection and heartfelt wishes,
Joanna Daniel Sheri Michael

Tribute to **Rabbi Lee Friedlander** of the Reconstructionist Synagogue of the North Shore
Rav L'kehilla: Avodah Kedosha
Honoree of the Jewish Reconstructionist Federation
April 6, 2000

He addresses you by name, as you enter the sanctuary 45 minutes late to *Shabbat* morning services. No, it is not a reprimand, and it does not embarrass. It is a welcome, a very personal, and specific welcome, so that you can be a part, immediately, since you have missed the benefit of the warm-up prayers and even much of the *Shaharit* service. He hands you a printed sheet and interrupts himself for 10 seconds to fill you in on what they are discussing, as they study the week's *parasha*. When it is time to read the next passage for study, he calls on you. It is like an embrace that folds you into the center of the *minyan*. Because you have come, he knows that you are ready to be fully present.

He climbs over the backs of the pew seats, stepping on the seats, stepping over congregants' heads, making his way from the back of the sanctuary to the front, in an act that might be just a little sacrilegious, or maybe only bad manners, if our children did this. He is dressed as a yellow M&M, with elfin-like M&M slippers on (as if M&Ms wore such footwear!), and a *schmata* hat that no self-respecting M&M (plain or peanut!) would be caught dead in. He yells *Haman*'s name and spins his oversized grogger with a passion that delights everyone who is a child and everyone who remembers being a child. We imagine he is a little embarrassed each *Purim*, but, nevertheless, he overcomes the natural adult tendency to be reserved and decorous, and outdoes himself in costumes each year, indulging and recreating the powerful connection to childhood, to memory, to celebration, to zaniness, to survival, to Judaism.

He listens intently when he is spoken to, whether the subject is celebration, study, struggle, or loss. In his listening, he is present in the full way in which he invited you to be present on that *Shabbat* morning. There is, for him, no ordinary *B'nai Mitzvah*, no ordinary baby naming, no ordinary wedding, no ordinary life passed. For he sees in each of these, the way in which the moment touches a family, and his words transform the moment so that it becomes a godly moment. He gives this gift to us, whether he sways laughingly with a newly-named, crying baby on his shoulder, or whether he speaks a eulogy, carefully putting together the many pieces of a life passed, so that we who might have been too close, can see with clarity. No, it is not about seeing, really, at all. **He** does the work, the work of listening, of reflecting, our words, feelings, intent, at just such an angle, that we may enter the moment fully—the *Bat Mitzvah* moment, the study moment, the marriage moment, the naming of our baby moment, the funeral moment—and know and feel the most important things that may be known and felt.

It is clear to all of us who journey this path with him, that Lee loves being a rabbi, a *Rav L'Kehillah*, and the work he does for us, with us, among us is, indeed, *Avodah Kedosha*, holy work. For what could be holier than anchoring us to a past replete with powerful, mythic meaning, connecting us to a present in which we are tightly woven and gently held in the threads of community, a community in which Lee teaches us how to share and celebrate the awesome and the ordinary together, and securing our future by teaching and living his splendourous love of the Jewish people.

Tribute to **Nathalie Solzberg** of the Reconstructionist Synagogue of the North Shore
Honoree of the Jewish Reconstructionist Federation
March 29, 2001

Modestly, she would tell you that she just loves children, and that what she does at our synagogue is really no big deal. But we, whose children have had Nathalie, know otherwise. If the word "rabbi" means teacher, then Nathalie is, indeed, a rabbi, for she is, for so many of our children, their first teacher of Judaism. And those of our children who begin their Jewish journeys under Nathalie's loving and protective wing, do not stray far from synagogue or Judaism. They grow up to work in our synagogue office and classrooms, and they go on to become leaders at their campus Hillels. Nathalie might tell you that her pre-Hebrew class is just a nice program, to get our children's feet wet, so to speak. But she would be very wrong. For our children's feet do not get wet. Being in Nathalie's class is like experiencing all the wonders and joys of crossing on dry land. She picks each one of them up, and carries them from their infancies across to the other side, and sets them down on the shores of home. She gives each a passport, and bids them *lech l'cha*, begin at *aleph*, go forth and find your way. But they have already begun before *aleph*. They go forth. And they find their way.

Tribute to **Allan Mendels** Honoree at the 40th Anniversary of the Reconstructionist Synagogue of the North Shore
May 20, 2001

His fingerprint is everywhere where something important is happening in the synagogue. For five years he was a kind of Moses, leading us from Plandome to Adelphi and back again, creating spaces in which we might sanctify our time together, spaces in which we might engage together in prayer. In this role he grew to be an essential member of our community, understanding important things about what makes holiness come about. He held us carefully in time and space, and he grew and changed along with us. While he no longer leads us in our ritual explorations, he continues to hold us, by ensuring that we maintain financial wholeness. In this way, he takes care of our basic needs, so that we and he may continue to tend to our "meta-needs," our journeys together in prayer, study, and mutual caring for one another. Allan also binds us to our "parent" organization, the Jewish Reconstructionist Federation, again, ensuring that we are part of the fertile exchange of thoughtful resources among our sibling congregations.

More important than what he has done, however, is who he is. Allan "moves in" and feels a sense of responsibility for this place, and for all of us who make up this place. He is not content to be a passive recipient of what RSNS offers. He feels, in an almost paternal way, a desire to protect what was created long before he was here. He is a man who comes to the table with distinct opinions, and who listens carefully to what others have to say, and he changes his opinions. He is not afraid of that. He actually loves that—that the RSNS community engages its members to think and to grow.

There is a story that Allan tells, about attending *Shabbat* evening services when he was a young child with his grandfather. For those of us who have sat next to Allan at services, and who have smiled and had to nudge Allan when his gentle snoring deepened into something that might be mistaken for the onset of a new and frightening plague, we should understand that Allan's grandfather once cradled him in his lap and stroked his head, as services grew late and Allan nodded off. There were no reprimands for falling asleep. In fact, his grandfather endorsed this, claiming that one only falls asleep when he is relaxed and comfortable and feels totally at home. His grandfather understood this as a wonderful expression of Allan's comfort in synagogue. We are grateful that this comfort continues! and grateful that Allan never sleeps for long, but tirelessly works to create "home" for all of us.

Tribute to **Arlene Silberzweig** of the Reconstructionist Synagogue of the North Shore
Honoree of the Jewish Reconstructionist Federation
April, 2005

"Living in two civilizations," for some, means feeling neither as fully Jewish nor as wholly American as they would like. Not so for Arlene Silberzweig whose life has exemplified the seamless melding of the deepest foundational principles of Judaism with the loftiest foundational principles of American democracy.

Having held numerous leadership positions, herself, including school board and synagogue president, regional chair of the Jewish Reconstructionist Federation, and member of its national board, Arlene understands that true representative government depends upon clear, full, and honest discourse. She understands that this is not merely conversation about "issues"; rather, it is about the essential questions that define us as human beings: how will we live together, what do we owe to one another, how will we protect and nurture each other and the world that sustains us. Her work on behalf of fellow citizens, advocating for civil rights and affordable housing, and building scholarship foundations, affirms Arlene's position that what is "Jewish" about these questions is indistinguishable from what is "American" about them.

In her passion, Arlene insists that our leaders understand exactly what has been entrusted to them. She will not tolerate "issues" replacing "people"; she will not tolerate easy immediacy replacing sustained vision; she will not tolerate elected officials hiding in offices and becoming complacent or detached from their mission—their sacred mission. Neither will she allow passivity and complacency in us. Arlene builds the types of bridges that ensure that we remain fully aware, and that we, together with our elected officials, remember that the future of our civilization is in our hands.

Tribute to **Rabbi Jodie Siff**
Honoree of the Reconstructionist Synagogue of the North Shore
November 9, 2009

It is not the show-stopping, flamboyant moon, at the peak of its fullness that calls us to gather each month, but the modest, unassuming slim crescent of light that despite its smallness, portends huge promise. It is the perfect symbol for our *Rosh Hodesh* group.

The new moon draws us together, but the promise that is latent in our gathering, is released and harnessed by Jodie. This is what she does: she creates for us a time to pause and breathe and study—a moment not unlike *Shabbat,* that many of us do not otherwise find; she chooses and prepares for us provocative and evocative texts; she helps us find a place into which we might enter those texts; she asks the kinds of questions that stir up, for each of us, the mud that we have allowed, complacently, to settle, so that we can again sift through the Jewish muck or personal muck, find what we have missed, and extract and possess the gold nuggets there for our taking; and, perhaps the hardest and most subtle thing she does, (and she does it so easily, because of who she is, and because of her clarity about what she wants this experience to be for us) is to pull herself into the background and allow each of us, alone, and all of us collectively to explore Jewish meanings, engage each other, and encounter God, whether we wish to or not, over and over, challenging and refining our definitions of this difficult, comforting, essential, primitive, ineffable, elusive Idea. *Rosh Hodesh* is not about Jodie, and she is careful, in an almost unconscious way, that this be so. I imagine the new moon exerting its gravitational pull on us, bringing us, like a tide, together; and I imagine Jodie, as a counterbalance to that pull, nudging us out, getting us started, and, like a good parent and teacher, allowing us to pick our way even if through thorny brambles, letting us test the ground, and find fresh intellectual and emotional Jewish footing that feels, if not solid, then at least possible.

Jodie provides for us a time and a way to honor the dynamic condition of the universe that we see reflected each month in the moon's face, encouraging us to embrace within ourselves this same capacity to change and grow.

For Karen Aaron on the Occasion of Her Retirement from Teaching

In our sleep we could say the words made famous by Dylan, and familiar by Geczik: "The times they are a-changin'."

And usually, without giving it much thought, we agree that this is as it should be, this is a good thing, and we will, like all organisms who survive, adapt.

But, sometimes adapting to changing times requires the sacrifice of things too precious, the giving up of things essential. This might be the reason that, walking past Karen's room we heard...a piano? in a classroom? and the earnest voices of 9 years olds singing *Happy Birthday* or Sousa-songs, or New York city songs, and were transported to a simpler time, a time of our own early school days, a half century ago, when just this type of singing was part of every day. Loving music and loving playing the piano were not personal indulgences; they were part of the gift of passion that Karen imparted to each child, instruction very different from that delivered at a Smartboard, a gift that has been silently and even unknowingly tucked safely into cerebral crenulations, stamping its fossil imprint, to lay dormant for an age and then to be re-discovered when **these** students send **their** 9 year olds off to 4th grade sometime near the year 2055.

Despite changing times, Karen continued to think of script as a thing of beauty, an unmeasureable but vital part of education. I remember loving writing in script, practicing alternative "selves" as I made my writing lean forward or backward. I have read decades of Karen's students' letters in script, and they, too, love this magical adult language opened to them, even in an age when other written languages—IMs and BBMs—abound. Their messages of having loved 4th grade and Mrs. Aaron are enlivened by the loops and chains that create weavings as mystical as the web of Charlotte, or a snowflake, their own hands, like still-unknown Michelangelos, reaching forth to touch a drop from the wellsprings of a creative fount they have barely met. It may be that penmanship fades from our grandchildren's curriculum, that, coming across old "letters" in some desiccated attic envelope, they delight in the quaintness of such old-fashioned writing, but for Karen, that time was not yet, and that loss would not be promoted under her watch.

It was not only love of that old upright, and grand-old-flag anthems, and penmanship, and penpals, and historical fiction that she bequeathed directly to some 1000 children, it was also her understanding that, despite changing times, 9 year olds are still children...that, in fact, they are smack dab in the middle of childhood and, as such, are consolidating competency skills on every front—intellectual, to be sure, but also on landscapes internal and external that would not even begin to bear fruit for many years. No, Karen did not have her head in the sand. She understood that there was something ahead to get prepared for, but she was not willing to have her students skip over this crucial time when Lego-like, brick by small-nubbed brick, they were building selves that they would carry into that next place of their lives. This was a time, once upon a time, when a student, not yet pretty, could feel her own gorgeousness as Cinderella, the lead in her 4th grade play, when students, sated with a chicken dinner from Karen's mother, could play the Beta Max over and over in Karen's living room, figuring out, together, the dance steps for Wizard of Oz. Tests? Oh yes, the state, the district, and the times demanded proof of what was occurring, an achieved number that would quantify the enormous and ineffable changes taking place for these 9 year olds. But, this was a time, the time spent in Karen Aaron's class, when childhood's cornerstones were laid, foundations cemented, when the full flowering of architectural possibilities of the self, could remain in a time still not even dreamt of. Karen understood that it is by slow accretions that human beings emerge, that these fine layered accumulations, like gold leaf, require the subtlest of scales, and that the finest things cannot be measured at all.

Karen has loved Shelter Rock with a reverence that we all reserve for those places and, more importantly, those holy spots of time wherein we have experienced deep and powerful transformation. Since entering our halls at the age of 21, and over the course of these last 38 years in Manhasset, Karen sculpted her life, sharing with us all the years of her coalescing adulthood. While in this place and this time, she has brought into being and given form and substance to the lives of her two daughters, one of whom follows in her footsteps as a teacher, the other following dad's path. In this place and in this time of her life, she has nudged generations of students toward wakefulness, opening them to the world in which they will create the selves they imagine they can be. And, she has enriched us, we who have shared this place and this time with her.

So, I ask us all, especially Rick, Stacy, and Lauren, to raise our glasses as we honor your wife, your mother, our colleague, our friend, a teacher: Karen Aaron.

(November 10,2010)

To My Mother at the Celebration of Her 75th Birthday

Four real scenarios:

October 13, 2002: Dessert is placed in front of us at cousin Seth's wedding. Within 2 minutes we have finished it. I look at my plate, on which remains 3 edge strips of white icing, a pile of whipped cream, and a feeble-looking, out of season strawberry. I have eaten only the small square of chocolate cake that had been nestled within butter-cream walls, and the small scoop of vanilla ice cream. I look at the plate next to mine. It is a near-duplicate of my own: a strip of butter cream icing, a pile of whipped cream, a pale, unripe strawberry. It is a little uncanny: of the 5 dessert items, we have both eaten the same two, in the same way, and left the same three.

September 28, 2002: The boys go shopping for a new cell phone battery. She and I take a walk. She tells me how she can't stand to sit around the house, how she always has to be busy, "futzing," she says. She can be happy cleaning the closets, tending her plants, always, always busy, especially her fingers. In her need for busy-ness, I recognize an almost mirror image of myself. Our dear friends, to this day, recall with bliss, a shared vacation when, having been invaded by an African parasite, I could not move from my bed for an entire week. They will tell you it was the most relaxing vacation they ever shared with us, because I was not orchestrating biking excursions, 5-mile walks around Lake Morey, water-ski escapades, and mandatory afternoon swims.

Any email at any time: "Dear Sher, Just a quickie: on our way to play golf, then doing a dinner party later with 50 people. Running the aquasize class tomorrow morning, then taking a 2 day cruise. Next week will pick up some supplies for the applique class I'm doing. Purim costume party over here the week after, so am busy cooking hundreds of mini empanadillas. Whew, I make myself tired just writing about it all. I need a rest." But we all know she will not take one.

Final scenario: October 13, 2002, Seth's bride Carol offers her marriage vows, which include the following: "And I vow to accept your family as my own." Michael discreetly (well, as discreetly as Michael is able to) leans over to me and whispers: "big mistake! I'm glad that wasn't part of our vows!" I, in turn, lean over to my mother, and repeat Michael's words. She leans to my dad, and passes the message along. The 4 of us have a laugh together. My mother leans back to me and whispers, "Oh, it could be worse." I quip, "Oh, yeah, give me an example." Neither she nor I can think of one. She jokes that this will send me back into analysis for 4 years. I counter with, "no, 10, at least!"

I have known, for some time, that middle age would bring with it hot flashes. I have been prepared for that. No one, however, prepared me for the other middle age scourge---that I would find myself agreeing with my mother about loud music, values of the young, investments, an impending war, politics, and even religion. Each time we visit, we seem to find more and more similarities, and I'm wondering just how it happened that after fighting it so hard for so many years, I have become my mother. Yes, I'm sure there are worse things, though even my mother could not think of them. The jokes we make at one another's expense are not things we used to laugh about 25 years ago. My mother has come a long way!

There is a universal curse that mothers love to cast upon their daughters. "I hope you have one just like you!" I'm pretty sure that I was the recipient at some point in my life of this curse. But, witch though my mother may be, she botched this spell royally. I did not end up with one just like me (which, after all, I don't think would have been so bad—I understand me). The curse got all turned around, and I ended up with one a bit like my mother.

I may regret ever saying this, but perhaps my mother, after all, did not get it so wrong. The curse came out just right, for in coming to love those qualities in Joanna, I was challenged to see them through different eyes in my mother.

This is what I have come to appreciate about my mother. She is impatient to get going. Do not stand in her way. In imitation of my mother, my first words behind the wheel of a car, at the age of 6 in an A & P parking lot were: "Jesus Christ lady! Move it." Yes, move it, for she has things to do and places to go.

My mother speaks her mind. You never have to guess where you stand with her or what she is thinking. It will always be clear.

My mother is a busy woman. She loves being active, productive, creative. There is rarely a moment when she is not doing something—playing golf, tending plants, planning dinner parties, needlepointing, knitting, crocheting, appliqueing, cleaning, reading. My mother is happiest, and paradoxically most relaxed, when she is busy. And how lucky we are, who have been the recipients of her creative, artistic talents: appliqued shirts and sweatsuits, Irish knit sweaters, afghans, cross stitch table cloths, baby blankets, decorated canvas bags, and my favorite, 2* of the most gorgeous and special *tallitot* ever made, that will become my family's heirlooms.

Her mind is as nimble as her fingers. If you've ever watched Wheel of Fortune with her, you will reach the conclusion that for her 80th birthday, we should abandon parties and roasts, and get her onto that show, with all of us cheering her in the audience. She will win big bucks. She can solve those puzzles before any letters are even up!

My mother is a party girl, even at 74¾ . If she cannot find some action, she will make some. *Purim* costume parties in Puerto Rico; an around the world trip when the strange message left on her answering machine had her children convinced that she and my father had "checked out"; a Halloween, 1967. I was 16 and far too old to go trick or treating. She was 39, and far too young to be missing the fun. She pulled me into her youth and we dressed up as farmers in overalls, plaid flannel shirts, and straw hats that we got from God knows where. Later we sat at the kitchen table like sisters, dividing up our goods, trading Good and Plenty for Babe Ruths, Mars bars for Milky Ways; I, setting aside my adolescent coolness for the zaniness that is my mother.

My mother loves to make a statement. I imagine that if she were born 2 generations later, she would be the first among her friends to have a pierced belly button. I'll just pause there for a moment while you all click on the visual for that one! She might have a tattoo, or be jumping from airplanes, like one of her granddaughters and one of her grandsons. But, because she was born in 1927 and not 1987, she had to content herself with putting firecrackers in piles of manure, dying her hair blue, and sewing (and wearing) a formal skirt with the kamasutra positions all over it. I must admit, that her statements were far more original than those of her grandchildren. But, if I had to say just what it was that my mother was making "statements" about, I would say that, like adolescents, her statements are all about celebrations of the body—its activities, its products, its possibilities. And though there was a time that such statements had the power to embarrass me, (I mean, who, at the age of 16, wants to think of her mother like THAT?) I would say now that I love my mother's celebrations of life. After we all had gotten to a certain age, ourselves, my siblings and I used to wonder if our mother would ever grow up. I think the vote is in, folks, as she nears 75; no, she will not, and that single fact, alone, may keep her (and my father), walking and golfing, aquasizing and knitting, cooking and partying, travelling, always, always making new friends and throwing herself wholeheartedly into life for another 20 years. (Of course, now that I've told her it's OK with us if she does these things, she will no longer need to do them!).

While many of my friends are caring for ailing parents, I become aware of how lucky my parents are still to have each other, to be planning, at the ages of 75 and 84, to take 28 hour plane rides half way across the earth, to be well enough and energetic enough to hop in the car and drive 9 hours to attend a graduation one week, and drive 7 more in the opposite direction for another, a week later.

So, mom, here's to dirty jokes that I finally understand, and mother's day gifts that **I** can give **you**, that can actually embarrass you. Here's to whatever antics you have up your sleeve, and here's to your friends and your family who await your next move, who will continue to laugh with you and love you as you bring life our way. Mom, here's to you.

(November 2, 2002)

* A 3rd, mine, was yet to come.

For Zade on His Second *Bar Mitzvah*

(Sheri) Since the limerick style's the thing
To Gene, of thee we sing
In this silly form
That's the Lipstein norm
A few thoughts of your life we will bring.

(Dan) A father he is to four
And Zade to seven more
There's Fred, Rob, Sher, and Sand
Becca, Matt, Bri, and Dan
And Jo and Julie and Lor.

(Jo) And let us not forget the four spouses
Who are far from retiring mouses
Cheryl and Gail now he's got
And Michael and Scott
Who've expanded the Lipstein houses.

(Michael) A brother he had so dear
Their two families did grow up quite near
Gene and Lenny had talks
'Bout life, vegetable gardens, and stocks
We all wish that today he were here.

(Sheri) There's a part of Gene we don't see
Except in limericks, you'll agree
But he once wrote fine rhyme
From a far place and time
In correspondence with cousin Siggy.

(Michael) Years before computers were in
Gene was busy with Fortran programming
Now spreadsheets he'll do
Email grandchildren too
As well as word processing.

(Jo) Those riddles of logic he'll pose
To see how smart you are, we suppose
Bottles, corks, hens, and eggs
Midgets with very short legs
The answer's a nickel, we knows!

(Dan) Gene loves to feel fit as a fiddle
Calisthenics he'd do just a little
He'll touch his arm to his nose
Reach halfway to his toes
And proclaim he is shrunk in the middle.

(Jo) It is a marvelous sight to see
Zade hit a small ball from a tee
The game's sometimes frustrating
Gets him ranting and raving
With his favorite word: "craminy."

(Sheri) When I was a little kid
Going swimming he rarely did
He hated the water
And thought it was smarter
To stay in the shade and keep hid.

(Dan) But now that his head is hoary
And in PR he lives half his story
In the water he goes
Though his limbs be froze
And does aquasize on the pool floor-y.

(Michael) Time waits for no man, regardless of needs
Forget time, it is Lee that he heeds
When she says hey ho
He can be no couch potato
But does whatever to please.

(Sheri) Gene is fond of quoting sages
Who love to speak of ages
He's mesmerized
By Ben Ezra's wise
Words that he finds on the pages.

(Dan) Grow old along with him
He has told us time and agin
For life holds in store
Oh, so much more
The best has not yet been.

(Michael) The correctness of this philosophy
We have witnessed, for we do see
Gene and Lee traipse
To every far place
No time to rest if you're weary.

(Jo) With some words of advice we will hit ya
On this, your second *Bar Mitzvah*
Relax, yourself pace
Admit stress no trace
Over small stuff don't break a *shvit-za.*

(All) Now he's made it to 83
A great milestone, you'll agree
Raise your glasses with me
Together again we will be
When Gene is a hundred and three!

(August 18, 2001)

For Dad's 90th Birthday

"Grow old along with me"
Gene loves this quote, you see
This rhyme that claims the best is yet to be.
This poem Gene would rate
As most things: "only great!"
Though lately questions its veracity.

Browning really did not know
As old he did not grow
With seventy seven years to his life only.
No match is he for Gene
Who's beat him by thirteen
And now might label Browning's words baloney.

If Gene rewrote this ditty
It might sound a mite less pretty
With ninety years to claim that are now his;
And anything he'd give
To remain positive
But his newly written verse might go like this:

Grow old along with me
It's not all it's cracked up to be
This last of life for which the first was made.
With shingles in my chest
Stenosis that bars rest
And hearing naught without a hearing aid.

Yet even with all this
There's nothing he'd want to miss
Another dozen years or more he'd choose to live
And as he's fond of sayin'
As each birthday comes to weigh in:
"Sure beats hell out of the alternative!"

All joking quite apart
I write this from my heart
With love and honor for your life well-lived
And hope that you have known
That from all the seeds you've sown
That good abounds, of this be positive.

So, we will grow old along with you
The best we still will view
Raise your glasses high and drink to dad
And like the poet said
To the years that lie ahead
And to all the ones behind that he has had!

(August 18, 2008)

V. When I Held the Staff

As Vice President of the Congregation, Presenting a *Tzedakah* Box to **Danny Seigerman** on the Occasion of His Becoming a *Bar Mitzvah*

December 2, 1995

Danny,

I'm glad that no one told you this in advance, just how dangerous your *Torah* portion was. Last year's *Bat Mitzvah* had to travel to the Southwest and ascend ladders into suspended Pueblo huts in order to experience first hand what that stairway to Heaven was like, and what it must have felt like to be as an angel, with free access between Heaven and Earth.

I know that you travelled all the way to Israel and faced certain death, hanging, at nightfall, suspended from our beloved Arbel Cliff, wrestling not, I suspect, with an angel, and uttering not, I suspect, very holy words. Studying *Torah* in our congregation, is truly a hands-on, or should I say, feet-on experience!

So I hope Rabbis Joy and Lee will warn the fated person whose *Bar* or *Bat Mitzvah* falls on *Vayetze* next year. He should know that he's in for a harrowing summer vacation!

As you know, Danny, it is our congregation's custom to give a *tzedakah* box on the occasion of our members becoming *Bar or Bat Mitzvah*. I have been asked why we don't give something "prettier" like *Shabbat* candlesticks. I must admit that I have even asked myself that. But in thinking about giving you this gift today, I think I understand why this is our congregation's gift of choice. It is easy to see and enjoy the beauty of *Shabbat* lights, as they are in our own home. But it is more difficult to see the beauty that you will spread in the world--far outside of your vision--when you live a life characterized by *tzedakah*.

For today, I can think of *tzedakah* as being like those huge metal staples carefully placed into Arbel rock. Those metal staples that held you on those rocks were also the things that allowed you to discover something essential about yourself--that you have strength inside yourself that you never imagined, and that you are surrounded by people who will help you find that strength inside, who will coach you and cheer you and stay with you as you tentatively or confidently place each foot along your path--whether that path be vertical or horizontal!

Whether *tzedakah* is given in the form of money, or in the form of books, or time, or food, or work, its goal is something that you found while suspended on cliffs above the *Kinneret* as the darkness of night rapidly approached one August night when you were still 12 years old. This goal of *tzedakah* is a double gift--of believing in oneself and finding in oneself courage to meet life in all its fullness, and of trusting in the loving support of community.

On behalf of our congregation, Danny, I am honored to present you with this *tzedakah* box, so that you may give to others, in some form, some portion of the gifts that you have discovered for yourself. And, to get you started, the Lindner family has made a modest, but truly heartfelt donation--of a half *shekel*!

As President of the Congregation, Presenting a *Tzedakah* Box to **Jenna Korobow** on the Occasion of Her Becoming a *Bat Mitzvah*

Jenna,

Your *Torah* portion describes what it is that God does that comprises the creation of the world. Essentially, what God does is to take nothingness, a void, chaos, and day by day pull from deep inside, definition, so that each piece of the world is given its own meaning and given its place within the scheme of the whole world.

It is this same work that we ask you to do in giving you this *tzedakah* box. We ask you to be mindful of the fact that there are many whose lives are characterized by chaos, by loss of meaning, by lack of defining values and supports, by large spaces of darkness and voids of many sorts. In choosing a life of *tzedakah,* you will do the work that God did in those first, prototypic 7 days: you will take your own sensitive awareness... that generosity of yours that is captured in picture after picture in my Israel photo album, of you taking care of the youngest members of our travelling family...you will take these gentle qualities that already define and identify you, and you will create somethingness from nothingness, you will impart meaning and worth for someone whose life is sorely missing these things that have so early been nourished in you.

Sometimes you will do this by giving food, sometimes by giving money that supports causes like *Yad Lakashish*, the Lifeline for the old that we visited in Jerusalem that employed the elderly, so they could continue to feel meaning and worth in their lives through the creative expression of their work; and sometimes *tzedakah* will lie in small, seemingly unimportant acts of kindness and of love that you will do for a friend, for a sister, for a parent, for a stranger.

So, Jenna, on behalf of the congregation I give you this *tzedakah* box, to place on your table, as a reminder of living a life of rightness, of continuing the work of creation that you read about today, of doing the things that God did "in the beginning," of giving definition, meaning, a place to start, a beginning to all of those fellow human beings whose lives, knowingly or unknowingly, you will touch. *Mazel Tov.*

As President of the Congregation, Presenting a *Tzedakah* Box to **Cary Adickman** on the Occasion of His Becoming a *Bar Mitzvah*

September 7, 1998

Cary:

Your *Torah* portion, in some ways, is the perfect *parasha* for you to have read to become a *Bar Mitzvah*.

Ki Tavo speaks of that time just before one of the great mythic transitions for the Israelites. Like you, these past months and weeks, they are preparing to cross over, to confront the moment when they will be given the gift of a canvas--a canvas that is filled with promise, on which they will envision and create their future in a land that is their own.

In the space of these last 2 hours, you have telescoped the Israelites' experience and you are now a few weeks ahead of them, and you now know what exhilaration and fulfillment lies ahead for them when they will make their crossing, for you have just made yours.

Today, I think you, too, have been handed symbolically a canvas and been given a glimpse, like Moses soon will be given, of the land that lies before you and of its promises and possibilities. This land before you contains fertile soil in which tender roots have already been planted for you and grown strong for you.

And at this moment, you are, indeed, as the Israelites, for with the gift of this day come prescriptions about what must be done with this gift. The land is rich enough, **they** are told, to provide for fruits for themselves as well as the strangers who are in their midst. This is true of the "land" that you inherit today--the land that is yourself, on which already grow deeply rooted trees of family, fragrant blossoms of Judaism, and bubbling streams of music. So, cultivate your fertile land well--keep it watered and weeded so that it flourishes with the full bounty of its promise, for yourself and for all who will casually or consciously walk upon the land that is Cary Adickman.

On behalf of our congregation, I present you with this gift of a *tzedakah* box. Like the land, like becoming *Bar Mitzvah*, it is also a gift that carries with it prescriptions about what you must do.

As you stand this moment on the shores of your Promised Land, and you know the sweetness of the milk and honey that flows so freely here, may you spread that sweetness and bounty so that others may know some measure of the fullness that is yours. *Mazel Tov*.

President's *Yom Kippur* Address to the Congregation of the Reconstructionist Synagogue of the North Shore 5757/1996

Recently at a Board meeting in which we were discussing the upcoming 36th anniversary of our congregation's incorporation, someone bemoaned the fact that we did not have a history written down of our congregation. This fact seemed especially poignant, in light of the loss of several founding members this past year. Rabbi Lee interjected that it was not surprising that we did not have such a history written down, as our founding members were not ones to sit around and reminisce about the "good old days," but rather were people whose visions carried them ever forward.

There are two parts to this brief and seemingly offhand interchange that to me are very significant. The first part pertains to the kind of community that we sustain here. It seems that there is always a tension within each of us (and sometimes among us) between our desire to look back and hold onto what we most cherish, and a knowledge, more like faith, that we must let go, move on, and trust that what we have been given, have created, and have to give will be safeguarded and cherished equally (even if differently) by the future.

This conflict of letting go and continuing on is one we recognize as our children grow up and as we grow up with them; but it is also the same conflict that characterizes our congregation in **its** maturational process. Certainly, we must not let go of the values that steer us, but equally certainly, we must embrace the fact that we now steer ourselves through different waters.

As a congregation we are no longer in the same place that we were even 5 years ago. Some think this is bad--that we have lost something along the way. Of course we have lost something along the way, just as we lose the precious, quiet intimacy of midnight feedings and the cuddled comforts of bedtime stories. Our families no longer spend their vacations or weekends at the same familiar park or beach as we once did. Yes, we lose much. But if we try to make time stand still, we accrue much greater and more significant loss.

And what are our recompenses? We need only look at the program calendar--at the breadth and depth and diversity of cultural offerings available nearly every week to all of us; we can also look at the eagerness, despite overwhelming intimidation, of our *B'nai Mitzvah* women and families, to tackle *Torah* and enrich our *Shabbats* by sharing their study with all of us; we can look further at adult members who decide finally to learn Hebrew, or our younger members who challenge themselves beyond what already seemed impossible, and determinedly learn the entire *Shabbat* liturgy; or we can remember what this *bima* looked like for the 5th *Torah aliyah* on day 1 of *Rosh Hashanah* last week. Who could look at this *bima* full of wriggling, adorable young life, at their families, many of whom have chosen to belong to and support our synagogue long before their children will enter Hebrew school...who could look at all of this and feel that we have made a wrong turn?

And so, as a congregation it seems we have no choice but to continue to grow up, to adapt to our changes, no...to create ourselves anew in the very process of these changes, the way our toddlers, our adolescents, our adult children, and the way we, ourselves, must continually do. It is thus that we all participate in the ever-evolving civilization that is constituted by our own families and that extends to and defines this larger community that we share.

This is what I have learned from our founding members

and from Lee's observation about them. I am often surprised and always inspired that our members who are in their 60s, 70s, 80s, and yes, 90s have **our** children's Jewish welfare as their priority. This is the kind of commitment that allows our community to perpetuate itself, where those who receive are eager, in their time, to exchange places with those who have given, and where value and meaning exist on all sides.

The second reaction to Lee's comment about our congregation being forward-looking is a more personal one. You see, when the first person bemoaned our lack of written history, it was easy to agree. Yes, what a shame that we don't have that. But, when Lee contributed his observation, it seemed that **he** was right. At first I felt silly to have ping-ponged so easily, agreeing with one and then with the other, seemingly opposite view. I often find, in study and even in casual conversation in the synagogue, that what I think I am certain about is turned on its head by others who are also thinking about an issue. This is one of the beauties and legacies of our community--that it engages me in thoughtful discourse, and I find myself growing when I didn't know that I needed to grow anymore.

When I came into this community 10 years ago, no one criticized me for not being the right kind of member, or for not having a clue about what Reconstructionism was; no one demanded that I be more capable of understanding commitment and participation in community than I was. But the opportunities for growing and changing were, and continue to be, all around me. This is the community that I was welcomed into, and it is this value that I feel a commitment to preserving as our community continues to renew itself in meeting the challenges that lie ahead of us.

What are these challenges that lie ahead for us? I think there is, and always has been, only one challenge and that is to continue "to create a spiritually fulfilling, intellectually enriching, and emotionally connected center for Jewish individuals and families to express themselves within the context of Jewish life."

In the context of this ever-present goal, we will, within the next month, find ourselves in changed circumstances from what we have grown accustomed to over the past 10 years, as first Rabbi Joy, and then Rabbi Lee, begin their sabbaticals.

I have heard from a number of you a variety of responses to what lies ahead this year for us. Some are nervous, wondering how we will be able to manage. Some, especially those who have been through many stages of our congregation's development, not only recognize this change as temporary, but embrace it as an opportunity placed before us to recreate and discover new things about ourselves through maximum lay participation.

Will the Rabbis' temporary absence from us be a loss? Without a doubt. But loss **can** be a powerful catalyst that impels us to move in some direction; in the best of cases, it calls forth from us our own creativity and ability to step in and fill from within ourselves what has been lost. Joy's and Lee's sabbatical, which we have been preparing for for the past year, has already engaged the congregation in important and stimulating self-understanding. We have been forced, once again, to contemplate and attempt to articulate our values, structures, and unspoken assumptions. For myself, this has been another of those ping pong experiences, where my first ideas quickly became **only** the first in a process of change. Our first response, my own included, to the dilemmas posed by our Rabbis' sabbaticals was to seek a traditional solution. We would be missing a Rabbi so we would need to replace the role with another Rabbi. In this automatic assumption of role replacement, we were blinded to the Reconstructionist possibilities which were at the heart of our situation. Necessity, however, soon demanded that we re-own our Reconstructionism--that we rearticulate, reassess, and revise what we thought we needed.

We would probably have been satisfied with either of the two talented and sincere substitute Rabbis had either chosen to join us. As neither did, we have embarked upon a different path, one that is replete with possibilities for growth and even greater enrichment. We are prepared to meet the challenge of our Rabbis' temporary absence with talent, enthusiasm, and love, all of which come from within our own community and from our new additions.

We welcome aboard, as the director of synagogue education, Phyllis Meyers, who is a learned woman who brings great energy, passion, and abundant ideas. Phyllis has aready begun in her role as principal of the entire Hebrew school; as co-ordinator of *B'Yahad*, our continuing alternative learning program in which families study together; as overseer of Bagels on the Bima, our monthly *Shabbat* experience for pre-schoolers and their families; and as co-ordinator of all intergenerational educational programs.

We also welcome Derek Miodownik who assumes a new role with us as teacher and director of our upper school. As a person who grew up in our congregation, Derek embodies the process and the value that I described above: like metamorphic layers over time, he has taken what was given him and transformed it at the same time that it was transforming him. He has crossed that threshold of exchange, and in Derek, our children now become the fortunate beneficiaries of our own congregation's reconstructed gifts.

And we are fortunate to have Sheila Case, a talented cantorial student who will help our *B'nai Mitzvah* students gain comfort and familiarity with liturgy, learn the musical cantillation system, and prepare their *Torah* and *Haftara* portions.

We are in the process of change, make no mistake. We do not yet have a concensus on what the shape of our solutions might be. One very challenging and exciting possibility is that next year for High Holidays we may turn to ourselves in large measure to lead our community in service, prayer, and renewal. We invite any of you who has an interest to participate in the many and complex decisions and processes that will be involved in this endeavor.

Know that I do not expect this year to be completely smooth sailing. But, then, our congregation never did go in for smooth sailing. Even on the calmest *Shabbat* evening, we can always count on one of our rabbis, or someone from the congregation to stir up the still waters. Sometimes I want to hang on tight and not allow myself to become unseated by these waves; but most of the time I find that taking the plunge, even when I didn't want to, is refreshing. We are a congregation that has never shied away from challenges, that in fact, comes alive in the face of new possibilities. We are a congregation that demands, of our Rabbis and ourselves, that we continually re-examine our understanding of Judaism, and re-create ourselves and our places as Jews. Few of us would feel content with tossing the same crumbs, the same dissatisfactions, into the same stream this year as we did last. And we must not lose sight that beyond renewing **ourselve**s as a community, we must also extend our reparative resources to the world outside of our own secure walls. These are not only Rabbinic values that have been gracefully handed to us; these are **our** ideals--they belong very much to us.

I have heard Rabbi Joy say, and I am sure I will misquote her, or at best misrepresent her, that the goal of the synagogue and rabbis should be to make themselves obsolete, unnecessary-- that the primary conveyors of Jewish life, learning, and values should be the family. Believe me, I do not look forward to Rabbis becoming obsolete or unnecessary. For me, teachers throughout my life have been makers of maps that have allowed me to chart the course of my life in new and unexpected directions; our rabbis have been cartographers *par excellence,* and I sometimes don't even recognize the "me" who is standing here, and who is a traveler in this Jewish terrain.

But it is not only Rabbis Joy and Lee who have helped me chart this new course in my life. This congregation--you, especially--have taught me much and given me Trip-tiks to guide my way. You: who years ago welcomed me so enthusisastically into the *Torah* study group, long before I was ready to join the *Torah* study group; you: who paid a *shiva* call to our home when Michael's father died, though you hardly really knew us; you: who dropped me a note just to say you enjoyed our conversation at *oneg* the other night; you all: whom I have watched or experienced do those things that may seem so small and yet are the seeds from which all that is really human springs.

My best teachers are not those who have given me knowledge, alone, but those who impart their humanity and their precious gift of passion-- those ever-renewable energy sources--so that I may continue to explore and travel and discover even in their absence. I, who have an infamously horrendous sense of direction, begin this new year knowing that we have maps and sextants, that we have among us good map readers, and some who know the way without even looking at maps, and some who prefer guided tours. I welcome this journey with you all, and though I will probably lose my way in the parking lot tonight, I'm pretty sure that together through this next year we will find each other as we find our way.

I wish you all a *Shana Tova.*

The circumstances of our Rabbis' sabbaticals necessitated that our congregation make decisions about how Rosh Hashanah *services would be conducted that year. A group of approximately 50 congregants worked on these services for nearly a year. The following is an account of that process.*

Cast Out, Or So It Seemed

Out of our ontogenetic pasts
Which often deal with loss
In raw ways,
We responded:
We felt abandoned, like Hagar,
Cast out, or so we imagined,
Not like Ishmael, the child,
But in need, nonetheless,
And fearful.

But we remembered
That we had been given
Bread and a skin of water,
No minimal provisions these
But the sustenance of life,
Food enough until we could find
More for ourselves.

A story is told in generations later
That the sea did not part
Until one person stepped a foot into it.
Not from the shores do such wonders happen.
Sanctification does not give itself to the edges of experience.
The sea did not transform,
Nor did we
Until we entered.

And what we learned we already knew:
That our path had been cut long before us
By a mythic river of wisdom and necessity;

That the best choice of place
For the road we would lay down
Was as close to the river as possible,
For it has made its way immemorially,
Carving itself through time, ages before we came.[1]

And we learned that we might find ourselves,
Like Hagar, in a desert, no oasis within our reach,
Thinking we might have to put aside our charge,
Worried of its survival;
Or we might find ourselves,
Like Isaac, atop a mountain,
Bound by our parent's dream
And simultaneously released from it,
Ensured of our survival;
Or we might find ourselves
Like Abraham, needing in the end
To return to our people,
Survival, alone, not having been enough.

Like Hagar, like Isaac, like Abraham
We journeyed our course,
Knowing, as they knew, the
Treacherous intersection—
The moment in which cleaving and sundering
Are indistinguishable,
Ready, as they were,
To follow paths set for us by inevitabilities,
To set out with hands that were not empty,
To lay down a new stone or two along our way
In places where old ones, now obscured by soil or time,
Had left their imprint,
To follow the river as we wandered in deserts and in mountains
Until we found our way back home.

(Spring, 1997)

[1] *I am indebted to the poetry of Edwin Muir for its rich elucidation of how the mythic and timeless (the river) is the background that informs the 'drama' of our time-bound lives (the road), and to Helen Gardner's* ***Edwin Muir:*** *(W.D. Thomas Memorial Lecture) Cardiff, 1961, for its elaboration of this imagery.*

President's *Yom Kippur* Address to the Congregation of the Reconstructionist Synagogue of the North Shore 5758/ 1997

It is a long way from *Eden* to *Canaan*. And there is a problem. *Eden*, really, is unremembered, as it was only ever briefly and dimly perceived, in the first place. The vision that we carry of it is one that was largely created by us, later. And *Canaan*? What do we know of *Canaan*? We are never really permitted to see it, and so here, too, our vision is of our own creation. Ah, but the journey--that we know. It is the journey to which we are to attune ourselves--that is our business.

And what do we do as we sojourn from one self-created place of vision to another? We do what those who have gone before us have done.

Like Eve, we hunger for knowledge. We study together, we desire to know, to understand, to appreciate. In our seeking, we come to learn that knowledge almost always means that we must pass through a gate--sometimes a gate that opens upon wonderful new vistas, and sometimes a gate that shuts us out of a comfortable place of pleasureable innocence we had come to feel as home--yet still we hunger and still we seek.

Like Abraham, we confront impossible decisions. Sometimes we follow and allow ourselves to be led, eager to suspend our own consciousness; and sometimes we look actively for signs that will guide us in our decisions. Like Abraham, we look around us, to take in information that might at first glance seem unmeaningful; we look again and again, trying mightily to understand what we are to make of a ram in a thicket.

Like Jacob, we wrestle, trying always to turn into angels that with which we struggle.

Like *Nahshon*, we have learned that the sea does not part until one person steps a foot into it. Not from the shores do such wonders happen; sanctification does not give itself to the edges of experience. The sea does not transform, nor do we, until we enter.

Like Miriam, we play music and sing and dance together. This, to raise our spirits and gladden our hearts and allow us to revel and give thanks for arriving together in safety and health.

Like the tribal leaders charged in *Devarim*, we make laws and decisions that we hope will allow us to govern ourselves well, so that we can remain together, stronger as a community than each of us, alone, better as a community than each of us, alone, yet aware, in any moment, of any one of us, alone.

Like the tribes we bring food offerings. We give to one another baskets of good wishes to mark another year of our traveling together. And, although I have been told that I should never trust my culinary instincts, I am pretty sure that a miracle like manna is in these baskets--that the honey cake might very well still be fresh when we reach our destination! And we try to remember, as our prototypic travelers before us were instructed, to set aside food for those without.

Like the Israelites, we turn to our "priests," our rabbis for blessings. Yes, we have been taught by them that it is we who are the source of blessings to one another, yet still we turn and seek this, for in our teachers, our understandings are deepened and our spirits nourished in ways we can not always define or articulate.

So, it is a long way from *Eden* to *Canaan,* and the distance we have left to travel is like an asymptotic line, ever closer, but never really meant to intersect. When the *Torah* ends, we have set neither foot nor eyes upon the land to which we have headed all those years. Only Moses has been granted a vision and this is as close as any of us is permitted. And after all, what would we do if we ever actually got there? We would do what we do now...we would continue this business of learning together, of living together, of loving together, trying with each new opportunity to get it a little more right. The journey, after all, is all.

Last *Kol Nidre*, we ended our addresses to you by saying that we **welcomed** our journey together; this year, after having served a year as your presidents, we are compelled to say...that we **cherish** this journey together. We know that it is your wisdom, your instincts, your generosity of spirit that show us the way. And we know, again, in this moment, what we had already known--that this is a community whose integrity touches us deeply, a community who engages itself with purpose and passion and decency in decisions small and large about which direction is the way to *Canaan*.

As we begin 5758, we continue together along our way, within us...always *Eden*, and before us ever...the place of Promise.

President's Address to the Congregation of the Reconstructionist Synagogue of the North Shore Congregational Meeting, June 17, 1998

There was a moment, sometime about a week before each of my children was born, that I sat on a couch and cried with fear that I did not know how to be a mother. In some enormous monsoon of hormonal activity, I felt overwhelmed at what was about to happen in my life. One would have thought that by the second time, I would not have experienced this--that by then I would have known that I **did** know how to be a mother. But, of course, I only knew how to be Dan's mother--I did not know how to be a mother to this other, unknown child, or a mother of two children together. And I only knew how to be a mother of a child up to the age of three--beyond that, I was as lost as any brand new mother.

So, how did I learn how to be a mother? How does any of us learn this? We learn how to be parents from our children. If we listen and watch with inner ears and eyes, we come to understand what they are telling us about themselves, and what they are telling us about what they need us to do for them. And perhaps, most importantly, we come to accept that we do not know the outcomes of our decisions until after we have made them. We make our best guess, with an accumulation of limited information, and we say "yes" when "no" would have felt much safer, or we say "no," when we wished we had had the courage and trust to have said "yes." Our decisions often feel like leaps of faith, and we must wait, sometimes for quite a while, before we know whether our judgment and our faith were right or not. And, so, it seems, we can only ever be sure of our mothering of the past--what we decided yesterday or last week, we can say, worked, or not; what we will have to decide tomorrow is likely to feel as fraught with uncertainty as our first maternal decision.

For Ellen and me, being entrusted with the well-being of this community has not been so different from this. For me, especially, I knew that I did not know how to do this. My inexperience scared and humbled me. But, I listened and watched, and little by little I learned from you what was required. Over these two years, we have been to the emergency room together, we have struggled with identity issues, we have bushwhacked new trails, without the certainty that these would lead us where we thought we should be going, we have taken, together, leaps of faith, hoping that we could find, in where we were at any one time, the subsequent clues to where we needed to go. We have said "yes" together, when "yes" felt full of risk, but perhaps full of possibility, as well; and we have said "no" together, when "no" meant closing a door, but, perhaps, a door that we were not ready, just yet, to open. As with parenting, certainty has not been a commodity that we have had the luxury of trading in. And, as with parenting, we have been given the gift of growing together.

We are grateful for the opportunity to have cared closely for this congregation, for the opportunity to have continued to learn about ourselves and our place within this community. I am grateful to Ellen for asking me to join her in this venture, which, like parenting, has presented us with both challenges and with a profound sense of respect for what we are a part of.

To Trudy and Linda and Julie, under your watchful care, may we go from change to change, from strength to strength, within us, always Eden, and before us, ever, the place of Promise.

Upon Being Honored by the Federation of Reconstructionist Congregations and *Havurot*

April, 1995

When I first walked through the doors of the Reconstructionist Synagogue of the North Shore in 1986, it was with selfish purposes, alone. I was there so that **it** would give something to my children. I did not really understand what the **it** was that would be doing the giving, or what the **it** was that would be given. I did not think about, or know, or understand that coming to the synagogue would entail caring about the other people who also happened to come there. Even as I participated over the years, I did so in order to change things so that the synagogue could continue to give what I thought my family needed. It was only gradually that I came to love this congregation, and only inadvertently that I found myself, in the process of meeting my own family's needs, caring about more than that. I continue to demand a great deal of this community-- more than I ever knew I would want from a religious community. But, gradually, I have come to understand that what I want for my family--the **it**--is that we embrace this community, accepting the responsibility and challenges it demands of us, and the enrichment and fulfillments it offers us.

Upon Being Honored by United Jewish Appeal

April 27, 1999

Since UJA so generously offered our congregation a Jewish continuity grant four years ago, I would like to address my comments to the issue of Jewish continuity.

I have a somewhat checkered relationship with Jewish continuity. Thirteen years ago, when my family and I first entered this synagogue, I did not know what Jewish continuity meant. I do not believe I had ever heard those words. And if I had heard them, I would have dismissed the idea as parochial. My family was dabbling in Judaism; our stay was to have been temporary--just so long as our then 5 year old son was interested in Bible stories. Judaism and this synagogue met a need, and we would stay as long as it continued to do so.

Ten years ago, I had probably heard of continuity, but did not care to give it much thought. We were in the midst of experiencing great pleasure and fulfillment in our involvement in being Jewish, but the idea of this pleasure, as well as the idea of continuity made us squirm. We still thought of ourselves as people who did not go in for this kind of thing, and really, in the larger scheme of things this being Jewish wasn't so important. We looked away from continuity, which tiptoed behind us, keeping a safe distance.

Five years ago, we looked the idea of Jewish continuity in the face, but we challenged it at the same time that it challenged us. While most identified Jews took this as a given, that survival and continuance of the Jewish people was a necessity, we asked, "why?" **feeling** that we were the recipients of something precious, but not understanding how this had come about in our lives, especially since we had intentionally avoided it for so long, and we still resisted its tug.

Nevertheless, we engaged ourselves in the struggle to articulate what was becoming so clear to us as a family (whether we liked it or not)--that in addition to pleasure, Judaism and our participation in it was allowing us to touch inner places that were not reachable outside of Jewish ritual time; Judaism was giving us a landscape in which to define our lives, a landscape of depth that extended far beyond the dimensions we could create for and by ourselves; Judaism was allowing us to feel a sanctity in our lives and a desire and necessity to extend that beyond ourselves.

And where are we now with this idea of Jewish continuity? We look at our son, who feels that being fluent in Hebrew is, for him, a Jewish imperative, that will narrow the gap between him, as an American Jew, and the larger "family" of his people; we are moved by his desire to step into the sea, as it were--not to remain on the edges of experience. We look at our daughter, for whom there are two odious experiences in life: the first is singing alone in front of people (so odious is this that she dropped out of high school choir because she would have to sing twice a year alone in front of the teacher); and the second is waking up before 1:00 on a Saturday. Yet, every other Saturday morning, (at 10 AM) you will find her standing amidst the *Haminyan* group, leading them in *Shabbat* prayer, and feeling that she wants to do this as service to this community. We are inspired by **her** ability to find a way for the sea to part. And then, there is Michael, who, in the midst of being the standard bearer for a group that might be called "They Who Are Disdainful and Contemptuous of Organized Religion," has just accepted the nomination, along with Lee Parker, to serve as President of the congregation for the next two years. Now, while I won't go so far as to assert that this is irrefutable evidence of the existence of God, I must concede that something on the order of miraculous is happening here!

So, it is no longer possible for me to resist the idea that

Jewish continuity is important. My life, and that of my family, has been so unfathomably deepened and expanded and enriched by being fully Jewish, that I support it even without fully understanding it. I have heard, often enough, that the three experiences that contribute most powerfully to Jewish continuity are Jewish summer camps, Passover *seders*, and trips to Israel. I am trying to figure out what it is that these provide, that our *B'Yachad* program, as a fabulous model of family participation in Judaism, also provided. Although I have not devoted nearly as much time to thinking about this as many of you have, I think that the power of these experiences is that they provide extended ritual time, ritual time that becomes an accumulation of transformative moments, moments in which we feel ourselves as different from the selves we have known, moments in which we feel the potential for our relationship with the world and with others in the world to be different, as well. I think that Jewish continuity occurs when our experience of being Jewish is large enough to enable us to locate ourselves, both communally and individually in a past that would seem to have nothing to do with us, and in a future that is not at all predictable. I think Jewish continuity also occurs when our experience of being Jewish is small enough for us to find ourselves, both individually and communally, in this present moment.

I am grateful to be the recipient of this UJA honor. But, I am not being modest when I say that this really belongs to you...to Lee, to Joy, and to all of you, for embracing my family and me wherever we were, for challenging us to go forth and explore and discover and create anew, and for rejoicing with us at every step along our way.

VI. The Ram In the Thicket

The Place

A long time ago
it was an ordinary place
where a father took his son
to murder him.

It has never been clear
whether the place became other-than-ordinary
because of the intended murder
or,
because the murder did not take place.

Thirty-eight centuries later
we are no clearer:
whether we can return this place
to an ordinary place
releasing it from its fetters of holiness,
like that father long ago
released his son,
or,
whether we must keep this place
a sacred place
celebrating the original intention there,
murder,
faith.

(July 26, 2000)

Published in *Jewish Women's Literary Annual*, Vol 7, 2006, p. 255

Abraham's Wisdom

Yes, Abraham almost did it.
He almost sacrificed his son for the sake of his God.
He came so close.
But he didn't.

In the end, he looked around
and found a way not to have to do it.
He found the ram in the thicket
and knew that it would do as well.
No! It was by far the better choice.

And we, who have revered or criticized Abraham's blind faith
for thirty eight hundred years,
will we, in the end, be as careful as he?
Will we look in every bush and tree
for the ram
that will save us from sending our sons up the mountain
with the firebrands of their own destruction strapped to their
    backs?

While you prepare to sally forth,
carried by what feels like a holy wind at your back,
I will not turn my ear to that god,
but frantically will I search
in the thorny, tangled brush:
"Oh, ram, please show yourself,
before it is too late!"

(September 20, 2001)

Appeared in the Reconstructionist Synagogue of the North Shore
Rosh Hashanah supplement of readings 5763/2002, Reading 13

Published in *Jewish Women's Literary Annual* Vol 7, 2006, p. 256

Isaiah's Return

Not ploughshares?
Then beat your swords directly into coffins.
Fill them with the shredded flesh of your sons,
and bury them deep.

Then go to the scorched places
that once housed your holy shrines,
and pray from the desiccated hollows
that once held your human heart.

Offer your prayers to whomever you think hears them,
and pray for a good harvest
of that which you have sown:
jagged fields of sword blades
and hectares of bloated coffins.

Or, are there among you
any with courage enough
to sow otherwise,
so that from those dead places
of rust and lead
will spring instead
blades
of grass?

(April 3, 2002)

Appeared in the Reconstructionist Synagogue of the North Shore
Rosh Hashanah supplement of readings 5769/2008, Reading 8

Published in *Jewish Women's Literary Annual*, Vol 7, 2006, p. 259

The following 10 pieces were written about the events of the school year 2001-2002. These events began with September 11th, during which 9 children at the Shelter Rock Elementary School in Manhasset, NY lost their fathers, staff members lost brothers, fathers, sons, and many other families lost first and second degree relatives, and friends. Later in the year, other tragedies befell students and families in our community.

Two Days After September 11th: (delivered to the faculty of Shelter Rock Elementary School)

It is good for us to come together…for many reasons. There are our practical questions:

--What do I say when a child asks if we are going to be bombed in Manhasset?
--How do I handle the 9 year old boys who parade their bravado, acting as if this is cool?
--What do I say when a child asks during a group discussion if their classmate's father is dead?
--What will we do when, finally, we know of someone in this community's bad news?

But, there are other reasons, besides the practical, for us to be together. As some of us manage 25 children in our classes, and some of us try to oversee 400 children at our combined grade levels, and some of us touch base with nearly all 760 children as they filter through our specials, and some of us attempt to keep the entire ship afloat and sailing smoothly, we forget that it is not only our children who need tending. We, too, are scared and off balance. We, too, will feel, all of a sudden, out of nowhere, a bottomless exhaustion, even though we might have slept the night before. We, too, feel the need to cry and hug one another in relief and release when we tell each other of the narrow escape of a brother, a husband, a friend. We, too, are shaken by the continual gnaw of anxiety and a feeling of dread because Connie has not yet heard from her son, and Robyn's son has not heard from his dear friend. We are terrified and we are in need. Even if our families and friends are unharmed, there is still darkness around us, and we grope toward one another to help find our way.

While yesterday was fairly quiet, and most of us managed OK, it is likely that in the days and weeks to come we will know of loss—of losses—very close to home. There will be so much that will be needed from us, as some children deal with very personal loss, and others absorb their classmates' tragedies through their own young and often fragile filters. Many children will be faced with the unimagineable, in terms that evoke their—and our—most primal fears.

And so, it is good to come together, to share what we know, to sip coffee, to rest a hand upon a colleague's arm, to offer our strength, to take what we need from each other. In our small world of Shelter Rock, we do all this so that we can take care of the children. But in the larger world, we do this for one another to begin to repair what has been broken, to affirm that life prevails.

(September 13, 2001)

I Pledge Allegiance

It has been a long time since I have pledged allegiance to my flag. I suppose that most adults do not have a daily opportunity to do this childhood ritual. But, it is different with me. I work in an elementary school where this is the first welcoming remark of each morning. I am often in my office beginning to return parent phone calls or sorting through what must be gotten to that day when the "announcements" come on. Sometimes, however, I am in a classroom talking with a teacher when the pledge is recited over the loudspeaker by a different student each morning. When I am in a classroom, I stand quietly in the back. I do not put my hand over my heart. I say no words. If I am near students I will assume the correct posture. I am aware of the necessity of being a role model for the students. I may even mouth the words. But I do not utter the words.

I cannot remember when I stopped saying the pledge, and I am trying to figure out now why I stopped. It had something to do with not pledging myself to an icon. It had something to do with being uncomfortable with that "one nation under God" phrase, when we are a nation that is, itself, pledged to separate religion from state. It probably had something to do with the fact that since my late adolescence, in 1969, it has not been cool to be or feel patriotic.

I still feel this cautiousness in pledging myself to the flag. It feels so easy to fall into the comfortable group rituals of our culture at this time. I am moved by the abundance of flags affixed to homes, cars, storefronts, and those smaller red, white, and blue ribbons that lie so close to human hearts. I want to join in with my own displays of patriotism, and I fear this impulse, at the same time that I want to be carried by its tides.

I think that these justifications for withholding myself from being an average American persisted for a long time because of one particular fact of my life (beyond simple immaturity). I have been given the gift of being allowed to take for granted my comfortable way of life, which has never been directly threatened. I am chastened, as I recall Cauchon's question in Bernard Shaw's *St. Joan*: "Must then a Christ perish in torment in every age to save those that have no imagination?"

Well, yes, I admit that I, and probably some others, too (although not everyone), required an apocalyptic reality to supply what a poor imagination has failed to enlighten. Listening to old men's voices break with emotion when they talk about America, its freedoms and opportunities, was not enough for me. In simple terms I have been deficient. But there is more. Not only have I been complacent in my enjoyment of the freedoms of my life, but I have also been critical of the country that nourishes and protects these comforts for me. That, too, is partially a remnant of a lingering adolescence that often has the luxury and privilege to reject the very things and people that support and nurture it.

I once thought that burning the flag was an acceptable expression of criticism. It has taken a long time, but I do not think so any more. Speaking out is acceptable, but destroying the thing you wish to improve is not. I have come to learn over these years, that a thing may be deeply flawed, and yet valued. So, I write this with an awareness of the exquisite irony that I have missed for most of this latter half of my life: that the American flag has represented to me the freedom not to pledge my allegiance to it; and therein lies the most important reason for me to pledge my allegiance to it.

(September 15, 2001)

Him

Written just after September 11, 2001 in response to images of hundreds of people standing in lines to donate blood, even after knowing how few victims would survive.

"Here is my body," he said,
"Take of it and use it for life."
"Here is my blood," she said,
"Take of it, so that they may live."

Is there a better way
To understand what He meant
Than this:
To witness thousands
Of ordinary human beings
Offering simply and without second thought
Only that which He once offered?

And witnessing
In this simple act
The miracle of Transubstantiation:
We become saviors
Just like Him
Giving body and blood
So that they—and we—might live, once more.

(September 17, 2001)

Post 9/11 Thoughts

So, I've been thinking about anthrax some these past few weeks. Now, I know that I am far too unimportant in the "big picture" to be a target and I do not work for a government agency that needs to be brought to its knees. It is highly unlikely that an anthrax-laced letter will come my way. This rational part of me has figured this out, and I do not spend too much time worrying about this. However, while my life goes on with this relative truth allowing me to feel, for the most part, secure, there are other awarenesses, perhaps less rational, that invade this "somewhat" secure life, as it "goes on." These are some of my "other" awarenesses:

--When my daughter calls me up from college to tell me she has a fever and feels achy and exhausted, I "wonder" when anthrax will infiltrate the general population, if she got a letter that had been in one of the "affected" postal clearing houses. I feel an uneasy weight of irresponsibility telling her to rest, drink fluids, take Advil, and go to the health service on Monday. It does cross my mind, I have to admit, that this may not be enough.

--When I get home and see the mail scattered on the floor of the hallway, having been shoved through the mail slot in the front door, I pause for an extra second. It is no longer merely a nuisance to go through the mail. There is that weight, again, of "wondering." It is not a worry, exactly—just a thinking that never used to exist.

--When I go into NYC, as I will be doing a few times in the next several weeks, I'm thinking that I will try to breathe real shallow and hold my breath as much as I can in Penn Station. I am not sure why above ground might seem safer; there's just something about being underground and vulnerable, though I truly have never thought about that before.

--When I go to the supermarket, I have an urge to hoard something—I'm not sure what. I already have Cipro that was prescribed years ago for some exotic travel. I am shallow enough that that makes me feel better. But I think I should be stocking up on other things. In a semi-humorous effort to address this vague need to hoard, I took an informal poll of family and friends, to find out what they like to hoard when faced with a hurricane or storm, or...anthrax. Here's a sampling: my son advises that I stock up on "2-ply," his short hand for Charmin toilet paper (now, you have way more information about him than you probably needed); my husband, always having a particular penchant for the apocalyptic, does canned tuna, powdered milk (just because it sounds healthy and necessary), canned mushrooms caps (don't ask), and the most essential item—several 3 pound bags of peanut M&Ms. After snow storms and hurricanes, I am always looking for unusual recipes that use up my four grocery bags of Michael's "end-of-the-world provisions." Don't bother digging one up for the M&Ms, however. They are never left over. As upset as I get with him for bringing such enormous quantities of junk food into the house, even I have to admit that the big Ms are popular and don't hang around for long. My daughter would insist upon bite sized Snickers, especially if we were going to be holed up for more than a month (those of you of the double X chromosome gender will understand this logic, that dictates the necessity of Snickers once a month for one's survival, and the survival of all those who come in contact with us). And me, I purchased a few cans of Ensure (which somehow makes me think of Depends), some peanut butter, and some bottled water.

So now you know: my family is way weirder than you might have imagined. But here's the thing. I'm generally a fairly "normal" person. I'm not one to entertain fears. (I am probably as bummed out as my son that his planned 4-month semester in Nepal had to be abandoned after the multiple murders of the royal family). My denial systems generally work really well. But lately, (and I wonder if you have been experiencing this too), I find myself working twice as hard to have my denial systems be half as effective as they usually are. And this takes a toll. It's not that I feel anxious or worried, exactly. It's just this vague, unsettled feeling that hangs around, not quite shakeable. It makes me a little cranky, a little tired. It gives me a pinch of an existential ennui at times, about doing mundane things. It makes me look at some strangers the way my mother-in-law might look at all Germans, and "wonder." It makes me feel like I have to work really hard to rise above some base human feelings that I usually feel free from. It makes me not like that such feelings find a hospitable host in me. It makes me wonder—no, worry—about a draft, and know that the selfish preservation of "my own" outweighs, by far, feelings of patriotism. The abstract ideals that I wholeheartedly support just can't seem to find a foothold when measured against the full ripeness of youth, the emerging adult, that is my child. I know, yes, I know, that the country that allowed me to raise my children as I wished, to nurture their souls freely, to choose religion or not, to allow them to flourish nearly unimpeded by hardship, that this country is worthy of protection, and yet... I wonder if these feelings represent a basic flaw of selfishness in me (yes, I do want someone to defend us, but not my child) or maternal protectiveness that is excusable. I'm not sure.

So, these are some of the thoughts nagging at the edge and sometimes forefront of my awareness, as I make my way through my days. I know that some of you have had your lives shattered, not just bent a little. And my "somewhat" altered consciousness cannot come close to touching the devastating mutation that has occurred in your lives.

(Fall, 2001 Unfinished....)

May 10, 2002

Dear George,

I will have to leave the funeral early, and may not get the chance to see you today, so I wanted to be sure and write this letter so you will know how much I am thinking about you.

There are so very many things you have lost in the space of a handful of days. And these losses will leave a hole in your life that might feel, right now, unfillable. But, in the midst of all that you have lost, there is one thing that you haven't lost—and that is you. I want this letter to be a gift to you, and the most important gift I can think to give you—that no one can take from you—is yourself.

It is hard for me to believe that I have only known you for 2 days. And I know that those 2 days will always be among the hardest and worst 2 days that you will ever experience. But, I came to know some really really important things about you in those 2 days. Here is what I learned about you:

I learned that in the midst of so much hurt, you still remained open—open to trusting people, open to receiving love and caring from people, open to your own overwhelmed feelings;

I learned that in the midst of so much that is incomprehensible, you remained clear headed. You asked the right questions. You sought for understanding. You could put into words your fears. You expressed your needs. Through all this, you remained grounded and anchored as solidly within yourself as anyone could have;

I learned that you are a gentle soul, who cares deeply for others and who reaches out to others to try and repair what might need fixing;

I learned that you have remarkable inner strength. That in the midst of a present that is so broken, you can imagine a future that contains good things for you. How amazing you are, George.

So, I want you to know and remember, that in spite of everything that is so awful right now, there will be a time that you will be OK. I know this, from everything I learned about you in 2 days.

Make sure that you stay open, no matter how much it hurts, that you keep talking to people who care about you, that you keep letting people give you what is in their hearts to give, that you keep asking questions, that you keep telling people what you need, that you keep caring, that you keep looking to the future for a time when some healing will have happened. Make sure that you and Nikos hug each other often.

I'm hoping to see you soon.

Love,
Dr. Lindner

(written to a student on the day of his mother's funeral following her murder by his father)

"My Kids Are OK"...Or Are They?

"My kids are doing OK." These words, so reassuring, were heard over and over this week as we canvassed many of your classes in the wake of the tragedies that befell two of our families, and by extension, our Manhasset community. So many of you are so very competent as you lead discussions among your students. And your assessment that your kids are "OK" is not wrong. They are OK. They are active, talkative, busy, involved in classwork, playing at recess. Even the child whose life was turned upside down was busy eating pizza in the cafeteria, selling baked goods, happily making change and handing out napkins filled with brownies, choosing his health expo project. Is he OK? Well, yes. By some awesome capacity that is a testament to human resiliency, he is functioning. And the fact that so many of our children can "look" so intact, can **be** so intact while they are with us from 8:30 to 3:00 is not to be underestimated. You are right. Your children, as marvels of adaptability, are, in some hugely important ways, OK.

But, in some other, deeply important ways, they are not OK. At the very same time that they are solving math problems, they have tucked away (until later) overwhelming worries that we, as adults, would go to the ends of the earth to shield them from. They are aware, in the most raw, exposed way, of the most primal fears that any of us ever faces. When dusk falls, what pushes itself to the front of their consciousness, is an incomprehensible, overwhelming, devouring fear. It is not just a touch of insecurity. I am talking about the erosion of a basic sense of trust in the safety and survival of themselves and the most important people in their lives. This is the stuff of which nightmares are made. They are afraid to play outdoors. They are afraid to be home alone, even for 5 minutes. Their 15 year old sibling is afraid to babysit them for an hour at 4:00 in the afternoon. They are afraid to fall asleep at night. These fears do not get verbalized all at once. One child, timidly and somewhat embarrassedly offers this experience; 6 others shake their heads, exhaling a nervous giggle of relief. The floodgates open. What has been tucked away is loosed. And then, all of a sudden, they are talking about mean and dangerous dogs in their neighborhoods, dogs that bite and attack littler dogs. They are off and running now on seeming tangents that pull them into symbolic worlds. It is just too hard to stay with the real possibilities of boogeymen, robbers, kidnappers, murderers, freak accidents. Ratweillers are still smaller than they are; there is the illusion that **they,** at least, can be avoided or controlled. So, are our children OK? No, not really. Not really at all.

How far should we delve into this internal scary world, that seems to remain successfully pushed onto a mental back burner from 8:30 to 3:00? I think it is essential for us to permit these bubbling stew pots of fears and worries to come to the "front burners"—in a controlled and carefully structured way. Such discussions do not, as some fear, introduce scary ideas to children; rather, they provide an opportunity to verbalize the unspoken, to organize the fuzzy-edged monsters that lurk around the corners of their young minds. It is through this process that the monsters are named…and tamed, and kids come to know they are not alone. Unspoken regressive needs push for expression in behavior—the need from a younger time, to sleep with mom and dad, to cling, to be afraid to come to school. Speaking the need allows children (us, too!) to hold it and contain it, rather than being constrained by it.

It is the deepest wish of all of us, that we can take from them the terrors that have shattered, yet again, their childhood worlds. We ask them to give us their words that define those feelings, and we hope, with desperation, that if they give them to us, they will be rid of them. But deeply within, we know better. We know that once the gate to the garden has been opened, there is no turning back.

So, while we can't take away from our children what they now know, we can, maybe help them be able to fall asleep at 8:00, in their own beds, having spoken what felt too babyish to speak. We might be able to help them begin to play outdoors again, with just a little of the old childish abandon. And maybe they can begin to feel independent and masterful in their encounter with their world, rather than handcuffed by inarticulate fear. And when all this starts to happen again, what looked like it was OK, will really be OK-- inside and out-- and they will resume their forward journeys, with only the usual sideways glance, along childhood's path.

May 20, 2002

Dear Robyn,*

It is an awesome responsibility to safeguard the well-being of almost 800 children and nearly 100 adults. I know that at Shelter Rock, there is never just an ordinary, easy day. But in these recent days of tragedy and trauma, I know that your job has been a challenge that you never imagined.

I think that the hardest part of your job, these past several weeks, has been to be one of us, grieving along with all of your children and staff for all that we have lost, and yet, to have to hold onto a vision, always, of how to move us forward, back into learning and life. I have seen those moments in you, when you wished for more time to do the first, when you felt you were not ready for the second. But what I have also seen, over and over again, was Robyn stepping into the door of a classroom, greeting and being a touchstone for children; Robyn stepping up to a microphone, dedicating a concert to the memory of a child whose life had only begun; Robyn standing before her staff and speaking dreaded or difficult words, always softened by comforting and assuring words. You have given us, these past weeks, the gift of your wise and compassionate leadership which has remained balanced and thoughtful, sane and humane, vulnerable and strong, despite whatever you were feeling within.

You know, Robyn, how often we have shared a joking moment about this place, Shelter Rock. The irony of these past several weeks, for me, is that I have never been more grateful to be a part of this place, to care so deeply for this place, and to feel proud of who and what we are. I am inspired by your capacity to demonstrate such "grace under pressure." I am so glad to be working with you.

Thank you for bringing us through this storm. May we have smoother sailing ahead.

Gratefully,

Sheri

*Robyn Mandor, principal of Shelter Rock Elementary School

May 20, 2002

Dear Robert,*

I needed to let you know how supported I have felt from you, and how much I have learned from you these past few weeks.

You said, offhandedly, at some point, that you can't do the counseling work that we, in the library, have been doing, but you could go into the fifth grade classes to speak about their anticipations of the memorial service. You were wrong about what you can't do. The work of counseling is to make possibility available—so that a wide array of feelings is possible, a variety of actions is possible, broad and fulfilling connections are possible, and deep experiences of the self are possible. You did all of that in your talks with children. You gave permission for them to experience anything that they might be feeling and thinking, and you did this by creating a cocoon of safety and calm, humanness and humor around them. There was room for sadness and laughter, grieving and living to coexist. You have done this each day for the past several weeks. Your presence in the building has given both children and adults a solid sense that we will be OK. It is inspiring to watch you at your work.

Thank you, Robert, for your openness and decency, for all the ways that you have taken such good care of all of us.

Gratefully,

Sheri

*Robert Geczik, vice-principal of Shelter Rock Elementary School

Thoughts About Two Boys

May 24, 2002

On most days, after arriving at school at 7:45, working through lunch, participating in countless meetings, and trouble-shooting with kids, teachers, parents, and administrators, I am more than ready and eager to leave school at 3:00. But these days, I find myself lingering in the office, the halls, the principal's office, the science lab. I cannot seem to leave.

I want to stay as long as possible, and put my arm on his shoulder as often as possible. I want to stay and laugh with him at the antics of his pet ferret, Ralph, an animal who, despite his odor, I look toward with a certain relief and wonder at how the ferret has adapted himself so quickly and well to his new home. I want to enjoy with him his chameleons who may, after all, be apt metaphors for what it might feel like to be him; as one of these clawed reptiles plays dead in Niko's hand, the poignancy seems to be lost on George and Niko, while it pierces me with immense sadness. I want to stay and watch his baby gerbils grow to their time of weaning, even though to watch them burrow under their mother as they blindly but assuredly nuzzle their way to her life-giving teats fills me with an ache for these two motherless, fatherless boys. How cosmically cruel that these gerbil babes live together with their mother and father. But still, in spite of the unfathomable ironies, the sadness, I need to stay. I cannot say goodbye first. Each goodbye feels like it would be a re-enactment of abandonment and loss.

And I am not the only one. Pam lingers. Sharon lingers. Robyn lingers. Robert lingers. Others do, too. And George and Niko linger, with foster care worker, Jason, who seems, in spite of his youth, to understand their need. Each of us finds himself and herself thinking about these boys late into the night. They evoke a primordial nurturing reflex. Each of us has entertained fantasies of adopting these children, of being loving mothers to them, of being tender, pillars of paternal strength and succor to them. In our most private moments, as we drive to or from school, we think about how to register ourselves as foster parents in our communities. Maybe we could have saved them some of the wrenching agony of so total an uprooting. We long to fill the gaping, ragged hole that has torn their hearts, which are as rent as if that bullet, which shredded their mother's life, had been shot straight through them. We think that if we purchase poster board for projects, make them cheeseburgers or brownies, buy their lizards sumptuous crickets to eat, intervene with detectives and law guardians to secure their treasured personal items—from gameboys and bicycles, computers and favorite pants, to photos of mom—that this will somehow be sufficient to fill in some of what is missing. These are games we play with ourselves, to lessen the despair we would know if we felt, for a moment, the utter helpless horror of what has befallen these children.

I listen every day, wherever I drive in my car, to the same song on CD, a song with the mournful pine of cellos, a song about leaving, and waiting for a loved one's promised return, for a time when the spaces of his heart will be filled. It is torturous and fulfilling, at once. But, I cannot listen to regular songs. I must do this sobbing when I am alone, over and over. In the space of a handful of days, I have fallen in love with this child. I will cry the tears that he will hold, for the time being, within him. For now, this is OK. I marvel at his capacity to sing with 100 classmates "The Rhythms of Life"...and lose, in the musical flow, the memory of how the rhythms of his life have become so dissonant; I marvel as I watch him shake up acids and bases in his chemistry test tube and laugh with real abandon at the resulting foam that rises to overflow its sides. It is OK that life grabs him in so many ways and pulls him forward. This is the only way he **can** go, if he is to go on.

And so, I will talk quietly with him each day, gently absorbing his questions about what will become of him and his brother. I will play chess with him, and help him safeguard his queen or, if she must fall, I will let one of his pawns get her back. We will talk about how powerful she is, how protective her role with her king. I will try to understand how those small pawns can flank their queen and protect her from hostile forces, how very important those tiny soldiers can be. I will try to play a defensive game, encouraging him to advance to my side of the board, to replace, one by one, my pieces with his. I do not want him to keep his king and queen and pawns safe in a small corner on his side. I want him to be brave, to know that he can move them out into the world, and that they will survive. I will try to listen carefully, as we talk chess talk, to the subterranean meanings vibrating within our words. And whether we are playing chess or not, I will help him hold onto his king and queen.

And I will linger long at the end of each school day. And so will they. And so will we all. Because school has taken on the sanctity of home, and our collective presence for George and Niko honors the silent, sacred covenant we have all entered. We will linger, also, because we know—and so do they, in the quiet, intact spaces of their hearts—that another uprooting is before them, and another large goodbye will need to be said. But we can do this and so can they, because the largest one has happened already. And so, we will linger and say small, daily, rehearsal goodbyes, and hope that each hug and touch of the shoulder finds its way to the beating places of their hearts.

Thoughts About Our School Year 2001-2002, Here at Shelter Rock

It was a year that began with the promise of each new school year. As it always does, September abruptly replaced the slow, renewal days of summer. For those of us who work in schools, there is the ambivalent blend of letting go of these halcyon days and rolling up our sleeves to tend to the new seedlings that will appear in our classroom doorways. For children, as summer ends, there is the recompense of trips to shoe stores, shopping sprees for new school clothes that will cover those extra inches of body sprung up like hothouse buds under the warming rays of the summer sun. There is the anticipated trip to Staples, for the purchase of brand new notebooks, binders, the latest in pen technology: the colorful gels that span the light spectrum, and that promise to make learning and writing an exquisite, artistic experience.

And so the year began, with the nervous excitement of a new teacher, a new group of students, a future spread before us all.

Before the end of the first week, the promise and the future were fractured. Within the space of two hours, on a bright, clear September morning, nine children in our school became fatherless; several more lost first degree relatives. The families of five of our colleagues and friends were irrevocably diminished. The ocean of loss continues to wash over them—and us—like aftershock waves of an earthquake, that threaten to devour all over again.

Months later, it is hard to say that healing began, for it never actually felt like healing had begun. But time did pass and daily life began to resume familiar contours and even rhythms though there was often a hollowness just underneath. Seasons did pass, and spring flowers pushed their way through the soft loam early this year, after a blessedly mild winter, a mildness we all needed to lessen the gray bitterness that had eclipsed September and the months we barely took note of afterward.

But, in our corner of the world, the promise of rebirth was betrayed again. One 6 year-old's young mother ruptured an aneurism and died a sudden death; another staff member lost her brother suddenly; two young brothers became motherless when an alleged masked intruder entered their kitchen in the light of a balmy, pre-summer evening, the night before their sacred Easter holiday and shot their mother in the head; these same boys became fatherless 2 days later when their father was charged with the murder of his wife; the horror deepened when a long history of domestic abuse was revealed, letting us know how deeply loss was heaped upon loss for these boys; and within the week an 11 year old, 5th grade boy fell off his bicycle, hit his head, and was functionally dead within moments.

Math became harder this year, as numbers were needed to compute an answer to the question: how many different ways have our children learned that they are not safe? They might be targets of random acts of violence, hatred that is ungraspably abstract, while at the same time unfathomably concrete and personal; they or the ones they love might be victims of random, ill-fated collections of blood cells, biology run off course; parental raised voices could result in unspeakable acts; an exuberant bike ride on a sunny spring afternoon could interrupt, just like that, their young and promising lives.

It is too much. It is hard to find anything left to say, though so much more needs to be said. We, perhaps, are talked-out. The children, however, are not speechless. Given the merest opportunity, they are bursting to put a frame around the thoughts that, like heated molecules, are bumping against one another within them. Just today, a teacher handed me 20 stories written by her students about colonial times. Having given this assignment for many, many years, she has never—never—gotten one story in which someone died. This year, 14 out of the 20 stories contained violent, unexpected deaths, often of parents, leaving orphaned children, often of children avenging their parents' death. Parents and children die in these stories in the variety of ways that these nine year olds have become, this year, accustomed to. No, there were no corncob checker games or flaxen dolls, no helping dad harvest the crops or baking pies in bricklined ovens. These survival or recreational activities are higher up on the scale of basic needs. Setting their fears in colonial times—long ago and far away—our children continue to wrestle with much more fundamental survival issues: how would they go on, if they, like their several friends, were to become fatherless, or, like their other friend, parentless. And what would happen if they, themselves, were to die? While this fear lies on the edges of the unconscious of nearly every child, it has become the backdrop of these children's daily lives this year. Trauma has been piled on top of trauma. The context of "OK" is buried too deeply to find an easy hand hold there.

Yes, this will be the moment in time, this year of 2001-2002, for many of our children, when they will chart the beginnings of their awakening. They may remember little about themselves and their world before this year. But they will begin to have something like continuous memory from this moment forward. And yet, while loss will become the catalyst for consciousness and memory, it will also become the catalyst for poetry. For in the midst of having been shaken awake, of knowing such sadness and terror, they can still imagine rightness in their world; they can still create solutions to unsolvable problems. Such poetry unfolded, on the spot, as one 8 year old girl, herself parentless, proposed that the mother and father who lost their only child in that bike accident should adopt the boys who were now without parents. And a 6 year old heard within himself a perfect harmony, when he expressed aloud that the man whose wife died of an aneurism, could marry his classmate's mother, whose husband died on September 11th. It does not matter that these matches will not happen. It matters only that these children can become visionary shamans, crafting solutions of symmetry worthy of the gods. They are composers, transposing the dirge handed to them into an exquisite symphony. It is not the solution that is healing. Rather, healing springs from their awesome capacity to participate in creation, to fashion possibility from within their own reservoirs of humanity. There is, after all, nothing better that we could offer. They, even better than we, can imagine a way to make their world whole again.

It is on this note that we will all leave for the summer in one more week. And we will renew ourselves. For, when September rolls around again this new school year, we will have only one week before we must look September 11th, and all that it evokes, in the eye. And we will need to feel such repair of our souls that we can look straight past September 11th to the 750 children, for whom all things are possible, again, in the new year that will be before us.

Wishing you all a summer of replenishment,

Sheri

A Lesson for Terrorists

I am struck
by the photographs
of the charred, hollow carcass
of the World Trade Center complex
how like it is
to Brueghel's *Tower of Babel*.
I suppose that was their point—
to punish us for what they perceive
to be our *hubris*
in building such a structure
that stretched itself
into the heavens
as if to touch God.

For a hundred reasons
they were wrong,
but for this above all:
it is not our arrogance
that compels us to create such things
but the one charge
breathed into us
at the dawn of our being:
to reach with all our might,
with paintbrush or plucked string
grace of movement or pen
with bricks or with our very breath,
to reach forward or upward
toward that finger reaching out to us,
to touch one moment
of the infinite wellspring
that was born
on that first great day.
This, within us each,
still stands.

(March 13, 2004)

What a Piece of Work

We tell ourselves
In white-robed gatherings
And in gilded or dappled chapels
That we human beings
Are the pinnacle of creation.

Our poets
Sing the sparks of divinity
Reflected in our 'noble reason,'
In our 'express and admirable' form,
Allowing us to hang our souls
On the trust
That what we see in such perfect verse
Is a mirror of ourselves.
If we believe them
And our ministers
We are the 'paragon of animals.'

Not even the most primitive forms of life
Do to their prey
What human beings do
Without end:
Schwerner, Goodman, Chaney, Pearl,
Hiroshima, the 16th Street Baptist Church, Warsaw,
The Killing Fields, Abu Ghraib, Babi Yar,
Darfur, Beslan...

It is impossible
That we
Are God's crowning glory.
It is more likely that we were created last
Because God had such doubts
About this particular piece of work.

(September 12, 2004)

A Parable for President Bush

A long time ago there was a man who, like you, believed that God spoke to him. He thought he heard God tell him to take his son to the top of a mountain and bind him upon an altar and make of him a sacrifice.

So, he took his son to the mountain and bound him on the altar. But then, something happened.

It is not clear exactly what happened: it might be that he heard a different voice; or maybe it was the same voice saying something different; or maybe he had been mistaken all along and could only now hear the silent articulations of his own heart.

Whichever way it happened, the man, Abraham, "flip-flopped," or maybe it was God who "flip-flopped." What is clear, is that somebody, Abraham or God, changed his mind. The original trajectory of events did not come to pass.

Our ancients tell us that we are to revere Abraham for his unquestioning faith in God. Sometimes even our ancients have missed the mark. I think we are to revere Abraham because he changed his mind. He took in new information (a ram in a thicket? a new voice?) and allowed himself to be changed by this.

Or maybe it was God who changed **his** mind. Maybe all along it was not Abraham's faith that was being tested, but God's faith in man, God's faith that we, when faced with new information, can change our minds, re-orient our perceptions of our world, edit what we thought we understood the first go-round, permit ourselves to be something other than static lumps of clay.

To invoke an image of God who demands that we send our sons up the mountain with the firebrands of their own destruction strapped to their backs, is to invoke a primitive God, a God who can only be a reflection of our most primitive selves, a God that in the end, even Abraham did not heed. To proclaim that such a God speaks directly to us, justifying our most primitive and least human actions, to hide behind such postures of "holiness" is the mark of a coward, one who is afraid of his own voice, or, perhaps, one who has no real voice.

I, for one, will always cast my lot with someone who has the courage to "flip-flop," to heed the world around him and make new decisions based on rams in thickets, based on voices heretofore unheard. Even Abraham did as much. Even God did as much.

(October 25, 2004)

Imprints

There is a kind of photographic paper
That my children once played with
On which the serrated shape
Of an autumn leaf
Emblazoned itself,
Wondrously,
In just a moment's time
On those days when the sun
Reigned peaceful in a perfect cerulean court.

It was just that kind of day
When twin images
In a moment's time
Were burned
Onto 300 million
Sheets of photographic paper
Leaving
The empty imprint of shadow spots.

My children knew
That photo paper,
Once exposed,
Could not be used again.

(September 7, 2004)

September 11th Again

Quiet
this Sunday morning.
Even joggers pushing
baby buggies ahead of them
fit the solemn stillness of the day.
Tangerine roses display
erotic layers of sueded petals,
and hibiscus open so large
they could be the delicate hands
of some loving god.

Is this jaunt of mine
to the Rite Aid
for nail lacquer
an irreverent disregard of
that day
when human shrapnel
obliterated sunlight
and flesh-bits drifted
the city
for weeks
or is my Sunday errand
permissible, affirmative?

I barter
with the unknown
arbiter of all that is decent...
buy that nail polish
but leave the package
sealed for the day
tomorrow, embrace,
like those reckless flowers,
frivolousness
and go forth with toes glossed.

(September 11, 2005
September 9, 2011)

September 11, 2006

Today, lambswool puffs, soft as whispers,
float on a pale blue sky;
not like the one five years ago
that would later be described as *severe clear*
only after the black engines of destruction
had wiped their sooty smear all over that sky.
Like a yin and a yang, folded together,
a perfect cerulean firmament
will never again exist
without our seeing also
the smoky stain of burning bodies,
the familiar signature of humanity.

(September 11, 2006)

Beyond Ground Zero

With no commissions or
architectural designs,
uncounted altars
are erected
all over this city
sprung unbidden
in the moment that created
need for memory
as fine dust ash
gray and black
hallowed drift-stuff settled
that late summer day
on window sills
of New York City apartments
whose tenants
can not bear to wipe it away.

(October 8. 2009)

Scents

On an evening walk at summer's start
I am drenched in the sticky-nectar-fragrance of honeysuckle,
the perfume-lather of lilac,
the dusk-released musk of mountain laurel.

In the company of these,
I cannot fathom
how we ever dreamed up
such things
as gunpowder
or a hydrogen bomb.

Mr. President, or Premier, or Prime Minister, or King, or Dictator:
set up your army training centers
in fields of lavender
and groves of orange blossom;

it is the only chance we have
that soldiers all over earth
might lay down their rifles
and their bodies,
take in the sex-scents that surround them,
then go home
and make love for all they're worth.

(June 19, 2005)

Published in *Jewish Currents*, March-April, 2006, p. 53

VII. Altars All Around

The Cubby

History is recorded so that we may possess and claim memory for experience that we never had. The visible evidence of the past imprints itself upon our consciousness and becomes part of us, almost as if we had lived it ourselves. And **we** record our own stories to affirm that we were here, that we embraced a time and place as it was handed to us, and we altered that time and that place by having been there. And it, irrevocably, altered us.

And so, it was a great sadness today, to witness the disappearance of a piece of recorded history, the erasure of art work far less masterful but no less treasured than that found on chapel ceilings or monastery walls. For this art work sprang from the same impulse as that. It was etched or printed into the walls; in fresco-like fusion, it became the walls, merged into each pore, which held tight the timelines of lives lived there, the genealogies of families, the precious baby-book albums of children growing up, the catalogued moment when one knew he was, for the first time, in love. These rich histories are gone now, painted over, thrown away to make room for new walls, clean walls. No museums are built to preserve those moments of youth breathed into camp bunk walls and cubbies.

I suppose it was inevitable that a new generation's history would come to replace ours. And, perhaps, it is a sign that the place still lives, that it changes in response to each decade of summer sojourners. And though I understand this, and accept the nature of time, still I am saddened that the tides have rinsed clean nearly all traces of our having been there at all. And so, I will have to re-create one very special lost moment now, as I imagine it occurred:

It must have been a cool, late August night, the chill a harbinger of summer's end. It would have been the kind of night that made us want to wrap our arms around ourselves, to coax from within, our own sources of warmth that we would need to call upon in the days to come. It would have been a night of immense sadness, because loss was imminent, just beyond the horizon, with the next sunrise. It would have been the last night of camp, when something like mortality comes into consciousness. And the brevity of time left to us evoked in all of us, a desire to immortalize ourselves, and to make known, for all of history, our presence there, in that place, in that time. All future generations should know: we had been there, as we knew, and revered, those who had been there before our coming. Their names, upon those walls, were mythic, we knew those names, they had lived where we lived, the place had made its imprint upon them, too. And so, whether we knew them or not, we knew them, for they were kin. And we would be kin and we would be myth to those who might never meet us personally. Like palimpsests these walls and cubbies were, with new histories never really obscuring the old, and with the oldest always giving a sense of richness and depth, context and continuity to the newer.

Do not mistake what we, and generations before and after us had done, as vandalism. There was no intent to deface, ever, but only to make those walls the holders, forever, of the most precious moments of our lives. Those walls and cubbies would be witness, year after year, bunk after bunk, to the unfolding blossoming of our best selves.

And so it would have been on such a night that a 13 year old boy would bequeath to the side of his cubby a thought, that had been pushing itself into consciousness all summer long. It was a private thought, that at that moment became public. The kindest response to that writing would have been a smile; a more likely response would have been a dismissal of this graffiti, as an impulsive declaration of a young adolescent boy's fantasy. But if it was a fantasy before that moment, it became a promise in the moment of its public appearance. I imagine that the boy felt a sense of relief and satisfaction in the moment just after recording his thought. I imagine also that there may have been a hint of embarrassment at the unlikely possibility of what he had just committed himself to, or fear, or maybe enlivening excitement, that now his feelings were real, and now, perhaps, he would need to move forward out of 13 and find a way to create the life that would fulfill his promise.

The thirteen year old boy turned 35 in the year 1988. As he wandered in and out of memories' bowers with the hand of his 7 year old son in his own hand, his 4 year old daughter upon his shoulders, and his wife of almost 18 years by his side, he came upon the cubby. There, on the side where his head would have been, where he could look at it on that last night of camp, was his declaration:

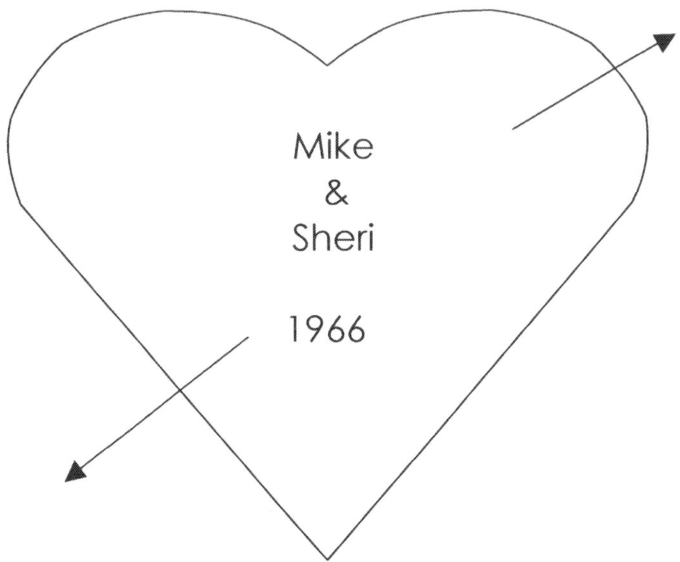

After a moment's calculation, I exclaimed, "Wait a minute! There was no Mike and Sheri in 1966." To which Michael replied, "There was for me."

It has been another 13 years since that visit to Saginaw, and a 20th, 25th, and 30th anniversary during which we have wished that we had taken the cubby in 1988. We have imagined it in our home, a testament to what Michael knew (long before I did). Our home would have been the right museum for the preservation of that moment in 1966. The story of the cubby is legend for us. It is the first recorded history of the birth of the rest of our lives together. It had also become the embodiment of all the possibilities of camp. On the eve of his first departure to sleep away camp, our then 10 year old son expressed distress over going. We assumed he was anticipating homesickness. We had missed the mark, big time. He asked, "How will I know?" He was worried that he would meet the girl he would love and not know it.

So, the cubby seems like it really should be ours. We decided on this April day in 2001, to find it again. And take it. We detoured to Saginaw on our way back from Washington today, and looked in every bunk. The cubbies were all new or newly painted. Most were light blue, clean, graffiti-less, history-less. The new owners generously unlocked the one place where a handful of old cubbies awaited "reprogramming." Excitedly we recognized the names of those with whom we had come of age 30 to 40 years ago, and the names it seemed we had always known, of those who preceded us 10 years before, and the names of those who had been junior campers, just beginning as we were leaving. We searched this cache of memory-treasures, our daughter, and the two of us, embracing spider webs and a winter's layer of dust. No Mike and Sheri cubby.

I was disappointed. I would have loved that cubby. I **have** loved that cubby. It does not exist any longer. No young boy will store his clothing there while he spends 8 weeks growing into himself in that Camelot. No young boy will stare at his cubby's walls at rest period, and absorb, subliminally, knowledge of the 80 or so others who, year after year, each, for a brief moment, shared that space. No young boy will know that once there was another young boy who declared, on that cubby, his love for a young girl, and made the improbable possible. But some young boy, will, this August, take up his laundry marker and begin to create history again, recording his presence and maybe, just maybe, his destiny.

We left Camp Saginaw empty-handed. No, that is not even close to the truth. We left with our youngest child, who stands on the brink of adulthood, with each other, and with the life that that 13 year old boy dreamt, and dared to write of on the side of his cubby, one late August evening, a half a lifetime ago.

(April 29, 2001)

My Husband Is an Infomercial Junkie

My husband is an info-mercial junkie. As a result, we own multiple versions of every song that was written in the '60s. We have a set of 4 *Real Rock* tapes, a set of 3 *Freedom Rock* tapes, a series of tapes entitled *The British Invasion*, and a host of others. Without doing a statistical analysis, I would guess that "One Tin Soldier" appears on roughly 4 tapes that we own; "Abraham, Martin, and John" on another 4; and "Reach Out in the Darkness (And You May Find A Friend)" on at least 3. And still, when one of those rolling song-title ads comes up, he will claim that we don't own a particular title yet, and want to buy a new set of 6 tapes—*Best of the '60s*. Even Napster hasn't dampened his urge to purchase a wonderful boxed set of Golden Oldies.

Our family's all time favorite info-mercial purchase (and, my husband's very first foray into the underworld of infomercials) came many years ago. It was a rainy day in Great Barrington, a ski day gone bad, so the four of us stayed in our jammies in our one motel room and watched TV for the better part of the day. Not having signed onto cable TV yet in our home, this was a real treat—80 some channels to dim our wits. It did not take long to stumble upon an advertisement for this product, that no self-respecting *homo sapien* could live without. A *Spanik* vertical roaster! I do not think, as a technological advance, it ever made its way to Stockholm for Nobel consideration. The idea here was that you could cook your chicken by impaling it onto this contraption and having it cook upright. Something about the juices and fat dripping off, leaving a healthier meal. It was especially exciting to contemplate cooking it in your bar-b-que this way. In his sheer joy at the genius of this wire cooking "thing," my husband forgot that he doesn't really like meat, that neither kid really liked meat, and that if they ate it at all they all ate the white meat (leaving me with an entire bird of dark meat and leaving them each with not enough of their color meat). Cooking a whole chicken never really worked for our family no matter what way we cooked it. He ordered it. It made our day. The kids thought it was really cool; I laughed, wondering how 2 AM discussions of politics and God and epiphanies with my soul mate had transmogrified into *Spanik* vertical roasters. But we were all humored for a time, eagerly awaiting its arrival 4-6 weeks later back home. While we were doing this waiting, my husband and I happened to stop into Zabars one weekend, only to find...*Spanik* vertical roasters! Perhaps we were to be on the cutting edge of chicken-cooking. Zabars even had them in several sizes. Before our chicken one arrived, we were the proud owners of a turkey one, also.

The *Spanik* roaster never made it past its maiden voyage. It really didn't fit into my oven, the chicken really didn't cook so evenly through, and I'm not sure where they found a bar-b-que grill 2 storeys high for the TV ad, since the roaster was miles away from fitting into ours. So, I made the difficult but necessary decision (after 11 or 12 years of having it be in my way in the pots and pans drawer) of donating it to St. Vincent de Paul's. At the time this had some logic to it, although now it makes no sense, whatsoever. If it didn't fit into my oven, why did I think that it would fit into the oven (or bar-b-que grill!) of someone less fortunate than I? Until writing this piece, this thought never occurred to me. Perhaps someone with technological or artistic vision came upon it, and it is now the base of a lamp, or the hub of some 21st century metal and wire sculpture. I imagine it has parted ways with chickens, if, for no other reason, than a St. Vincent de Paul's shopper would have no earthly idea what its original use was. Our *Spanik* vertical roaster, even years after it has left home, has provided our family with many a warm memory and a pot-load of howls and hoots at my husband's expense. I have to admit, it was worth every penny.

Now, his latest purchase arrived last week. As he tried, clandestinely to hustle the box into his office and sequester it there, so he could open it without the jibes that were sure to come, he was caught "brown-box"- handed. "What's that?" I asked, eager to see the newly-delivered goodie. Looking somewhat sheepish, he responded, "Something I ordered." I knew. An info-mercial acquisition. I thought we had had it down to a science: one of us, my son, daughter, or myself, would place our bodies in front of the tube and loudly sing as soon as Michael's channel-surfing washed him upon the shores of one of those info-mercials. We could sing those songs from the '60s to pass the minutes of the infomercial, preventing him from writing down that fateful telephone number. Those tapes served their usefulness, after all. But, one informational commercial must have slipped through. And here were the "goods" to shame us with our lapse.

So, the 3 of us left at home have been dutifully making carpet tracks with our "ab-slider" for 2 weeks now. We weren't too hard on Michael, as this appealed to my daughter and me, too. She, being a bit too much like her dad, might even have ordered it herself, had she been surfing at just the right time. (She confessed to having gotten as far as writing down the number!) So, we slide out an arm's length, and, the trick is, to roll back in. The thing has this spring in it, to help you get back "home" again. My abs are in such pitiful shape that the first week I got out and collapsed flat, leaving the ab-slider to find its own way home. This week I can get back in. But, woe to me when I sneeze! For the past 20 years, since having children, the only thing I had to worry about when I sneezed was peeing myself. Now, a sneeze triggers an ab muscle response that mimics the onset of labor. So painful was it today at work, that I grabbed my stomach, hunched over, and groaned aloud, having to explain to a fellow worker nearby the whole, sad story of rolling myself out like a slab of dough. She gave the predicted response: "then it must be working, no?"

Now, here's the thing. I'm sure the ab-slider sellers are counting on us to use just this line of logic—for at least 30 days. If I am in pain, especially abdominal pain, it **must** be working. And if it is working (here's where the fantasy part kicks in) then at any moment, my abs will begin to morph and sculpt themselves into a semblance of a 6-pack (that's what the guy on TV said—in just 3 minutes a day--and he had 6 gorgeous, individual little muscle groups to prove it). That's surely what is happening. It's definitely working. I will keep doing it; in fact, I will overdo it until sneezing, coughing, and rolling over in my sleep are impossible acts, to hasten these abs along, fit into a bikini I do not own and have not even contemplated since child number 2 and those 10 pounds moved in.

Honestly, I don't see it happening, and I think the ab-slider inventors knew this all along. The thing was designed to cause pain in the ab muscles and delusions in the body-image centers of the brain: end of story. My husband is no closer to a 6-pack than he ever was; my daughter actually does seem to have a flatter belly, but she has also been working out at the gym 4 days a week, (and is young enough to have the right shape without making carpet tracks with this info-ab gadget). And me? It's not meant to be. But we are the perfect consumers. We will keep rolling ourselves out, deluding ourselves that this pain means it's working, for about 31 days. We will tire of the pain, desire to sneeze in peace again, and decide we can accept ourselves as we are, soft abs and all. We will retire the rolling wheel to the attic, along with the cross-country ski machine, the bike puller machine, the bread machine (which promised to yield healthy bread which we could eat and grow thin on. Right!) And after several years, we will clean out the attic, while singing and grooving to a blaring tape of "Let the Sun Shine."

(January 23, 2001)

How My Husband Almost Made it onto QEFTSG

Dear Family and Friends,

Well, some of you know about this news and some of you don't, so we thought we'd update all of you about the latest Lindner escapade.

OK, so, picture Michael--not exactly a fashion template, right? Joanna, who tells us that the show Queer Eye for the Straight Guy, is a huge hit in Australia, decides that the creators of this show absolutely had Michael in mind, though they did not know it. So, she decides to introduce them to their prototypic straight guy in need of a makeover. She fills out an online application Wednesday night, sends it in. It includes such delectables as: his infamous glasses string, his Merrell shoes (worn with everything from shorts to black suits), his other infamous dashiki, the fact that he hasn't had a professional hair cut in 36 years, his yo yo dieting, etc. By noon Thursday we have a message on the answer machine that they want Michael to come in to NYC for an interview. They schedule it for Monday and ask him to bring some digital pictures.

I share this news with some friends from school who know Michael and each one wants to know if we included a particular quirk that she knows about: "Did you tell them about the bacon thing?" (Michael takes scissors and cuts the fat off bacon before cooking it so he begins with 2 pounds but ends up with about 2 ounces.) "Did you include how he wears a belt pack in Vermont with a hunting knife on it so he can kill a bear when it attacks the dog?" The quirks are endless and endearing. So we go to the casting studio Monday, Jo brings her digital camera which includes a random view of some of Michael's "quirks," such as: a can of spam in the cupboard, our really messy kitchen bulletin board which contains our lives, the section of floor in the bedroom that Michael uses as his dresser (smelly sweat suit that dries out every day to be worn the next for several humpf humpf....weeks, assorted jogging socks, shorts still unwashed from last summer), his death mask that he made when the kids plaster-casted their hands ages ago, some amazing shirts (a bright yellow one with colorful parrots all over it, some purple tie dyed ones, a few seersucker ones, an elephant safari one, all askew on wire (poo poo) hangers). Jo and Michael make a bet that the Fab 5 will love that parrot shirt ($100 is riding on this bet: Jo says they'll toss it out the window, M says they'll love it--stay tuned). Among the photos is also Michael's dresser top which hasn't been cleaned up in about 20 years and contains an assortment of *chotchkas* from travels, from kids, from who knows where.

OK, so he has the interview and we assume he passed with flying colors (yeah!) because they tell him that he'll hear in about 3 weeks and he gets the call in 12 hours. We think what clinched it is when they asked him if he'd be willing to lose the glasses string and he responded with, "maybe, but I think that glasses straps are making a come back." Jo figures that the minute we left the studio, the woman was on the phone to corporate headquarters saying: "Hold production, we got the guy for the next 8 seasons!" The number they leave on the machine is a 617 area code. So, having just had the Noons here for the weekend, we are certain that this is a joke and that David had one of the women in his office make this call as a spoof. But, alas, the number really is Tighe and Doyle Casting Co., headquartered in Boston. So, now they're ready to come to the house.

They came. He had an in-home interview (the footage wouldn't be on the show--but used to show the director to see if he was good material). He shows them and tells them about some of his famous infomercial purchases (cross country ski machine, bike puller machine, hanging upside down back stretching out machine, gazelle, and of course, our most significant....the endless pool. The casting young woman is picturing the Fab 5 in their speedos playing in the pool current, toasting. We get to pull out the dashiki which he admits that he thinks is beautiful and yes, he would wear it again (watch out when you invite us to your next affair....), and the parrot shirt. He gets to show them the coffee table in the family room that has been screwed and hot glued together a dozen times, his office, which is a plethora of mismatched greens and more *chotchkas* including the Sigmund Freud action figure which he has hung next to the patient chair, still in its plastic and cardboard wrap. They seemed to enjoy him a lot, and we certainly enjoyed the interview.

So, they said 3 more weeks before we hear again. We're thinking: tomorrow. Well, whether he gets on QEFTSG or not, we are having SO much fun with this. He might get a haircut, he might get some cool clothes, his office might lose the green and make it out of the 50s. He's back on Atkins so he will look sleek and gorgeous if they actually choose him, and the new clothes won't be chubby clothes. We'll keep you posted.

Shorn

Not so unusual
for you to take the scissors
from the pen cup on the desk
and give yourself a haircut
when you are feeling shaggy,
the weather too warm,
your hair pastes itself uncomfortably to your neck.

But this time
when I saw the orange-handled scissors by the sink
and your pewter curls
silent in the bathroom trashcan,
not five days since your mother's last breath,
I thought of Samson,
shorn,
severed from his primordial well-spring.

We will mark together
the new season's arrival,
the irrepressible debut of crocuses,
the steady climb of the sun from equinox to solstice
when your hair, at least, will have grown back.

(March 10, 2006)

Published in *Jewish Women's Literary Annual*, Vol 7, 2006, p. 162

After Death

Hundred dollar bills
are dealt
—rapid fire—
        fanned out, Vegas-style
as if this summed her life.

The dealer loads his truck
and we close the door on the empty house.

There, by the front entry,
I spot one more thing we should have tossed:
a single plant stem,
its two waxy green leaves,
striated with blushes of yellow and red,
hugging the edge
of an old plastic cup,
a cutting, started weeks earlier from a mother-plant.

As my husband packs our bags
for the long ride north
I move the cup
with its mass of tangled root-threads
so the sprinkler system will keep it watered
until the new people arrive.

(December 1, 2006)

Published in *Jewish Currents,* Winter 2009-2010, p. 40

Seedpods

The old maple
behind the house
strews my yard with millions of seedpods
from May through November,

tossed with bountiful abandon from branches,
like confetti from skyscrapers
in parades that welcome weary soldiers home
or celebrate a new year.

Each spring,
and then again in fall,
I come upon five or six
saplings, sprung up in beds of ivy,
waving jubilant greetings.

So profligate is nature:
millions and millions of seedpods
and hardly a dozen take hold.

It makes sense to me now
When my husband tells me
he thinks about sex
all the time.

Published in *Jewish Currents*, May-June, 2005, p. 19

Snow on Trees

Overnight they become old men
osteoporotic
bent over to less than half their height
heavy with the weight of the world
on their shoulders and backs.

I work loose
limbs that have been buried
before their time,
comb the heaviness
from their frost-shocked heads.

In my hands
for just this moment,
the secret of the fountain of youth
time turned back
wise old, cocky young saplings
proudly erect again
waving at God
their whole lives before them.

(December, 2007)

Published in *Performance Poets Association Literary Review,* Volume 12, 2008

Vermont Snowfall

From a leaden desolate sky drift
these weightless stars spun of
air
and water
that disappear on touch
so light
I might have dreamt them up
these gossamer prisms
holy geometries.

Though I cannot hold them
they press one against the other
lovers each to all until
they tuck right into the sides of earth
like a starched clean sheet
on a birthing bed.

(November 30, 2003
February 26, 2007)

Published online in
http://womenspiritualpoetry.blogspot.com/2013/01/vermont-snowfall-by-sheri-lindner.html

Snow Memories

As many times as I waxed,
with a fresh brick of Ivory soap,
those rusted runners
of my Flexible Flier
(the old, small, driftwood-faded one
that we four knew was just better
than the sleek, shellacked, red-bladed, extra-long,
Chanukah-new one),
and went sailing down my driveway,
the street below guarded by my brother
who would make my flying safe
even as I competed with him
to see how far we could glide
across the wooden bridge
that spanned the frozen creek;
as many times as I screamed down that golf course hill
dizzy and nauseous and breathless with a two-year old
wedged squarely between my legs
or splayed across my back
attached as if by marsupial instinct;
as many Nordic trails as I have traversed
through powdered diamond-stippled glades
stopping to suck a naked bough,
heavy with heaven-spun water;

still I sometimes yearn
to return to and edit
that one night
fifty years ago
when I stood measle-spotted and fevered by the window
and could only watch
as all the neighbors, sleds in tow,
gathered atop our driveway hill
to revel in that falling snow.

(February 14, 2006)

Waking to Snow

It looks as if
an author
unsatisfied
with the effort
has ripped
the paper to shreds
tossed them,
the opus that was to be
now in pieces
infinite tears
that fill all space,
yet in each ragged-
edged flake
a delicate weaving
beyond the hold
of words
and for one
fugitive moment
I know
just what the author
meant to say.

(February 19, 2010)

Solstice

Arboreal candelabra
empty tree branches
lit this day
by dawn's faithfulness.

(January 2, 2012)

Vermont Forest

In dense Vermont woods
snow sifts
draping pine boughs
with thousands of filigreed veils.

The silence is so vast

(I never knew there were degrees of silence)

as if all sound
were locked within these million crystalline lattices.

This must have been
the ready, no-sound
the moment before creation
burst forth
or perhaps
the sublime quiet
the moment after.

(March 14, 2006
December, 2007)
Published in *Poetica Magazine: Reflections of Jewish Thought*, summer, 2009, p. 13.
Published online in *Soul-Lit*, November, 2012

Swimming

From a place within
that is so old it is beyond memory,
I feel the perfect grace
of this movement,
this movement that sometimes urges its way
into the shadowy, predawn images
of my unwillful consciousness
with the insistence
of the chemical poetry
that tells a salmon
to fin its way through the currents to home.
So consummate is it
that I am almost compelled
to inhale great chestfuls
of water
trusting my gills
to filter out what I will not need.

But a cortical message
overrides this primordial urge
as I capitulate
to my species'
pulmonary necessities
roll my head to the side
drink a goblet of air
and then return
to this exquisite movement
that is surely the way a fish tastes God.

(December 7, 2003
March 5, 2007
January 22, 2013)

Creamer Pond

At the waning hour of a mid-summer evening
the edges of the pond
are swaddled in lavender dusk.

But, as if it were God's gathering vessel,
Creamer Pond is still bathed
in bright, mid-day light
texturing its surface
velvet gloss.

Frogs and crickets
chant their vesper hymns
slow
and rhythmic.

I hang my robe
on the splintered, weathered pole
while the small creatures
sing and sing
their urgency
calling me
to take part
in their noisy, swelling chorus.
Drawn,
like the light,
I step my feet
into the pond.

Here I am.

(July 17, 2002
February 6, 2005
August 11, 2005
December, 2007)

Published online in *Soul-Lit*, November, 2012

Leaves

Not all at once,
But one at a time
They float determinedly down.

No change of wind is necessary;
It happens when the time is right,
When, simply, there is not enough light
To sustain the hold.

They do not cling unnaturally
To sapless limbs
That have nothing left to offer,
But sunder themselves
From the canopy aflame
That presages darker days,
Then cluster themselves in great masses
Near the root-source,
Remembering,
In a silent, wordless place
That is surely deeper
Than anything we ever know,
That what is nurtured
On a gray autumnal eve
Bears leaves of deepest green
Come spring.

(October 31, 2004
November 2, 2004)

Day of Days

The Sabbath was a brilliant creation:
after a spell of hard work,
a day of rest.

But God did not imagine
the last day of school
the first week of summer
the holy experience
of friend shouting to friend
one leg swooping over a bike seat
pedaling miles and miles
out of town
under a jubilant sun
droplets of sweat seeping from
the small of backs
and the crease behind knees
arriving at the old marble quarry
leaning bikes in careless haste against
a scattered pile of marble blocks
pausing for only the intake of a breath
atop a sheer rock wall
then leaping into a cold
(so cold!)
glacial-green pool
surfacing with a
seemingly meaningless whoop of a noise
that means *awake now!* and *yes!*

God can have that day of rest.

(July 16, 2008)

Land

Like a despot
thirsty for sport after a slothful winter
I declare battle
every spring
staking my claim
on yet another parcel of land.

I steal it from under the noses
of its inhabitants
mercilessly uprooting them
banishing them
outside the borders of my land.

I have become *Qin Shihuang,*
building walls of rock
to keep out marauders
who, nonetheless, in broad daylight,
under my very nose,
stage sorties, gain ground.

It is weary business
occupying land,
demanding continual vigilance
and a willingness
to don, almost daily,
battle gear.

Yet, each year
I seize more,
unsatisfied with my lot.

I could say
that I am trying to make the world safe
for hibiscus and primrose, bee balm and mallow

but in the end
I know that they
and I
will be claimed
by the common grass and dandelion.

August Day

Butter-hued hair,
body bare and smooth
as the milky-beige inside an almond,
she alights, momentarily,
like a delicate dragonfly,
first in the sandy, shallows at the pond's edge,
next on the grass berm
where, with the carefree ease of a pup,
she squats,
calling to her mother:
"Just a minute, I'm peeing!"
all the while
watching the bikinied older girls
tease and dunk,
laughing and shouting
as they overturn each other's kayaks,
and swim out toward the raft.

If I could,
I would place this moment
in a frame,
beneath glass,
away from time's reach:

this day,
when she could hardly have been three,
delightingly naked,
held between a robin's-egg-blue sky
and the cool rim of a mountain pond.

Before a handful of years have gone
she will be pushing hard on the gate of this *Eden*
as she swims out
into the deep.

(August 11, 2005)

August Night

Another day
heavy with steamy heat
settles to stillness
as the lilies wrap themselves closed for the evening.
The garret loft
holds tight the day's dense hot
that cannot escape
through the meager skylight window
above the bed.
We switch on the roof fan
hoping to draw in night coolness.
It hits us
like a fairy spell
air washing over us
drenched in flower fragrance
drugs us
until we are breathing
only colors.
All night long
with every sleeping breath
we inhale
the sweetness of this musk liqueur.
By morning,
along with our dreams,
the mystical flower vapors
are gone,
and in their place,
freshly bathed, scentless air
to which our eyes
and a thousand buds
open.

(August 6, 2005)

Published in *Jewish Women's Literary Annual*, Vol 7, 2006, p. 135

Summer's End

Carefree this
hot August day moving
so fast to the end
of summer,
a boy on his bike approaching
twelve
everything ahead
pedaling his heart out
down the hill
to the pool.

Of what ungodly use was it
when we learned
how to calculate the moment
of impact
of two vehicles
travelling at different speeds
each toward the other?

(September 4, 2008)

Va y'hulu

It is as if the earth bursts her seams
And the colors of her splendid insides spill forth.

Forsythia-daffodil-yellow,
Tulip-crocus-purple,
Magnolia-dogwood-pink,
Pear blossom-hyacinth-white,
And green, always green.

It is written
That after six days of creating,
On the seventh day,
God rested.

This day of rest was crucial
So that on the eighth day
God could create these colors.

(April 24, 2004)

Once

when Mount
Saint Helens erupted
hot rock seared life out of
every pulsing thing; gray ash and
dust entombed the char that a second before
had been plant and animal and person, sealing all in
graves the size of cities, the depths of seas. Scientists, who are
schooled in such matters, avowed that nothing would live in that place
for decades. They could not account, just five years later, for the sing
that appeared, each leaf stalk a perfect six-pointed star, green spears pointing in
every direction, the tangle of amethyst flowers, laughter bubbled up from the belly of earth.

(June 18, 2008)
Appeared in the Reconstructionist Synagogue of the North Shore
Rosh Hashanah 5770/2009 Supplement of Readings, Reading 9

Awarded Honorable Mention in the First Annual Nassau County Poet Laureate Society Poetry Contest, April 29, 2012.

Published in the *Nassau County Poet Laureate Society Review*, February, 2013, p. 10.

Published in *Jewish Women's Literary Annual,* Volume 9, 2013., p. 241.

Published online in *Soul-Lit*, November, 2012

Winter Moon

From straight above the skylight window
full-moon-glow spills
luring me to this place
that until now
was ordinary.

Sleep does not come;
held in white,
under this phosphorescent spell,
I dare not close my eyes
against the mystery.

If I were a certain kind of believer
I would build a sanctuary
on this spot,
my pillow,
brushed by this other-worldly
luminous face.

At last, I sleep,
bathed in this milk-pool
and when my husband comes to bed
the earth has shifted.
He knows nothing
of the hour before,
of the light
that ravished his wife.

(February 5, 2007
February 7, 2007
November 4, 2009)

Published in *Jewish Women's Literary Annual*, Volume 8, 2011, p. 138

Winter Moon 2

A giant eyeball in the skylight, this
midnight full moon fixes her gaze
on my pillow...

we play the staring game:
she blinks first through tears
in shredded charcoal clouds
that slide by so fast I can
feel the earth spin.

Open-close-open she winks
to seal some sisterly secret that
drifts just out of reach as
sleep displaces it from memory.

(February 21, 2008)

3 A.M. Sky

Skeletal trees
silhouetted in blueblack night
a treasure chest
shaken out into the universe
shimmering
gems placed on every finger
of every tree
in betrothal

nine-tenths asleep
I imagine
a nine year old girl,
an empty piece of black
construction paper
before her
new metallic silver
glitter pen in hand
and she
has just learned to make stars.

(February 21, 2010)
Published in *Jewish Women's Literary Annual*, Volume 8, 2011, p. 137

Awake

Like gravity
envy tugs me
each time I toss back
the covers
turn over
and spoon again
to your quiet body
still in the same position
it was four hours ago
your inhalations
rhythmic and regular
tidal whispers
midnight waves folding
themselves onto the sand
while I, magnetized to consciousness,
thoughts swirling,
wonder if these floating
fragments
will, like the earth's crust,
cool, coalesce
into poetry.

(September 26, 2010)

Birch

Bursting her seams at every moment
Bark-peels
hang from
this bronze birch
metallic in the winter sun,
the forest's golden scepter
against a royal sky.

I want to kneel before her,
honor her courage
to cast off, even that gorgeous, shiny skin
trusting the new one to be a perfect fit.

(March 5, 2008
March 29, 2008
April 1, 2008
November 5, 2011)

Passing By

That woman
sitting on the bench
at the town dock
is not holding
a phone
to her ear
like the woman
two benches away
or reading a newspaper
like the man
three benches beyond that.
She is not briskly walking
a circuit around town
as I am,
grabbing, with a glance,
geese, rippled shimmer, gulls, her.

She sits
eyes closed
hands at rest in her lap
the descending October sun
illuminates her face—
an annunciation
right here, right now.

And I, I
pass on by.

(October 29, 2009)

Easter Sunday

Last week when I
walked this route
collar turned up
against a needling wind
tombgray clouds snatching
the water into twisted peaks
not a soul sat at any station
upon the way
all benches yawned, empty.

Today, every bench is full:
a baby draped across
his mother's lap
fills his lungs with the world;
an old couple props each other up
leaning together
unselfconsciously asleep;
girlfriends chatter, drinking coffees;
lovers spoon
ice cream into each other's mouths;
a man alone reads, intermittently
turning his face toward the sun
receiving that blessing;
two sit quietly
watching the still bay
this being quite enough.

(April 2-4, 2010)

Spring

According to solar reckoning
spring arrived three weeks ago,
but I know that spring arrived today
for today I tossed fleece headbands and mittens
Into the wash
to rinse away the stuff of sweating winter heads and hands.
And today I took my down jacket
and tufted, down comforter
to the cleaners
to prepare them for their long summer hibernation,
bedded down in sheets of tissue and blankets of plastic.
And today my husband went into the garage
and untangled the arms and legs
of deck chairs and tables
that had lain in one another's embrace through
the long winter,
and put them out for air and for a stretch
in their ritual, yearly places.
And today my husband and my daughter
plummeted through the sky
like some latter day prophets,
leaping from their speeding chariots.
With an urgency,
they fell to earth.
They fell at the speed that falling bodies fall,
obeying invisible laws
while breaking human boundaries.
In celebration of this
season of rebirth
miraculously
they touched down to earth.

(April 13, 2002)

Spring Finally

Clocks ahead one hour
Afternoon light sticks around
Crocuses are up!

(March 11, 2010)

Rain on the Pond

Raindrops on the pond
Make hundreds of eyes blinking
Open closed open.

(May, 2009)

Sequoia

Giant sequoia,
world's largest living thing, stands
mute: earth's testament.

(June 16, 2009)

Cat on a Front Stoop

The tabby cat sits
blinks at an adoring sun
like a reigning queen.

Winhall River

After heavy rain
the still, dreamy stream ferments:
frothy, amber ale.

(July, 2008)

3 A.M.

Today, pelting rain
shrouds of draping darkness. Now
star chunks stud the night.

(Summer, 2010)

Labor Day Weekend

The stack of novels
along with summer daisies
is almost finished.

(September 5, 2010)

Wildflowers

August wildflowers
Queen Anne's lace and goldenrod
Mean summer's ending.

Winter Solstice
3 *Haiku*

December descends;
days are devoured by dark
and souls are weary.

Two more nights until
the solstice arrives; the days
will finally lengthen.

Yesterday's solstice
a shroud of smothering dark;
today: emergence.

(January 20, 2009)

Silent Soundings

(imagining the loss of the sense of hearing)

I do not know
The liquidness of language,
The tides that ebb and swell
From the poet's tongue;

I do not hear the crinchy-crunch
Of my step on day-old, crusted snow,

Or the bubbled-burbled breath
Of my underwater exhalations,

Or the murmured moan
That catches in his throat
At passion's crescendo.

But oh how I drink in
The poet's printed picture
Tasting the sweetness
Of unheard melodies,

And hear to perfection
The full silence of falling snow
Swaddling a still-untrodden wood,

And feel the steady stream of life
That leaves and fills my lungs
As I make my way from lake-end to lake-end
With primordial cadence,

And know passion's pinnacle
By the wild hurtling
Of his heart
As it launches itself beyond
Earth's pull.

(November 3, 2004)

Passage

I say goodbye
As you slowly take your leave,
My friend of forty years.

When you entered my life
On October 12, in 1963,
I did not know
How I would come to treasure you.
You were a nuisance,
Cramping my ways.

But I learned to know you as the keeper of the rhythm of my
 life
As I circled your arrival each time on every calendar I owned
From twelve to fifty-three,
Those three-ringed ones
That yearned to record dates neither solarly nor lunarly
 determined
But that merely held deadlines for English papers;
And later, the ones
That reminded me of mammograms and parent-teacher
 conferences.

As we grew together,
There were times that I worshipped you,
Greeting your arrival as evidence that there might just, after
 all,
Be a God;
And there came a time when your absence
Was sure evidence of a bountiful universe
Drawing me forward
Into mystery.

You were unjealous,

Staying away for nine and eighteen months
While I fell in love
With what you made possible.

I learned from you
To tune myself
To the waxing and waning
Spaces within,
Swellings and ebbings that heralded godly possibilities

Once upon a time.

The markings on my calendar
Are nearly gone
Yet I celebrate you still
Each February 29th (or March 1st)
When I mark your first presence
In my daughter's life
By sending her Advil and flowers.

(November 25, 2004)
Joanna's 21st birthday

The Gates

(Inspired by Christo and Jeanne-Claude's 7,503 gates and saffron flags along 23 miles of paths in Central Park)

Far more
than the saffron robe of a Buddhist monk,
the yellow-orange flame of a *ner tamid*,
the consecrated light of a hundred votives,
or a million gilded mosaic chips
studding a domed mosque
in celestial geometric mystery,
these
invite us
to be astonished
by a simple walk in the park,
and dare us to smile
at another
from whom, just yesterday,
we might have averted our eyes
and hurried past
in indifference
or in fear.

(February 14, 2005)

A Walk at Week's End

The scratch of a lone rake
scraping together the last stray leaves
that lay half-buried
beneath the season's first powdering of snow
is a metronome,
marking my pace
as I walk at week's end,
untangling and loosening
all that had bound me to the week.

Almost imperceptibly
the sun has dissolved,
light brushes into deepening gray,
and the air begins to exhale
the chill of descending night.

Four girls, 11 year-olds I would guess,
sashay their way toward me,
laughing, squawking,
doubled over in delight
of nothing in particular,
singing at the top of their lungs,
in desperate need of a choral master.
As if she had hit upon the solution
to end the world's problems,
one says:
"I know, let's scream. OK, one, two, three!"
And the four let loose their
discordant, piercing shrieks,
a *halleluyah* chorus
to Friday afternoon.

(December 12, 2003
December 13, 2005)

To Teenagers

It was teenagers
(you'll see why I say that in a moment)
who wrote that
in the drying sidewalk near my house.
It is not the foulness of that 4 letter word that bothers me,
so common as to be almost trite,
but my uncertain vision for those imagined 15 year olds,
my hope, on the one hand
that a decade from now
they will have grown into people
who would hardly recognize
the fifteen year old for whom
a night of naughty desecration
was an unparalleled thrilling experience,
and my fear that those 25 years olds
would have entombed themselves as 15 year olds
forever in that hardening concrete.

E-O

Many answered the ad
Who could barely care for themselves,
Let alone my newborn, firstborn child.

But she was different:
A baby nurse in Israel in 1940,
A daughter my age
Who lived a mile from me,
Who had recently had her own
Firstborn.

While I went to school two days a week
To learn how to understand
The ways that minds and hearts
Can keep people from being fully in the world,
She warmed my breastmilk
Equally with her abundant joy
And with our new microwave technology.

She sang playfully to my child
"*Chupa chupa rider…*"
And sat on the floor for hours
Creating Farmer Jones scenes
With his dozens of plastic Fisher Price people
And farm animals.
They left the red barn and white fence
Standing
So I could join them for harvest when I returned home.

She made chicken soup each day for lunch,
Chopping carrots and celery
Onions and parsnips
Cooking them so soft
For a tender palette and a handful of teeth
That would learn, soon enough,

How to chew upon the tougher stuff
That the world would serve up.

On those two days a week
She introduced my child to the world
Strolling him around town
So that he could greet,
Like a political candidate on a campaign trail,
All who passed.

People who did not know me
Would tell me of having met my child
When he was out with his grandmother,
This woman whom my son lovingly called E-O
Until he could say Susan.

My husband bumped into E-O in town today.
She asked him his name
Nearly a dozen times.
She asked what our son's name was again
And how did she know us?
Had we known her in Dusseldorf?
My husband told her only
That we had loved her.
Her companion,
Who does for her,
What she once did for our child,
Echoed my husband,
Affirming for her
All that she once had been.
"I was your babysitter?" she asked.
"No," my husband replied,
"You were a gift from God."

While I was in school
She held and rocked and fed my child,
She sang and talked and strolled with him,

Helping me build, from the haze of his infancy,
A history trove, rich in love;
I never did learn in school
How to understand
The empty spaces
That have consumed Susan's lifetime cache
Of memories,
Of which we were once
A small part.

(August 12, 2004)

Letter from Prometheus to Eve

Would you do it again?
I've always wanted to ask you that question.
No one, it seems, has ever considered that
You are the real hero of Genesis
(Actually, I think you are the hero of that whole book)
Oh yes, some god got you there
But you set the world in motion
Nothing would have happened without your move
So simple so necessary
Adam...Adam was milquetoast
But you, you dared
To be
To leave that unbearably perfect
Garden where no time was
And walk in the world of possibility
When you defied God
Only then did you know how to live
That apple...the antidote
To so many hungers.
So I did what you did
I disobeyed
Knowing in a way
(Just as you knew)
That fire was put before me
So I would take it
They couldn't have meant to keep it for themselves alone.
So I guess my question really is
Would I do it again?
A thousand thousand livers
Are nothing
Compared to the nothing
That would be
Had I not brought to them that torch
Had you not opened them to the world.

(December 7, 2008)

Diving the Great Barrier Reef

The more outlandish the shapes and sizes
and especially the colors
of the fish sliding by me
in this foreign underwaterworld
where the only sound I mark
is my own windy in-pull of air
followed by its bubbled release,
the greater my delight.
I forget to be afraid
even as a 900 pound
aquamarine and neon green
Maori Wrasse—
with patterns like fern fronds
woven into his sueded skin
and watchful, spiral turquoise
eyeballs that shift cartoon-like
from side to side
and enormous blue velvet lips
so deliciously kissable
it really almost takes my breath away
(as I smile too broadly, take in water,
and nearly lose my oxygen lifeline)—
moseys up to me.
He stays by me
holding steady by means invisible to me
as I run my hand
over his pulsing side
just above the open-close-open
of his huge gill-slit.

Much later
back in my own familiar world
air is not metered
no one notices the in and out that keeps us alive,
or delights in the fantastic variety of skin
hues that should
elicit wonder.

(August 15, 2006)

Old Ski Pants

Wiggle into ski pants
unworn for ages and
check out each zippered
hideaway storing protective provisions:
hand and toe warmers,
chapstick, and look here,
a flattened, still-wrapped
tampon, just in case.
Don't need that anymore.
And here, wadded up
a cache of bills
from when we all
skied together, each taking
a twenty, also just
in case, with me,
the banker, collecting the
unspent at day's end.
These pockets:
time's witness bearers.

(April 10, 1007)

Jacks

Burnished and darkened, the rust-brown of a pond whose source runs over rocks rich in iron ore, these heavy metal jacks smoothed and oiled by three generations of fingers newly competent at ball-toss-pick-up-ball-catch, my own fingers so skilled I could sweep a tensies hand larger than my own 10 year old hand on the concrete playground pavement and hardly scratch my finger tips or palm, and never break a nail, or sweep-the-parlor, or be nimble-as-jack on an old wooden bunk floor eluding splinters though we quickly learned to write home for 2 foot square swatches of contact paper to play it safe, the bunk floor checkered with stick-on jack-fields, ready for tournament heats, though the most satisfying (and most competitive) games were on the kitchen floor with mom, sister and both brothers, all of us jacks jocks of the first order.

Hard to believe, that since we each turned 18 and left home, we have never once, all four of us, gotten together without our parents as hub to our wheel spokes, but here we are, our first ever sibling weekend, just us kids 61, 59, 56, and 53, an accountant, a Ph.D., and two lawyers, searching for a common denominator, finding ourselves on a black and white linoleum kitchen floor, playing jacks.

(October 4, 2007)

A Daughter's Early Memory

His square, sure hands
slide each plank carefully toward the teeth of the saw blade.
In concentration,
he is aware of little around him.
He works to build shelves
for books.

In my smallness
I do not care about books
yet
but there is nowhere else I'd rather be
than sitting on the cool, damp floor of the garage
scooping together overflowing handfuls
of silky curled shavings.
To him: useless detritus;
to me: fairy-floss treasures.

Each of us is in love with wood.
He: because of its sturdy strength
and its willingness, nonetheless, to be fashioned and formed,
cut and combined into utilitarian perfection;
I: because of how it can become, inexplicably,
as light as frothy, whipped egg whites
with a sharp piney pungency that imprints itself
deep within the ancient part of my young brain
as I breathe in
the aliveness he has released from dead wood.

Work in Progress…

You would think, given that pistol in your hands
That you knew something of the world of 1954.

But you are just three
and brown is the color of the fringes on your new Dale Evans
vest,
not a plaintiff against the Board of Education;
and red is the color of tulip tops,
not an idea that makes a senator from Wisconsin desecrate
your country's most sacred founding principle.

You will not know of these things for a long time.

You also do not yet know
that there is a young buckaroo
now only half your age
who will see you barely 9 years from now,
and will claim
thirty years thence,
that he knew by his 10th birthday,
still years away from his first wet dream,
that he would marry you.

There is danger in turning the clock forward,
by fifty years, or even by minutes,
tempting the "evil eye,"
or just robbing you of the splendors of uncertainty,
--of all possible choices—
so I will tell you only this:
the world will need more saving than you could ever muster
and you will not need anything like that little plastic pistol
in the place that you will call home.

(April 5, 2006)

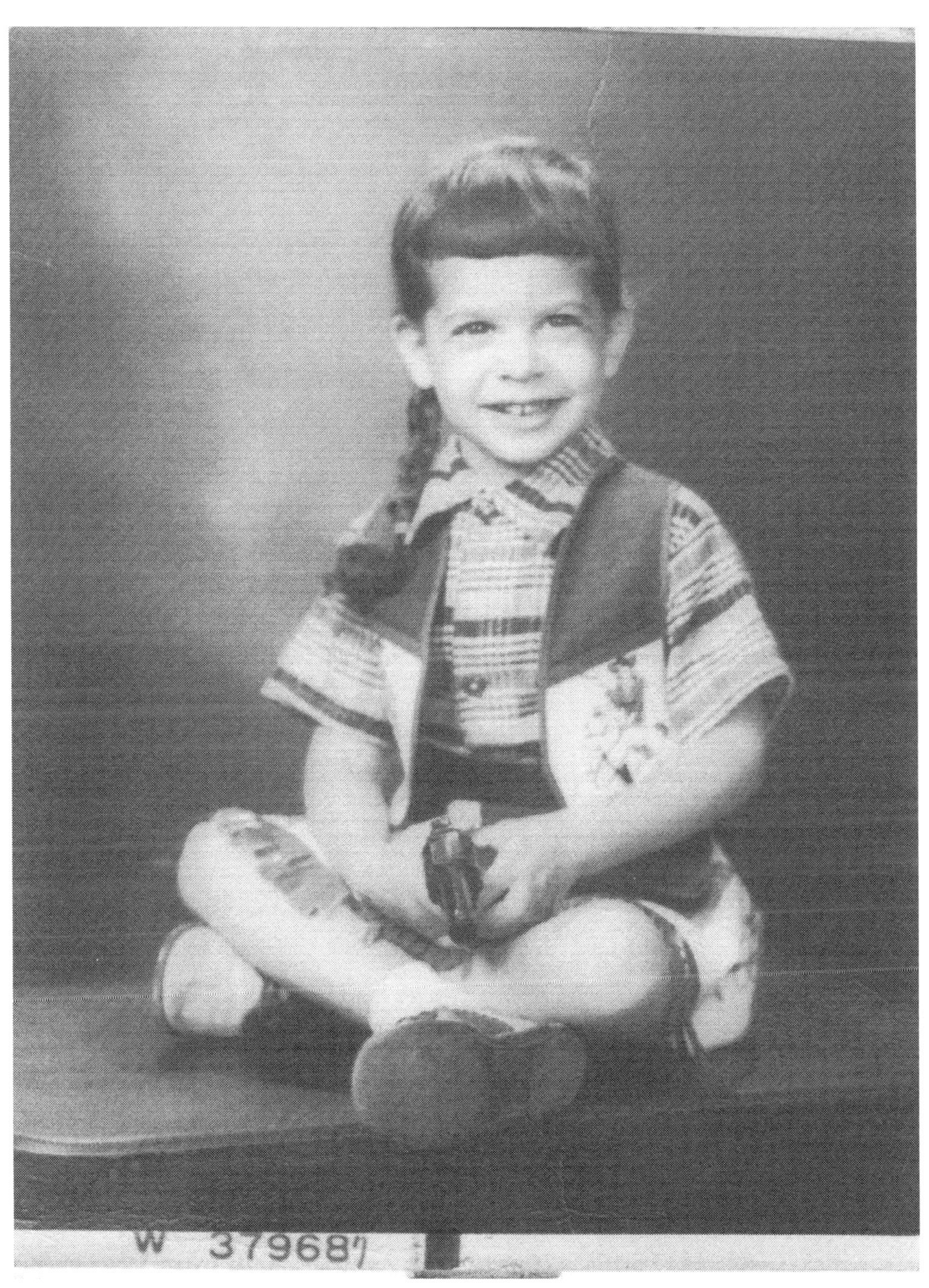
W 37968

A Poem Born

(An Ethere where each line increases by a syllable and then decreases)

Un
worded,
sleeping rest-
lessly in knot-
ted, shadowed forest...
awakens, wanders a-
bout, stumbling on underbrush,
almost curls back into itself
to drift again into a sleep of
non-being; instead, stretches itself to
the edge where wood meets meadow, darkness
light. Blinded, unfocused vision
comes slowly to clear. Hostage
to sunlight—even a
small, dappled shaft—it
grows words, cannot
retreat, a
poem
born.

(November 25, 2006)

Before a Poem

It stills my
breath

and then
the long wait
as it
attaches to me
like my own shadow
tagging along
nagging
for days
months
sometimes years
when I turn it pivots with me
elusive
allowing a glimpse only
hovering
just behind
yet insistent
that I breathe
back into it
there
always there
just
out of reach
like a name
caught in a synapse
unable to ride
the pulsing current to the tongue
until the effort is let go.
Wrapping my soul around
the shoulder
of this thing-that-words-will-not-yet-stick-to
I go in silence
until we are ready to speak to each other. (April 21, 2009)

Poetry Workshop

They're not here
because they don't
need to be here
oh, I know they
write verse
aching, soul-plumbing
iambs and trochees
but their real poems
unfold unwritten
as their lives
ripen
verdant and sweet
while we
whose fertile fruit
long ago burst
its seams and flowered
anew
need to do this
to transform
the already-known
into the
not-really-ever-known-
until-this-moment
astonished
to find ourselves
attached once again
to the vine.

(April 30, 2012)

Christmas

Her fourteen year old
lies in a hospital bed
as they wait for a heart
for another mother's child to die.

(January 4, 2008)

Christmas Morning

From chimneys
smoke
spirals
lazy sky
disappearing dovegray
into the
from which

silent

snowflakes

float

unhurried.

On my way back

from the country store

cup of coffee in one hand,

quart of milk in the other,

I match my walk

to the gentle mingling

of warm and frozen vapors.

This morning's

harp string plucked

the undulating wave herding everything

into its harmonic corral.

(December 25, 2011)

I Love Christmas

Growing up, I was more comfortable singing: *It is the night of our dear Savior's birth* than I was singing *Mi Chomocha*—both were merely songs to me, equally non-meaningful, and *Oh Holy Night* was by far the prettier and more compelling melody.

So, what's my issue with the proposed Santa Hat Day at Christmas time in the elementary school where I work? It brings out happiness in everyone, it gets everyone excited about the upcoming 10 day vacation, probably 800 of the 900 people in the building will wear one, I have one in my attic, it doesn't hurt anybody, and it will be something that the "entire" community of adults and children will enjoy together. Why am I spending so much time trying to figure out if I will wear one or not?

I wish it felt as easy as my youthful caroling. I feel, curmudgeonly, a Jew who has little use for "belief," yet who seems to be taking all of this too seriously. I cannot have a discussion about this with anyone at my school. It would make both me and my Christian friends feel awkward, and, like politics, a topic that is off limits. I wouldn't even feel comfortable broaching it with fellow Jews, as it would seem to set up an "us" vs "them" schism. I would wish to hide from fellow Jews my desire to participate in and my enjoyment of what would to them be obvious Christian symbols. I would wish to hide my ambivalence from my Christian friends about what would, to them, be so very obviously symbols of American holidays and end of the year celebration.

I think this is not about Christians and Jews, at all. It is about the place of religion in an American public institution. Santa Hat Day, as a sanctioned activity in a public school, is out of place, not because it is Christian, rather because it is anything religious. It feels out of place because it puts me in a quandary about my place among my colleagues. And if it does that to me, it does that to 20% of the staff who are Jewish and perhaps 10% of the students who are Jewish, and other students who are Muslim and Hindu and Buddhist. This problem is compounded by the sense I have that many Christians feel that their religious symbols are not inappropriate in public display, as their public expression is commonplace in our country. There is likely to be offense taken were I to suggest that our school is not the place for religious expression. And when offense is felt, the possibility of honest discourse evaporates, and an institution of learning becomes a parochial place where dissent is discouraged and only *some* ideas permitted. And then a place of learning becomes a place of darkness. And expression yields to oppression.

I do not wish to interfere with anyone's right to practice, believe, or express personal religious feelings. In fact, were I invited to a friend's home to share this holiday, I would enjoy, unambivalently, singing about the *holy infant so tender and mild* (even understanding what I am singing about), and I would experience a sense of reverence and holiness. I would wear a Santa hat in the cold, darkness of a winter's night, and be made happy by the bright lights that illuminate our way. But I would be doing this in the realm of my personal life, choosing to join Christian friends in the celebration of their sacred holiday, in the space of our personal lives.

It is different in school, where my freedom to choose compromises me no matter which choice I make: if I wear a hat, a part of me will feel happy, and a part will feel uncomfortable that I've capitulated to the silent pressure of a majority of which I am not a part; if I do not wear a hat, a part of me will feel like Scrooge, ruining the fun, making some political statement about an abstraction, and part of me will feel like a person willing to risk discomfort for standing for something larger than the immediacy of a good time.

What is it exactly that I would be standing for? For the principle that true religious freedom cannot occur when the presence of religion becomes an easy assumption, as it makes its way unthinkingly into the public sphere.

As much as those fuzzy red and white hats have entered American iconography, they are not secular but are inextricably tied to the religious holiday of Christmas. As much as I would like to join in the fun I will not be wearing a Santa hat and I will feel uncomfortable in this abstinence. Ironically, this discomfort of mine makes it all the more important that I not don a Santa hat. I want to protect religious freedom—everyone's. I also want to protect Christmas so that it does not devolve into an unthinking assumption; I like Christmas too much to see this happen.

Note: This proposed day occurred several years ago and a decision was made by the school not to have a Santa hat day.

Some Holiday Musings from your Editor

I had what I thought was a really neat experience last Thursday night. The "winter" concert at Weber Jr. High School in Port Washington featured the 7th and 8th grade chorus singing the Yiddish and Hebrew songs "*Oif'n Pripetshik*" and "*Yerushalayim*" which the general public has recently been introduced to through the movie *Schindler's List*. The introductory music to these numbers was the theme from *Schindler's List* played on the piano by the chorus director, Mr. Capobianco, and accompanied by a cellist.

When I first heard from our son, Dan, that this was Mr. "Capi's" choice, I was touched, and felt that this was a courageous undertaking for the chorus director. There must have been close to 100 students who spent the past 4 months learning Yiddish and Hebrew words. I will guess that 80% of them were not Jewish. It was beautiful to hear the haunting and uplifting Jewish melodies, and to know that some appreciation or feeling for this music, and maybe this culture, penetrated so many kids' sensibilities. I remember feeling equally moved last year when 100 students had all learned the Latin words of "*Kyrie Eleison*" for the same concert. Mr. "Capi" succeeded, both years in injecting thoughtfulness and meaningfulness into a celebration that often lacks both. It is not clear to me if these concerts are supposed to be truly "winter" concerts, or if they are supposed to be concerts featuring religious music of various religions. Either way, I guess the issues of birth, barrenness, death, and imminent renewal are all somehow appropriate themes for this time of year. And with those themes are attached the emotions of joy, desperation, struggle, victory. I think that holiday times are times of remembrance and reflection. The depth of emotion and pleasure during holidays comes as much from these, as from the event, in the present, all by itself.

The next day I was walking into the winter concert of

my daughter, Joanna, at the elementary school, and I struck up small talk with another mother I did not know. We talked about how early one has to arrive to get a parking spot, etc., and she mentioned how early she had been to Weber's concert the night before. I sympathized, as I had sat for 45 minutes in the auditorium the night before, also. She asked me what I thought of the musical selections. I said I thought they were great. I thought they did a wonderful job with some very difficult music. She said to me that she thought it was an odd holiday choice of music--"not exactly uplifting or in the spirit of the holidays. I mean *Schindler's List* is not what I'd call joyful music. At least he could have thrown in some Jingle Bells!"

I wondered for a moment if my horns were showing. I felt momentary embarrassment at having felt pride in this music the night before. I felt angry, foreign, simultaneously less-than and better-than. Is that all she wants from this time of year? Is that all she wants for her 14 year old--that he or she keep singing "Jingle Bells" every December with no more thought for this time of year than that? Did she not feel proud that her child had felt the pathos of another people and expressed it in the beauty of another language and in music? I felt proud that Dan had learned words and music from a Catholic mass last year...that he had learned about something outside of his tradition, that his world had expanded.

Don't get me wrong. I'm not a scrooge. In fact, I love Christmas. But what I love more is that (most of the time) I do not have to feel strange for not celebrating it. I love the similarities in traditions, and I love the differences. And I especially love watching children feel wonderfully comfortable in learning about each other's traditions. When Christmas is celebrated and sung with its origins in mind, the celebrants pay homage to a person/deity. In Judaism, most of the holidays pay homage to a people. So "*Kyrie Eleison*"

(Lord have mercy) is appropriate, and songs that speak of family life and learning, and a people's collective vision of a city of prayer and peace are also appropriate to celebrate these holiday times. And cello music that reminds us of just how tenuous is this freedom to honor each other's traditions is also appropriate.

I would like to hear your responses about experiences during the holidays, or reactions to my experience. I'm interested in kids' and adults' thoughts on this. If you like to write, write a short piece and I'll put it in next month's *Shaliyah*.

Appeared in the *Shaliyah*, 1995

Climbing Bromley Mountain

At the end of the rocky, rooted, dappled path that switchbacks and winds through wood rot and pine growth and rich loam-fragrance, four times criss-crossing the mountain stream flowing like an artery from the mountain's head to its foot, we emerge above trees into unshadowed sunlight, welcomed by carpets of wildflowers, woven into green like prayer rugs—Queen Anne's lace, daisies, black-eyed Susans, thistles of pink and white and purple—and summit the mountain, walking through grasses taller than ourselves bowing in the afternoon wind. We just have to yodel!

(June, 2008)

Taming the Woods

If only I could walk these woods
and feel solitary silence,
become primordial as this hemlock,
alive with only
my essential breath
and the indelible imprint
of pervasive beauty,
smell the sequent stages
of wood rot from birches
downed by last summer's storm
or maples felled years ago
from unremembered winds,
twigs and trunks crumbling to
velvet loam, melting back into earth,
without also feeling this niddling
fear tapping my shoulder
though I swat it away
that danger lurks
in as many forms as
this forest's trees—
a bear stretching hungry
from hibernation,
a shady woodsman coming upon
a lone wandering woman,
my own abysmal spatial sense
that could direct me to veer right
at that juncture ahead, launching
me into an orbit around
an unknown center—
I could be lost forever and die
with the path home
a scant few steps away.
So I nail metallic blue can lids
to tree after tree, front and back,
on my right the way out,

left the way home,
from anywhere I stand
I can see two lids ahead of me,
and in this way,
with some sadness
and shameful security
I tame you,
wild woods I love.
I tame you,
thudding heart afraid
of losing my way.

(March 23, 2012)

For Michael, the true hammerer of beacon can lids, in whose accompanying presence and partnership, I fear nothing.

Can You Hear Me Now?

Friday afternoon
huddled on the sidewalk outside
Dunkin' Donuts
a gaggle of girls,
barely adolescent
make urgent
plans for that night;
like bees whose
hive has been disturbed
those evolutionarily advanced
opposable thumbs
slide furiously over
flat screens, send texts, BBMs
to batch address-book entries
touch nothing.

(November 5, 2010)

Keys

You are the keys to the universe, you dozens of smooth-cupped, digit-rest-stops with single Braille dots on each side to see me safely home. I love the feel of your perfectly–sized wells where each of my finger's pads is gently embraced like a breast in a lover's palm; and like that, from there I can go anywhere. My fingers fly across your monogrammed squares, feeling every single one and though each is smooth and sure it is the ecstatic rhythms of how my ten fingers dance in infinite patterns—like a balletic choreography or the crocheted weavings of water crystals tumbling as snowflakes from the sky—that simultaneously raises my pulse and calms it as if the intricate digit-dance created the wakeful, yet meditative beta wave pattern, but was no more effortful than the easy inspiration and exhalation of air.

After completing my *pas-de-dix* I find your one button (like that other core node that, when touched, opens the world's gates), and I hit that button—ENTER—and it all goes mysteriously into an unseen world, traveling with the help of the new age transmitter, silicon, not unlike, I imagine, the release of serotonin, epinephrine, dopamine that carry unseen thoughts, translating them into neuroimpulses, that jump across synaptic gaps as if some gentleman, with a flourish, took off his cape and lay it down across a mud puddle for a distressed damsel to get from here to there. I can't say that I really fathom how it actually works, no more than I can understand exactly where my finger-clacked message enters once I open that door. I've heard that it beams up to the moon or somewhere near there and then back down again in the time it takes me to breathe deeply in and out again. So, I will tap my fingers in their pulsing dance across these keys and open the magic door and send it to the moon and *voila*! there it will be before the eyes of anyone I choose, anywhere on earth…or beyond?

(November 11, 2006)

The Only Prayer Left

Not "why?"
but this, the only prayer
that I will ever again
be able to utter:
how to unring the phone
hush those sinusoidal waves
I did not yet know gathered
into them loss as colossal as the universe,
just place my hand lightly,
as if on a drum gut stretched tight
and halt those reverberations
like concentric rings
from a stone tossed carelessly into a pond
at whose center,
a black hole that pulls me
into it, takes from me all air
stops—but not for long enough—
the thudding in my chest
that keeps alive loss that until lost
is inadmissible into the chambers
of consciousness, and after—
a conflagration consuming everything
that once had residence there.

O Merciful Universe,
let me set my clock back one hour
unring my phone.

(March 17, 2011)

Imagining the mothers,
upon hearing of the death of Nicholas Pellaton, 29 years old
and the suicide of Joshua Lipstein, 21 years old

My Musings on Melons, Mammaries, and More: a 39.3 Mile Walk

With team names like: *MILK DUDS* and *SAVE THE TA TAS, MAGNIFICENT MAMMARIES*, and *HOOTER HEALTH,* the theme of this weekend was ostensibly, breasts. But, while bras were worn abundantly on shirts' exteriors (by women, street crossing volunteers, and even vans and motorcycles), and while breasts were definitely celebrated, this weekend was not really about breasts, at all. This event, organized in 9 cities across the U.S. each year by the Avon Corporation, was about hopefulness and life.

Here are some of the highlights:

🎗 Over 2500 women walked 39.3 miles in Boston; 214 of them were breast cancer survivors.

🎗 Together, over 5.6 million dollars was raised. These were not corporate dollars; these were $10 and $20 and $50, or $100, $500, or $1000 donations from regular people, from all of you. A quick calculation of 5.6 million dollars times 9 cities each year is an amazing statement of what can happen when people care.

🎗 The number 1 in 9 is now 1 in 7. Every 3 minutes a woman is diagnosed with breast cancer. Over the course of the weekend, Avon workers draped one woman, at random, every 3 minutes, with a sash to denote this statistic. It was frightening and overwhelming to see how many women were "sashed" by the end of the weekend.

🎗 Neighbors all over Boston stood outside their homes all day cheering us on, supplying us with coolers of water bottles, lemonade, Hershey's kisses. Three year olds gave thousands of walkers "high fives" as we passed.

Volunteer men and women came from far cities on their Harley-Davidsons to stand at intersections for hours, helping thousands of walkers cross safely, making sure we were hydrated, and feeling well, and boosting our sometimes sagging energy. Strapping, macho bikers wore pink. Many do this in multiple cities, for multiple years.

Twelve year old children stood in front of a microphone before thousands of us and spoke of losing their mothers to breast cancer. These same children cheered us, served us, filled our water bottles, and cared for us as part of the Youth Crew all weekend long.

The reading material for the weekend consisted of the backs of people's shirts, on which were written the names of all for whom they walked: many were honored, and too many commemorated.

I walked with the SnowAngels team, captained by Erica Snow, my son's girlfriend. She and her sister, Stef, did this walk last year, as their mom, Marybeth, was undergoing treatment for breast cancer. Marybeth shared with me that she has wanted to do this walk for 25 years, since she, at the age of 26, lost her mother to breast cancer. She walked this year, in memory of her mother, in celebration of her own survival, in hopes that her daughters will never get any closer to cancer than this.

I walked in honor of Marybeth, who is a one year breast cancer survivor

I walked in honor of Ronna who is a 22 year breast cancer survivor

I walked in honor of Gail who just celebrated her 10 year breast cancer survival anniversary

I walked in honor and in memory of Effie who survived breast cancer for nearly 40 years, but was not so lucky with another cancer

I walked in honor of Marion who will soon celebrate 1 year breast cancer-free

I walked in honor of Bobsy who will celebrate 10 years free and clear of breast cancer this fall

I walked in honor of Barbara who has passed her 7 year breast cancer survival anniversary

I walked in honor of Jean who is coming up on her 20 year anniversary as a breast cancer survivor

I walked in honor of Anne's sister and sister-in-law, who have both just passed their one year breast cancer survivor anniversaries

I walked in honor of Maria's sister who continues her treatments for breast cancer

I walked in honor of Nancy's mom who is a 25 year breast cancer survivor

I walked in honor of Marsha, Gloria, Jill, Liz, Pam, Joanne all breast cancer survivors

I walked in honor of Will and Eileen and Fern and Jonathan and Gregg surviving other cancers

I walked in memory of Aunt Sis

I walked in memory of John's mom, Gerda

I walked in memory of Marsha's mom

I walked in memory of Rod's sister

I walked in memory of Allison's friend, diagnosed at 25, who fought for 7 years, and did not win

I walked in memory of those who fought other cancers: Alex, Katharine, Jim, Joan's mom, Shelly's dad, Khalil's mom, David's friend

"I walked for our daughters, our mothers, our sisters, your wives

I walked for you and me

I walked for life."

We begin: May 16, 2009 6 AM (Stef, Marybeth, Nicole, Sheri, Erica. We go to meet Tanya, our other team member)

Our sherpas: Dan, Tom, Michael, Jeff. They set up our tents for us. So nice!
They cheered us (and several hundred others) on at lots of corners along the way. So nice!

Hope springs eternal!!

Entering the Wellness Village, after 26.2 miles! WOO HOO!!
(Stef, Nicole, Marybeth, Sheri, Erica, Tanya)

An amazing blue sea of tents!

Very tired SnowAngels after 26.2 miles on day 1 and 13.1 on day 2 (plus 5 additional miles to and from several dozen porto-potties)

WE DID IT TOGETHER! (No energy to raise arms or say WOO HOO!) but WOO HOO!!!!

Most of you receiving this email made generous contributions in support of this walk and this cause.

I am grateful to all of you who have supported me, our team, and this cause that touches us all. Thank you for joining me. You make a difference.

With humble appreciation and love,

Sheri

On the LIRR

Their fingers clack away on tiny keys
fretting, as if counting rosaries,
heads bowed in homage to the deity
to whom all praise is due, the Blackberry.
Ipod wires into their brains infuse
music that eclipses any muse.
Time and space around them they invade
as phone talk scars my quiet, makes me trade
reading and thinking to hear of what they spent
or ate or who said what, my ears are bent!
No quiet stillness can they seem to hold;
to small machines their restless souls they've sold.
One might have the makings of a poet,
but plugged in thus, will probably never know it.

(December 11-13, 2008)

Published in *The New York Times*, February 23, 2009, Metropolitan Diary, p. A24.

December 3, 2011

Dear Family and Friends,

It is with great sadness that we share with you that we said goodbye to our dear Hallie today. All of you have known her—in New York, in Vermont, in your homes. Even in those snapshot moments of your visit or hers, she had a way of entering your life, the way she entered ours, making each moment happier, and filling us with pure goodness.

Over these nearly 15 years, as she walked the Port Washington circuit with Sheri or jogged with Michael or ambled with us down to Winhall Market every morning, she brought with her a spark that made others stop, talk with her, pet her, and reach out of themselves to connect. Honestly, people took out earplugs or said "call you back" and put away mobile phones when they encountered Hallie. They just had to say hello. In more recent years, when her walking circuits needed to be smaller—just around the block—people have stopped us regularly to ask where our dog was. Some of these people we do not know, we don't even recognize, they don't know our names, but they know that we are the people with that wonderful dog.

There was a time when we would let Hallie out that she would bound off the deck, flying in the air. Her spirit was uncontainable. When she ran, she was almost part kangaroo, going so fast that her front legs didn't have time to touch the ground. In Vermont, she would race down to the lake and sploosh in the water. As a swimmer, she was never going to win any medals. But sputtering and snorting, she would follow us out to the raft, wanting only to be where we were. Her moxy was evident, as we dove back into the lake and she was left dancing and positioning herself, gathering her courage to take the plunge and swim back to shore with us. She would soar off that raft, clearly trying to cover as much distance as she could in the air, so she'd have to swim less! It made **us** feel more secure, in later years, to zip her into her Fido Floats life vest, though I'm sure it was a yellow badge of shame to her water dog-ness identity.

Her life was a daily fulfillment of her name—*Halleluyah*—for she embodied the exuberance and love, the reaching out with her soul to everyone, the being IN life that honors and celebrates all creation. She possessed and radiated the spark of creation. Her life was a long and pure song of praise to the essences of existence. In this she was a rabbi, a guru, a master teacher, showing us how life should be lived.

Thank you for loving her, for holding her, for being a part of the circle of her life and ours.

In friendship and sadness,
Sheri and Michael and Dan and Erica and Jo and Dave

VIII. Crossing the Sea

The following was how our family experienced the Exodus story, as the first 3 children of the next generation, my son and 2 nieces, were preparing to leave home for college. It is repeated here (see page24), as it was the first *Pesach* piece, and began a tradition.

Exodus in Our Time:
A Story for the Children,
Especially for Those Who Will Begin Their Journeys Soon
for *Pesach* 5758/1998

You know, don't you, that the Exodus story is about you, you sitting
around this table.
Tonight, especially, it is your story: Daniel, Rebecca, and Loree,
And soon it will be yours, Joanna, Matthew, Brian, and Julie;
It once was our story, mine and Michael's, Sandy's and Gail's,
Ronna's, Freddi's and Scott's, Robert's and Cheryl's;
And before us, it was Leona's and Eugene's, and Effie's and
Harold's;
And it was a true story for those who came before them, too.

But tonight, it is your story
And we will map the ways in which you **are** the Hebrews.

Do you remember how the Hebrews came to be in Egypt?
They came because there was food, life in abundance,
there for the taking.
It was there that they could thrive, and grow into a people.

You, too, arrived nursing eagerly at the land,
Growing strong on the abundance, there for your taking,
Growing into people.

Eager Josephs you were, who paved the way,
Becoming rulers in your new homelands!
Ready to test and then to welcome your kin,
When they would chance to arrive.

For a long time, 400 years the story says,
The Hebrews and the Egyptians lived together.
We do not hear a word about them for this long time.
We assume, therefore, that all was well:

The Hebrews were not slaves; the Egyptians not oppressors.
Together, they thrived.

So it was in our homes.
For timeless years: uninterrupted living.
Continual genesis.

And then, without knowing exactly when it happened,
The Hebrews feel enslaved.
Yes, a new Pharoah arose who knew not Joseph.
How could it have been otherwise?
For Pharoahs,
Like Josephs,
Change with time.
And the Hebrews are instructed by God that it is time to leave.
They are ready, and they are not ready: Moses equivocates, but
knows that he will be ready.

And you? Yes, this happened to you, too.
There was a point in time,
A moment that you probably cannot even remember,
When you, too, felt that you were no longer recognizable to us.
That we did not know you anymore.
And though we remember Joseph
(Oh, how we remember Joseph!)
It is not enough,
For you needed to set aside your Josephness
In order to receive the mark that time would put upon you,
In order to respond to the silent call, as irresistible as God,
The magnetic pull that tugs insistently at your body and your soul
And tells you to prepare to depart--the time is near,
And you are ready and not ready, but, like Moses, becoming
ready.

What have the Hebrews been doing when we hear of them again?
They have been making bricks.
They have been learning how to build,
To know what is the stuff that protective shelter is made from,
To know how to build a home.

And why, all of a sudden, do they feel themselves slaves,
when they had not begun that way?
Because, all of a sudden, they know how to make bricks,
Well enough;
They do not need to be taught this anymore.
And so the practice, in the narrowed walls of Egypt, stifles.

And you?
Yes you, like the Egyptians, have also been learning about
what is the stuff that makes a home
And though perhaps you could use a tad more practice with the
toilet seat thing, or the dirty underwear on the floor thing,
Still, you are nearing readiness for your apprenticeship to end.
You are nearing readiness to leave Egypt,
The land that has begun to feel too close, enslaving.
Yes?

What of the plagues? What of them?
The land of Egypt can barely imagine itself without its Hebrews.
The Hebrews' presence has enriched Egypt in untold ways.
The Pharoahs love to tell stories about the old days,
When the Hebrews first arrived,
And the golden years, when the Egyptians and Hebrews lived
a synchronous life.
But these are no longer the same Hebrews.
They do not want to hear these stories--not because they do not
love them--because they do.
They love hearing of former times, when all was well,
When they were afforded places in the palace.
But they know that these stories could lure them from their mission,
Their purpose,
Which is to leave.
And they cannot risk being deterred.

They know that they must
'lose the earth they know,
for greater knowing;...lose the life they have,
for greater life...leave the friends they've loved
for greater loving;
to find a land more kind than home, more large than
earth...[1]

And you? So it is with you.
You will rain petty plagues upon us to help us know that the time
is right.
And we, like Pharoah, will loosen our hold, as we have been doing
little by little since the beginning.
But we will, no doubt, have you make just a few more bricks,
to make sure you really know how.
You will throw plagues our way to distract us from the real issue
at hand:
That you are leaving.
And we will watch to see how **you** weather your own plagues.
And we will know, when you find your Goshen, your safe harbors
from your own storms,
That it is all right for us, finally, to let go.
And we will.
We will let our people go.
And you will go.

But we will, because we must, follow you to the edge
of the Sea of Reeds.
And there we will remember, because it was only a breath ago
When we stood at the shores
And dared to step our feet into a sea much like this one
And how we thrilled as the way parted for us.
We will remember that we wandered for a time
And then we found our way to our Promised Land
This same place that once you knew as Eden
And only now is known as Egypt
But will forever, for us, be our Place of Promise.
We will remember all this
Because this was our story, too
Oh so long ago
And not so long ago.

We will watch you for a long long time, as you cross
to the other side.
We will be more wise than Pharoah: we will know that where
you go we cannot follow,
And so we will watch
Until even our vision no longer binds you to us.
We will watch

Until all that binds us are the invisible threads of memory's
treasure trove
That will always be filled with the awe, as great as creation itself
that we both felt
When once we taught, and once you learned
How to make the bricks
That you would someday use to build your life.
We will still watch
Bound by a gigantic and ephemeral hopefulness about the life
that you will build.
We will forever watch
Because of something bigger than memory and bigger than hope
Because of that thing that was the first thing.

And we will whisper a prayer that you will not hear
A prayer for the wandering and the discovering and the creating
that lies ahead for you
As you leave Egypt and begin your desert journey.
Whatever words we use,
We will mean something like this:

We hope you come to know the desert as the place where
creation begins, a place of utter quiet, ready to echo the
strains of music you will play;
We hope the oases you find fill you with such wonder and
nourishment that you forget you are in the desert;
We hope you feel, at each new tent site along the way, surely
this must be the Promised Land.
We hope you find yourself, one day, in a Promised Land, and
not quite be able to remember a time when you were not
always there.*

---

[1] Thomas Wolfe, *You Can't Go Home Again*

I was tempted to include one last stanza:

> "We hope that you remember Egypt as the place that fed you and held you
> Until you could do this for yourself."

but that would be pulling them back before they had ever left. And I imagine that that is a verse they must write for themselves in a time distant from this one, in a time when **we** may not hear, perhaps when they are holding and feeding those who come from them…or perhaps when they are saying goodbye to them.

Published in *Reconstructionism Today*, Vol. 8, No . 3, Spring, 2001, pp. 11-13

In Celebration of Our Lives Together
Pesach 2000/5760
2001/5761

Around this table
We gather
About to tell a story
About to offer our thankfulness
For having been granted
More time
More time alive
More time alive in health
Shehehianu, v'kiyamanu, v'higianu...
To be together
To rejoice together
To eat together
To remember together.

In the next hour
We will tell a story,
A story of a people
Growing up,
A story of a people
Coming of age,
A story of a people
Dancing and singing together.

And while we, sitting here, will remember, tonight,
A crossing that **we** never made,
Yet we have grown up together,
We who sit around this table,
We have commemorated and celebrated together,
We, and many others
Who have been our friends,
Whose paths have crossed with ours,
Whose paths have crossed with those of our fathers and our mothers:

(Each person reads the name, event, and date inscribed inside of his/her kippa*)*

So, we have celebrated and grown up together, all of us,
And while not one of us has ever stepped his feet into the
muddied bottom of the Sea of Reeds
Yet we have made such momentous crossings together
That the followers of Moses, 3200 years ago, could barely
have dreamt for us
This moment
This table
This gathering.

It is these crossings
That will help us remember, tonight,
The story we never lived,
The story we have exquisitely lived
The journey we have made together—
Mud and manna and all.

Who Is a Jew?
A *Pesach* Poem in response to the *New York Times* article April 19, 2000 p. A3
Pesach, 2000/5760

Can you be sure
That your grandfather
Or perhaps his grandfather
Five hundred years ago
Did not make a guilty
Or relieved
Conversion
To some Christian official in a Spanish court?

Can you be sure
That this grandfather of yours
Did not choose life
Then
Over a glorified but meaningless
Martyrdom?

Can you be sure
That a grandfather of yours
Two thousand years ago
Did not capitulate
To a Roman officer,
In a town like *Zippori* or any other;
Did not sport a statue of a Roman god
Upon his mantle
In the name of peaceful existence?

Can you be sure
Nineteen hundred years ago
In the time of Hadrian
That an ancestor of yours
Did not vow, upon all that was sacred,
To disavow his Jewish practices

And then secretly sit
In an underground room
On *Shabbos*
And read from the book of Prophets
Instead of the *Torah*?

Is it possible
That you are here
And that you are a Jew
Because one grandfather
At some point in the past
Three thousand years
Chose life, instead of death?

And if that were so
Would you not revere
With honor
Such a choice,
Such a person?

Do you not applaud the Maranos
Their ingenuity
To become Christians
Yet remain Jews?

Do you not honor
By continuing the practice today
Those who found parallel
Prophetic readings
To remind them of *Torah*?

Yet you deny
That Mitiku Yalew
Is a Jew?

Surely his father
In the remote, Ethiopian village

Of Gondar
Did no less than your father
In pretending a conversion
To perpetuate a family.

Or is it that Mr. Yalew's
Ingenuity
Is diminished
By the color of his skin?

No! You are not the arbiter
Of who is Jewish.
The blackness of Mikitu Yalew's skin
Makes him no less a Jew than you or I;
And the blackness of your coat and streimel
Makes you no more a Jew than he or I.

But your righteousness and your racism
Will sow, like a Roman army or a Grand Inquisitor,
Such seeds of death to the spirit of a People
That you, alone, will be called The Destroyer of People.

Will you be counted among them,
Or among us?

Roasted at the Reed Sea

Pesach, 2000, 5760

(An assignment for our *seder* guests of 2000: How would each of your family members have responded to the hurried exodus)

Joanna:

When Joanna first heard that we were leaving Egypt, she was feeling very mixed up. This was a moment she had waited for for years, but all of a sudden, she did not feel ready for this. This confusion led to a very bad mood. Soon, however, she decided to make the best of this situation and get herself properly outfitted for this trip. Finding everything she would need at Amenhotep and Tut, she immediately got in a better mood. She thought of those tawny skinned *Canaan* boys and was eager to set out. Not even the frizz-inducing, misty dew of the Reed Sea at parting could dampen her spirits. It is a good thing for us that the math has not yet occurred to her, and she does not realize that she will be 56 when we arrive in *Canaan*. We will not tell her this—this could put her in some mood for the next 40 years. But look at it this way, when we arrive, we will not have to worry...ah, you will not have to worry about PMS anymore. And, I guess there are some hot guys who are 56! But most important, Joanna would want to be like manna: she would want to make this journey by falling from the heavens, free-falling and landing gracefully and effortlessly on the other side of the Sea.

Daniel:

When Dan hears we are leaving Egypt, he tacks a few signs up around Cairo. This arouses the interest of about 400 people, none of whom have been slaves. The 600,000 swells in number to 600,400. Dan has promised that on the other side of the Sea, there will be a party and a keg. Instant Jews, these newcomers! Dan throws a few things into his duffles, and petitions his parents to purchase an extra cart or two to haul his stuff. He chooses 5 of his most special guitars and slings them over his shoulders. Just at the edge of the Sea, he spots several attractive girls. Sauntering over to them, he introduces himself, and asks one if she would just hold this for him for a second while he adjusts his knapsack straps. He crosses the Sea with empty hands, and his several female friends wonder how they ended up carrying this guy's stuff. One very special and lucky girl is carrying his pillow.

Michael:

When Michael hears of the leave-taking, he can't believe how stupid all these people are to follow this guy Moses. He's a little intrigued by the guy, whose hair is long, but paltry compared to his own. This Moses is clearly a wannabe. Michael grumbles about what a simple minded bunch of cattle we all are. He grumbles about what a long walk it will be and thank goodness he did not run that morning because of the Angel of Death thing—that was a real gift—as good as a rainy morning. Pretty soon, reluctant to admit it, he finds himself enjoying the trip. He totally changes his mind about this Moses. He's having a really good time, especially when he overhears someone say that manna is loaded with carbohydrates. He's breakin' his diet for the next 40 years. This is one happy fellow! He might even grab a timbrel and dance a little with Miriam and the women. Just keep the manna, coming—he'll deal with the milk and honey later.

Sheri:

When I heard of the trip, I compressed the entire family's belongings into a single 3 inch by 5 inch sack on wheels. I was very excited. My hastily-cooked *matzah* was no worse than anyone else's. And I would not have to cook for 40 years. This excited the whole family. When we got to the Sea, though, I was totally bummed out about that miracle thing. I had been so looking forward to swimming across the

Sea. I was going to count the strokes and be able to tell you exactly how far it was. I grumbled about how we'd just have to come back there once we were settled in *Canaan*, so I could swim it. I soon became content to walk, especially once I realized that Michael would have to walk with me. I had a walking partner for the next 40 years. I promised him we'd go to Abe's cycle shop the first thing when we got to *Canaan*. Then we could get the Honda 3000, the one that looks like a house-trailer, with 3 rooms, surround-sound, lazy-boy reclining seats. Because, of course, by then, I'll be 88; oh, but maybe we could downsize to the Honda 2000, because you'll still be a spry 86!

Next Year in Jerusalem

Pesach, 2001/5761

We come to the end of our service
The time when we utter the words:
"Next year in Jerusalem."

But wait. I do not want to be
Sitting at a *seder* table
Next year
In Jerusalem.

I want to be here
With my family
And my friends.

Why would we want to be
In Jerusalem?

We could,
Like the wicked son,
Challenge these words,
Refuse, pugnaciously,
Or on principle,
Or out of self-assertion,
Or out of political conviction
To utter these words.
No, next year,
Right here.

We could,
Like the simple son,
Say the words,
Perform the ritual
Not understanding what it means
Or why it is there.

But, out of orthodoxy,
Or habit,
Or compliance,
Or comfort
Utter the words,
Complete the service:
Next year, in Jerusalem.

We could,
Like the son who does not know how to ask,
Remain silent,
While others say the words.
Listening,
Looking,
Uncomprehending,
Unasking.
Next year, in Jerusalem
As good as here, I guess.

Or we could,
Like the wise son
Pause in our proceedings
And ask of one another
What is the meaning of this: "Next year in Jerusalem"?

Ir Shalem, a city of peace,
Is not, I suspect,
A place 7000 miles away from here.
Not, I suspect,
A place, at all.
But maybe this:

> the moments when who we are
> are synchronous with who we can be;
>
> the moments when what is real and what is true
> are indistinguishable;

the moments of choice when what is right
shines with such clarity, that the choosing, itself, is
liberation;

the moments when the fullness of our fortune
spreads itself before us;

this moment, a moment sufficient unto itself.

We have a choice,
Each of us here:
What to utter
At this close of our ceremony.

Let us raise our cups--
Not Miriam's, not Elijah's—
Not what has been, not what is to come.
Let us raise **our** cups
And say together:

"Next year, may we be gathered
In the full numbers of our family
And our friends,
Next year, wherever we shall be
We will, together, become a people
And we will create a moment just so
That we will be
Wherever we are
In Jerusalem."

(May 1, 2000)

A Modest Proposal

Pesach, 2002/5762

(An assignment for our *seder* guests of 2002: Write a proposal for peace in the Middle East)

> *I realize that the following proposal may be considered unorthodox, but sometimes Orthodox problems demand unorthodox solutions. Here is my proposal for a lasting Middle Eastern peace:*

Before the end of the year 2002, every Israeli family that is expecting a baby would be paired with a Palestinian family who is expecting a baby. As soon as the baby is born, the Israeli family will give its baby to the Palestinian family to raise. The Palestinian family, likewise, would give their newborn baby to their partnered Israeli family to raise. These paired families would raise each others' children for 20 years. Liberal visitation by the origin family would be encouraged, but the children would remain in residence with their "host" families. It would be the responsibility for the host families to educate the children. The agreement would entail education in both Muslim and Jewish cultures for all children. It would be understood, of course, that if Israelis were to inculcate their Palestinian charges with the "politics" of religion, rather than the ethics of religion, that their children, too, would be raised with such parallel distortions. Liberal visitations would ensure that those families of greater means share their prosperity with their partnered families, ensuring that their own children thrive because their host families thrive.

It would take no Delphic oracle to understand that if the agreement is broken, a ghoulish mass Oedipal scene would result, in which children, upon returning to their families of origin as young adults, would murder those whom they would have otherwise loved.

Yes, this would entail a sacrifice of the children, but there is Biblical precedent for offering our children as sacrificial fodder. This time, however, the sacrifice might yield something beyond the divided households of Sarah and Hagar. There is also Biblical precedent for a child being raised in the household of his "enemy." Perhaps the Hebrews would not have been enslaved if law had decreed that Pharoah's son be raised by a Hebrew mother.

This plan would remain in effect for 40 years, for the length of time the Jews wandered in the desert, the length of time it takes for the current generation of adults to die or to pass the torch to the next generation.

Yes, it may be a radical solution, but talking borders and holy places will never yield peace. These things may carry some emotional valence, but they are really only symbols. Now our children, that's a whole different ballgame. In a matter of only one generation, that which has raged for thousands of years would be *swiftly* resolved.

Pesach, 2002/5762

Over *Pesach*, last year, my daughter, traveling with her aunt in California, found herself seated next to an Orthodox Jewish woman in a spa waiting room. The woman, part of a group of 700 people who spend *Pesach* week at this spa, as an alternative to *kashering* their kitchens for *Pesach*, asked my daughter if she was part of the group. When she answered "no" the woman asked if she was Jewish. When she answered "yes" she asked her if she was keeping kosher for Passover. My daughter said "no" which shocked the woman, whereupon she began "proselytizing," asking Joanna if she knew the story of Passover. The woman expressed to my daughter that she felt as if they were "losing a beautiful one," because Joanna does not eat *matzah* for 8 days.

Joanna had the grace (or perhaps it was discomfort) not to engage this woman in a discussion about her Judaism. Put on the spot, I might also have backed away from such a discussion. However, this is a fragment of the response I have since fantasized, and would have loved for Joanna to have made to this Orthodox woman:

The beauty of this Judaism of ours is that it calls forth from each of us—it demands from each of us—that we find ways to recreate it, renew it, with each encounter we have with it. You, perhaps, connect with Judaism through *halakhah;* I do not. You, perhaps, feel that *halakhah* is the only legitimate place to enter Judaism; I do not. But you needn't feel that I am lost to Judaism. There are a thousand ways that it is a part of my life; eating *matzah* for eight days happens not to be one of those ways.

Yet, though I do not adhere to the dietary restrictions of *Pesach,* I do not back away from "Judaism-Wrestling," to paraphrase Arthur Waskow. I engage with this Judaism again and again. Isn't that what we are meant to do? Certainly, we do not read the same *Torah* each year in order to think the same things with each reading. I was taught to ask questions, to challenge before accepting, to create. I do not submit to *halakhah*; but I do challenge it in an ongoing effort to create ways to embrace it, to understand it, to make it mine.

No, I do not eat much *matzah*. But I read *Torah* on *Yom Kippur*, before my entire congregation, sharing the 7 *aliyot* with other young adults, both male and female. I could lead a *shiva minyan*, if called upon. I served as my synagogue's junior congregation cantor for a year, leading young families in prayer, and being a role model for young children about what is possible for them as they become knowledgable Jews. I write essays and poetry—some published in the *Jewish Week* recently—trying to reconcile the land of Israel's promise with all that remains unfulfilled there. I have written a dozen other poems, with titles like "*Lech L'Cha*," "*Midaberet B'Midbar*," "I, *Hagar*," and "Jacob's Ladder" in which the rich metaphors of *Torah* have become a frame for understanding my life's experiences. And, I stand on the brink of my adult life, intending to immerse myself in religious studies as I begin college in a handful of months, studies that will open vistas for me, vistas that may not be about God but will most definitely be about humanity.

Some of these activities are not possible for you in the Judaism that you know. But there is so much that is possible in the Judaism that I know.

Matzah Balls

As dry and bland as sun-parched earthen crust
These powder flakes, first cousins to sawdust.
Mixed with oil and egg, a pasty gruel is made,
Fit food for the oppressed and enslaved.
But then with oiled hands, like Pharoah's own masseuse
I shape the gruel to hail-sized balls, then loose
Them gently into frothing, roiling water
Like the Nile when she spills her silty matter
Upon her banks, where sprouts fertility
Yearly wakening possibility;
Then watch the miracle, like the parting of the sea,
Cast into water, the gruel finds air to breathe,
Engorges itself on a people's memory
To feed the freed, as we tell our best story.

(April 14-18, 2004)

Eight Commandments: Ways to Live, Written by Human Beings for Human Beings

Pesach, 2006/5766

(An assignment for our *seder* guests of 2006: If you could rewrite the 10 commandments, what would you say)

1. **It is a sin beyond all others to presume to speak in God's name.**

   Commentary: There is a reason why "God" is "known" through so many different guises: *Adonai,* Jesus, Buddha, *Allah*. It is because the idea of God is so compelling to explain all that is not understood about life. While the **idea** of God has some uniform features across cultures (God is bigger than we are; God is very powerful), the **experience** of God varies widely (God is love, God is vengeful, God is punitive, God is merciful, God demands obedience, God demands that all human beings experience God the same...) It is the highest form of arrogance to presume to "know" "God," to act in "God's name," or to claim to possess "the truth." These are not static, fixed ideas, that can be pinned or frozen or contained within a wall, a rock, a dome, a book; these ideas must remain alive, fluid, organic, capable of challenging every human being who is brave enough to wrestle with the "angel" of uncertainty, and honest enough to acknowledge that ephemeral understanding—a momentary, fleeting, partial glimpse, is all that will ever be possible.

   > "I declare with perfect faith
   > that prayer preceded God.
   > Prayer created God,
   > God created human beings,
   > human beings ceate prayers
   > that create the God that creates human beings." --Yehuda Amichai

"Men never do evil so fully, so happily
as when they do it in the name of God."

--Pascal

2. Love

Commentary: Do not teach your children about God. The old 10 commandments had it all wrong. Learning to love "God" never did lead to learning to love one another. First, teach your children about love—by loving. Only in the saving of humanity, is there any hope of redeeming God—not the other way around.

3. Grow and change

Commentary: Human beings are supposed to change, to grow, to be flexible when they encounter new experiences or new information. Just as human beings are supposed to allow the God idea to shift and grow and change, they are also supposed to allow the "human" idea to take continuous shape throughout their lifetimes. These ideas should expand thinking and understanding, not narrow it. If one's idea of God or of meanings in human life can not be challenged, and in this challenging, changed even a little, then those ideas are *ipso facto* wrong.

"We shall not cease from exploration
And the end of all our exploring
Will be to arrive where we started
And know the place for the first time."

--T.S. Eliot

"The moment of change is the only poem."

--Adrienne Rich

"When you're through changing you're through"

--Bruce Barton

"We can easily forgive a child who is afraid of the dark. The real tragedy of life is when men are afraid of the light."

--Plato

4. Live a life worthy of being honored

Commentary: Honor each other. Honor your children, so that they grow up whole, able to honor all life, able to honor their parents who honored them.

"If you always assume
the man sitting next to you
is the Messiah
waiting for some simple human kindness—

You will soon come to weigh your words
and watch your hands.

And if he so chooses
not to reveal himself
in your time

It will not matter."

--Daniel Siegel

5, Wonder

Commentary: Be willing to feel awe for what you don't understand or for what overwhelms you. Resist the urge to call this God, because this concretizes what should stay fluid. Stay in the moment of wonder for as long as you can. Be open to feeling it again.

> "To see the world in a grain of sand
> And Heaven in a wildflower
> Hold infinity in the palm of you hand
> Eternity in an hour."
>
> --William Blake

6. Participate in creation

Commentary: Dance, or make music, or write, or paint, or look, or listen, or teach or learn.

> "It's all been said better before...[But] we
> each have to say it, to say it in our own way...
> We have to try to put it down in pigment,
> or words, or musical notations [or movement]
> or we die."
>
> --Madeleine L'Engle

7. Eschew God

Commentary: If you would follow the previous 6 commandments, you will come to know that which is divine, which is not at all what "God" has come to mean these days. "God" is the result when one participates in humanity in the deepest, fullest way. Religion has been all wrong in starting with God. One cannot become human by claiming knowledge of God. One *can* come to know the most profound experience which some call God, only by being fully human at which point, the God part will not matter.

8.Hike the Appalachian Trail with someone you love

Commentary: This is no joke. In walking the earth's terrain, climbing her mountains, bathing in her streams, living in the sun's light and warmth and the stars' glitter, hearing the wind's whisper, being baptized in the rain, sensing the nights' dark mysteries and the forests' still silence, smelling the musk of each other at day's end, and lying together embracing your shared journey, you will come to find a deep inner reservoir of manna.

> "When the spirit of evil reached its height,
> Nature maintained for me a secret happiness."
>
> --William Wordsworth

Should Religion be Brought into Space?

Pesach, 2008/5768

(An assignment for our *seder* guests of 2008: If human beings ever settle in space, should religion be brought along?)

Given: Human beings, as a species, can not refrain from the religious impulse. William James posits that it has existed in every culture throughout known history.

Premise: The religious impulse is one of humanity's most noble impulses.

It arises from humanity's irrepressible and insatiable need for meaning and understanding, especially in relation to experiences of awe and mystery that penetrate too deeply for words. It is in this paradox that the **idea** of religion and religion part ways. The **idea** of religion honors the moment of mystery; **religion** codifies that moment, pinning it, like a rare butterfly, to a 2-dimensional mat, thereby rendering it lifeless.

Religion is an expression of our capacity to think about thinking, and, as such, may be the defining element that sets us apart from all other creation.

Therefore: Religion is a good thing, as it embodies our acknowledgment of all that is ineffable and essential about life.

As such, it should come into space with us.

However: How can we conceptualize a form of religion that remains true to the origins of the religious impulse?

This is a proverbial slippery slope, as the nature of an impulse is to be fleeting, the nature of the ineffable to be indefinable, the nature of mystery to be beyond conceptualization.

Having said this, if I were in charge of the world (and after all, that is what this is about!), here are some of the religious ideals that I would like to see brought into space.

Religion should not be about God. It is about humanity... about the ways we come to touch the wellsprings of our humanity, at the center of which is love. Not ladders to heaven but pathways that paradoxically allow us to ascend into the depths of our own souls is what religion should provide.

There are experiences and vehicles that take us to this place. In fact, almost any experience can do this: the birth of a child, listening to Beethoven's Ninth Symphony, reading *The Book Thief*, watching *Les Mis*, reading the Bible. It is not the vehicle that matters....it is the process of having our being "cracked open" that matters, like a seed whose wondrous potentials are released (but still need to be nurtured). If being "cracked open" is like the revelatory moment on the mountain top, then the subsequent nurturing is like Abraham's return from the mountain, the necessity to surround ourselves with all that will help us sustain our connection to that moment of holy awakening. The awakening and the growing are both at the core of religious experience. The experience of the transformative potential, and the capacity to feel, to watch and reflect upon that experience takes us into the inner sanctum of ourselves where an alchemy occurs whereby we become something other than we were in the moment before. One writer described that the only moment of transformation comes when we let go of one trapeze bar before we have grabbed the new one swinging toward us (Danaan Parry). It is only when we allow ourselves to be unsettled, unmoored, that we can see and experience life as if for the first time. This is rarely if ever possible when we are safely anchored.

Religions, as they are most often practiced, have strayed from this understanding. They have taken it as their mission to "teach" us what we are to do or think or be...to moor us and anchor us with a set of rituals, texts, behaviors, beliefs. Rituals are, I believe, intended to provide an "unanchoring," a time to unmoor ourselves from routine and familiarity so that we can let go of what we know and know something deeper. Unfortunately, more often than not, they function to structure and impose rules upon the moment, and thereby rob the moment of its transformative possibilities. Religions have set up ministers and rabbis and priests to interpret words or actions for us. It is no wonder that so many of us leave the suffocating nest of religion...and then return asking nothing more of our priests or of ourselves than what we turned from.

If there are to be "heads" of religion at all, these persons must only provoke thought and question, and then step back out of our way, allowing us to wrestle, as Jacob did with an angel, with these questions, journeying within and between as we attempt to answer these; as soon as the teacher shows the way, imparts knowledge, religion is no longer a process of journeying inward, but rather a set of directives that keep us on the surface of our lives. No one tells us how to absorb *St. Francis in Ecstasy* or *My Fair Lady*. The artists create a reflection of ourselves and leave us to find ourselves in it. Some viewers, listeners, readers remain on the surface, feeling entertained or amused or cultured. But some find a deep and essential reflection of the possibility of change that is brought about through loving in these mirrors of our humanity.

Religion has become insecure. It does not trust us to discover the deepest meanings of our texts or celebrations. It feels the need to teach us, to codify itself, thereby relinquishing all of the best that religion can provide. It needs to honor the fluid, not the fixed; it needs to cherish the process, not the product, and it needs to revere the inner discovery, not the outer form.

This, I think is why we ate the apple in Eden...because we have a deep inner yearning to know ourselves, our world, each other. This is why Francis left Assisi because its narrowed walls limited who he could become. This, I think, is why we had to leave Egypt...because we had become slaves to our own lives, had stopped growing. This, I think, is why we wandered for 40 years, the length of a generation, in the desert...because it is only in the journey that we might feel foreign to ourselves, and thereby find or create new possibilities. This, I am certain, is why we do not enter the Promised Land...because the visionary creators of the Bible understood that once there, everything that was fluid would be fixed, we would hold too tight to that particular trapeze bar, we would possess it and never let it go, (indeed, have done exactly as the visionary had foreseen, had known us so well) and, paradoxically, having arrived, we would cease to grow. The Promised Land, for each of us, is in the moment when we have the courage to release ourselves, the trust to reach into the yet-to-be-known, and the vision to create, just as we ascribe to God, what did not exist in the moment before. This is the essence of the religion I would want a brave new world to be brave enough to embrace. And its credo would be:

We shall not cease from exploration
And the end of all our exploring
Will be to arrive where we started
And know the place for the first time.

Why Is This Night Different from Other Nights?

Pesach, 2010/5770

In anticipation of this year's family *seder*, some family members expressed that Passover *seders* were not meaningful, and while they would be willing to come to a family dinner gathering, they would no longer attend a *seder*. Our challenge, this year, was to attempt to articulate whether or not we would abandon a *seder* in favor of a simple family dinner.

This question forms the core of the *seder* celebration. And each year we recite the prescriptive answer to this question: we eat different foods, we dip them, we recline...we do this because once we were slaves in Egypt, but, with a mighty, outstretched hand, God freed us from slavery.

Tonight, this question raises its head again, forming a hot center for our family's *seder*. The question has arisen for us, in various forms:

--why should this night be different?
--does this night have to be different?
--doesn't "the repetition wear you down?"
--how "serious" should our *seder* be?
--what is the essence of doing a *seder*?

These questions come in the context of and at a time of family transformation. Many of us here tonight and some not here, did not grow up with a as part of family tradition. But the question has arisen not only on behalf of those, but as an expression of alienation on the part of some who did grow up with this tradition. As the ranks of our family swell, as we continue to welcome the beloved significant others of each generation into all of our celebrations, it is, perhaps, appropriate that we place these questions before us and ponder them. The *seder,* after all, is a night where questions are not only welcomed, but encouraged, where the prescription of a *haggadah* can get us going, be our starting point, but need not be our ending point; where our four children's questions need not be hierarchically judged, but might be something like: the ones to whom the *seder* does not speak; the ones for whom the *seder* is meaningful; the ones who are not certain but enjoy parts of the evening; the ones who will come but would not miss it if it did not happen.

So, as this particular challenge sits at the table among us, I will attempt to posit not "the" answer, but "an" answer, "my" answer offered tonight.

Does this night need to be different? Why can't we just have a family dinner together, with *matzah* ball soup? We all have salient memories of cousins, extended family, and special foods. These questions are valid, especially since family gathering and memory would appear to be the essence of the *seder* celebration.

I would offer that all of this is essential, but still, for me, would miss the most elemental experience of the *seder,* which I struggle to articulate but will try, nonetheless.

Growing up, we had many dinners with our first cousins. Unlike this generation, we lived close and saw each other frequently. I know this but do not have a clear memory of any of it, except our *seders*. The aroma of Gorham's silver polish, the gray, wine-stained *haggadahs*, the search for the *afikomen*, the fancy dresses and new shoes, the silver dollars, the ability to read and participate, the time when each of us was honored as the youngest and could chant the 4 questions in Hebrew, the valiant stab at Who Knows One, the discovering of exactly what tongue was, the ancient grandparents (who were not even as old as I am now!), the younger cousins, the kids' table, the firstborn. The ushering of the next generation into all of this. But these are my immediate memories, the ones that occupy the foreground.

Behind, beneath, above, and within this foreground, there is a background: the ritual enactment that somehow gives dimension to these memories--the *seder* ritual that, like any effective ritual, transports us somewhere deeper than this foreground. As we light the candles, we set the stage. And we step onto this stage, not because we are "acting" but so we become conscious of the role we occupy. And we tell a story. It does not matter if it is real history; it matters that it is mythic in proportion, ancient and huge in import, and resonant with truth about our humanity. Here are some of the elements of our story upon which our own lives overlay: our protagonist is born to humble origins, but raised a prince (which of us has not wished for or been grateful for the good fortune to be raised in the wealth of essential things—dignity, respect, the having and giving of love?); the wealth of his upbringing does not eclipse who he is as a human being (which of us does not yearn to be the kind of person who will make personal sacrifice to stand up for those oppressed?); through many trials with his symbolic father, in spite of a speech impairment, the need for his brother to speak for him, he comes to find his own voice and to use that voice, that self-understanding for good (which of us has not stood before our Pharoahs, insisting upon being born, being let go, knowing our own readiness for membership in the tribe of humanity?). This story includes image after image of birth (the plague of the red Nile; the parting of the Reed Sea waters), suggesting that we are always to be works in the making, that creation and re-creation, not complacency or completion, are somehow at the core of our humanity. This is a story about becoming, about growing into one's self; about locating one's self in one's own time; about coming to know one's place upon a canvas larger than family; about enacting this primal, ancient saga. I would suggest that this is a story that transcends its Jewish context, a story that is emblematic of us all as human beings.

I think this is why a Passover *seder* often (though I understand, not always) has powerful emotional resonances…because it elicits responses that are immediate and those that hover at the edges of awareness; responses that are personal and those that are collective. I would propose that a family dinner gathering, lovely as it might be, does not do this. I offer, that it is only in agreeing to create ritual time together, in allowing ourselves to enter this sacred time, in participating, for instance, in this *seder* that there is potential to have a transformative and transportative experience, an experience in which we may touch the tap root of our own humanity, the yearning not only for freedom, the more obvious theme of our evening, but our inner yearnings to be connected to our best selves, to struggle through mighty roadblocks, as Moses did, to have faith in what is possible, and do what is not popular, like *Nahshon* who stepped into the sea and in that act effected his destiny and the destiny of a people; to open ourselves to all that is miraculous and mysterious; to insist, over and over, on being born; to celebrate that we are here, and to remember why.

IX. Letters

February 27, 1995

Dear Yuda and Ziva,

I need to re-introduce myself to you. In the summer of 1972 many unhappy things happened in Israel. At the beginning of the summer was the Lod airport massacre. And at the end of the summer, Israeli Olympic athletes were killed in Munich. In between those two very sad events, Michael and I travelled in your country, we discovered the beauties of Israel, and we met you.

I do not know if the two of you remember us, but we have remembered you and thought of you very fondly over these 23 years. We were hiking up *Har Harmon* in the Golan Heights, on a 3-day outing from the *kibbutz* we were working on (*Rosh Hanikra)*. We had met up with another traveller (Jeff Rubinoff? or Rubinowitz?) when we were looking for a youth hostel in *Kuneitra* the day before. You were on a kind of second honeymoon, celebrating your 25th anniversary, I believe, and you picked us up, knowing that there was nothing for us to see and nowhere for us to go in that deserted area of Israel. You took us on your day's outing--we went with you to *Hameshoshim*, where we all took a dip, and to *Tsefat* where you generously treated us to dinner. We had the most wonderful and memorable day in Israel.

We were also young, and I do not know if we properly expressed to you then or even after our return to the States, how grateful we were, and how touched we were and still are by your generosity to us. Perhaps as we have gotten older, we have come to appreciate your picking us up even more. I only remember that you had wanted *Time* magazine, and I think we sent you a subscription (I hope we did, and didn't just think about it).

Well, as you must be celebrating your 48th anniversary (I

make the presumption that you are both well, and I hope this is so), we approach our 19th in August (we were not yet married that summer in Israel), and anticipate with great excitement a trip to Israel this August. We have not been there since 1972. Although we have reminisced often about Israel, this upcoming trip has filled us once again with wonderful memories, and particularly with warm thoughts about you.

We will be travelling with a group from our synagogue, and our trip does not have time in Tel Aviv. However, we would love to find a way to meet you, to take you to dinner, to introduce you to our family (Daniel, who is 14, and Joanna, who is 11), and to thank you again, after all these years, for a very special day you gave to us 23 years ago. I hope that this letter arrives to you.

With warmest regards,
Sheri and Michael Lindner

June 1, 1998

Dear Shel,

I am missing you a lot. Besides not being able to share our day to day lives (like how your job is going this year and how you've changed it and it's changed you), I especially miss that we cannot go have a 3 hour cup of coffee and have a wistful conversation about our children growing up. Today is Jo's 2 year anniversary of her *Bat Mitzvah*, and she will get her braces off in 2 hours. Enormous moments that will be marked in small ways and will pass into tomorrow too quickly.

There are moments when I think of Lisa graduating that it just feels normal, exciting, wow, Lisa's graduating high school and going to college. And then there are moments when Michael and I are in your Palo Alto apartment with Lis in the kitchen sink, or we are walking down the block with her in her pram accepting compliments at how beautiful our child is. And there is the moment when Dan's lip begins to quiver because he got a puzzle as a gift, or Lisa reminds Dan to put his napkin in his lap, or Joanna and Amy look like Siamese twins, sprouting upper bodies and adorable heads out of a common strawberry patch nightie, or Lisa and Dan are nestled into your arms, each with a thumb that must be the perfect reciprocal shape to his and her palette, because the fit is right and the attraction of thumb to mouth is magnetic.

There are thousands of such memory-moments, with our children together and with each one, alone. But somehow, if we could add all of these memory-moments together, they do not add up to our grown-up children. It is as if the essence of their growing up happened between or around these moments; and for me, in spite of marking them all, and remembering so much so vividly, I still can't exactly figure out when they grew up. I somehow didn't see it happen.

Michael and I saw a special on TV a few weeks ago where David Crosby (I think that's who it was) was interviewed. Hair still long, frizzy, moustache, about 250 pounds. Flashes back to 1971 or so, where he is thin and oh so young looking. Looks like Dan. There is a wiggly picture quality--a then and now, with us then and us now alternatingly visible, and with us then and our kids now also alternating, so that our youth is replaced by their youth. There is something so sweet about the young David Crosby (Michael described it as "juicy"). Yes, there is a ripeness that our kids have, and although they will be ripe for some time, this is such a pivotal moment it seems.

So I am feeling wistful about our babies who now belong more to the world than to us. This is not at all a sad feeling, or only a little bit so, but more a very full feeling. There is a sense that all things are possible for them and all things lie ahead for them. Because of this and because we love them so much, it gives us the feeling that all things lie ahead for us too--because of the pleasure we will take in the blossoming unfolding of their lives.

Did you guys ever get my poem from *Pesach*? I realize that I am saying something of the same thing here. Would love to hear, read, whatever, your thoughts, your conflicts, your joys about what this transitional moment in Lisa's life is for you. Sit with a cup of coffee and write me a letter, and I will sit with one and read it. I look forward to a long, ambling walk together, whenever our next opportunity for that will happen.

Love,
Sheri

January 6, 1999

Dear Bill,

As the cold weather breathes its chill upon us, I realize how long I have held your book--since the sunshine warmed us when we met on Mitchell corner as our walking paths converged.

I enjoyed your words very much. I am moved, especially, by your desire and motivation to seize an emotional moment and hold it in words, and frame it for time's safekeeping. It seems that you never let your appreciation--for a teacher, for a speech, for courage, for a window, for a hill, and most importantly, for a child and a life companion--go unspoken. What you feel, you express, and you take such matters seriously enough to choose carefully how you will express these precious thoughts and experiences, so that they are fully yours and also more than yours, alone. Your pieces convey a man who always finds meaning and importance, vibrancy and love even in the mundane. What is disregarded by others is held in regard, and held in light, by you.

Thank you for sharing your life's perceptions. I look forward to meeting again on Mitchell corner next spring, when you will be walking slowly and I will be walking quickly; but we both will be translating the images and experiences of our lives into language as the world enters our souls.

Best Regards,
Sheri Lindner

August 18, 1999

Dear Derek and Tam,

What a very neat idea. At first we thought: "Oh God, what are we going to do?" And then we got some ideas. So, here is a tour guide of our patch for your *chuppah*.

We learned a great word about four years ago. The word is "palimpsest." Of course we thought the person who used it was pretty pompous, using a word that we didn't know. But when we looked it up we liked this word a lot, and here we have made a kind of palimpsest for you. It is not etchings upon etchings in stone with underlying and older meanings influencing the shape and existence of newer meaning (which is the literal idea of the word,) but it is layers upon layers of cloth "etchings." We thought this was a fitting patch, as our lives together have been like a palimpsest, with layers upon layers of newness, each layer never totally obscuring the one before it, so that origins and earlier experiences are still visible (either directly or in derivative forms).

Here are the components of our patch: The square, itself, is cut from a sarong that we wore in Guadaloupe on our honeymoon. Michael wore one tied around his waist all week and Sheri wore one tied across her chest. We have always imagined that the Chinese letters said things like: 'prosperity,' 'happiness,' 'contentment,' etc. So when we were faced with your *chuppah* idea we took it to the Chinese laundry guy to pick which character was the best one to use. We found out that the characters were names of chess pieces: knights, warriors, soldiers, etc! Oh bummer! Well, we thought they said happiness...what did we know...and we've been pretty happy. So, as far as we're concerned your patch says something like 'contentment,' OK? We saved this cloth all these years thinking, insipidly, that we might wear these sarongs around here! (It is not a pretty picture!) We are glad to include a piece of our honeymoon-- our beginnings, into your beginnings.

One corner has a Kliban cat in it. This was the picture (actually the cat in red sneakers) on a hand towel that became Daniel's "ditty" when he was 16 months old. "Ditty" (his rendition of "kitty") was his blankie, a near appendage that seemed to hang right from his nose, gripped in just one particular way. When we moved from our first house, when he was almost four, we found thousands of "Ditty hairs" -- the terrycloth loops of the towel -- along the molding of the wall where his bed had been. Now, while we don't imagine that he will pick some future wife's head bald, one hair at a time, we do know that Ditty was a very important step along the way toward learning about love -- holding it to oneself fiercely, protecting it with one's soul, being fully committed and involved. Ditty allowed him to venture away from mommy and daddy and go out into the world. A very important container of safety, in fact, of humanity.

One corner has a "My Little Pony" in it. Yup, this was Jo's "Cuddles"--and if you promise not to tell anyone, you can still find "cudsies" under her pillow right now. Tomorrow, when she arrives home from 8 weeks away, she will reach under her pillow, hold Cuddles in the ancient way, take in an enormous sniff, as if it were her first breath of life, of Cuddles' mane, while curling the tail hair of the pony around her finger. She may secretly sneak a suck of her thumb, an instinctive act that is inextricable from holding Cuddles. I imagine she performed this sacred act the night before she left for camp also. Cuddles, like Ditty, has been a crucial container of all that is human and all that is worthy in the world.

In another corner is a little scrungy piece of fleece which is a snippet of "Baby." You guessed it... this one is Hallie's. It came with her when we got her. We can't say it contains humanness within, but it does hold crucial necessities, generosities, mother meanings, and the ability to venture forward unafraid. While she will chew other stuffed toys to shreds, she mouths this carefully, knowing, somehow, that it is not just for sport, but is more important than that.

So these three corners contain the icons, textures, and smells that allowed each of our babies to go forth into the world, to leave their moms and dads, with a feeling of security. We included them here because they are important symbolic, maturational referents, and because Ditty, Cuddles, and Baby are relics who once were as important as mommy and daddy, and because we wish for you two to develop your own set of ditties and cuddleses, so that as you venture forth you do so in strength and security.

The cow, well, you can imagine what that is. Now that all the young Lindners are so secure and enjoy venturing forth (far and wide), we, too, are venturing into new territory -- Vermont. You both could tell us a heap about what Vermont means. We are coming to it later in life than you, but while you both have grown up with a Vermont sensibility, (yes, unmistakably, as awful as it is to admit, you both got there first!) it has been percolating in us for many years as fantasy (and given how important we know fantasy is, perhaps, and we don't mean to be too competitive, but maybe we got there first?!) But we must tell you that we feel absolutely as young as you guys as we pull into our driveway at #3 Burnt Hill Road. Vermont is *Shabbat* time for us. And beyond that, it represents how wonderful change is, taking a risk, trying something new, seeing ourselves as new.

And the *mezzuzah*, well, beyond the obvious, it, also, represents the excitement we have discovered in our own capacity for change. We found something beautiful in the least likely of places (for us) and that's just neat. You know how you meet a person and decide quickly for some reasons that you don't like him, and then you discover at some point later that you really do. The ability to change your mind, to find meaningful attachments in things you once spurned, that is what the *mezzuzah* represents for us.

Oh, and the flannel sides -- well, that's just some old nightie, but life should be edged in something soft and warm.

The whole thing is stuffed a little, both for softness and for dimensionality -- life should also have depth.

And, inside is a surprise, fun, and something that will make you smile, maybe laugh. Life should be filled with these too.

So, that's the story. It's not a real elegant patch -- we won't quit our day jobs -- but it is stuffed with love for you both, from us 4 (plus one).

May you go forth, encircled by a communal equivalent of flannel, may you build layer upon layer of life's rich offerings, may you feel safe and secure, may you moo together for your lifetimes, and may you both find warriors... oh, I mean contentment and happiness!

Love,
Sheri, Michael, Daniel, and Joanna, and Hallie

P.S. Give your *chuppah* square a little squeeze, just over the cow's heart!

April 7, 2002

Dear Thelma,

My mother lent me your book of poems, *High White Moon*. What a treat! I held it for a few weeks, knowing that I would want to read it when I had a stretch of uninterrupted time. It saw me across the country, on my flight from San Diego to New York last week. And now, my mom will have to wait for its return, until my husband has the chance to read it!

I love your images that make the ordinary awesome. I am moved by your use of religious metaphor, also, which infuses into daily experience feelings of sanctity. I love "High White Moon" with its references to the Eucharist. I smiled at "Who could have guessed/God was a whale with bad breath." I nodded at "but have always been rooted, here,/in the heart of that for which we searched." Yes. I enjoyed "These black Christs/nailed to their own arms," and "I am hesitant to choose morning/over the night palaces." I liked "A Bouquet of Guemes Poets." "The Tool Shed at Lake Campbell" felt nostalgic to me, and inspired a poem that I am working on about projects once done with my dad. There is sweet sadness in the poems about your mom, particularly the last stanza of "Separating The Milk." The simultaneous closeness and distance, immediacy and wistfulness stay with me. And "If Only They Could Speak." And I liked the one for Bradley, with his map spread before him. What a great image, of a small red-eyed bird shitting on it! I love the poem to Evan, particularly the last verse: "And like Coyote, who never/contemplates the shit on his tail,/may you show us the pads of your paws/as you race headlong/into mystery." I have thought of this line already, as I watch my dog prance and gallop on our muddy Vermont paths. There is such unmodulated exuberance that it makes me twice as happy to be out on the path. I can see the pads of her paws, and I know, concretely, what you have captured in that image, and yes, I wish that confidence for my children, to "race headlong into mystery." What a beautiful, perfect expression. I will use these lines of yours, I am sure (and I will credit you). That was definitely one of my favorites. And The Darrell poems convey so poignantly blessing and fullness, sorrow and loss, holding and letting go. I imagine that your poetry gave you, in some measure, Darrell and you again, that your talent was a healing gift to yourself, even through loneliness. And I laughed at American parents catching the Guemes Ferry.

So, Thelma, thank you. I really really enjoyed your poems.

I know my mom "*kvelled*" (Yiddish word for expressing lots of pride) to you about my writing. It is nice to have her as a fan! I am collecting a few diverse pieces to send to you, and will send them in a few days. I would welcome feedback, including critical feedback. Also, e-mailing might be easier, so my email address is: SheriAL@aol.com

I look forward to some correspondence with you.

Best,
Sheri Lindner

Letter to Bates College Magazine
Summer Magazine, 2002, p. 2

I enjoyed reading the many comments honoring President Harward in the Winter, 2002 issue of *Bates*, all of which resonated with my own experience of President Harward upon first meeting him at an accepted students' reception in Manhattan.

Taking some liberties with his wording, I remember him saying something like this: 'If you know exactly what you want to do when you come into Bates, and you leave having done exactly that, then we will have failed you.' He went on to speak of his vision of a liberal education, which was also his mission for Bates. He hoped that our children would enter Bates, and whatever they thought they knew about themselves would be tossed on its head by the time they leave Bates. He hoped that they would explore, and discover, and nurture talents and interests, proclivities and passions that they didn't even know, at that moment (when they were still high school seniors), existed. He did not want them to enter Bates as fully fashioned and completed; he hoped, instead, that they would engage themselves with purpose and passion with the people, the place, and the time that they would be given, that they would be fashioned and refined by this experience, and emerge, four years later, perhaps hardly recognizable, even to themselves. We knew, upon listening to President Harward, that our son would be faced with many decisions over the next four years. What he would major in and what he would do in the world would be among the decisions he would make; but most importantly, Bates would help him make decisions about who he would become. President Harward understood what was important.

Dr. Sheri Lindner
Parent of Dan Lindner, Class of '03

Letter to the Editor

Re: "The Rise of the Six-Figure Teacher" (LI Section, *New York Times*, May 15, 2005)

I'm wondering: what salary do you tax payers feel a teacher *is* worth? You're willing to pay an accountant or a gardener to manage your money or your dirt. But, I guess, your children are not worth the same investment.

You entrust us, every day for 13 years, with what is most precious in your lives. You ask us to teach your children how to read and write, to reason and problem solve, to sing and draw, to use their bodies and their minds so that they will learn how to make sense of the world in which they live. You ask us to teach your children to think, to understand, and to appreciate so that they will become decent, ethical, educated adults, who can earn a living (maybe even a six-figure salary with which they would still be unable to purchase a home in most Nassau county neighborhoods).

But you ask even more. You ask us to give your children all the tools they will need so that they not only will become leaders in the world that they will inherit, but they may even be able to shape and create and change the world they will inherit. You entrust us with your children and in doing this, you ask us to guarantee the future. In doing this, you affirm a profound hope for the world.

And we do ALL that you ask--because we love your children, because we believe in your children, because we, too, wish to launch your children into a future that they are prepared to hold. No, Richard Graham, we did not become engineers. The bridges we build require more than what engineers understand. On our bridges rests the perpetuation and the possibility of the betterment of civilization.

--Sheri Lindner Port Washington, NY

Correspondence between Tam Smith, Joanna, and me

From: SheriAL@aol.com
To: tsesmith@gmavt.net
Date: Sat, 5 May 2007 09:42:35 EDT

Hey Tam,

Wanted to send you along this poem that just appeared in *Jewish Currents* (hot off the press). While it was inspired by Hallie, it also, at its core, was inspired by Joanna and written for her. I'll attach it. (see page 84: *On Observing a Dog in a Meadow)*.

In "answer" to your question "how to get her there" (Zory) (ha ha, who do I think I am trying to answer THAT question??? which is the biggest most important question not just for parents but for all of us in trying to fulfill our humanity...but, hey, I'll give it a try!) perhaps the easiest to say-hardest to do answer is just to get out of her way. Which doesn't mean of course not to parent. Just watch her unfold (I'm thinking that all the new green growth that comes up in spring starts off looking like a spear of green--all pointed and stiff to push its way out of all that ground, and then it gets bigger and softens and spreads out and is beautifully lush). Take lots of photos or let John do that and look at them in moments when your only interaction with her is to sit and look at her eyes that can't wait to conquer, control, master all that life bombarding her each minute. If she is not equal to the task now (of course she's not and that makes her frustrated and mad at the person most responsible for why she's not a teenager already (you!)) she certainly will be. I was serious, too, about photos and videos (not that they're the key to parenting), but when you're IN the moment, it is probably rare to be able to see and process all this about her without you having to be alert to managing other things at the same time. Michael and I occasionally pull out the videos and photos and it makes us cry to be filled with how sweet and how overflowing they were at young ages. That feeling is good to find in yourselves as often as you can. Jo was an intense little kid (Dan was mellow and became more intense but still basically easy going) who got easier as adolescence approached. She always talked buckets to us needing us to be vessels to contain her dramas (still!). Her favorite put-down of us is: "People pay you for your advice?? We're still learning our dance together that when she asks for advice she doesn't really want it, but if we don't give it she tells us that's not helpful either. We haven't always been good at understanding this process with her (better with patients!) that she needs to dump it all, make us the possessors of some part of it, and then fight it in us so she can get clarity about what she wants/needs. And we do HAVE to fight back just a little to give her something to push against. Then she can be mad at us; and if we don't fight back she's also mad because she needed that from us to get her feet planted better for herself. From this moment of describing it to you, it's funny! And from Australia and age 23 we all now seem to understand this and do mostly better at it. But from within any particular moment along the way, it would only be after some major blow up that we could all articulate what happened, and "get it" about what she needed. I would say that she has come to understand this even better than we. And might I say (just to give you a pinch of wonderful anticipation...)that these blow ups pretty much came once a month on schedule! until we all caught on (you'd think for people with the number of years of education that we have, it would have come faster, but it took some time). Now all of that is funny, she has learned from herself what to anticipate and how to manage it, but we were the battering ram recipients until she could beat that particular sword into something else.

So, I'm sure none of this is really helpful and I could talk about Jo forever (I think the less she needs me the more I miss her). You won't avoid all the potholes. Maybe just try to take them slowly so no axles get broken along the way (or none that can't be fixed). Pay attention not just to her but to who she insists you become as HER mother (different from Luc's mother), and become that mother for her. Be amazed at what you have learned about yourself from her. Enjoy how you continue to grow up and be transformed by parenting and family life. And.....get lots of rest!

Love, Sheri

(Joanna's emailed response):

hey,

maybe i will write to tam, but its nice to hear you describe the experience of being my mom. and if it seems like i need you less you've misread the situation. i continue to derive so much of my strength and ambition and drive from you, and from dad. If i need you less on a daily basis (though i'm not sure if that's really me needing you less or not having access to you as much) its because you've done a great job giving me everything i need to get through everyday with a smile. anyway, its 2am so i'm off to bed. loved catching up with you. will have to fill you in on jake at some point!

MWAH
love

August, 2007

Dear Shelly,

This seems to be an end of many eras—some difficult and sad, and some, for all of us, sweet and fulfilling.

We have marked so many of life's milestones together: our developing friendship, which, as we all have recounted together, seems to have evolved, like the earth, itself, in an unseen, inevitable way; our marriages; the birth of our children; their growing up—how some liked napkins and some hated puzzles, how some were easy-going and some far feistier, how they all grew up in thrilling ways committed to possessing and improving the world; their *b'nai mitzvot*; the illnesses and deaths of some of our parents; the sadness that you and Jeff have endured together and each in the deepest reaches of your hearts.

It has always been a source of comfort to us that our children would have joined your family had anything happened to us along this path of the past 25 years. We have always felt a deep gratefulness for your willingness to have had that happen, and for the images this has given us, hard as that has been to imagine, of what our children's lives might be, without us. Believe us, the prelude to each trip we took was the emotionally wracking scene of "what if." We would sit at our computer, write a good-bye to Daniel and Joanna, be sleepless the night before leaving, and cry our hearts out at the terrible possibilities before us. We often said to ourselves that we wished we hadn't planned these vacations. But we did take trips, and we gathered ourselves together to do it, knowing that everything was "in place" and our children would be loved and raised in the awful event of "what if." For that peace in our hearts, we forever thank you.

As we looked through our wills from 1992, time fast-forwarded in front of us, with the children's grandparents and our executors Harold and Effie no longer here, and our children no longer minors in need of custodial care in our absence (care: yes.) So, we just updated everything, making Dan and Jo the trustees together of whatever they will inherit. Going through the legal motions is just the "clerical"; pondering the emotional implications is still way beyond that, into the "awesome" — how far life has brought us all, and with whatever bumps and valleys along the way, we have emerged more or less whole and able to hand over the managing of the world to these precious no-longer-children.

Shelly, thank you.

We know you are biking your legs off in Provence and hoping that in the movement of your body, the beautiful landscape, the finding of new friends, and the discovering of new yous, you are finding and taking in everything that you need.

The enclosed forms need your signature, witnessed by a notary public, in all the purple-flagged places, for us to transfer the trustee-ship from you to the kids. Thanks for getting to this as soon as you can.

We love you and hope we can get together soon—in Boston or Vermont or wherever.

Love,

Sheri and Michael

March 24, 2008

Dear Mary,

I can't tell you how wonderful it was to see you, though heartbreaking, as well. I left you with such a mixture of amazement, to have found and seen and hugged my best camp friend, and an aching sadness, at what you have had to absorb in your life and into your sense of self. And I was amazed all over again, at how utterly positive you seem and how fully you grab hold of life (our visit, friends' children, your description of your mom) in every form that it presents to you.

It feels so odd that we did not stay in touch for so long, that we did not continue to know each other as adults, that there was so much we never really knew of each other even as kids. And yet, what we each remembered of the other was the part of the other that we cherished most, that we respected, and that we could learn from. That felt so lovely (and loving).

And, after the catching up, the funny memories and the important memories, there is still so much of you I want to drink in. I do not know whether I step over a line or not, but I want to ask you how you come to terms with MS and with the loss of your husband. What philosophy or faith or inner reservoir of strength, courage, or OK-ness do you draw upon to manage this. Did you, do you feel anger or despair. I do not want to reduce you to your disease, but I also do not want (if we can remain connected now) to ignore it, or pretend that some monumental part of your life now does not exist. I will be guided by you as to how we can talk about this (if you have the energy or desire…or not). As always in the past, I know how much I have to learn from you.

More than anything, though, I felt such a desire just to stay there forever and fill in a lifetime of years: what college was like for you; what inner crises you weathered as a late adolescent; what wonderful anchors did you find or create along the way; who have been the most special people to you through your adult life; what have been your regrets; what experiences are your favorites; what have you discovered about yourself, about life that you treasure...and on and on.

So, if you wish, start anywhere and let's be penpals once again. Will it be odd or uncomfortable to dictate a letter through Divita or another of the people who help you out? I imagine that you have developed a deep bond and a kind of understanding and knowing that is beyond words with those who share your days.

Your friend,
Sheri

September 24, 2008

My dear dear Mary,

Where to begin? First, I must tell you that I missed you terribly this past weekend at the Saginaw reunion. You were such a part of the fabric of that place for the many people who asked about you. For me, you were, of course, the golden threads that wove me into my own life.

There were over 300 people, who spanned many generations of Saginawers. Dozens of people asked after you (Jackie Wilen, Steve Greenblatt, Billy Shapiro, Sharon Korman, Sandi Sherr, Wendy Miller, Nancy Buckhantz, Sandy Katz...) I shared with them that you still, as you always did, have a light that shines from within you, powered by an awesome positive energy. They all remembered you the same way: beautiful, athletic, kind, spirited, and upbeat. Do you remember Sharon Sydney? I hadn't remembered her until this weekend. She was one of our counselors in Bunk N (1965). The other counselor was Sharon Silver (whom we didn't care for as much). Sharon Sydney only came to camp that one year, but she met her husband that year, so both of them were Saginaw alum. She came to the reunion specifically to see you, me, and Nancy Buckhantz. She remembered the three of us as kids who made her summer wonderful and made her job as a counselor easy. Francine Elion was there (bunk 12 counselor) who also asked about you. I must tell you that though you were not there, you were absolutely there in spirit.

It was a wonderful weekend that called for us to regress to certain feelings we had as teenagers, while at the same time holding onto our adult selves. It was like those "wiggly pictures" that used to be in Cracker Jack boxes: we were then and we were now, back and forth. It was actually a very pleasureable experience to keep our feet in both "camps" so to speak: the past and the present.

In my thank you note to the organizers of the reunion I wrote:

I left this weekend full of Saginaw and its people, but very soon afterward felt the lack of all I did not say, all the extended conversations I did not have, and I yearned for more time to go beyond the sparkle-eyed excitement of being there, and "merely"! having fun, and finding somewhere in memory song-words that came together once again in the stunning poetry created by the utter ripeness of 20 year-olds eons ago.

Saginaw always was, and still is, a religious experience. Michael said this also, but I am filled with gratitude for the gift that I was given--that we all were given-- to grow up in "ritual" time where every moment held transformative possibilities. The reunion created this space anew for us, allowing us to open, again, the possibility of transformation as we relived, renewed, repaired our connections to one another.

It was not the Hill or the Acropolis that was ever so important. It was the opportunity, at every moment, to become who we could become. When we returned, year after year, we did not come back to the same place, ever. If it happened right, we were different, and what we gave and what we took from Saginaw was, each time, different. And a time came, for all of us, when we had to leave even this garden. But, as we each, in our own way, wandered in deserts, heading toward our own promised land's creation, we had within us a reservoir that had been filled by Saginaw. We had within us Eden, because we had been there.

Brian, Ira, and everyone: thank you for opening the gates to the garden once again, for creating Camelot for one brief, shining moment. The weekend flooded my soul with where I began and with all of you who once, as we walked on be-

rooted paths together, entwined your arms around me while mine encircled you, allowing us all to say "yes" to what spread itself before us.

Mary, you were always the person whose arm was entwined around me and mine around you. Thank you for being a steady presence in my life, even through the years when we were not in touch with one another.

L'shanah tova: I wish for you a year of peacefulness and quiet contentments, a year filled with the presence in your life of those who love you.

With loving feelings...from then and now,
Sheri

Letter to the Editor, *(New York Times)*

Evaluating teachers based on student standardized test performance seems, in theory, to make sense. It makes sense that the "product" is a direct result of its "manufacture," if one accepts certain assumptions.

It makes sense if we assume that students are equivalent to products. In corporate parlance, the more we make and sell, the greater our profits, and the only measure of success that is valued is quantity (in the case of students: how high we can score on that test).

It makes sense if we assume that what comes out of students bears an equal and reciprocal relationship to what goes into students, and that this occurs and can be measured in real time.

It makes sense if we assume that all students bring with them to school the same level of having had their basic needs satisfied, that students who come to school hungry, unrested, angry, or anxious can learn equally to students whose basic safety and security needs are met daily.

It makes sense if we assume that the most important thing we do as teachers is to put knowledge into students' brains.

It is only if we accept these assumptions that it makes sense to evaluate teachers on their students' test scores.

When I became a teacher over 30 years ago, none of these assumptions was part of the landscape of my training or my idealistic enthusiasm about teaching. Corporate and battlefield lingo (strategic initiatives, outcomes) was not applied to educational thought. When I became a teacher I understood that what students and I shared in a classroom might not have its full flowering until many years later. I took it as my charge to help students create the paths along which they would find their most meaningful encounters with the world. I was aware of the holy trust I shared with my students. They were not products, or data, or test scores, or outcomes; they were young minds on the verge of wakefulness, and it was my job to paint a dawn upon which they would open their eyes, their minds, their emerging humanity.

I understand that doing all of the above is not mutually exclusive with teaching basic skills; students must learn to read and write and do math, before any of these more lofty things can occur. When I was a teacher, we read and we wrote, and they took Regents' exams. But, more importantly, they stepped into the currents of adult consciousness and adult awareness, and adult humanity, and it was my freedom to follow their inquisitive minds that permitted such sublime transformations.

It saddens (and frightens) me to think of how one-dimensional teaching might become when teachers' worth is calculated on student data, which may or may not be an accurate reflection of a teacher's value, at all, when teachers become afraid to follow their students' leads, and stumble, together, upon an intellectual place beyond where the teacher had imagined she or he would go that day. It is the freedom to do that that allows the teacher to grow every day along with his or her students, that recharges a teacher's batteries daily, reminding him or her of all the most important reasons he or she became a teacher.

I find myself drawn to quote the wisdom of someone who always understood children, far better than those who are entrusted to create educational "policies."

It is easy to convince people that children need to learn the alphabet and numbers. There are too many reasons to enumerate, ranging from 'it'll help 'em when they get to first grade,' to 'we've got to use these early years to get in as much as we can.' How do we help people realize that what matters—even more than the superimposition of adult symbols—is how a person's inner life finally puts together the alphabet and numbers in his outer life. What really matters is whether he uses the alphabet for the declaration of war or for the description of a sunrise, and his numbers for the final count at *Buchenwald* or the specifics of a brand new bridge.

--Fred Rogers

For Melissa Noon, on the Occasion of Her Wedding Shower

Someone, in the interest of commercialism, decided arbitrarily that anniversaries should be celebrated with particular items—paper, silver, gold, diamonds—as if such metals, stones, materials could hold within them an expression of our dearest and most important feelings.

I imagine for you and Ian something different each August 7th as you commemorate the official beginning of your lives together. I imagine the two of you sitting together over a bowl of *matzah* ball soup, a fitting remembrance of the event you both happened to find yourselves at the first time you knew of each other's existence.

As you make and eat your yearly *matzah* balls, may you keep in mind a few things about this humble food and your now special connection to it:

--all by itself, it is closer to sawdust than to anything edible, let alone delectable. Now, the comparison is not exact, but some miraculous things happen when the right ingredients are combined.

--that it was your "gameness" to go to a gathering called the "*matzah* ball" that created the moment when you would just happen to find yourself outside of a bathroom next to a person whose ingredients would mix and balance with yours, resulting in a love that every human heart yearns to know.

--that within the corniest of moments lies the holiest of possibilities.

--that there is virtually nothing that represents and provides comfort and a sense of well being like a *matzah* ball (well, except for chocolate, but you didn't meet at a chocolate hop!).

--that sometimes—not always, but sometimes—following mom's advice is not at all a bad thing.

So, while silver, gold, and diamonds are OK, I hope for you that regardless of how hot and muggy it may be each August 7th, you and Ian find yourselves sitting together, a *matzah* ball shared between you.

With so much love,

Sheri . Michael . Dan . Jo

(May 15, 2010)

For Suzanne Davis on the Occasion of Her Wedding Shower

Joanna, a bridesmaid, arranged for each guest to write a card to Suzanne and Jeff that would be opened only on a specified date or a specified event in their lives in the future. Our assignment was to write a card for them to read when they had their first marital argument.

Dear Suze and Jeff,

We hope that we do not have the dubious distinction of being the first card in your box that you are opening!

So, you've just had your first fight as a married couple—unless you are unique, it was about money, or cleaning up, or who leaves a mess in the bathroom, or how much more one of you is doing than the other one, or who does or doesn't want sex, or whose parents are coming (again!) to visit, or whose family expects you (again!) for holidays, or whose driving is terrible. Did I cover all bases?

Here is what you need to remember when one of the above occurs (since one just has). None of those comes close to being as important as the two of you together. When measured against your love, whatever you just argued about is very small potatoes. To continue the food metaphor, just toss it out before it spoils the master chef creation that is your marriage.

So, if you carelessly shoved that metal cookie sheet into the cupboard above the refrigerator, and your loving spouse opened that cupboard and got clobbered on the head for the 5th time...say you're sorry, don't laugh too obviously, and don't do that again (a recurring Lindner scenario!)

Different from what you may think, each of you is not 50% responsible for your relationship. Each of you is 100% responsible. If one of you is feeling strong and solid and secure inside and can fix the "fight," that one is responsible to do it—right then. If you find yourself waiting for the other person to apologize, you need to know that in waiting "to win" you are digging yourself into a place where you have already lost.

In this moment, the two of you are not filled with the certainty you had as you stood together on your wedding day. Jeff, in this moment, you must bring you and Suzanne back to that center. Suzanne, help Jeff bring you back to that place. Suzanne, right now...go back to the moment of hope that you both had on July 3, 2011 and bring Jeff with you. Jeff, allow yourself to be brought back there, as you both restore your loving, pure center where everything again is filled with promise and possibility and love.

We have some friends who, when they argue, call each other the worst names they can think of (our favorite of theirs is "dickwad")! They do this back and forth until it becomes so absurd they just laugh. We can't say we'd recommend this, for reasons that are obvious. But, we thought we'd throw in another "conflict resolution" technique for you. Nah, don't do this one. You'll never regret being kind.

So, have you made up? If this worked, recycle this card and pull it out again, if the need arises.

We love you and wish for you that your lives overflow with the dreams you create together and the realities you live together and the love that pervades your lives always.

(April, 2011)

Letter to the Editor *(American Educator) in response to the article:* ***Why I Force My Students to Memorize Poetry*** by Andy Waddell (*American Educator*, Summer, 2011)

This was a beautiful article that articulated so clearly the gift that we open again and again throughout our lifetime when we have memorized a poem, and how the meaning of a poem has roots that only really take hold when they have been nourished by soil enriched by years.

Years ago, in a retirement tribute to my 12th grade English teacher, I wrote:

...She filled our heads with words, with gorgeous rhythms and melodies, and we came to feel awe for the beauty and majesty of the sound of language. I would put honor on it that many of us can still, on a long car ride, in a traffic jam, or on a sleepless night, quote the first 18 lines of Essay on Man, or the first 18 lines of the Prologue to the Canterbury Tales ***in*** *middle English, or words from* Meditation 17, *or lines from* To A Skylark, *or passages from* Paradise Lost, *or any number of Blake's or Wordsworth's verses. There is great power in the memorization of such language. We, the lucky ones, had neural pathways forged in our brains and our synapses filled with poetry. And while we are likely this hour to forget where we put our keys or our glasses, we will have with us always the lyric wonder and promise of renewal of: "Whan that Aprill with his shoures soote" etched deeply within us, claiming a place of permanence in our memory's treasure trove...*

Other teachers helped us chart our course through the topographies of history, of chemical and quadratic equations, of cells and laws of motion, of foreign idioms and conjugations. These are no small tasks, and their successful accomplishment is not trivial. But Karen was a cartographer of a different sort: she gave us sextants and maps (of words and images and metaphors, of poetry and art and human urgings) so that we could chart the quiet, essential streams that flowed deeply within us, streams, that in the end, would be the only true paths by which we find our way. Most of us, before then, had not even known of the existence of these subterranean sources of nourishment that bubbled within us, whose rich silt would come to fertilize our souls.

I hope Mr. Waddell's students come to appreciate the gift of language with all its transformative possibilities, that has embedded itself within their souls.

--Dr. Sheri Lindner
Former HS English teacher
Clinical Psychologist

Published in *American Educator*, Fall, 2011, Vol 35, No. 3, p. 2

Letter to the Editor of *Jewish Currents*

I was just reading the discussion of the possible place of psychedelic drugs in society and of a need for reform of drug policies. I said to my husband: Where else would someone be willing to talk about this stuff? Regardless of any "conclusions," the fact that such a discussion was featured seems courageous, and the fact that the participants didn't feel the need to pretend that they hadn't been part of their own generation felt more than refreshing. Its sheer "un-PC-ness" was so honest, and that fact, alone, makes it important. There aren't many circles where such a conversation could even be imagined; I feel fortunate to be involved in a few where it is almost unthinkable *not* to have such discourse.

I look forward to seeing each issue of *Jewish Currents* and what it tackles. Ah, the pressure is on!

Published in *Jewish Currents*, January-February, 2006, p. 2

X. Songs of Sojourneying

Our Israel Trip (to the tune of *El ha ma hayan*)

We arrived at JFK
Ready to be on our way
We were 12 families when the trip we'd begun
But soon we were one.

We were moved at *Mod'in*
Planting trees for our lost kin
Though for a moment we did grieve
A future legacy we did leave.

When we went to the wall
A lady yelled that we were dressed for the mall
Undaunted we did not go home
But together sang *Oseh Shalom*.

Leaving the wall we got on the bus
Thinking this was all of us
Some girls were missing we said, "OY!"
But they were with Joy.

Ben Yehuda street was fun
Something to buy for everyone
People, things, and places to eat
Soldiers with guns on the street.

To *Ohlmert* and *Abu Zaid* we spoke
Approaching them with our deep hope
That between men like them real peace could come
A Middle East *Shalom*.

Through the Lost Communities we did wander
As our ancestor's hometowns we did ponder
We listened to John's tale and cared
Grateful he was spared.

While in *Mea Shearim*
We could not expose a lot of skin
Their lives are very different from ours
They don't even own cars.

On the Temple Mount a Mosque now stands on the rock
Where *Av'ram* went to sacrifice his son, *Yitchak*
But we learned that holiness is not in land, or things or places
But in our acts and hearts, reflected in our faces.

Ancient Hebrews we've met now
On *Pesach* we'll remember how
They escaped across the desert sand
To embrace the Promised Land.

In *Ma'ale Adumim* we were in their modern homes
With running water, TV, and phones
Although from Ethiopia they hail
They're now *Am Yisroel*.

We left Jerusalem on a bus
With some of us singing and some throwing up
But at *Sachne* we all felt renewed with a dip
In the water falls or jumping off a cliff.

Then we went on to *Tsefat*
In the ancient synagogues we learned a lot
Of the *Talmud*, the *Mishnah*, the laws, Lee did list 'em
And, oh, "Fack the System."

Down the Jordan River we did float
On our bodies and inside a boat
We splashed and had a day of glee
Even Rabbi Lee.

While arriving at *Nof Ginosaur*
Yitzhak said, "let's hike, it's not far
Bring water for your thirst to slake
But it's a piece of cake."

To the *Arbel* cliffs some of us set off
With our trustworthy guide, *Yitzhak* Sokoloff
Who assured us we'd be back to dine
Ha! What a line!

By now it was seven fifteen
The sun's dying rays made quite a gleam
Ytizhak said, "don't worry, we'll sleep out if we have to."
We said, "he's crazy."

Through the *Golan* Heights we rode on a jeep
Replaying the victory Israel did reap
And what is so important about this land
We struggled to understand.

We learned about the *Zipporians*
Who capitulated to the Romans
And now their culture stands only on the floors in mosaic
For the Jews who chose not to be Hebraic.

Now *S'dot Yam* was a real *kibbutz*
Cleaning our trays in the kitchen of all our *schmootz*
It's where *Hannah Senesh* stood by the sea
And wrote, "*Ay li, ay li.*"

The British blockaded Jewish refugees
To us they said: "Don't enter, please!"
But we were determined to create
A Jewish state.

To *Tel Maresha* caves of yore
To dig up shards of ancient lore
Vivian found a bowl and Steve a lamp
From a *Maccabean* camp.

To *Arad* we next were sent
Where we ate with the Bedoins in their tent
They made us lamb and beef and bread and rice
The camel ride was nice.

Five fifteen and up we get
Camels in a silhouette
Up the Roman ramp and down the snake path too
Derek, I got in the bus before you!

So on to the Dead Sea we progressed
Defying gravity was the best
Onto the *Ein Gedi* spa
To refresh us all.

We came back to Jerusalem
Feeling we were home again
We'll hold dear to all that we did learn
Awaiting return.

El ha ma hayan
Bagadi, bagadi katan
el ha ma hayan
bagadi katan.

Chorus

Ha shalom lo
Le lu van ben bet tu el
Ha shalom lo
ulel, Rachel.

On the bus she would get us to sing along
So, thanks to *Tahel* for this little song
Many a morning we'd awake when the night
had seemed so long
'Cause we couldn't stop singing *Bagadi Katan!*

And now you'll be singing *Bagadi Katan*!

Sheri . Michael . Dan . Jo

(August, 2005)

Western River Expedition Rafting Trip Through the Grand Canyon (written and performed by the Lindner family)

To the Tune of Uncle John's Band

Oh the first days are the hardest days don't you worry
anymore
Soon you'll sleep on the beach at night and hear Joel and
Dolores snore
Come along with me, don't you cry or yelp
Oh, oh what I want to know -oh-oh is who has the NEED HELP.

Before we came on this rafting trip we had some fantasies
Of sleeping under the stars at night in the quiet and the
peace
Well eat some sand with me, now that we are here
Blow it out of your nose and mou-ou-outh, and pick it from
your ear.

Chorus:
Come hear a geologic moment by the river side
Here are rocks and there are rocks, everywhere we look are
rocks
Come raft the Colorado, please just hold on tight
Rapids rate from one to ten, just tell me what to suck and
when.

Wilson has to relieve himself very frequently
But without these regular Wilson stops, we'd all be holding in
our pee
Women there may bathe, men make your own shade
We know when you gotta go-oh-oh, you got-ot to go-oh.

Travis helps us to pass the the time by posing riddles and
telling jokes
Trevor gives us deep thoughts and true stories and fixes
engines when they're broke

Contemplate the view, wateralls and canyons, too
We are a lucky few-ew-ew to be here with you.

The walls we pass are old and deep geologic time is vast
Igneous, sedimentary, metamorphic rocks from the past
My what time can do, a billion years or two
Oh-oh if you're cold and wet don't get pissed, enjoy-oy the Vishnu Shist.

Here comes a number ten get your front and rear grip
Mike and Joel think that it's too tame and they'll take a different trip
Almost off the boat, now show us dead man's float
Oh-oh but we want to end this trip on an alive note.

Chorus:
Come raft the Colorado all you have to do is sit and listen
Come along but come with us, Western River Expedition.

To some brave souls the pontoons call cold water splashing them in walls
We others would prefer to stoop safely in the chicken coop
Ride a natural high, water, rock, and sky
Oh-oh what I want to know-oh-oh is when will I be dry.

Let's go on a hike today it's always optional
This one's not very strenuous, but yes...it's slightly technical
Fording streams and taking dips, jumping off of cliffs
We don't have a li-i-ine to rhy-hy-hyme with this!

Well the last day is the hardest day it's just like the brochure said
How can we possibly adapt to hot showers and a bed
So we bid *adieu*, farewell to all of you
And now we'd like to say to Travis, Trevor, Trent, and
Drew...**Thank you!** (August, 2006)

Appendix

Two Roads To The River

בִּרְכוֹת הַשַּׁחַר

BIRḤOT HASHAḤAR / MORNING BLESSINGS

בָּרוּךְ אַתָּה יהוה אֱלֹהֵינוּ חֵי הָעוֹלָמִים
הַמַּעֲבִיר שֵׁנָה מֵעֵינַי וּתְנוּמָה מֵעַפְעַפָּי׃

Blessed are you, AWAKENER, our God, life of all the worlds, who removes sleep from my eyes, and slumber from my eyelids.

בָּרוּךְ אַתָּה יהוה אֱלֹהֵינוּ חֵי הָעוֹלָמִים
הַנּוֹתֵן לַשֶּׂכְוִי בִינָה לְהַבְחִין בֵּין יוֹם וּבֵין לָיְלָה׃

בָּרוּךְ אַתָּה יהוה אֱלֹהֵינוּ חֵי הָעוֹלָמִים
רוֹקַע הָאָרֶץ עַל הַמָּיִם׃

Blessed are you, THE PROVIDENT, our God, life of all the worlds, who gives the bird of dawn discernment to tell day from night.

Blessed are you, THE FASHIONER, our God, life of all the worlds, who stretches forth the earth upon the waters.

בָּרוּךְ אַתָּה יהוה אֱלֹהֵינוּ חֵי הָעוֹלָמִים פּוֹקֵחַ עִוְרִים׃

בָּרוּךְ אַתָּה יהוה אֱלֹהֵינוּ חֵי הָעוֹלָמִים מַלְבִּישׁ עֲרֻמִּים׃

בָּרוּךְ אַתָּה יהוה אֱלֹהֵינוּ חֵי הָעוֹלָמִים מַתִּיר אֲסוּרִים׃

בָּרוּךְ אַתָּה יהוה אֱלֹהֵינוּ חֵי הָעוֹלָמִים זוֹקֵף כְּפוּפִים׃

Blessed are you, THE LAMP, our God, life of all the worlds, who makes the blind to see.

Blessed are you, THE COMPASSIONATE, our God, life of all the worlds, who clothes the naked.

Blessed are you, REDEEMING ONE, our God, life of all the worlds, who makes the captive free.

Blessed are you, THE HELPING HAND, our God, life of all the worlds, who raises up the humble.

בָּרוּךְ אַתָּה יהוה אֱלֹהֵינוּ חֵי הָעוֹלָמִים
הַמֵּכִין מִצְעֲדֵי גָבֶר׃

בָּרוּךְ אַתָּה יהוה אֱלֹהֵינוּ חֵי הָעוֹלָמִים
שֶׁעָשָׂה לִי כָּל צָרְכִּי׃

בָּרוּךְ אַתָּה יהוה אֱלֹהֵינוּ חֵי הָעוֹלָמִים
אוֹזֵר יִשְׂרָאֵל בִּגְבוּרָה׃

בָּרוּךְ אַתָּה יהוה אֱלֹהֵינוּ חֵי הָעוֹלָמִים
עוֹטֵר יִשְׂרָאֵל בְּתִפְאָרָה׃

Blessed are you, THE WAY, our God, life of all the worlds, who makes firm a person's steps.

Blessed are you, THE GENEROUS, our God, life of all the worlds, who acts for all my needs.

Blessed are you, THE MIGHTY ONE, our God, life of all the worlds, who girds Israel with strength.

Blessed are you, THE BEAUTIFUL, our God, life of all the worlds, who crowns Israel with splendor.

בָּרוּךְ אַתָּה יהוה אֱלֹהֵינוּ חֵי הָעוֹלָמִים
שֶׁעָשַׂנִי בְּצַלְמוֹ׃

בָּרוּךְ אַתָּה יהוה אֱלֹהֵינוּ חֵי הָעוֹלָמִים
שֶׁעָשַׂנִי בֶּן/בַּת חוֹרִין׃

בָּרוּךְ אַתָּה יהוה אֱלֹהֵינוּ חֵי הָעוֹלָמִים
שֶׁעָשַׂנִי יִשְׂרָאֵל׃

בָּרוּךְ אַתָּה יהוה אֱלֹהֵינוּ חֵי הָעוֹלָמִים
הַנּוֹתֵן לַיָּעֵף כֹּחַ׃

Blessed are you, THE IMAGELESS, our God, life of all the worlds, who made me in your image.

Blessed are you, THE FREE, our God, life of all the worlds, who made me free.

Blessed are you, THE ANCIENT ONE, our God, life of all the worlds, who made me of the people Israel.

Blessed are you, RENEWING ONE, our God, life of all the worlds, who gives strength to the weary.

THE LITTLE MERMAID'S BIRKAT HA-SHAHAR

I'll tell you a tale of the bottomless blue
And it's hey to the starboard, heave ho.
Look out, lad, a mermaid be waiting for you
In mysterious fathoms below
Fathoms below, below
From whence wayward Westerlies blow.

Where Triton is king
And his merpeople sing
In mysterious fathoms below.

Isn't this great--the salty sea air, the wind blowing in your face!

Prince Eric revels in the wondrous feeling of being alive and being in nature.

PRAYERS OF GRATITUDE FOR THE WORLD'S WONDERS AND FOR OUR ABILITY TO PERCEIVE AND PARTICIPATE IN THEM

1. *Asher Yatzar:*

בָּרוּךְ אַתָּה יהוה אֱלֹהֵינוּ מֶלֶךְ הָעוֹלָם אֲשֶׁר יָצַר אֶת הָאָדָם בְּחָכְמָה
וּבָרָא בוֹ נְקָבִים נְקָבִים חֲלוּלִים חֲלוּלִים:
גָּלוּי וְיָדוּעַ לִפְנֵי כִסֵּא כְבוֹדֶךָ שֶׁאִם יִפָּתֵחַ אֶחָד מֵהֶם אוֹ יִסָּתֵם אֶחָד
מֵהֶם אִי אֶפְשַׁר לְהִתְקַיֵּם וְלַעֲמֹד לְפָנֶיךָ:
בָּרוּךְ אַתָּה יהוה רוֹפֵא כָל בָּשָׂר וּמַפְלִיא לַעֲשׂוֹת:

Our gratitude for the openings and vessels in our body so that we are able to see and hear, taste and smell, touch and feel all of nature.

---

2. *Elohai Neshama:*

אֱלֹהַי נְשָׁמָה שֶׁנָּתַתָּ בִּי טְהוֹרָה הִיא:
אַתָּה בְרָאתָהּ, אַתָּה יְצַרְתָּהּ אַתָּה נְפַחְתָּהּ בִּי וְאַתָּה מְשַׁמְּרָהּ בְּקִרְבִּי
וְאַתָּה עָתִיד לִטְּלָהּ מִמֶּנִּי לְחַיֵּי עוֹלָם: ←

Elohay neshamah shenatata bi tehorah hi.

Our gratitude for our soul.

---

3. *Ahavah Rabba:*

אַהֲבָה רַבָּה

אַהֲבָה רַבָּה אֲהַבְתָּנוּ יהוה אֱלֹהֵינוּ חֶמְלָה גְדוֹלָה וִיתֵרָה חָמַלְתָּ
עָלֵינוּ: אָבִינוּ מַלְכֵּנוּ בַּעֲבוּר אֲבוֹתֵינוּ וְאִמּוֹתֵינוּ שֶׁבָּטְחוּ בְךָ וַתְּלַמְּדֵם
חֻקֵּי חַיִּים כֵּן תְּחָנֵּנוּ וּתְלַמְּדֵנוּ: אָבִינוּ הָאָב הָרַחֲמָן הַמְרַחֵם רַחֵם
עָלֵינוּ וְתֵן בְּלִבֵּנוּ לְהָבִין וּלְהַשְׂכִּיל לִשְׁמֹעַ לִלְמֹד וּלְלַמֵּד לִשְׁמֹר
וְלַעֲשׂוֹת וּלְקַיֵּם אֶת כָּל דִּבְרֵי תַלְמוּד תּוֹרָתֶךָ בְּאַהֲבָה: ←

Our prayer for having placed "into our hearts [the] ability to understand, to see, to hear, to learn, to teach, to keep, to do, and to uphold with love all that we study [in the] Torah."

ARIEL'S PRAYER OF GRATITUDE AT THE WORLD'S WONDERS:
HER DAWNING AWARENESS OF HER SOUL & READINESS TO FIND HER PLACE IN THE WORLD

Maybe he's right
Maybe there is something the matter with me.
I just don't see how a world that makes such wonderful things
Could be bad.

Look at this stuff, isn't it neat?
Wouldn't you think my collection's complete?
Wouldn't you think I'm the girl,
Girl who has everything?

Look at this trove, treasures untold
How many wonders can one cavern hold?
Lookin' around here you'd think
Sure, she has everything.

I've got gadgets and gizmos a-plenty
I've got whozits and whatzits galore
You want thing-a-ma-bobs?
I've got twenty.

But who cares
No big deal
I want more.

I want to be where the people are
I want to see, want to see 'em dancin'
Walkin' around on those, what do you call them,
Oh, feet.

Flippin' your fins you don't get too far
Legs are required for jumpin', dancin'
Strollin' along down the, what's that word again?
Street.

Up where they walk
Up where they run
Up where they stay all day in the sun
Wanderin' free
Wish I could be
Part of that world.

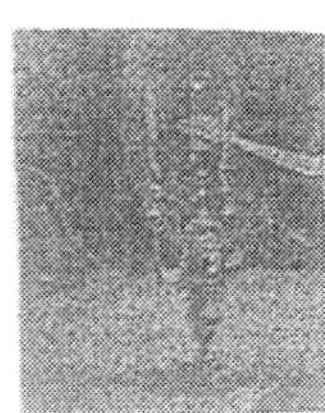

What would I give if I could live
Out of these waters?
What would I pay to spend a day
Warm on the sand?

Betcha up on land they understand
Bet they don't reprimand their daughters
Bright yong women
Sick of swimmin'
Ready to stand.

And ready to know what the people know
Askin' my questions and get some answers
What's a fire
And why does it, what's the word, burn?

When's it my turn?
Wouldn't I love
Love to explore the shore up above
Out of the sea
Wish I could be
Part of that world.

Reprise:

What would I give to live where you are?
What would I pay to stay here beside you?
What would I do to see you smiling at me?

Where would we walk
Where would we run
If we could stay all day in the sun?
Just you and me
And I could be
Part of your world.

I don't know when
I don't know how
But I know something's starting right now
Watch and you'll see
Someday I'll be
Part of your world.

THE IMPORTANCE OF LANGUAGE אשר בדברו

1. *Asher Bidvaro:*

ברוך אתה יהוה אלהינו מלך העולם אשר בדברו מעריב ערבים
בחכמה פותח שערים ובתבונה משנה עתים ומחליף את הזמנים
ומסדר את־הכוכבים במשמרותיהם ברקיע כרצונו: בורא יום
ולילה גולל אור מפני חשך וחשך מפני אור: ומעביר יום ומביא
לילה ומבדיל בין יום ובין לילה יהוה צבאות שמו: אל חי וקים
תמיד ימלוך עלינו לעולם ועד: ברוך אתה יהוה המעריב ערבים:

Words give creation form and meaning. "Our word, like God's, gives expression to a depth beyond language."

---

2. *Baruch She-amar*

ברוך שאמר והיה העולם ברוך הוא:
ברוך עושה בראשית ברוך שמו:
ברוך אומר ועושה ברוך הוא:
ברוך גוזר ומקים ברוך שמו:
ברוך מרחם על הארץ ברוך הוא:

ברוך מרחם על־הבריות ברוך שמו:
ברוך משלם שכר טוב ליראיו ברוך הוא:
ברוך מעביר אפלה ומביא אורה ברוך שמו:
ברוך חי לעד וקים לנצח ברוך הוא:
ברוך פודה ומציל ברוך הוא וברוך שמו:

"Blessed is the one who spoke and all things came to be."

---

3. *Ilu finu*

אלו פינו מלא שירה כים ולשוננו רנה כהמון גליו ושפתותינו שבח
כמרחבי רקיע ועינינו מאירות כשמש וכירח וידינו פרושות
כנשרי שמים ורגלינו קלות כאילות אין אנחנו מספיקים להודות
לך יהוה אלהינו ואלהי אבותינו ואמותינו ולברך את־שמך על־אחת
מאלף אלף אלפי אלפים ורבי רבבות פעמים הטובות שעשית
עם־אבותינו ועמנו: ←

"Were our mouths oceans of songs, our tongues alive with exultation like the waters' waves, our lips filled full of praises like the heaven's dome..." we could never express sufficient praise for the goodness that exists in our world and which we are the recipients of.

---

4. *V'ahavta*

ואהבת את יהוה אלהיך בכל־לבבך ובכל־נפשך ובכל־מאדך:
והיו הדברים האלה אשר אנכי מצוך היום על־לבבך:
ושננתם לבניך ודברת בם בשבתך בביתך ובלכתך בדרך
ובשכבך ובקומך: וקשרתם לאות על־ידך והיו לטטפת בין
עיניך: וכתבתם על־מזזות ביתך ובשעריך:

"...Speak them when you sit down and when you rise up."

---

5. *Amidah*

אדני שפתי תפתח ופי יגיד תהלתך:

"Open my lips so my mouth can declare praise."

WHY ARE WORDS SO IMPORTANT?
HOW CAN YOU DO GODLY WORK WITH YOUR WORDS
WHAT DID YOUR WORDS CREATE THIS WEEK?
DID ANYONE SEARCH FOR YOUR VOICE THIS WEEK?

THE IMPORTANCE OF LANGUAGE

1. King Triton's daughters are introduced and given identities by being named:

> We are the daughters of Triton
> Great father who loves us and named us well.
> Aquata
> Andrina
> Arista
> Atina
> Adella
> Allana
> And then there is the youngest in her musical debut
> Our seventh little sister, we're presnting her to you
> To sing a song Sebastian wrote, her voice is like a bell
> She's our sister, Ari....

We have a king, we have the number 7, we have names that begin with the initial letter of the alphabet, we have a shift in name endings --from those ending in A--to Ariel, which means light of or warrior of God. References to creation can not be overlooked. Ariel's name is not fully spoken here, as she is being introduced, because she is not fully created yet. Her identity is in formation, as is her name.

2. Scuttle, the seagull names Ariel's treasures from the human world. Like Adam, he assigns them names and functions. We should not miss the fact that the "dinglehopper," a fork, is used to create something that is aesthetically pleasing (human beauty), or that it is triton-shaped, suggesting that humans are indeed to be co-creators with God, of beauty. Similarly, the "snarfblatt," or pipe, is given the function of creating music, another way that humans bring beauty into the world in imitation of the creator.

3. Triton reprimands Ariel for going above saying, "As long as you live in my ocean you'll obey my rules! Not another word!" This occurs after Flounder has tried to tell Triton that their missing the concert wasn't really their fault, but he is unable to say what he means in clear words. Ariel must leave the ocean, because her voice is not adequate to express what she needs to express.

4. Ursula takes Ariel's voice. She will need to find the mature capacity to love to get it back.

5. Prince Eric searches for Ariel's voice: "That voice. I've been looking for it everywhere."

חֲצִי קַדִּישׁ

יִתְגַּדַּל וְיִתְקַדַּשׁ שְׁמֵהּ רַבָּא בְּעָלְמָא דִּי בְרָא כִרְעוּתֵהּ וְיַמְלִיךְ
מַלְכוּתֵהּ בְּחַיֵּיכוֹן וּבְיוֹמֵיכוֹן וּבְחַיֵּי דְכָל בֵּית יִשְׂרָאֵל בַּעֲגָלָא וּבִזְמַן
קָרִיב וְאִמְרוּ: אָמֵן:
יְהֵא שְׁמֵהּ רַבָּא מְבָרַךְ לְעָלַם וּלְעָלְמֵי עָלְמַיָּא:
יִתְבָּרַךְ וְיִשְׁתַּבַּח וְיִתְפָּאַר וְיִתְרוֹמַם וְיִתְנַשֵּׂא וְיִתְהַדָּר וְיִתְעַלֶּה
וְיִתְהַלָּל שְׁמֵהּ דְּקֻדְשָׁא בְּרִיךְ הוּא
לְעֵלָּא (*On Shabbat Shuvah add:* וּלְעֵלָּא) מִן כָּל בִּרְכָתָא וְשִׁירָתָא
תֻּשְׁבְּחָתָא וְנֶחֱמָתָא דַּאֲמִירָן בְּעָלְמָא וְאִמְרוּ: אָמֵן:

Reader: Yitgadal veyitkadash shemey raba
be’alma divra ḥirutey veyamliḥ malḥutey
beḥayeyḥon uvyomeyḥon uvḥayey deḥol beyt yisra’el
ba’agala uvizman kariv ve’imru amen.

Congregation: Yehey shemey raba mevaraḥ le’alam ulalmey almaya.

Reader: Yitbaraḥ veyishtabaḥ veyitpa’ar veyitromam veyitnasey veyit-hadar veyitaleh veyit-halal shemey dekudsha beriḥ hu le’ela (*On Shabbat Shuvah add:* le’ela) min kol birḥata veshirata tushbeḥata veneḥemata da’amiran be’alma ve’imru amen.

ARIEL'S HATZI KADDISH:
The end of one phase of her life and the start of a new phase

POOR UNFORTUNATE SOULS (part)

(Ursula): The only way to get what you want is to become a human yourself...

(Ariel): If I become human, I'll never be with my father or sisters again.

(Ursula): Life's full of tough choices.
Oh, and there is one more thing.
We haven't discussed the subject of payment.

(Ariel): But I don't have...

(Ursula): I'm not asking much, just a token really, a trifle. What I want from you is your voice.

(Ariel): But without my voice, how can I...?

(Ursula): You poor unfortunate soul. It's sad, but true:
If you want to cross a bridge, my sweet
You've got to pay the toll
Take a gulp and take a breath and go ahead and sign the scroll...

Palooga sarooga come winds of the Caspian Sea
Now rainsus glaucitis et max laryngitis la voce to me...

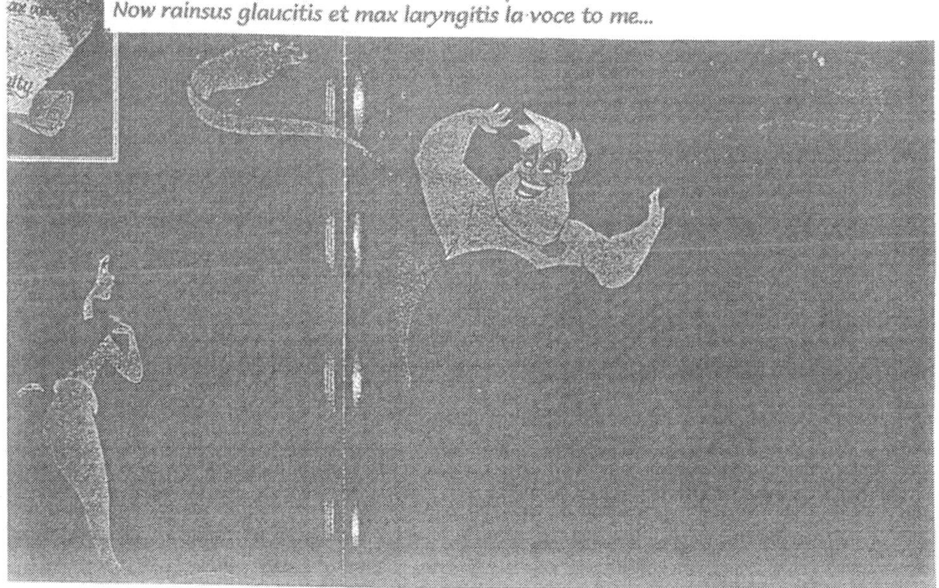

* תְּהִלּוֹת לְאֵל עֶלְיוֹן בָּרוּךְ הוּא וּמְבוֹרָךְ מֹשֶׁה וּמִרְיָם וּבְנֵי יִשְׂרָאֵל
לְךָ עָנוּ שִׁירָה בְּשִׂמְחָה רַבָּה וְאָמְרוּ כֻלָּם:
מִי־כָמֹכָה בָּאֵלִם יהוה מִי כָּמֹכָה נֶאְדָּר בַּקֹּדֶשׁ נוֹרָא תְהִלֹּת
עֹשֵׂה־פֶלֶא:
*שִׁירָה חֲדָשָׁה שִׁבְּחוּ גְאוּלִים לְשִׁמְךָ עַל־שְׂפַת הַיָּם:
יַחַד כֻּלָּם הוֹדוּ וְהִמְלִיכוּ וְאָמְרוּ:
יהוה יִמְלֹךְ לְעֹלָם וָעֶד:
*צוּר יִשְׂרָאֵל קוּמָה בְּעֶזְרַת יִשְׂרָאֵל: וּפְדֵה כִנְאֻמֶךָ יְהוּדָה וְיִשְׂרָאֵל:
גֹּאֲלֵנוּ יהוה צְבָאוֹת שְׁמוֹ קְדוֹשׁ יִשְׂרָאֵל:
בָּרוּךְ אַתָּה יהוה גָּאַל יִשְׂרָאֵל:

ARIEL CROSSES TO DRY LAND

Like the *midrash* about Nahshon ben Aminadav, who stepped his feet into the Sea of Reeds, Ariel "takes a gulp and takes a breath" and takes the plunge. She, too, goes through water, risking drowning (as a human now) to arrive in another world. Like Nahshon, Ariel knows that the sea does not part, life does not change, unless we go forward, leaving safety behind. As in the *Mi Chomocha*, Ariel is grateful for her emergence from water, which had threatened to suffocate her both psychologically (in her father's ocean) and literally (in her new human form). She begins to be less recognizable to her sea friends, but her identity in the human world is not yet known. She will wander for a time, moving steadily closer to her promised land, the full humanness she will attain through love.

עֲמִידָה

אֲדֹנָי שְׂפָתַי תִּפְתָּח וּפִי יַגִּיד תְּהִלָּתֶךָ:

אָבוֹת וְאִמּוֹת

בָּרוּךְ אַתָּה יהוה אֱלֹהֵינוּ וֵאלֹהֵי אֲבוֹתֵינוּ וְאִמּוֹתֵינוּ

אֱלֹהֵי אַבְרָהָם	אֱלֹהֵי שָׂרָה
אֱלֹהֵי יִצְחָק	אֱלֹהֵי רִבְקָה
אֱלֹהֵי יַעֲקֹב	אֱלֹהֵי רָחֵל
	אֱלֹהֵי לֵאָה: ←

Open my lips, BELOVED ONE,
and let my mouth declare your praise.

1. AVOT VE'IMOT / ANCESTORS

Blessed are you, THE ANCIENT ONE

God of Abraham	God of Sarah
God of Isaac	God of Rebekah
God of Jacob	God of Rachel
	and God of Leah; ↵

ARIEL'S AMIDAH

Ariel is silent for 3 days, meditating and reflecting on what is around her, on where she fits into this scheme of things, on how she will bring herself into this world and create holiness in her life in this world. During this time, she is open to all experiences around her, continuing to take risks as she goes forward to get what she needs in order to live (love). She has her "ancestors" with her as she experiences all of nature's harmoniousness (metaphoric and musical, as Sebastian summons "percussion, strings, wind...words") through new senses, as a human. Scuttle, Flounder, and Sebastian, as her ties to her old world, stay with her to usher her into her new world. Like in the Amidah, these "ancestor"/friends, parts of her past, sustain her. Sebastian reminds us, again, of our role in the world: You want something done, you have to do it yourself." We should not overlook that the Amidah is the "standing" prayer. For Ariel, standing on her new feet is a holy act. In this act she pays homage to her human world and her human self, even if her voice is still silent. Our recitation of the Amidah is the same.

עָלֵינוּ

עָלֵינוּ לְשַׁבֵּחַ לַאֲדוֹן הַכֹּל
לָתֵת גְּדֻלָּה לְיוֹצֵר בְּרֵאשִׁית
שֶׁנָּתַן לָנוּ תּוֹרַת אֱמֶת
וְחַיֵּי עוֹלָם נָטַע בְּתוֹכֵנוּ:

It is up to us to offer praises to the Source of all, to declare the greatness of the author of Creation, who has made us different from the other nations of the earth, and situated us in quite a different spot, and made our daily lot another kind from theirs, and given us a destiny uncommon in his world.

עָלֵינוּ לְשַׁבֵּחַ לַאֲדוֹן הַכֹּל לָתֵת גְּדֻלָּ
לְיוֹצֵר בְּרֵאשִׁית שֶׁלֹּא עָשָׂנוּ כְּגוֹיֵ
הָאֲרָצוֹת וְלֹא שָׂמָנוּ כְּמִשְׁפְּחוֹת הָאֲדָמָ
שֶׁלֹּא שָׂם חֶלְקֵנוּ כָּהֶם וְגוֹרָלֵנוּ כְּכָ
הֲמוֹנָם:

וַאֲנַחְנוּ כּוֹרְעִים וּמִשְׁתַּחֲוִים וּמוֹדִים לִפְנֵי מֶלֶךְ מַלְכֵי הַמְּלָכִים הַקָּדוֹשׁ בָּרוּךְ הוּא:
שֶׁהוּא נוֹטֶה שָׁמַיִם וְיוֹסֵד אָרֶץ וּמוֹשַׁב יְקָרוֹ בַּשָּׁמַיִם מִמַּעַל וּשְׁכִינַת עֻזּוֹ בְּגָבְהֵי מְרוֹמִים: הוּא אֱלֹהֵינוּ אֵין עוֹד: אֱמֶת מַלְכֵּנוּ אֶפֶס זוּלָתוֹ כַּכָּתוּב בְּתוֹרָתוֹ: וְיָדַעְתָּ הַיּוֹם וַהֲשֵׁבֹתָ אֶל לְבָבֶךָ כִּי יהוה הוּא הָאֱלֹהִים בַּשָּׁמַיִם מִמַּעַל וְעַל הָאָרֶץ מִתָּחַת אֵין עוֹד: ←

עַל כֵּן נְקַוֶּה לְךָ יהוה אֱלֹהֵינוּ לִרְאוֹת מְהֵרָה בְּתִפְאֶרֶת עֻזֶּךָ לְהַעֲבִיר גִּלּוּלִים מִן הָאָרֶץ וְהָאֱלִילִים כָּרוֹת יִכָּרֵתוּן לְתַקֵּן עוֹלָם בְּמַלְכוּת שַׁדַּי: וְכָל בְּנֵי בָשָׂר יִקְרְאוּ בִשְׁמֶךָ: לְהַפְנוֹת אֵלֶיךָ כָּל רִשְׁעֵי אָרֶץ: יַכִּירוּ וְיֵדְעוּ כָּל יוֹשְׁבֵי תֵבֵל כִּי לְךָ תִּכְרַע כָּל בֶּרֶךְ תִּשָּׁבַע כָּל־לָשׁוֹן: לְפָנֶיךָ יהוה אֱלֹהֵינוּ יִכְרְעוּ וְיִפֹּלוּ וְלִכְבוֹד שִׁמְךָ יְקָר יִתֵּנוּ וִיקַבְּלוּ כֻלָּם אֶת עֹל מַלְכוּתֶךָ וְתִמְלֹךְ עֲלֵיהֶם מְהֵרָה לְעוֹלָם וָעֶד: כִּי הַמַּלְכוּת שֶׁלְּךָ הִיא וּלְעוֹלְמֵי עַד תִּמְלֹךְ בְּכָבוֹד כַּכָּתוּב בְּתוֹרָתֶךָ: יהוה יִמְלֹךְ לְעֹלָם וָעֶד: וְנֶאֱמַר: וְהָיָה יהוה לְמֶלֶךְ עַל כָּל הָאָרֶץ בַּיּוֹם הַהוּא יִהְיֶה יהוה אֶחָד וּשְׁמוֹ אֶחָד:

ARIEL'S ALEYNU

Ariel has always known that she was the "different" one (even her name was different from those of her sisters). She was "made different...situated...in a different spot" with a daily life and destiny that is different from that of other creatures. In a supreme act of selflessness and godliness, her father restores to Ariel "the breath of life" and the capacity "to walk about." Ariel completes her differentiation as she says goodbye to her friends, Scuttle, Flounder, and Sebastian. They are now internalized "ancestors" who will forever sustain her. She is grateful for the capacity to have become different as she grew, to feel herself as different, unlike other creatures' whose consciousness does not foster this self-awareness. Perhaps this is what chosenness means, after all--that we, as human beings, are chosen above other creatures, to exercise responsibility through consciousness and conscience.

קַדִּישׁ יָתוֹם

It is customary for mourners, and those observing Yahrzeit, to stand for Kaddish. In some congregations everyone rises.

יִתְגַּדַּל וְיִתְקַדַּשׁ שְׁמֵהּ רַבָּא בְּעָלְמָא דִּי בְרָא כִרְעוּתֵהּ וְיַמְלִיךְ
מַלְכוּתֵהּ בְּחַיֵּיכוֹן וּבְיוֹמֵיכוֹן וּבְחַיֵּי דְכָל בֵּית יִשְׂרָאֵל בַּעֲגָלָא וּבִזְמַן
קָרִיב וְאִמְרוּ אָמֵן:
יְהֵא שְׁמֵהּ רַבָּא מְבָרַךְ לְעָלַם וּלְעָלְמֵי עָלְמַיָּא:
יִתְבָּרַךְ וְיִשְׁתַּבַּח וְיִתְפָּאַר וְיִתְרוֹמַם וְיִתְנַשֵּׂא וְיִתְהַדַּר וְיִתְעַלֶּה
וְיִתְהַלַּל שְׁמֵהּ דְּקֻדְשָׁא בְּרִיךְ הוּא
לְעֵֽלָּא (*On Shabbat Shuvah add:* לְעֵֽלָּא) מִן כָּל בִּרְכָתָא וְשִׁירָתָא
תֻּשְׁבְּחָתָא וְנֶחֱמָתָא דַּאֲמִירָן בְּעָלְמָא וְאִמְרוּ אָמֵן:
יְהֵא שְׁלָמָא רַבָּא מִן שְׁמַיָּא וְחַיִּים עָלֵינוּ וְעַל כָּל יִשְׂרָאֵל וְאִמְרוּ אָמֵן:
עוֹשֶׂה שָׁלוֹם בִּמְרוֹמָיו הוּא יַעֲשֶׂה שָׁלוֹם עָלֵינוּ וְעַל כָּל יִשְׂרָאֵל וְעַל
כָּל יוֹשְׁבֵי תֵבֵל וְאִמְרוּ אָמֵן:

KING TRITON'S KADDISH

King Triton acknowledges to Sebastian what has become inescapable to him: that Ariel really does love the prince and that there is only one thing to do about it. As he turns Ariel back into a human, his mer-daughter is lost to him forever. His words, however, are not about her loss; his words are for the ending of her study as a child, under his parental tutelage. He has done his job well; she has emerged, she is formed, she is full, and she has the capacity to love and be loved. Like the Kaddish, his words evoke sadness, but they are also, like the Kaddish, celebratory of the world of which his daughter has now become a part. Whatever shape she takes, he cannot fail to recognize within her adult self, his former child. And he cannot fail to let her go because, after all, she has found the thing he would have had her find.

His final act, before diving back into the sea, is to paint a rainbow from the sea to the heavens, embracing Ariel and Eric, and all that is in their world. *Oseh shalom bim'ramov...*

אֲדוֹן עוֹלָם

אֲדוֹן עוֹלָם אֲשֶׁר מָלַךְ   בְּטֶרֶם כָּל יְצִיר נִבְרָא:
לְעֵת נַעֲשָׂה בְחֶפְצוֹ כֹּל   אֲזַי מֶלֶךְ שְׁמוֹ נִקְרָא:

וְאַחֲרֵי כִּכְלוֹת הַכֹּל   לְבַדּוֹ יִמְלֹךְ נוֹרָא:
וְהוּא הָיָה וְהוּא הֹוֶה   וְהוּא יִהְיֶה בְּתִפְאָרָה:

וְהוּא אֶחָד וְאֵין שֵׁנִי   לְהַמְשִׁיל לוֹ לְהַחְבִּירָה:
בְּלִי רֵאשִׁית בְּלִי תַכְלִית   וְלוֹ הָעֹז וְהַמִּשְׂרָה:

וְהוּא אֵלִי וְחַי גֹּאֲלִי   וְצוּר חֶבְלִי בְּעֵת צָרָה:
וְהוּא נִסִּי וּמָנוֹס לִי   מְנָת כּוֹסִי בְּיוֹם אֶקְרָא:

בְּיָדוֹ אַפְקִיד רוּחִי   בְּעֵת אִישַׁן וְאָעִירָה:
וְעִם רוּחִי גְּוִיָּתִי   יהוה לִי וְלֹא אִירָא:

ARIEL'S ADON OLAM

The *kavannah* of this prayer centers us on those aspects "of reality which elicit from us the best that is in us and enables us to bear the worst that can befall us." This is a fitting ending for Ariel, for she has discovered and created a reality that has elicited from her her humanness and that will sustain her in her new world.

Made in the USA
Lexington, KY
28 February 2014